"Claire Jia's confidence is intoxicating. Her deft prose and deliberate unfolding of plot, the way she lays her characters bare so that we understand their deepest wanting just as they begin to grasp it for themselves, all her literary choices make this a debut that feels like it was written by a master."

—Jade Chang,
author of *The Wangs Vs. The World*

"Claire Jia's *Wanting* is a mesmerizing exploration of ambition, self-delusion, and the complicated bonds of friendship. Ye Lian and Luo Wenyu are unforgettable characters—two women whose lives have taken starkly different paths, yet remain inextricably bound by shared history, simmering rivalries, and unspoken betrayals. In evocative and emotionally rich prose, Jia lays bare the ache of longing and the illusions we cling to in order to make sense of our pasts."

—Alexandra Chang,
author of *Tomb Sweeping*

"*Wanting* vividly traces the arc of adolescent friendship and love into adult hunger and hope. Whether for a wealthy immigrant YouTuber or the lonely strivers of the world she leaves behind, Claire Jia's attention to her characters is at once compassionate and unflinching. This is a dazzling portrait of both modern China and the unrelenting ambitions of the human heart."

—Belinda Huijuan Tang,
author of *A Map for the Missing*

"Written with emotional precision and tremendous wisdom, *Wanting* depicts the subtle and often inexplicable ways that friendship and romantic love evolve over time. Compassionate, perceptive, and totally absorbing—I loved this novel."

—Hanna Halperin,
author of *I Could Live Here Forever*

"Claire Jia's novel brings us right into the fray of the complicated, human dramas of Beijing's urbane elite. She delightfully illuminates both the quotidian and surreal details of our multicultural, interconnected worlds and of the unexpected connections between the US and China, between old friends and old grievances. Her novel is a thoughtful and thought-provoking exploration."

—Emily Feng,
author of *Let Only Red Flowers Bloom*

"A deliciously observant social inquiry into the regrets, discontents, and might-have-beens that haunt us from youth to quarter life to old age, *Wanting* sweeps us into the summer three Beijing residents face a crossroads: set fire to the lives they've been living and start anew, or make do with what they already have? Jia raises a magnifying glass to the narcissism of our age, dissecting how we use the lives of others as mirrors for our paltry selves. Combining moments of high drama with perceptive insight into friendship, love, self-comparison, and envy, *Wanting* is a sharp-eyed debut which is unsparing on our human foibles—but also gentle, understanding, and wise."

—Cleo Qian,
author of LET'S GO LET'S GO LET'S GO

WANTING

WANTING

A NOVEL

CLAIRE JIA

TIN HOUSE
PORTLAND, OREGON

Copyright © 2025 by Claire Jia

First US Edition 2025
Printed in the United States of America

EPIGRAPH CREDIT: "Fragment" by Bian Zhilin (trans. Mary M. Y. Fung and David Lunde), from Mary M. Y. Fung, ed., *The Carving of Insects* (Hong Kong: Research Centre for Translation, 2006), p. 94. Reprinted by permission of the Research Centre for Translation, The Chinese University of Hong Kong.

Manufacturing by Kingery Printing Company
Interior design by Beth Steidle

Library of Congress Cataloging-in-Publication Data

Names: Jia, Claire, 1993– author
Title: Wanting : a novel / Claire Jia.
Description: Portland, Oregon : Tin House, 2025.
Identifiers: LCCN 2025008163 | ISBN 9781963108279 paperback | ISBN 9781963108347 ebook
Subjects: LCGFT: Novels
Classification: LCC PS3610.I25 W36 2025 | DDC 813/.6—dc23/eng/20250307
LC record available at https://lccn.loc.gov/2025008163

Tin House
2617 NW Thurman Street, Portland, OR 97210
www.tinhouse.com

Distributed by W. W. Norton & Company

1 2 3 4 5 6 7 8 9 0

For my family and my friends:
I know you under every sky

The moon adorns your window—
you adorn someone else's dream.

—BIAN ZHILIN

WANTING

L

ian sat on the front stoop, her arms wrapped around herself so tightly her thumbnails created pockmarked valleys in the flesh of her biceps. She wished she'd put on a jacket before coming outside. She couldn't go back in the house now.

Police officers milled about, unrolling caution tape and snapping on blue gloves. Lian could see Wenyu sitting in the back seat of the police car, talking calmly with the paramedic. He was checking her blood pressure, and Wenyu's face was serene. What struck Lian most was how her friend's curls still sat in perfect barrels. How was this possible? So many things had ended that night and yet Wenyu's hair looked pristine.

A few neighbors had come out of their houses and stood in the street, staring eagerly at the spectacle. She couldn't believe that a mere three hours ago they were clinking glasses of champagne, eating seared scallops off toothpicks, and discussing which electric cars were best. Zhu Zixi swore by her Tesla, but those weren't allowed in most parking lots, Yang Qinru had argued. The Chinese-American political situation and whatnot. Her husband drove a speedy little blue NIO whose battery charged in the exact time it took her to stand in line at the Hermès store.

And then the squall of the car debate was replaced abruptly by a more recent memory: an agonizing scream.

Lian mashed the rubber of her slipper on the too shiny face of the obsidian slab leading down to the driveway. Try as she could, she couldn't scuff it. She regretted the silver pedicure she'd gotten especially for the party; the metallic was inappropriate given the tableau before her.

Two officers stood on the driveway, looking up at the facade.

"What a pity," the shorter one said.

"It's gorgeous," the tall one concurred. "How much money do you have to make to afford a place like this?"

"Don't think about it. You'll work your whole life and maybe afford a toilet in one of these."

"It's gonna be a damn good toilet, though."

The shorter officer caught her eye and coughed. He walked over. "We just have a few questions for you, miss."

She nodded. The lump that had lodged itself in her throat was getting bigger.

"Are you the owner of the property?"

She looked in Wenyu's direction. "No," she said.

"What's your name?"

"Ye Lian," she said. "'Lian' for water lily."

"What happened tonight, Miss Ye?" the officer asked her now.

His question was part official business, part curiosity. Did he want the story—or the truth? She looked at him, her eyes blank.

What had happened? A few words came to mind. *Revenge. Retribution.* They weren't quite right.

Kismet. Karma. These were tidy, curious words, and perhaps not perfect, either. She rolled the last word around on her tongue. *Karma.* The only thing that separated *karma* from *revenge* was that one was predestined, the natural consequences of one's actions; the other, a human plot. Both pointed to some initial debt.

"I don't know," she finally stammered. "It was supposed to be a party."

PART ONE

I

June

The woman who would soon become known as Vivian Straeffer-Kenney looked perfectly American: her full lips curved orange-slice plump and outward, her hair billowed off her shoulders in fat, blondish waves, layers of mascara gave her eyes that perfect half-vernal, half-vampish shimmer irresistible to men everywhere.

She was recording herself in her living room, while the screen flashed with an architectural rendering of a mansion she and her new fiancé planned to build in the Shunyi district of Beijing. The house was palatial, vaulted ceilings rendering it nearly holy, a tiled pool reflecting aquamarine onto its pale stone walls. She gushed about the views they'd get from the rooftop terrace. It was gorgeous, the kind of home only the most abundant of money mountains could afford.

She'd gotten work done on her eyelids; Lian was sure of it. She stared, pausing the video on her phone and zooming in on her face. She had never had that crease before; it caused the midpoint of her eye to pop up in a look of constant delight—the kind that was once reserved for the moments that really deserved it.

Lian hated how she rushed to watch every new video Vivian posted. She couldn't help it. She was looking for something— something only she could see.

"Lian? Lian. We're almost there."

Her boyfriend was gesturing at the elevator doors. Their floor was coming up. A projector splashed an advertisement for a new food delivery app on the wall.

"Right," Lian said, putting her phone in her pocket. The elevator pinged and the doors slid open.

A woman in a stiff maroon suit was standing outside, her left arm dutifully gripping a clipboard. Her gold name badge read SANDY. She stuck out her hand. "You made it!"

They were viewing a condo in the Chaoyang One subdivision, an appointment her mother had brownnosed upwards of a dozen acquaintances to secure. Sandy was allegedly the best of the best. She'd sold Zhu Zixi her luxury condo for 100,000 kuai under asking, nearly impossible in this year's housing market, and because of that, Lian was expected to put her future in Sandy's hands. Zhetai wore his nicest shirt; there was something jittery in his step.

Sandy opened the door to the apartment. Her first impression was that it was quite expansive; the living room and dining space bled into each other seamlessly. It had been outfitted in a mid-century modern style, currently popular in the West, according to Sandy. A low leather couch spilled across an orangey rug while a single drop lamp arched perilously over an armchair whose back was so vertical she couldn't comprehend how one would sit in it comfortably.

Zhetai sat down on the couch, leaning back in a pose of uncharacteristic casualness, the faint grid lines of his shirt creasing as he stretched his arms out. "I love this couch, Lian," he said. "I want to get this exact couch." Western light streamed in, bathing Zhetai's face in a sherbet glow. Lian smiled. For a moment, she could see the two of them here, years older, their faces more rugged and lined, sitting on this very couch. Sandy was beaming at them, no doubt dreaming of her own family in her own high-rise condominium one day. On the wall, the ductless air conditioner oscillated soundlessly. This was a place where joy—or at least contentment—was expected to grow.

"It's a great couch," Lian agreed.

They walked into the guest bedroom, which had its own balcony with a sliding door.

"The second balcony is <u>so</u> rare," Sandy said. "You two can enjoy your alone time on the primary bedroom balcony, while your child can entertain himself on this balcony."

"We don't have children," Lian clarified. She wondered what a child would do with a balcony. Use it to smoke cigarettes, probably.

"Oh, but you might someday!" Sandy chirped. Her face was trained right on Lian, her eyelashes thrumming, and Lian smiled again.

She opened the sliding door and stepped, precariously, onto the stone base jutting out forty meters above the ground. She surveyed the landscape of the subdivision before her: seven perfect obelisks rose in a cluster of glass and concrete, imperious in a sea of slightly shorter, slightly lesser buildings in the city beyond them. In the middle of the subdivision was a playground, a prerequisite for paradise, its clementine exercise bikes and shamrock swings providing whimsy and respite for child and adult alike. She saw a small boy sitting at a pectoral fly machine, his shoulders splayed unnaturally as his hands gripped the lacquered metal bars. Together the hands came—thwack! A little look of surprise startled his features out of place. And then back out the metal bars went, threatening to rip his arms from their sockets. He wore a bright green shirt and Velcro shoes. His mother looked on, her hair swept up by a plastic claw clip, which she unclasped and clasped as she chatted with another woman, whose own young child did belligerent half somersaults at her feet. Surrounding them were cobblestone paths and grassy patches in the shape of koi fish. Rotund bulldogs dragged their lumpy bodies across the Astroturf. Young couples pushed their baby strollers by the water while BMWs crawled past on their way home.

Sublime, she thought.

Idyllic.

Halcyon. She grinned. *Halcyon* was a good word.

The boy slammed the machine closed in front of him so swiftly Lian could almost see the look of surprise on his face, all the way from the twelfth floor. She remembered sitting at similar machines as a kid: You always thought the weight would be heavier than it ended up being. You thought those machines were real weight machines and expected to feel the way bodybuilders on TV looked: burdened, heroic for having mastered them. When the arms clanked shut, for a moment you marveled at yourself—wow, I am stronger than any bodybuilder. In the moment immediately after that, however, the truth slid over you: about the machine, about you.

"On a clearer day, you can see Jingshan Park from here!" Sandy pointed at a murky blur in the southwest distance.

"I think I can see it," Zhetai said. "Isn't that the pagoda overlooking the palace?"

"Yes, yes!"

Lian couldn't see a thing, but she smiled and nodded. The three of them stood there, staring out at nothing.

MINUTES LATER, Lian and Zhetai walked out of the building. The June day was unpredictably cold, whipping wind through the loose sleeves of her blouse. They nodded to a young couple who tugged along two small children, the first sporting a onesie emblazoned with Thor's hammer, while Loki's signature green-and-gold helmet shined brightly on the other's.

"A Thor onesie <u>and</u> a Loki onesie?" Lian whispered to Zhetai. "How 'One China, two systems' of them."

He chuckled, in that hollow, polite way he always did when he hadn't understood a joke but wanted to appear like he had. At the entrance to the complex, there was a flashy promo going on: Close before the new year, and you get a FREE three-month subscription to the Pilates studio down the street.

Everyone was living in a place like this now. Everyone successful, that is, and most everyone Lian knew from high school and university was now successful. Zhu Zixi had just purchased a 7 million RMB penthouse condo at Dongchengmen, Yang Qinru a 9 million RMB one at Guomao. Their San Diego and Shanghai degrees had produced the expected fruits, and so too would Lian's Beijing pedigree. Life was evolving as planned. She and Zhetai agreed that the apartment was splendid indeed. There could, perhaps, be more light in the kitchen, Lian said, and Zhetai nodded. More light in the kitchen, yes.

"And be careful, are you gonna have to take up Pilates?" She pointed at the promo sign.

"Maybe I will," he said. He turned to her. "Come on, Lian, it was nice."

"It was nice! Didn't say it wasn't nice."

Her phone pinged.

"*I know this is your favorite, but I think Some Like It Hot is a bit too silly. I like the really romantic ones. Like Charade. Cary Grant is perfect.*"

Lian smiled, rolling her eyes slightly. Everyone in the world loved Cary Grant. He was charming, sure, but there was something unapproachable about him. She much preferred the jokey boyishness of Jack Lemmon.

"*Romance is subjective,*" she typed back. "*I think Some Like It Hot is very romantic.*"

She looked over at Zhetai, wondering if he had seen her screen. But Zhetai was checking his own phone, typing up a message to the real estate agent.

They passed by Dongdan Square, littered at this time of year by matchmaking papers: the detritus of desperate singles flinging their degrees and BMIs into the ether, hoping to attract a partner. "Female. 27 years old. 163 centimeters. Bachelor's degree in English from Tianjin Normal University," one read. "35 years old. 170 centimeters. 20,000 RMB salary a month. Wanting: a wife with cooking and needlework skills," read another. Lover's Day was around the corner, and people wanted someone to hold, or at least to sit across from in an expensive restaurant. Posters crowded tree trunks, trash cans, and makeshift laundry lines strung up between branches. "Hobbies: pop music, hiking." "Owner of a brand new high-end Toyota." "Owner of an eight-hundred-square-meter condo in Chaoyang." Courtship was now calculation. The tech evolution, urban anxiety, Westernization, the economy, or some combination of these things had made numbers of them all. Romance was dead and replaced with a BMW and a lifetime membership to Space Cycle. She clutched Zhetai's arm more tightly, feeling a need to anchor herself to him, the kind and smart boy she'd met organically, that some higher being had plunked down in front of her one winter day her senior year of college so that she needn't ever participate in the grueling rat race of mate selection.

An elderly woman sat next to a tree trunk, carefully guarding the prime real estate of the towering oak. Lian read the poster taped above her head: "39 years old. Female, master's degree, violinist." The elderly woman cradled a framed photo of a woman with shoulder-length hair and a smile that showed two front teeth jutting in opposite directions. Lian avoided the woman's gaze as she walked past on Zhetai's arm.

LIAN AND ZHETAI rode the subway back home to Lian's place, their hands nestled comfortably between them. They had been together for eight years. He was sweet and reliable, better at caring for her when she was ill than being romantic when she was happy, but she figured it was more important to be there for someone when they were down, anyway. His squarish inability to understand jokes made her want to protect him. He was also the only person she'd ever met who was more punctual than she was. He was a physicist, and she was a junior executive at an American education company—the perfect mix of left- and right-adjacent brain intelligence, seven figures between the two of them. His father had worked with hers years ago at the China Petroleum and Chemical Corporation. They had officially met in college, but twenty years before that, they'd actually attended the same New Year's dinner, although neither of them, being toddlers, had remembered. That was called destiny. Yuan fen. On Fridays Zhetai came to hers for dinner. On Saturdays they went to his. On holidays the two families ate together, sometimes at his house and sometimes at hers. Their mothers would sing karaoke and their fathers would clink bottles of Qingdao beer and compare their latest tech purchases. It was a comfortable, often blissful, routine. Her future was a sunny ray of light shooting straight to the end of her life. She could see everything: her husband, her home, a precocious child in three to five years.

As of late, both pairs of parents had begun surmising, "Wouldn't it be nice if you kids hosted these dinner parties? Then we wouldn't have to clean up after you!" And so one joke had turned into two, which had turned into a series of appointments from Fengtai to Chaoyang, all of Beijing's most sunlit two- and three-bedroom condos blurring into one perfect mass before her eyes.

As the subway churned on toward Princess Grave, Zhetai told Lian to take a nap on his shoulder. She nestled her head into the crook of his suit jacket—his shoulder was the perfect height—and looked up at his face. He stared at the blinking light of the subway map, the faintest stitch between his brows. He was always like this: so focused on his mission to get them to their stop, he didn't even notice her gaze.

Comfort.

Solace.

Destiny.

She closed her eyes and felt the rumble of the train beneath her. The last thought before she fell asleep was that he would wake her up before they got to their stop; he would always wake her up.

"MA!" ZHETAI CALLED out when they entered the apartment. Lian had grown up here, and she was comforted by the sight of her family's shoes crowded together in the front hallway, sneakers and plastic slippers forming a clump that never ceased to look messy despite her mother's best efforts. The evening news tittered in the background, her father's profile lit electric blue by the television as he sat, half-asleep, beside a beer bottle nestled precariously in the grooves of the couch's majiang-tile mat. They lived on the sixth floor of an old building that had once been the newest in their complex, where their family had proudly moved when Lian was eight years old.

"Son!" Lian's mother called back, hurrying to hang up Zhetai's jacket. Lian's mother loved Zhetai. He was everything she had wanted for her daughter: smart, dependable, close to his parents, with a fine education and background. He was reasonably tall and had good posture and a high metabolism. He had started calling her "Ma" immediately upon meeting her—a move that was uncharacteristically bold and yet so rigidly within the bounds of social norms that it came all the way back around to conservative—which Lian knew delighted her to no end.

Her mother had made Zhetai's favorite, as she always did on Fridays: stir-fried black bean noodles. Every weekend they ate the same thing, because Zhetai only liked a handful of meals.

They discussed the condo showing. Zhetai was emphatic, praising the views, the floor-to-ceiling windows, the granite counters. Her mother had stewed red dates, which Lian hated but forced herself to eat on her period to ward off anemia. She plopped a date into her mouth, grimacing at the saccharine sweetness.

"What about you, Lianlian?" her mother asked, spooning another mound of dates into her bowl.

"I liked it," Lian said. "Great amenities." She nudged her mom's shoulder. "You did good, Ma."

"Don't say it with such hesitation!" her mother said, clapping her hands. "Would I send my only child to live in a garbage bin? So, am I hearing you found the perfect place?"

Lian allowed a smile to creep across her face. "Maybe. But maybe we should see a few more just to be safe . . ."

"Well, there's also a condo near Renmin I heard had an opening. It's in the same building where Peng Ayi's daughter is living."

Lian knew that condo; it had sky-high HOA fees but, as a result, amenities like you wouldn't believe. Peng Ayi's daughter had an elevator for her car.

"Let's see it," Zhetai said, grinning at Lian. "Though it'll be hard to top this one."

It was nice to see Zhetai so energized. He was usually the kind of man wholly contented with his routine, his 8–7 job at the Renmin physics lab, his two daily allotted "The Walking Dead" episodes, and badminton in the mornings on weekends, never distinctly passionate about anything but always satisfied. In discussing condos, however, Lian saw a twinkle in his eye that was usually reserved for the most groundbreaking of discoveries at his lab. Zhetai was a Virgo, which meant he loved a project. She could see him starting to lay out the chess pieces in his mind, planning their negotiation technique, crunching the collective totals of their bank accounts, his mouth working out his plan in tiny, nearly imperceptible circles.

She stuffed a date into her mouth. "Let's do it," she parroted.

"Ooh, that reminds me! You know who has a nice house?" her mother said, gasping. She hurried over to the kitchen and grabbed a thick white envelope. "Luo Wenyu! She's coming home! Luo Mama told me she bought a beautiful home in Shunyi. I guess becoming an actress really paid off!"

Lian spit out the date core. So the news had reached her mother. Luo Wenyu was coming home. Lian grabbed the envelope. Her name was embossed in silver on the front.

"She's not an actress, Mom," Lian said. "She's a YouTuber."

"I heard she's marrying an old outsider," her mother continued, conspiratorially. "Won't her babies have weird skin and big noses?"

Lian slipped the invitation out of its envelope and came face-to-face with a woman with long, shimmering curls and fake eyelashes. A Caucasian man hugged her from behind and grinned with a set of blindingly white teeth. "You are cordially invited to the engagement party of Thomas Straeffer-Kenney and Vivian Luo . . ." Vivian Luo. This was who Luo Wenyu was now.

"Luo Mama says Wenyu wants to see you," her mother said. "Give her a call."

She wanted to see her? "She has my number," Lian said, hoping her voice sounded nonchalant. "She can text me."

"Who's Luo Wenyu?" Zhetai said absently, looking down at his bowl. By the time she had met Zhetai, it had been years since she and Wenyu had spoken.

"Just an old friend," Lian said.

AFTER DINNER, Zhetai gathered his things to go home to his parents' place on the other side of town. Lian's mother gave Zhetai several boxes of noodles, wrapped in a red mesh bag, and he was happily on his way.

Lian sat at her desk and opened her laptop. She had a student on Friday nights, a rising high school senior with dreams of attending Yale. Lian worked at an American college prep company, Genius Tree Education, that specialized in sending the children of wealthy Chinese executives to American universities. She had started in the curricular department, developing curricula for test prep and application prep classes, and had over the years ascended the ranks, so that now she managed the entire department—at twenty-nine, the youngest manager they'd ever had—and no longer had to teach students of her own. But she kept a few private tutoring sessions a week. The sessions reminded her of the rush of possibility she'd had as a seventeen-year-old; they were her private joy. Her students were high school seniors and recent college grads looking to go abroad for graduate school, and she often felt she had more to say to these kids than to people her own age, whose ascendance into wealth and stability had stultified their ability to be interesting or interested.

She swiveled on her baby blue desk chair as she waited, rubbing lotion on her hands. Her room was a grown-up version of her childhood bedroom, the oration trophies and Harry Potter books stored away to make room for succulents and handmade pottery pieces painted in swathes of primary colors. She still had the Doraemon plushie, however. He would stay.

She examined the invitation again. Wenyu and her American Prince Charming stood in the clearing of a Generic American Forest wearing puffy jackets and tall brown leather boots. Puffy jackets were domesticity incarnate, the comfortably committed declaring their love to the world in the form of an unflattering synthetic fiber casing. Look how secure we are! We are secure enough to look like plastic balloons. The most offensive part: a glassy-eyed Pomeranian, patches of fur bursting out from between Wenyu's manicured fingers.

Lian had been waiting for this invitation. Ever since Luo Wenyu had left a decade ago, Lian had kept a quiet watch on her American life. At first, the two of them had still talked, sending each other quotidian updates on their university lives. But the messages dwindled with time and distance. Years later, Luo Wenyu resurfaced in the form of a YouTube personality, *Viv Like Vivian*, her channel dedicated to skin care and fitness and which prix fixe Italian restaurants were worth the splurge. Lian had discovered Wenyu's videos on a late-night stumble through the internet shortly after graduation, and she nearly didn't recognize her. At the time, Wenyu had dyed her hair strawberry blonde. She wore fake eyelashes and an off-the-shoulder top. She had developed a wide, toothy smile that Lian had never seen before. Most jarringly, she spoke with the jaunty cadence of an American sorority girl. Her voice was higher in English, more measured, without any of the rough animation Lian knew it possessed.

By the time Lian discovered Wenyu's channel, she already had a reasonable following. As she scrolled back, she realized Wenyu's channel had once been more focused on her art history studies, Chinese recipes she'd cook when she missed home, observations she had about the strange American world around her. But as she followed Wenyu's journey, from the dorms at UC Santa Cruz to an apartment with a view in San Francisco, Wenyu's content morphed. She met a man. The man was some sort of Irish-German blend with skin that looked perpetually flushed, giving him the appearance of an asthmatic baby. They frequented pop-up restaurants and white-water rafted with venture capitalists and danced at music festivals in the desert. They weekended in Napa and summered in Mykonos. Two years in, she moved into his four-story house in the coveted Cole Valley neighborhood.

Her subscribers skyrocketed. But despite Wenyu's new upper-echelon lifestyle, she still managed to seem "*relatable*," a term that her fans flung relentlessly in the comments section. She admitted to eating too much, or going to sleep with makeup on, or getting in fights with her boyfriend. Her channel was the land of low-hanging fruit, completely sanitized and pleasant, the kind of stuff Lian and Wenyu would have once mocked. But despite her annoyance, or perhaps because of it, Lian observed Wenyu's updates with the piety of a Red Guard. Each Sunday morning she'd sit on her bed, her phone nestled in her hands, and watch as Wenyu waved her shiny nails about and offered up an opinion on going vegan versus paleo. She couldn't stop; despite the way the new Wenyu grated on her, Lian felt she was looking for something: some evidence that perhaps the Wenyu she knew was still there, or that underneath the layers of concealer she was actually quite unhappy. And once in a while—in a long while—Wenyu's voice would crack or her grammar would reveal a slight mistake—"*I went to beach last week*"—and Lian would feel a pang of glee. See? You're still the same person. Still a Chinese girl with a Chinese voice who couldn't care less about followers or fad diets or American grammar. These people can't see you, but I can.

Three months ago, Wenyu had uploaded a video with the title "*surprise*." Cryptic. Lian had clicked on it immediately and was greeted with an image of a blue ocean. A second later the video cut to the inside of a helicopter, where Wenyu sat nestled in the arms of the asthmatic man, her now tan shoulders poking out of a blue puff-sleeve shirt. Even the wind seemed on her side, whipping her hair in fluid ribbons like she was the star of an anime.

The man rested his hands on her shoulders and pointed out at the water: Look, there's the Richmond Bridge. Look, there's Angel Island. She could see the Golden Gate Bridge in the distance, shrouded in cloud. Someone was holding the camera behind them, catching small moments: the man's hand ruffling Wenyu's hair, Wenyu turning and giving him a kiss on the cheek. Over the thrum of the helicopter blades, Lian could hear Wenyu say to the man, "*There's the rock where we, you know.*" Bursts of laughter. As if on cue, the helicopter dipped around the bend toward the rock and suddenly, as the first few notes of light piano began playing over the video, Lian saw it, milliseconds before Wenyu did in the video: a fleet of red, blue, and green boats lined up in perfect formation along Paradise Cay, spelling out that terminal question. WILL YOU MARRY ME?

When Wenyu finally saw it, she slapped a manicured hand to her mouth. The old Wenyu would have hated something as gaudy as a helicopter proposal. "*Thomas?*" she gasped, and the Caucasian man looked to her. He pulled out a blue velvet box, revealing a diamond engagement ring the size of an engorged ladybug. "*Will you marry me?*" he said aloud now. She cupped his face in her hands and kissed him deeply, her answer a foregone conclusion.

The video concluded with a montage of the couple's sweetest memories set to the tune of a warbling pop song. Lian felt her stomach twisting as she watched. As the song quieted, Wenyu's face reappeared, announcing that she and Thomas had purchased a summer home in Beijing and were going to spend several months in the city overseeing renovation. They'd have a party in Beijing before their real wedding back in San Francisco in the new year.

"*Don't worry,*" she reassured her faceless fans. "*Can't keep me away from Tartine for too long!*"

Heartbreak resounded in the comments: *we'll miss you Vivian!!*; *Brb on a flight to Beijing now!*; *Beijing seems soooo beautiful.*; *I'm so jealous you'll get to eat chinese food allll the time!*; *Thomas is so lucky!*

Twelve years ago, Lian and Wenyu would never have predicted this future. Back then, the whole world knew it was Lian who was destined for America.

Lian and Wenyu had gone to the same elementary school, but they did not become friends for some time. Lian's signature from a young age was her obedience; all adults loved her, praising her for her ability to follow directions, stay focused on her studies, and not get distracted by shiny things. This included friendships. Occasionally she consented to playdates with the other well-behaved and high-scoring girls in her class. Wenyu was not one of these people; Wenyu was a girl of an entirely different ilk.

It was a day in fourth grade when everything changed. Lian's mother sent her to the convenience store with five renminbi to grab her a sachet of black tea. This was a task her mother had started entrusting to her regularly, and she took on the responsibility with reverence and glee. She donned the outfit she always wore on these errands, a button-down shirt that made her feel regal and mature, because only adults wore shirts with stiff collars as opposed to the flat, round collars children wore that she, in her nine-year-old mind, already thought looked juvenile. She walked breezily out of their apartment, down the stairs, and two blocks south to the grocery store with the red-and-yellow sign. Inside, she proceeded to the leftmost aisle. She'd committed the grocery store and its contents to memory, lest she look like a lost child wandering around. She was not lost—she knew that aisle 1 contained the teas, spices, and medicinal remedies; aisle 2 the soy sauces and chili pastes; aisle 3 the dried noodles and rice; aisle 4 the dried mushrooms and mung beans; aisle 5 the snacks (puffed chips, chocolate biscuits, wafers); and so on. She walked swiftly to the middle of aisle 1, and glee escaped her lips as her eyes landed on the white-and-brown cardboard box that contained her mother's preferred tea brand. She clutched it in her hands and turned around to walk toward the cashier, the five-renminbi note in her pocket feeling heavier and more important with every step. This was always the most exhilarating part, when she'd walk up to the register and slide her grocery items across, pulling out the cash from her pocket with utmost nonchalance, while the cashier lifted her eyebrows at Lian. She'd stare the cashier down, dare her to ask where her parents were, and each time she'd watch an impressed look cross the cashier's face.

Today, as she prepared to make toward the register, she heard a shout. "Hey! You didn't pay for that!"

She followed the sound of the cashier's voice until her eyes alighted on a girl standing by the door. She had a frizzy bushel of hair tied so tenuously with an elastic that her head was mostly flyaways, the tiny wisp of a tail making a mockery of the elastic entirely. It was the kind of ponytail her mother warned her never to have; it was the mark of a careless girl. Her own at this moment was securely fastened at the nape of her neck with a pair of green plastic dice, her short hair fanned in a perfect semicircle across her shoulders. The girl was wearing an oversize blue windbreaker, clutching something in her hand. She had been about to cross the threshold when the accusation from behind had halted her midstep. She turned now, her face a mixture of smarm and surprise, her lips smushing upward in a bashful smile, as if to say, So you've finally caught me.

Lian recognized the girl from class. She couldn't remember the girl's name, only had a vague memory of her bushy head bobbing up and down in the back of the classroom as she thumped her foot against the side of her desk. She was kind of annoying. Lian saw the girl's fingers curl more tightly around whatever it was she was holding.

"What do you mean?" the girl said now, pushing her hand behind her back. "I was just looking." She smiled sweetly, her voice so full of disbelief that Lian doubted what she'd seen. Maybe the cashier was overreacting, playing police after a long day of work.

But the cashier didn't let up. She stood and marched over to the girl. "Don't think you can lie to me, girl. I'm not a fool." She made to grab for the girl's arm, and the girl jolted backward.

"What are you doing?!"

"There are consequences for little girls who steal."

Lian could see several thoughts cross the girl's face. She was thinking that she could run, which would confirm her guilt and make it impossible for her to ever come back to the store. Or she could give in, and show the cashier what was in her hand, which would produce the same result. She watched these rapid calculations unfolding on the girl's face, until desperation began to emerge, her eyebrows arching upward in a plea to something, someone. Her eyes caught Lian's at that moment, and then, suddenly, her name came to Lian: Luo Wenyu. Wen, for "hear." Yu, for "universe." I hear the universe. Yu was a boy's name, and the other girls had snickered. But Lian had been jealous of this name.

She was not sure what made her do what she did next. Normally an incident like this would have scandalized Lian; she'd have sided with the cashier, sided with propriety and justice. Stealing was for petty criminals and people without impulse control. But something else cracked open in her young brain: it had something to do with power. There was not much children could do in this world, but she realized there was something she could do now.

"Hey! Luo Wenyu!" she yelled out.

The scrabbling between the cashier and Wenyu stopped. The cashier turned with a puzzled look.

"Why'd you run off ahead of me? Do you have the thing my mom wanted?"

The groove between the cashier's eyebrows deepened. But the look of surprise on Wenyu's face was even greater. She realized that Wenyu recognized Lian too, and, in fact, knew her to be an uptight, straight-A student, and what Lian was doing now was the last thing she ever expected.

"Oh, yeah," Wenyu replied, slowly. "I couldn't find you, so I ran outside."

"I was just getting this," Lian said, holding up the box of tea. She could feel her hand trembling. "Zhang Ayi, can I check out now?"

The cashier was bewildered; Lian could tell that she didn't totally buy what was occurring, but she also couldn't come up with any reason why it wouldn't be true—Lian was such a good girl and had a reputation at this grocery. She hurried back to her station, frazzled, and scanned Lian's box of tea. Lian motioned for Wenyu to come over, and Wenyu approached gingerly, before placing the object in her hand on the conveyor belt. It was a wrapped piece of haw-fruit candy, now sweaty. Lian gave the cashier a wide smile as she checked them out. The cashier fixed on Wenyu a death glare, but there was nothing more she could say.

"Have a good day, Zhang Ayi!" Wenyu said now, smiling. Then she looped her hand into the crook of Lian's arm, and they marched out the door. Lian's heart was pounding, more exhilaration pumping through her than she'd ever experienced coming to this grocery alone. If before she had felt a fuzzy, joyful kind of pride in fulfilling her tasks, now she felt ecstasy, a thrill that made her entire body thrum. She and Wenyu traded gleeful looks as they walked out the door and onto the street, where they were nearly bowled over by a bicycle. Lian realized in this moment that her truthfulness, her obedient reputation, had a higher purpose. She had gained the trust of adults and could wield that trust in ways she'd never anticipated.

"Thanks," Wenyu said, once they were out of earshot of the grocery. "I thought you were one of the goody two-shoes."

Lian narrowed her eyes, then smirked. "There's a lot you don't know about me."

And then Wenyu reached into her pocket and pulled out an entire handful of haw-fruit candy. "Want one?" she said, grinning. She held up a sweaty piece and popped it in her mouth. "I got impatient this time. My bad."

This was the initial dramatic spark of their friendship, and eventually, they became the best of friends. They discovered that they'd both grown up on the west side of the city and knew its bus system from memory, knew which sidewalk grandpa made the best egg pancakes, knew which kiosk sold the crispest green tea, knew which grocery had the freshest chestnuts in the fall and the juiciest strawberries in the spring. They held deep convictions about the correct way to drink soy milk (hot and sweet), and the best items at McDonald's (the spicy chicken wings and the chocolate milkshakes). Wenyu was brash and careless and clumsy, so Lian called her Yutou. "Silly Yutou," she'd say, when Wenyu fell and bruised her ankle. "Like a taro tumbling down the stairs." In the mornings, they'd find each other on the exercise field and windmill their arms together crazily. The other girls would look at them with disgust, and Lian would feel a twinge of embarrassment. But on the other side of that embarrassment was unbridled freedom and joy. Wenyu was not afraid of all the things that Lian had spent her entire young life frozen in fear about: the rejection of peers, the retribution of adults. She always spoke at a volume too loud for the situation, showed up to class late, and didn't mind being scolded. Sometimes she didn't come to class at all, electing instead to hang out with the girls who stood inside the small photography studios and hair salons crowded together on Donggongzhuang Boulevard, girls who'd come to Beijing from faraway provinces, seeking a better life.

Wenyu lived in a more run-down building a few blocks from Lian's, and her mother, bedridden from an illness Wenyu never liked to talk about, let her roam free. Lian became envious of this freedom. Wenyu's life was exciting, Lian's boring in contrast. Her own mother's constant attention—the additional preening and smoothing she would do to Lian's hair and clothes before Lian walked out the door each morning for school—began to feel stifling. The things she'd once taken such pride in began to feel a bit trite. Who cared about a neat ponytail? Wenyu's devil-may-care attitude electrified Lian; she wanted some of it for herself.

They began going to the grocery together, Lian acting as decoy, Wenyu squirreling away chocolate bars and melon gummies and, if she was being brave, the occasional noisy bag of chips. Lian would never pocket the items herself, but she was integral to the plan, chatting up the cashier, asking exhaustive questions about the different types of ice cream bars in the freezer next to the cash register. With Lian, Wenyu could steal more, better things.

Wenyu told Lian that she stole because she'd tried it once, when she was seven, and had gotten away with it, and from then on, every time she went to the store, she wanted to push herself to the limit, see how far she could go before getting caught.

"I did it because I could," Wenyu said, shrugging.

As Lian got to know Wenyu, she never again saw on Wenyu's face the look of desperation from that first day at the grocery. Wenyu was always cool, confident, charming. Even as they grew into adolescence, she seemed untouched by teenage self-consciousness; she never doubted herself, even when doubting yourself was the hallmark of living. This was perhaps what most bonded the two of them—the fact that Lian had glimpsed Wenyu at her most fragile.

Eventually, Lian's bump with rebellion translated into a desire to go West. She'd already demonstrated a clear talent for English in class. On the first day of lessons in second grade, Lian had stuck her hand out to her teacher, speaking clearly in a ringing American accent. "*My name is Ye Lian*," she said. "*It's a pleasure to meet you.*" The shocked teacher asked if Lian had been born abroad. No, she responded. She had watched "*Titanic*" the previous week. She was just imitating the sounds she'd heard.

You have a special talent, her teachers said to her. Eventually they told her: You should go to America. America is where good things happen. Older students from the high school were already sending back stories of racking up accolades at Harvard and Stanford, striking it rich at Microsoft and Intel. At first, Lian thought this idea was silly. Her, riding on a ship like the *Titanic* to go pursue love and success in a country like America? But with every story she read in her English classes, thrilling tales about young girls who defeated evil stepmothers or siblings who set witches aflame in the woods, her curiosity deepened. What was the magical world of the West?

A cousin gave her a copy of "*Harry Potter and the Philosopher's Stone*" when she was ten—the English was too hard for him—and she found herself devouring it. In seventh grade English class, she gave herself the name *Luna*, for the eccentric white-haired girl who had a special connection with animals. The English language was her special comfort. When she was nervous, she'd practice her vocabulary, whispering the words until her stomach stopped flipping. *Perseverance*, she'd say to herself. *Diligence. Tenacity.*

Lian began to dream of what it'd be like to live abroad, perhaps in New York City or California. She became enamored of old Hollywood films, Western actors with their bare shoulders and cloudlike blonde hair. Grace Kelly in her monochrome dresses and Audrey Hepburn in her pearls: these women possessed a glamour that riveted her. She showed Wenyu her favorites, hoping to infect her with the same dream. She discovered the sitcom "*Friends*," and she and Wenyu would watch the show for hours, copying the accents of the swaggering men and women, imagining what it would be like to recycle boyfriends like clothing, hang out all day with your friends in a coffee shop, run through an airport to declare your undying love. There was something romantic and careless about American life. She coveted it.

"When I go to America, I'm going to own an entire floor of a mall," Lian would declare, wearing her mother's heels as she posed in front of the hallway floor-length mirror. "I'm going to become a true capitalist traitor!"

"When I go to America, I'm going to eat french fries every meal and pay people to clip my toenails!" Wenyu would jump up and expound.

"I'm going to build my own swimming pool and have attractive lifeguards bring me shrimp cocktails and ketchup and celebrity gossip magazines!"

"I'm going to own twenty dogs and dye their hair twenty different colors, and then my eight children will walk my dogs for me!"

They would laugh and laugh and pull their faces into exaggerated expressions and stuff underwear down their shirts so that they were busty like the old Hollywood actresses. They said they'd one day live in mansions on green lawns right next to each other, and their children and dogs would be best friends. Some would say it was playacting, but for Lian it was preparation for a life. One day, she and Wenyu would take on America together.

In high school, Lian began entering competitive English oration tournaments and would spend many of her weekends on the road, traveling with her teammates to Shijiazhuang or Jinan to give meticulously prepared speeches about famous historical figures: JFK, Winston Churchill, Richard Nixon. Lian took home a trophy every time. She dreamed of walking under the spindly gothic spires at Yale, losing herself in the stacks of Harvard's Widener Library, becoming a member of one of Princeton's elite eating clubs. She felt feverish planning for her future. The city around her seemed to feel similarly. Beijing the summer before their final year of high school was unlike they'd ever seen it. The 2008 Olympics were right around the corner, and Beijing was brimming with hope. Every day throughout the fall of 2007, Lian and Wenyu would pass the to-be Olympic Village on the bus on their way to school, and little by little they watched the opening ceremony stadium rise, the metal hatches clicking together so that they formed the sloping tire shape of the Bird's Nest. Every billboard and bus stop was emblazoned with grinning athletes drinking Bud Light and driving Bentleys, various Western brands clamoring for attention on the streets of a Chinese city. Liu Xiang in Nike, Zhang Yining in Adidas. They'd snatch gold on the backs of American luxury, leaving the actual Americans in the cold.

Lian felt the fervor of the city, channeling it into her applications. Like an Olympian, she'd be a representative of her country abroad; she'd bring back the metaphorical gold, much to the envy and admiration of everyone she'd left behind.

Meanwhile, Wenyu fell in love. This had started during their second year. He was the class rebel, a boy with hair in his eyes who refused to wear his uniform and instead showed up to class in a multicolored array of baggy clothes. While Lian was staring in the mirror practicing her *hows* and *lows* and preparing for her future, Wenyu was sneaking out of prep class more and more frequently to pull petty pranks with her new boyfriend. Wenyu's scores slouched down the rankings. The shoplifting of their youth translated to more flagrant defiance. Suddenly, Lian was no longer Wenyu's main conspirator. Her boyfriend would steal bigger, riskier things—shoes, clothes, MP3 players—pushing Wenyu to a new limit. She was now the person electrified, as opposed to the one electrifying. When her boyfriend's antics got Wenyu suspended for the first time the winter of their second year, Lian confronted Wenyu, pleaded with her to get her act together: Why are you tying yourself to an idiot like that? Wenyu shot back, He's the smartest boy I've ever met. He's destined for greatness. He could be anyone he wanted. Just you wait. Just because he doesn't have his nose stuck in a book all day and night like you do doesn't mean he's not just as smart. Smarter, probably. And he doesn't need to go to stupid America to prove it.

What about our dream? Lian cried. What dream? Wenyu shot back, cruelly. That was just for fun.

But in the end, Lian wasn't the one to go to stupid America.

ONE CHILLY MORNING in December of their senior year, Wenyu appeared at Lian's door, holding two ice cream bars that cut a teeth-chattering profile against the frigid winter landscape. Lian was in the middle of an essay for Harvard. "*Why Harvard?*" Why not? she always wanted to respond. It's the best university in the world. Who wouldn't want the best? She opened the door deep in thought, English phrases still dangling on her lips. She sat back down at her desk while Wenyu threw herself on Lian's bed and grabbed a magazine in one hand, holding her ice cream in the other. Then, in one quick breath, Wenyu told her the thing that would change her life:

"I'm moving to California."

Lian couldn't understand what she was hearing. She turned around, mouth agape.

"My dad's friend lives in San Jose, so they're gonna put me in high school there. Isn't that exciting, Lianlian?" she said, as if she'd just discovered that their favorite band was coming to town, or that their favorite tea shop now sold lychee flavor. Not the kind of voice you use when you're telling your best friend you're moving halfway across the world.

"I thought—I thought you hated America . . ." was all Lian could think of saying.

Wenyu shrugged. "Just because you love it doesn't mean I hate it." She turned the page of the magazine and took a chilly bite of her ice cream. A dribble of white threatened to unleash its milkiness across the vulnerable expanse of Lian's pillowcases. "They're not gonna let me take the Gaokao. I've been suspended too many times. So my dad asked his friend, they happen to have an extra room in their house, and yeah."

"Yeah," Lian parroted. "Well, that's a good thing then, yeah." This had been what she'd feared for her friend, that Wenyu's grades would slip so low she'd cut off all paths to any future. What she'd hadn't predicted was that the one path remaining would lead to America.

Wenyu sat back up. "Maybe we'll both end up in California. We can buy our mansions on the beach!"

"Yeah!" Lian said again, more forcefully now. But a strange feeling lashed at her. Wenyu's departure was one of necessity. Her dream, Wenyu's last-ditch effort. She returned to her essay, hastily unwrapping her own ice cream. It tasted sour in her mouth.

TWO WEEKS LATER, Lian stood in Wenyu's bedroom, watching her stuff underwear and blouses and pads into her suitcase. Wenyu was afraid there'd be no pads in California—Americans only wore tampons, according to an older cousin. There was a frenetic energy about Wenyu. She had put on her best dress for the plane ride over. She was supposed to leave for the airport in an hour, but Wenyu was debating whether or not she should bring her rain boots. "Does it rain a lot in San Jose?" she asked, to no one in particular. Neither of them knew.

Lian thought Wenyu might be scared, but Wenyu seemed preoccupied with the trivial things—tampons, rain—and Lian couldn't muster up the nerve to ask.

"See you in California, right, Lianlian?" Wenyu asked again, locking eyes with Lian. "Stanford's gonna snap you right up."

"Of course!" Lian said, her heart thrumming.

Wenyu tried to stuff her Doraemon plushie into the suitcase, but Doraemon bounced back, refusing to deflate. Wenyu turned and handed Lian Doraemon, his eyes two perfect black-and-white orbs peering out at her. "Take care of him," she said.

In the end, Lian told Wenyu to leave the rain boots. There was only so much space in her suitcase, and she could always come back for them if it turned out San Jose was a monsoon city.

It was not, and Lian never saw her again.

THE REJECTION LETTERS did not come in a swarm, like in her nightmares. They were a slow trickle of thin envelopes that reached her one by one, her dream chipped away piecemeal. Like *Titanic* and the unseen glacier, she whispered to herself. There was no explanation, only trite apologies that there were too many qualified applicants that year.

Throughout that spring, she thought about Wenyu, steadily becoming a California girl. Wenyu went to stay with that classmate of her father's, who had two sons of her own. Lian was jealous that Wenyu got two built-in brothers, and Wenyu reported back with frequent news of their quirky behaviors, the loud video games they loved, the "*Transformers*" shirts they wore. Wenyu sent Lian real-time observations about the strange weather, the overwhelming supermarkets, the stick of fried butter she'd tried at a thing called a *fair*. At first, Lian responded exuberantly, laughing alongside Wenyu at the weirdness of American traditions. They said they missed each other, and

Wenyu counted down the hypothetical days until Lian could join her in California. Her father's friend took Wenyu on trips into the city to eat samples from the Ghirardelli store, to walk the Golden Gate Bridge. As Lian's dreams crumbled, she told Wenyu with more and more conviction that soon it would be the two of them, romping through San Francisco together.

When the last rejection came, from Berkeley, Lian was almost relieved. There would be no her and Wenyu in California, no cleaving of her American dream to share between the two of them. Now, she could throw herself fullheartedly into the Gaokao. She'd sit with thousands of her peers, dripping sweat in a classroom in June, and she would outscore all of them. She'd take the traditional route, the one she'd always been expected to excel in, anyway. She'd get into a Tier 1 university at home, and no one would fault her.

She did exactly that. She tested into Beijing Normal University, one of the nation's top schools. Wenyu got into a state university in California, and Lian texted her congratulations. Slowly, however, their updates grew sparser. Wenyu's reports from California suddenly felt braggadocious, pompous, Wenyu rubbing in Lian's face the spoils she'd never get to enjoy. Lian stopped responding, eventually. She met an intelligent and caring man. She landed a high-paying job at an American company before she even graduated. She influenced scores of students with dreams like hers. They spoke of literature, film, politics, history. And other friends returned from America with stories of gun violence, racism, a crippled health care system. It was not the land of her dreams. She told herself that America made more sense for Wenyu anyway. It was a land devoid of rules, of shame, a place that had no respect for tradition or convention—perfect for Wenyu, the girl who stole and yelled and rebelled because she was never satisfied with what life had given her. But Lian could be content. She would be content. So she focused on her own path: career, husband, luxury high-rise. And indeed, twelve years later, she'd achieved almost all of this. She didn't need Wenyu roaring back in, reminding her of a wish she'd long since buried.

STILL, SHE PEERED at the Golden Gate Bridge in the hazy background of the invitation to Wenyu's engagement party. She looked at her perfect curls, her manicured nails. Her fiancé with his hammy smile, made hammy by too many meals of expensive ocean fish. What could her life have been? Her eyes landed now on the photo taped to her wall: Wenyu and Lian standing in front of their high school, both wearing their uniforms. The electric blue of their track pants had faded to robin's egg in the sunlight. Lian stood with her back rigid and arms pinned to her sides, pinned by Wenyu, who wrapped her arms around her, her head cocked to one side and her left leg kicking out behind them. Wenyu's eyes were crinkled shut, her smile wide and luminous, her dimples two miniature teacups of sunlight. Her hair was wild and free, the bushel careening down her back, while Lian's was, as always, neat and shoulder-length. Lian wore a look of faux annoyance, her mouth slightly open as if to say, Get off me! But the tiny smile tickling the side of her lips told a different story.

IT WAS 7:55. Five minutes until her session. They would be going over application essay questions today. She pulled up the website listed on Wenyu's invitation.

RSVP: Yes or No.

Lian clicked Yes.

2

It took them fifteen minutes just to find the door to the bar, which was at the back of the building, behind a dumpster. Lian teetered across the gravelly alley, holding on to Zhetai's arm. This was a trend that had seized Beijing in the last few years, and Lian loathed it. Americans called this phenomenon "*speakeasy*." There was nothing easy about it. What was wrong with a bar with a charming front entrance prominently displayed on a central street? Why did she have to hunt and squint for the entrance, buried deep behind a trash can, inside a janitor's closet, through the freezer section of a refrigerator? It reminded her of a children's novel she'd read years ago. The tiger and the wardrobe or something.

"Are we in the right place?" Zhetai kept asking.

They were on their way to Wenyu's engagement party. Lian had RSVP'd and received a generic confirmation email from Wenyu with more details about the event. She'd felt slightly shafted, receiving an email like that, as if Wenyu was speaking to just any acquaintance. Then she reminded herself that that's what she and Wenyu were now. Acquaintances.

They pushed open the unmarked door behind the dumpster and heard low bass thrumming from inside. A man in a black suit and black turtleneck asked for their names.

Under the bouncer's scrutiny, Lian grew self-conscious. There was a slight pilling on Zhetai's right sleeve, and his jacket was a tiny bit too long for him. She wished he'd worn the dark gray blazer; navy was much too daytime for this hour. But the bouncer waved them through, and Lian felt her heart beating in her chest as the hallway grew shorter and the music grew louder. Twelve years. What would Wenyu be like? What would she think of Zhetai? What would she think of her?

The bar was dark, low recessed lighting throwing sensual shadows across brown leather booths. Waitresses in tight black dresses handed out goblets of rose-colored cocktails. The space looked like the hollowed-out underbelly of a ship, and Lian could tell the drinks alone cost more than a typical date-night dinner. A recent Drake ditty echoed throughout the space. Distinct groups of people milled about the bar: some older people and girls with teenage faces she assumed were Wenyu's family members; a cluster of middle-aged men in suits; and a few Caucasians, who clung together chattering aggressively. The groom's friends, Lian assumed, perhaps in from Silicon Valley on an extended vacation, groupies on Wenyu and Thomas's international wedding tour. And then there were the familiar faces: Zhu Zixi was there in rapt and feverish conversation with another classmate of theirs, Liu Bin, probably trying to finagle a down payment's worth of investment out of the poor guy. Zhu Zixi, like Wenyu, had gone to school in California, at UC San Diego, though she'd come back shortly after graduation with a heavy distaste for American food, traffic, and values, as well as a PowerPoint presentation for a startup that would later turn her into a millionaire. Yang Qinru stood by the bar ordering a drink, her wisp of a husband holding out her Chanel purse like it was a crying baby. Lian was more surprised to see some other faces: Cao Jingqing had stopped in, evidently, from Tianjin, where she managed an explosives factory. Ge Zunhuai, who was at the London School of Economics for his PhD, sat beside her.

Lian and Zhetai walked with the easy, unhysterical intimacy of long-term partners, their arms grazing but their hands never meeting. Lian felt that those couples who insisted on traveling everywhere with their hands glued together exposed their insecurity; if their hands broke apart for a single second, would their relationship follow suit? A waitress approached with a tray of canapés, tendrilled things oozing with uni. Lian selected one, balancing it on a tiny square of napkin. Flanking the bar stood two long banquet tables overflowing with more hors d'oeuvres: tuna tostada bites, shrimp tartlets stuffed with Gouda, skewered five-spice duck tongue, deviled quail eggs, pillowy Japanese baked tofu on individual beds of cabbage. Beside these frilly appetizers stood a gilt-framed brushwork painting of Wenyu tucked into Thomas's arms, her hair swirling in the wind per usual. It looked so out of place in the darkened bar that Lian nearly coughed out her uni with laughter.

"Ye Lian! Ye Lian!" Zhu Zixi had seen her.

She and Zhetai walked up to Zhu Zixi, who threw her arms around Lian's shoulders.

"There you are," her friend screamed, handing her a purplish drink. "Here, drink this for me."

Lian gulped down the liquid, not caring what it was. She felt it burn her throat as she swallowed, and she was thankful for it. Where was Wenyu? They'd all gathered for her. Then she chastised herself for forgetting. It was just like Wenyu to make them wait.

"How's closing going?" Zhetai asked Liu Bin, absentmindedly. This was the only question anyone asked Liu Bin these days. He and his wife had been attempting to purchase a condo for months now, but competition was fierce. When they'd finally secured one—an admittedly impressive unit in a coveted subdivision just past the Fourth Ring—they encountered numerous issues in the heating system that gave Liu Bin headache after headache. And so the questions went, on and on.

"Almost there. Thirty days until I can get out of my mother-in-law's house," he said, his eye bags heavy as stones. "We can't all be as lucky as Zhu Zixi."

Zhu Zixi smiled a gummy smile, reaching behind her and pulling her portly husband, Bo, seemingly out of thin air. The man stood there, chubby and moonfaced, a heavy Rolex hanging off a disproportionally thin wrist. The men her friends chose were all brainless, dependable types, the draw their net worth rather than their personalities. In Zhu Zixi and Bo's case, they had met through their parents; her father's elementary school friend had struck it rich mining nickel, and her father was giddy to marry his daughter off to the man's well-fed son. Zhu Zixi had been the one to pursue Bo, which made sense: She had always been the type to chase after what she wanted with the ruthlessness of an osprey diving for an unknowing fish. "It's called consolidating wealth," Zhu Zixi had said, with grave solemnity. "You can't drag your feet." Within six months of knowing each other, they were engaged, and the two had just moved into their multimillion-renminbi penthouse in the heart of the city.

A ping.

"I am thinking about Double Indemnity. I think everyone did a lot of trouble for not a lot of money. If I was Phyllis, I would have waited longer and done a better job of making it look like suicide. Do you ever watch a crime movie and think about all the ways you could do it so much better than these idiots?"

"Sorry if this makes me sound like a crazy person."

"I do not think about killing anyone."

"I am not thinking about killing anyone."

"Should I use 'think' or 'thinking' in this case?" The texts came in rapid-fire, green filling up Lian's phone screen. She looked at Zhetai, who was now talking to Bo, nodding politely as the louder man giggled about some play investment in ore or silver that his father had thrown him to keep him occupied. She was about to respond when she heard a spike of laughter behind her, and she turned to see a man sitting at the next table, dangling a skinny shot glass as he leaned in to talk to a group of people Lian

didn't recognize. He stood out sorely in the crowd in baggy jeans and a T-shirt so large it reached his thighs.

Su Mingzun, Wenyu's itinerant first love, was alive and in front of her. They'd all heard what had happened to Su Mingzun in college—the meltdown on campus, the sudden disappearance from school—and it was surprising to see him here, looking quite fresh despite everything. The main difference between then and now was that he'd buzzed off his unwieldy mane, so that his hair at present was short and spiky. She felt a strange urge to march up to him, reach out and brush her hand across the top to see if it would cut her. She was shocked that Wenyu had invited him, but of course she had. If this evening was meant to show the people of her past what she had made of herself, he was a necessary audience.

"What's he doing here?" she turned to Zhu Zixi to ask.

Before she could get her answer, the opening notes of Ed Sheeran's "*Shape of You*" cut abruptly through the bar. The back of the stage slid open, and Wenyu and her husband-to-be appeared.

Wenyu was draped in a magenta dress with a slit all the way to her thigh. Her hair fell in big waves that glinted gold, movie-star glossy, her legs terminating in pointy heels. She looked as perfect as a wedding cake. Gone was the careening bushel of hair. Gone was the diamond shape that would crater between her eyebrows when she frowned. This Wenyu had buffed away every imperfection.

Wenyu's fiancé followed, smiling wide, yet again showing off those large, white teeth. Send my regards to your orthodontist, Lian thought. Everyone began clapping. Wenyu laughed, shrugging, as if the whole hullabaloo hadn't been her idea, and waved her hands to quiet the music. "Hey, everyone!" she exclaimed, beaming from face to face in the crowd. Lian stood just off center in the front row and watched as Wenyu's eyes slid over each of them in an egalitarian fashion. She waited for Wenyu to make eye contact, to stick out her tongue and wink, to hint that she knew how orchestrated this whole thing was. But Wenyu didn't even linger on Lian. Her heart sank.

"Thank you so much for coming! I am absolutely thrilled to introduce you all to Thomas, an incredible man and my best friend. And I'm so happy he gets to meet all of you, my family and my dear friends. We know that not all of you will be able to make it to our wedding all the way in San Francisco, so we're delighted we get the chance to celebrate with you here at our engagement party, and we look forward to celebrating together throughout the summer. We've been away from Beijing for so long, and it feels wonderful to return home into the embrace of those who know me best. *Now everyone, please eat, drink up! The rum cocktail is to die for!*"

"Return home into the embrace of those who know me best"? It was so formal, like the propaganda slogans they used to mock that would blare over the speakers at school. When had Wenyu started talking like that? As the music resumed, Lian grabbed Zhetai's arm, determined to retreat into the shadows before Wenyu could see her. It had been a mistake to come. She was no one to Wenyu.

Affectation.

Superciliousness. She was proud that she'd remembered this term despite her thrumming heart.

"Slow down," Zhetai said, putting his hand on her glass. Lian realized she'd been angrily sucking down her cocktail. She'd lost count of how many she'd had. "You don't want to get sick."

Sure, sure. Drinking makes you sick. She didn't have the patience for a lecture at the moment.

"What's that, your fourth one?"

She softened. So he'd been watching her. She was often struck by the things he noticed, even when she was sure he hadn't. "I'm fine," she said, collapsing into a booth. She suddenly felt exhausted. "Could you get me some water?"

He stood wordlessly and removed his jacket, folding it into a perfect square. He set it down on the leathery seat. As he departed for the bar, Lian sat back, surveying the scene before her. Ge Zunhuai was sitting next to Yang Qinru and her husband. He leaned back with one leg slung over the other. Yang Qinru chattered on enthusiastically, occasionally pistol-whipping her husband's thigh with her bag to get him to chime in. Zhu Zixi had ambled over to one of the middle-aged businessmen and had arranged her cleavage in prime investment-capturing form. The husbands all sat, inert and thick with money. Wenyu made her way from table to table, clinking glasses with her aunts and uncles and her father's business partners and all their high school friends. Lian watched as she greeted the table of Caucasians with tight hugs, Wenyu hopping on her heels like a child at a birthday party, her American voice sailing over the heads of the gathered crowd and sending piercing notes of English into Lian's ears. *"So happy you made it!" "I'm soooo jetlagged!" "Love your dress!"* Wenyu seemed lighter amid the Americans, her arm slung languidly over an ice-blonde girl's bony shoulders, her fingers ruffling the girl's fringe. It reminded Lian of the way the two of them would topple to the floor together, half play-wrestling, half hugging, every time they'd had to separate for even a few days. Wenyu had always been free and comfortable with her body, and since she had left Lian had felt herself fold in, becoming rigid. She certainly did not topple with Zhetai; she did not topple with anyone.

And then, suddenly, Wenyu was walking toward her, surging with that same trudge-cum-stomp that was her signature, her posture only slightly better than it had been twelve years ago. Finally, this was something Lian recognized. "Lian!" she called out, her voice brash in the way Lian remembered. "Why are you sitting by yourself?" Up close, contrasting layers of bronzer and shimmer threw dramatic shadows and highlights across her face, lighting her up like a disco ball. It was dazzling, but hard to look at it.

Lian stood and allowed herself a smile. "Hey, Wenyu."

Thomas flanked her, sticking out a large paw for Lian to shake.

"*You must be Lianne!*" he practically shouted, dragging her name into two syllables. He looked younger than she'd thought, nearly cherubic, and his voice had a disarming boyish lilt.

"*Nice to meet you,*" she said. She tried to catch Zhetai's eye at the bar, but he was turned away from her, asking for her water.

"*I've heard so much about you,*" he said, an empty American phrase all the more hollow in this context. What could Wenyu have told him about her? They no longer knew anything about each other.

"*I've heard so much about you too,*" she said back. From Wenyu's YouTube videos, but she didn't add that.

"*Oh, stop,*" he said. It was funny to Lian that he immediately thought this was a compliment. He moved to sit down in the booth across from Lian, as Wenyu slipped in next to her. So they were staying.

"Lian," Wenyu said, grabbing her arm and giving the fleshy part of Lian's tricep a squeeze. It was an act that was so familiar, and yet she couldn't help thinking about Wenyu caressing the Caucasian girl's hair. Perhaps this was simply what she did with everyone now. "I'm so happy you're here. Isn't this so ridiculous?"

Lian laughed, her heart springing; yes, she wanted to say, thank god you think so. I was starting to think you actually believed in all this stuff. But before she could respond, as if catching herself, Wenyu switched into English. "*We're so excited to catch up,*" she said, looping her arm around Thomas's. It jarred Lian, hearing her speak English, like the three of them were practicing lines in a play. "*It's been . . .*" And here Wenyu faltered, for one nearly imperceptible beat. Lian knew she wanted to put a number on the years, but when she realized the years were myriad enough to form a decade, she stopped herself. "*. . . too long.*"

Too long. That was one way to put it.

Lian felt shy, thinking about the way they'd faded from each other's lives. After she left, Wenyu didn't come home for two years, not until she'd started at UC Santa Cruz, and the first winter she returned, Lian was in Hainan with her family. They'd text each other on birthdays, holidays, but even those well wishes got more tepid over time. The last time they'd spoken had been one winter three years ago, when Wenyu mentioned she was coming back to Beijing for the new year. "I'm gonna be in Beijing for a week! Always such a short time," she messaged. Lian had contemplated asking her to hang out, but Wenyu's text seemed to gesture that it was a quick stop; she wouldn't have any time for her. So all she'd said was, "Hope you have a great holiday."

"*We hope you're enjoying the party,*" Thomas said. "*We got the brush painting from this amazing artist . . . babe, what's her name again—*"

"*Candy—*"

"*Oh right, yeah, Candy, which I thought sounded like a stripper, but her art is bomb!*" Lian hadn't heard that term before, *bomb*. She didn't quite know how to respond, so she smiled.

"*It's a nice picture. And the appetizers were delectable,*" Lian mustered, digging up a word from her TOEFL. *Delectable*. A little more refined than delicious. Thomas chuckled.

"*Okay, Lianne, Miss SAT over here!*" he said, laughing. Wenyu burst into giggles, covering her face with her hands. Lian was confused about what was so funny. She watched them for a beat, Wenyu's glossy fingernails like butterfly wings across her lipsticked mouth. What could they talk about? There was so much to catch up on. Her job. The trip to Europe she and Zhetai had taken three years ago. They'd taken boats down the canals in Venice and ridden bicycles through Copenhagen. The trip to Japan they'd taken the previous year, where they'd stumbled into some sort of sex mall that had ignited an enormous fight, Zhetai accusing her of purposefully provoking him. The condos they were looking at. Suddenly Lian's heart sank. Was there really all that much to catch up on?

Finally, Wenyu spoke. "I love your dress. Where did you get it?" The game of catch-up was always like grabbing leaves in the wind. You scrambled and snatched and the thing you finally caught hold of, in the end, wasn't the thing you cared to know about at all.

"Oh, just Zara," Lian said.

"Cool," Wenyu said.

"Yours is nice as well," Lian said. Then, for some reason, she felt compelled to add, turning to Thomas: "*If this party is this grand, I'm sure the wedding will be even grander!*"

Wenyu and Thomas laughed again. "*I love the way you describe things!*" Wenyu said.

A waitress walked by. Thomas hailed her down. "Excuse me, miss," he began, in stilted Chinese. "Can I have—*Vivian, how do you say, the wings—*"

"The fried chicken we have in the back." Wenyu leaned over, giving the woman a conspiratorial look. "Could you bring it out for us?"

The waitress nodded. "Thank you!" Thomas shrieked. The jauntiness of his English became clownery in Chinese; as most Americans tended to, he overemphasized the tones, turning the affirmative solidity of the fourth tone into a harsh command. He turned back to the table, an apologetic look on his face. "*Sorry, I'm starving.*"

"*Very good,*" Wenyu cooed, as if praising a dog. "*Thomas is brushing up on his Chinese,*" she said, turning to Lian.

"*I studied abroad in Shanghai when I was in college,*" he said. "*Forgot all of it.*"

"*I was so impressed on our first date! He was telling me about his work, and I said he sounded like such a successful guy, and he goes,* na li na li. *It was crazy!*"

"How authentic," Lian said, nodding.

"*Our first date, actually, it's a pretty funny story,*" Wenyu said. "*I was doing my master's at Davis, right, in art history, and I got this summer internship in the city. I'd take the train in three days a week. San Francisco was so exciting, but I didn't know anyone, so I started using Tinder.*"

"*Who wasn't?*" Thomas said, a slight note of defensiveness in his voice.

"*I was swiping, just having fun, then I landed on Thomas's profile. At first, he seemed like any other successful, good-looking guy. But okay, this is stupid, I liked that he didn't go by something cutesy like 'Tommy.' So I swiped right.*"

Thomas had graduated from Stanford a few years before and was, as were most men Wenyu had met in the Bay Area, in the tech world. For their first date, he and Wenyu met for drinks at a rooftop bar and he paid for everything; the margaritas, the red snapper ceviche, the tiny tiramisu cups, and even her Uber to and from the bar. He was an old-fashioned gentleman, and from the very beginning, she felt that she could rely on him. He told her about his company; he and a Stanford friend had created an extension that allowed one-click shopping across social media platforms. He was modest about it but hardworking; they called it an early night because he had to get back to work. When they parted, she found herself wanting a kiss, but he merely gave her a hug before opening the door to her Uber.

"*I didn't think you wanted me to come on too strong!*" he said now, playfully indignant.

"*Well, it worked,*" she said, scrunching her nose and giving him a peck.

She thought she'd never hear from him again, but the very next day, he invited her to be his plus-one at a company mixer that weekend. He kissed her on the rooftop of the Ritz-Carlton, the San Francisco lights twinkling.

"*It was a great first kiss,*" Wenyu said, leaning into Lian. They began seeing each other regularly, shopping on Hayes Street and eating at izakayas and boulangeries. When school started again in the fall, he would visit her every weekend. She began doing YouTube full-time. Two years after they met, Thomas sold his startup and bought his house. They got a dog, a fussy but *"brilliant"* (Wenyu's word) Pomeranian that she named *Lucky*.

And then, six months ago, on their five-year anniversary, Thomas took her on the helicopter ride that Lian had watched so many times on YouTube.

"It was the happiest moment of my life! You should have seen it, a little buoy formed the dot on the question mark," Wenyu said, smiling at the memory.

Despite Wenyu's enthusiasm, she recounted all this with the practiced cadence of one who has had to relay her life story often. Lian nodded and interjected occasionally with a soft gasp or "hmm." She felt torn between rabid fascination and annoyance; with the exception of the bit about Thomas's name, these were all details Lian had already gleaned from her YouTube channel. How had twelve years smoothed the edges of their friendship so that all Wenyu could talk about were the sanitized highlights she'd share with anyone on the internet? Worse—she behaved as though it was the most natural thing in the world for her to end up with someone like Thomas. But he was as far from what Lian had pictured for her as could be.

"Babe, you tell that story so good," Thomas said, leaning in and giving Wenyu a giant, loud kiss on the cheek. She pushed him away, playfully. *"I fought off all the suitors,"* he said, puffing up his chest.

Wenyu rolled her eyes. *"If you call psycho fans suitors."*

"They're kind of nice," Thomas said. *"I love when they send chocolate."*

This Lian did not know. "You have some secret admirers, Wenyu?"

Wenyu blushed. "I don't know about admire. They just send a lot of gifts." This exchange tickled Lian; it was a kind of faux modesty limited to only the beautiful and famous, Wenyu diminishing her devotees as merely crazy to make herself appear just like any-one else. But it didn't erase the fact that she had devotees to begin with. "*Oh, Thomas, I didn't tell you, this new one sent me clothes.*"

"*Ooh . . . he wants to dress you up?*" He grinned and squeezed her waist.

She rolled her eyes playfully. "*Oh, stop. The clothes are pretty cute, actually.*"

There was a stale beat. "*Well, what about you?*" Wenyu asked, training her big eyes on Lian. Then she slipped back into Chinese. "How's your love life?"

Lian was flustered. How could Wenyu not know about Zhetai? But then she chastised herself: There was no way Wenyu would have watched her with the same sort of rapt attention as she had Wenyu over the years. "I've been dating someone for a while," she said. "He's here, actually," she added.

Wenyu's face lit up. "Ooooh! Is it the guy from your Moments?"

Again Lian was surprised; so Wenyu had watched her too. She nodded, then gestured toward the bar, where Zhetai was still waiting for a glass of water.

"He's so tall!" Wenyu said, glee in her voice. "Good for <u>you</u>." Then, "Is he anything like Ma Zhongshun?"

Ma Zhongshun had been a star athlete in their class, flirta-tious with all the girls. He was smart and temperamental and Lian had loved him quietly all through high school because once she had arrived to an exam without a pencil and he had let her borrow his. He wrote his entire exam in pen and didn't make a single mistake. Zhetai, who always worried he'd left the stove on, was nothing like Ma Zhongshun.

"Oh, he's way smarter than Ma Zhongshun," Lian said. "And he's not a big flirt. He's super loyal."

"Awww, Lian!" Wenyu said, beaming. "You're so happy!"

At this moment, Zhetai reappeared at their table with Lian's glass of water. He didn't seem startled to see Wenyu and Thomas sitting there—evidently he'd seen them from the bar and had probably been waiting to see how long he could loiter before having to return. "Wenyu, Thomas, this is Zhetai," Lian said, extending her hand and placing it on his sleeve. She let it linger there briefly, feeling the warmth of his hand like a hot iron, just millimeters away but far enough not to be touching. She took it and gave it a squeeze, sending a look of alarm into his face.

"Hello," Zhetai said. "Congratulations."

"Sooooo nice to meet you!" Wenyu said, standing and giving him a hug, which sent bursts of red up Zhetai's cheeks. "Lianlian was just telling us about you!"

"That's nice," he said, giving Lian a smile.

Thomas gave Zhetai a slap on the back. "*Great to meet you, man. You keeping our Lianne over here out of trouble?*" He winked at Lian, and she winced. Thomas had known her for approximately six minutes. In no way was she "his." But it was unsurprising, this penchant for an accelerated and faux intimacy—it was very American; every American she'd ever met had been *so excited* to meet her, pelting her with embraces and nonspecific flattery.

Nonetheless, she gave a brief, affirming snort. Zhetai imitated her chuckle, moving to slide into the booth next to her.

"How did you two meet?" Wenyu asked, turning her large eyes on Zhetai.

"At school," he said. "At a film screening."

"Film screening! That's so cute. So old-fashioned," Wenyu said, fluttering her fingers.

"We've been looking at condos," Lian said.

"Oh my god, so exciting!"

"We saw one at Chaoyang One yesterday," she said, letting that emblem of luxury, Chaoyang One, roll casually off her tongue.

But Wenyu's face registered only a generic excitement. "Congratulations!" she said. "What a big step!"

"It was nice," Lian said. "Lemme see if I can find a photo—" She pulled out her phone.

"Lian wants to keep our options open though," Zhetai said.

"Well, of course," Wenyu said. "You can't ever fall in love too quickly." She cocked her head and put her face in her hands. "You're so cute together."

Lian laughed weakly, patting Zhetai on the arm. But Wenyu was already moving on. "*Oooh, Thomas, show them the photos of our new place,*" she said, tugging Thomas eagerly on the sleeve. "*We spent months looking online for houses in Beijing. We finally decided on this house in Shunyi, but then we weren't totally happy with it, so we decided to tear it down and build our own!*"

"*Right!*" Thomas grabbed his phone, the oil from his fingers slick against the screen (the fried chicken had materialized, dissolving at breakneck speed into a pile of bones). He pulled up a digital mock-up. "*They're still building, so we won't get official pics for a while, but these were our original designs,*" Thomas said.

Lian felt instantly silly for having bragged about Chaoyang One. Theirs was a towering mansion, three floors with a nearly all-glass facade, the living area spilling into a pool and a spacious backyard. In the mock-up, robotic ladies dangled their bare legs over the side as muscly men sloshed around in the water. It was being built in the Heavenly Earth residential complex in Shunyi just outside the Fifth Ring, a bit of a trek, sure, but the neighborhood was—Lian had heard among her friends and parents' friends—a suburban paradise worth the commute.

"*This is beautiful,*" Lian said, and put down her phone, embarrassed by the photo of the Chaoyang One condo she'd finally found. Even Zhetai was leaning in, nodding appraisingly.

"Thanks," Wenyu said, grinning. "Thomas and I designed it together; I wanted it to be a dream home for both of us."

"*The pool was a me thing,*" Thomas said. "*And Vivian did the rest.*"

"What will you do about your San Francisco home?" Lian asked.

"Oh, we'll be back," Wenyu said. "We'll go between this house and SF, maybe spend the first half of the year here, second half there."

"*The SF place is smaller,*" Thomas said. "*But we love it.*" He pulled up another photo. "*Check her out,*" he said, revealing a homey living room with white throw rugs and low-lying oak chairs, a single abstract painting hanging on the wall. Large bay windows overlooked a hilly neighborhood. In the distance, the ocean ebbed. Lian could see the whorls in the wood, the Craftsman details that made the space seem quaint while also telegraphing its high price tag. Wenyu sat by the window, nursing a cup of coffee, a knit blanket thrown over her legs. The blanket looked soft and the view looked spectacular.

So this was wealth. Having the palaces and skyscrapers of Beijing and the forests and mountains of California. Making the entire world yours, giving up nothing. Wealth was owning both sides of the Pacific Ocean. And it seemed to have come so easily.

"*We live near my favorite bakery,*" Wenyu said dreamily. "*I get a croissant there every morning after yoga. On weekends we go to the coffee shop down the hill. They make an amazing Earl Grey coffee.*"

"*There's a bookstore by the coffee shop that has every book you could possibly imagine,*" Thomas continued. "*And there's this hilarious old man who sits outside the bookstore and sells tiny poetry collages he makes from the books that are so old even the bookstore doesn't want them.*"

"*Thomas bought me one on our anniversary. I think it was made out of old Sears catalogs and some romance novel paperback. It was something like, 'Her hair was like the sun / One-time opportunity / but / 50% off / she'd be just as beautiful.' Silly.*" She smiled at the private memory. They just sounded like words to Lian.

Throughout the conversation, it did not get any less strange, hearing Wenyu speak English. She seemed so comfortable with it, her tongue slipping deftly over the idioms and local phrases. Back when they were kids, English was a flat language that, in their melodic, middle-school mouths, became pitchy, like an out-of-tune song. But sitting in front of her now, Lian could tell that Wenyu's English no longer carried with it the tones of her

Mandarin. She hated to admit it—it was better than hers. She envied Wenyu's ability to blend in like a shadow and also felt a stone in her heart, as if something had died.

"*That sounds lovely*," Lian said. And it did. There was no equivalent word to "*lovely*" in Chinese, but it seemed to be the perfect English term in this case. She had learned the term while reading "*Pride and Prejudice*," and she knew that people used it to describe all sorts of things: a plate of eggs, a blood-red sunset, a warm home, a person they loved dearly, a person they didn't love but still thought was lovely, nonetheless.

LIAN SPOKE A BIT about her job, about how she'd finally started watching "*Game of Thrones*." Wenyu told Lian she was making more vertical content now; she said her mother's health was better these days. Then the conversation was over, and Wenyu and Thomas stood up from the table. Wenyu snapped a selfie of the four of them, so swiftly it felt perfunctory, an impulse rather than a desire. They parted with one of those half-hearted but full-throated declarations that we absolutely must catch up one-on-one, I'll text you, yes, I'll text you. They'd talked about houses and parties and proposals—easy, fun things. Maybe this is what happened when people achieved their dreams. There was nothing left to talk about. Lian watched as Wenyu made her way over to a table of middle-aged people, presumably aunts and uncles, who greeted her with a cacophony of chirps and eager fingers reaching out to grab at her cheeks. Thomas wore that face that Americans wear when they are being shown off but can't understand the compliments—a dopey, unspecific smile, a slight bobble of the head as he agreed to whatever it was Wenyu was telling her seated relatives about him. They didn't even bother to sit down; Lian knew this stop would not be a notable one, and for an instant felt a bolt of joy, knowing that Wenyu had cared enough to sit with her.

Zhetai and Lian were now alone in the booth. She wanted to ask what he thought of Wenyu, of Thomas, but Zhetai was beckoning her to stand. "Let's join the others," he said. They found their way back to the table where her high school friends were sitting, and Lian perched next to Zhu Zixi.

"Did Wenyu come by?"

"Yup," Zhu Zixi said, through bites of a tartlet. "Her makeup was wild. I even told her, wow, Americans like everything big, their houses, their sodas, their . . . well, their lashes too."

Lian stifled a giggle, though she felt a bit guilty. "Don't forget about their nails." Out of the corner of her eye, Lian could see Wenyu doing her flurried goodbyes, clasping the hand of one particularly needy aunt before moving on to the next table, a group of men in suits.

"Oh my god, yeah," Zhu Zixi said, widening her eyes. "She could've blinded me with those things."

They both watched Wenyu for a beat, as she whipped out her phone to film what would probably show up in a vlog by the end of the week. Lian watched her lips moving, narrating the events of the night, but she could not read them.

"You think we'll make the cut?" Zhu Zixi smirked.

At that, a projector began throwing gauzy images of Wenyu and Thomas across the back wall of the bar, the two of them wearing large plastic sunglasses and cut-off T-shirts and Hawaiian leis in shades of pink and orange. Thomas in a leather jacket, Wenyu in a pink felt skirt as big as a tent, a black poodle prancing across its hem. Wenyu in spandex and a black mask with ears, holding a long tail in her hand; Thomas wearing a cape. The two of them in matching white T-shirts, hunched over a plate of ribs as blond children run shrieking in the background. Coupledom in America seemed mostly to be about Halloween and barbecues.

Lian and her classmates sat around the table, enjoying an easy familiarity. Ge Zunhuai poked fun at Liu Bin. "I just got off the plane and you look more tired than me!" Ge Zunhuai said, slapping Liu Bin on the back.

Liu Bin had always been a good sport and could dole out insults the same way he took them. "That's the price of making money, brother," he said, smirking. "Oh, you wouldn't know, you're on your, what, sixth degree?"

"Fuck your mom," Ge Zunhuai laughed, flicking a shred of napkin his way. "It's only the third, excuse you."

Cao Jingqing complained about her good-for-nothing husband, whom she had married young and who now sat on the couch all day watching sex thrillers. Zhu Zixi bemoaned the funding difficulties she'd encountered with her new app—"Everyone's broke these days. This cleavage used to get me millions!"

Lian joined in the light laments, gossiping about a coworker who was constantly trying to show Lian up at work by baking brownies on the weekly and wearing monochrome pantsuits on the daily.

"Very Martha Stewart meets Hillary Clinton," Zhu Zixi said. Her friends laughed and laughed. It was this sort of complaining that made them equals; it was necessary to voice a little discontent about one's life.

"We getting sentimental over here?" Lian turned to see Su Mingzun, who'd previously been sitting in the corner all night, standing at their table with that languid but defiant stance from high school, canting slightly to the left, one shoulder dropped so that his fingertips grazed the edge of his pant leg, his head cocked in a look of perpetual recalcitrance. Up close, she could see crow's-feet at his eyes.

The group laughed politely. Everyone remembered him, but no one at the table had ever been close to him.

"Su brother!" Ge Zunhuai said, clapping him on the back. "It's been a while."

Su Mingzun sneered in a way that was not entirely bad-natured, but not good-natured, either. He collapsed in the booth next to Ge Zunhuai. "I see we're all here to support the institution of marriage."

"We're here to drink," Ge Zunhuai said, grinning. He poured a shot and offered it to Su Mingzun.

He took it and downed it. Everyone shifted uncomfortably. The people seated at the table were mostly to blame for the rumors that had proliferated about Su Mingzun. After high school, he'd gone to Wuhan University, but he'd had to drop out, Lian had heard, after an anxiety attack. Many had claimed he'd been found in the middle of the school quad late one night, rocking on his heels and muttering. Zhu Zixi insisted on a more salacious truth, that he'd stripped naked and exposed himself to a few teachers, bellowing the words to "Understand You" as he did so. Either way, he never finished school, an unheard-of fate for the people at the table. Lian had thought he'd stay in Wuhan after, but apparently he was back in Beijing.

"So, Su brother, what're you up to?" Ge Zunhuai asked.

Su Mingzun flashed him a smile. "Oh, just the same as all of you. Got a promotion, buying a house, getting married."

Lian couldn't tell if he was being facetious. Zhu Zixi's eyebrows flew up. "Really?"

Su Mingzun laughed but ignored her pointed question. "I've been working in sales," was all he cared to elaborate.

"That's tough stuff," Ge Zunhuai said. "Good for you."

Su Mingzun gave him a hard look, but then a smile stretched back across his face. "It's bullshit," he finally said. "You don't need to humor me." He said this without any bitterness. He said it the way one would talk about a bad hand they'd been dealt but had made peace with. "I think it's really beautiful, what all of you are doing here. Growing up, settling down. Pointing your finger in one direction and saying, I'll go there." He closed one eye and pointed to a spot on the far wall. "You can't see exactly where you're going, but you're doing it anyway."

There were polite murmurs around the table. Su Mingzun spoke with his classic tenor—it was impossible to tell if he was mocking them or praising them.

"Do you all remember the story of the farmer and the rabbit that ran into the stump?"

"Of course," Zhu Zixi said, laughing. "Who doesn't remember that?"

"Yes, yes," he said. "A farmer tends to his crops, dutifully, diligently. He reaps corn and vegetables for his family. He is hardworking, but the labor is tiring. Then one day, a rabbit bolts across his field and hits a tree stump. It dies on impact. The farmer goes over and picks it up. He's filled with glee. Dinner! He calls it an early day in the fields and goes home to his wife. They skin and steam the rabbit and enjoy a nice meal of soft rabbit seasoned with chili pepper. The farmer realizes, hey, why am I toiling in the fields so hard, day in and day out, when I can just wait for dinner to deliver itself to my door? He starts sitting down in the field, waiting for the rabbit to come. He waits for days. Days turn into weeks. Another rabbit never comes. The farmer's crops, without the farmer to tend to them, all die. There is no harvest. He and his wife go hungry."

Lian snorted. Of course Su Mingzun would force everyone, at Wenyu's engagement party, of all places, to listen to a trivial story they'd all heard as children. Everyone knew you had to keep tending the fields. Rabbits would not always serve themselves up to you on a silver platter. Stupid expectation. "It's a story about how instead of waiting for life to reward you, you should work hard to achieve success for yourself," she practically snapped, surprising herself with her boldness.

"Ah, Comrade Ye!" Su Mingzun whipped toward her. "Guan Yu getting feisty in her old age, I see." He grinned, using that old nickname that everyone had used for her in relation to Wenyu. Liu Bei and Guan Yu, the fearless leader of the Shu-Han Kingdom and his loyal commander. Before she had the chance to retort, he continued: "That's what they want you to think is the moral of the story. But here's what the story's really about. You see, after he and his wife go hungry, she leaves him for a salesman who has invented a clever rabbit trap. He sets them all around his field and catches ten rabbits a day. She and her new husband eat like kings for the rest of their lives, and the old corn farmer dies alone." Lian made eye contact with Zhu Zixi and they both rolled their eyes.

"I don't remember this part," Zhu Zixi whispered. Lian didn't either; she realized Su Mingzun must have made it up.

Su Mingzun continued. "The actual moral is that no, we should not give in to blind risk, but we also should not think the only alternative is the one we attempted to reject in the first place. The farmer could have spent his days devising his own clever device to hunt rabbits. Better yet, once he caught the rabbits, he could have made the skin into leather shoes and bags and sold them on Taobao. The world is not an either-or game. We need to be smarter about finding a different way out of this wretched, dull life. We need to find our own rabbit traps."

He pointed at Ge Zunhuai. "Why are you really on your third degree, brother? Are you scared that when you enter the workforce, you'll lose your way without tangible markings of status and rank? Does only the world of academia, with its rigid hierarchies and clear reward systems, make sense to you?"

Liu Bin interfered. "Now, Su brother, I think that's a bit harsh—"

"He's right," Ge Zunhuai said, quietly. "What you all do, it's too scary to me. Making money and being entrepreneurs, it's not my game."

"Liu brother," Su Mingzun said, swinging around to Liu Bin. "I heard you just bought a condo, but it's not going so smoothly. You want your house to be cold and utilitarian. Your wife wants it to be stylish and cozy. The both of you have reduced the selection process into one of two choices. This is why you and your wife can't seem to agree. Maybe the house isn't the problem at all."

"You—" Suddenly Liu Bin's face was tomato red.

Only Su Mingzun would have the gall to disappear for years and walk into an engagement party with a lecture on how to live their lives. Ge Zunhuai attempted to hand him another drink, and Su Mingzun pushed his hand away, gruffly. "Let's cut it out with the nice guy shtick, okay?"

The table fell silent. It was at this moment that Su Mingzun stood up again and called out Wenyu's name. He grabbed the glass that Ge Zunhuai had left on the table. "Luo Wenyu! Let's drink to you!"

Wenyu looked over, and her face remained unchanged. Lian felt frightened at how she could look upon someone she'd once loved with eyes that betrayed nothing.

"Thank you," was all she said. She lifted her drink and downed it.

Su Mingzun dropped his glass on the table. "It's been real, my old classmates," he said, before trudging away. Everyone looked quite unsettled, their previously cheery mood deflated.

Zhu Zixi looked at her watch. "We should get going," she said, tugging on her husband's sleeve. "What an asshole."

One by one, the seated couples began rising, with murmured promises that they'd all get together soon. Zhetai rose, too, his arms crossed. Lian knew he disapproved of what he'd just seen, had probably never interacted at close quarters with someone like Su Mingzun. When he got upset, he tended to wrap himself up tightly in this fashion, as if building a blockade against any chicanery that could slip in. Lian, however, stayed put, wanting not to follow the tide of her friends dissipating—wanting, for some indescribable reason, to prolong the night.

"I'll be outside," Zhetai said. Lian nodded.

The only other person not to leave was Ge Zunhuai, who had gotten progressively drunker throughout the night and now seemed ill-equipped to rise.

"Another?" he said, offering a bottle in Lian's direction.

"Yeah," Lian said, not caring what was in the bottle.

They drank their liquor—whiskey, as it turned out—for a moment. Lian's phone buzzed.

"*I try Citizen Kane for the third time tonight and I still do not understand why Americans love this movie so much.*" Then, uncharacteristically, in Chinese: "They're obsessed with regret!"

"*Regret,*" she typed. "*New vocabulary.*"

"*I do not understand why people regret. It is a waste of time.*"

Ge Zunhuai seemed heavier than he had minutes prior, and Lian wondered if he was bothered by Su Mingzun's outburst.

"That was pretty crazy, what Su Mingzun said," Lian said. "Nice guy shtick? You're not even that nice."

Ge Zunhuai stared at her for a wry second, before letting out a laugh. "Gee, thanks, Comrade Ye."

She grinned. "You'd think he'd grow out of his asshole thing by now."

Ge Zunhuai shrugged. "Maybe he's right though," he said, hunching his shoulders in a manner that suddenly reminded Lian of their high school days, when he'd have the answer to a question in class so quickly he'd be embarrassed to say it. "We're all kind of, doing this thing. I don't know how I ended up here, either. Well, not here-here. London. Grad school. It's crazy. Sometimes I'm convinced I stay in school because I don't want to make a decision about my real life."

He chuckled, holding his glass to his mouth. Lian looked at him. It was clear from the way he spoke that Su Mingzun had said nothing Ge Zunhuai did not already feel.

Lian spoke. "Maybe we're all making the mistake of 'one stubborn will, one stubborn path.'"

He laughed again, hiccuping this time. "You were always more the literature buff, Ye Lian, but I don't think you're using that right."

It was her turn to laugh. "What I'm saying is, maybe you're right to not make a decision. Maybe everyone else is just being stubborn."

Ge Zunhuai downed the liquid. "Isn't 'stubborn' just one way to describe someone who has conviction?" He let his arm fall as he contemplated his empty glass. "I'd like to have some of that conviction one day."

She stood. She didn't want to be here any longer. "Hey, have a safe flight back. Let us know next time you're in town."

He nodded, blearily.

She made her way toward the door. The bar, now nearly emptied, felt cold and random. The businessmen had left; the girl with the ice-blonde hair was gone. Wenyu and Thomas had disappeared.

Lian walked outside, the wet June night immediately cloaking her in sweat. Zhetai stood at the foot of the steps, one hand in his pocket, the other thumbing through his phone.

"Hi," she said.

"DiDi's coming in a sec," he said.

She stood outside the door to the bar, contemplating the evening. She thought again of how she and Wenyu had parted, and now wondered if the two of them would ever see each other again, or if they would pass each other by the way they'd done for the last twelve years, allowing excuses and schedules to wedge another decade-long space between them. She thought about Su Mingzun's speech, the way he'd jabbed at them all with that holier-than-thou look in his eyes. What would he think of Wenyu's life now? Wenyu was beautiful and wealthy and successful, and she had fallen in love with a man who loved her. She'd taken the right steps, and now she got to reap the rewards of a job well done. Lian realized that she'd been attempting to search for some evidence tonight, some sign that maybe Wenyu wasn't so happy, that she regretted going away to America. She thought of that look on Wenyu's face as she sat down next to her: Isn't this so ridiculous? A conspiratorial moment that was probably just an illusion. Maybe Lian had her answer: Wenyu really was so happy.

Zhetai got a call, probably from the DiDi driver, lost somewhere in the back alleys of this labyrinth. Lian watched Zhetai walk on to the main street, his head tilting from side to side as he waved down a car that could not see him.

And then she heard something. A low murmur, soft chuckling. She craned her neck to look around the corner of the bar and caught the gleam of a cigarette, a pinprick in the dark. Wenyu stood underneath the alleyway awning, a trail of smoke snaking from her fingers into the night air. Beside her stood Su Mingzun, his body curled inward so that the tip of his cigarette drifted toward hers, the two ends meeting until his ignited in a burst of amber. His hand rested on the curve of Wenyu's purse, tugging the strap just slightly toward him. Lian looked away, a blush spreading quickly across her cheeks.

The lights of a white car finally pierced the alley, and Zhetai reappeared, jogging toward Lian. She hurried to meet him. He opened the car door for her, and she slid in quickly. She sat and stared straight ahead. She could feel her heart thumping, her face ablaze.

"Are you okay?" Zhetai asked.

"Yeah, yeah," she said, and she knew immediately she did not want to tell Zhetai what she had seen. "Just so hot."

He nodded. They sat with their seatbelts tightly fastened. Lian turned toward the window and watched the skyscrapers blink past, the city disappearing and reappearing a thousand times before her eyes.

WHEN THEY GOT BACK to hers, Zhetai collapsed into bed. He was asleep before Lian even had a chance to change out of her party clothes. She watched his back rise and fall, then slowly undressed, unzipping her dress and letting it spill into a pool at her feet.

She stood there in her underwear and stared at her reflection in the mirror. Her hair still fell in the same neat manner across her shoulders as it always had. She held her shoulders with the same slight hunch. As a child she'd been tall, but her growth spurt had come early and now she was of a respectable and entirely generic height. Sunspots studded her cheeks, but she felt ageless. When did an adult become so? After they traded their zip-up sweatshirts for suit jackets? After the gangly edges of their pubescent bodies became soft and grief-laden? And yet, she did not feel different from that girl with the dice-clasped hair, windmilling her arms wildly on the early morning track field.

She lay down in bed next to Zhetai, her body stretched out like a board. As if he sensed her presence, he turned over to face her, his hands cradled near his chin. His lips mumbled a phrase, their movements dictated by some dream. "Go, go," she could hear him saying. He had told her once he had a recurring nightmare in which he was stuck behind a large crowd on his way to work, and no matter how he tried to cut through, the mob would seal up and prevent him from moving forward. She wondered if this was happening now, or if he was on a clipped stroll in his subconscious or was pushing some imaginary son or daughter out the door.

What had she seen as they were leaving? Wenyu sharing a cigarette with Su Mingzun. It could have been innocent, but the thudding in Lian's chest told her it was not. The June heat was heavier than ever, and she flung the comforter off her body so that her bare stomach lay glistening under the moonlight that streamed through her window. She was sweating—oh, how could she stop sweating? As she gazed at the moonlight, everything about Su Mingzun flooded the front of her brain.

SU MINGZUN HAD MET Wenyu and Lian during their first year of high school. The three of them were all in the same class. It was a vulnerable year, when those who'd been accumulating social prowess throughout middle school solidified their standing. But Wenyu couldn't care less about status or standing, and the bewilderment with which the girls looked at Wenyu in middle school turned to spite in high school. She sought no one's approval, least of all theirs. There was also the fact that she was beautiful, and people are always threatened by beauty. Her dad had started working in Shanghai and would only come home on weekends, prompting rumors from the cruel minds of their classmates: that he had a second family, that he was a drunk who couldn't keep a job, that he'd gone away because he hated being around Wenyu.

Su Mingzun, too, had an absent father. He, too, did not have friends. He made many jokes, and the boys in class joked with him, but everyone thought he was too weird to be close to. He was sent to the principal's office every week for refusing to wear his uniform, but he persisted in his rebellion. He once showed up to class wearing only his underpants.

One day in their second year—that flimsy, penultimate year of high school upon which it feels the rest of one's life hinges—Wenyu showed up to school in a red dress. It was her birthday. She'd stolen her mother's blush and dotted her cheeks with cherry. Su Mingzun appeared in class wearing a black T-shirt over black running shorts. The two of them stood out sorely among the sea of blue-and-white tracksuit uniforms. Lian, who always sat in the middle of the classroom, wanting to be seen neither as teacher's pet nor rebel, watched as their mathematics teacher dragged the two of them out of the room, a handful of Wenyu's red dress in one hand, a handful of Su Mingzun's black T-shirt in the other.

In the principal's office, Wenyu told her later, Wenyu said that she believed students had the right to self-expression, especially on special days such as their birthdays. Su Mingzun agreed with her and said that he had dressed this way, too, because of her birthday. It was of course a lie, but nice lies can be crucial.

They began dating and would arrive at school in matching nonuniform outfits, Su Mingzun in his yellow graphic T-shirt and Wenyu in her yellow blouse. Lian found this a bit paradoxical, the fact that the two of them would risk retribution to stand for individuality and yet wear corresponding ensembles, but she was happy for her best friend. When Su Mingzun kissed Wenyu for the first time, Wenyu ran up to Lian on the exercise field red-faced and out of breath and shouted the news in her ear. Lian screamed and they jumped up and down like children.

"What's a boy's tongue like?!" Lian asked, her eyes bugged out.

"It's muscly and slippery, like an abalone wriggling out of its shell!"

"EWWWW!!" Lian shrieked and slapped at Wenyu, who stuck her tongue out and gagged. But Lian could tell she was very happy.

Then Wenyu started asking Lian to defy the dress code with her and Su Mingzun. Lian, too scared of punishment, said no, joking that she didn't want to third-wheel her and Su Mingzun.

"You're too afraid of everything these days," Wenyu told Lian. "It's no fun."

"Well, fear is important so your head doesn't spin off into traffic because you're sticking it out the window trying to catch raindrops on your tongue, and you get hit by a passing truck."

"You're too morbid," Wenyu said. "If you weren't so morbid, maybe Ma Zhongshun would ask you on a date."

Looking back, Lian felt that it was over this specific issue—the dress code—that their friendship had begun to branch. Lian realized she liked the mundane certainty of their uniform. The fact that everyone wore the same blue polyester jacket over a white T-shirt and a matching pair of striped pants meant that no one had to feel threatened by another's sartorial creativity. It made everyone look equally mediocre, and Lian felt that was good for children growing quickly into adults. Each morning, she put on her uniform sitting on her bed and tied her tennis shoes kneeling by the front door. She felt safe in the routine. On the exercise field, the teacher would shout, "Bring about unity to the nation! Show your devotion to community by kicking higher! Working harder!" Their uniform really did bring about unity. No one was better than anyone else.

Finally, Wenyu stopped asking. And that was when Lian looked at herself and no longer saw the girl in the uniform. All she saw was a girl without a red dress.

Then the other rumors started: Su Mingzun and Wenyu had had sex on the exercise field at night; they had gone to Tibet and gotten secretly married; Wenyu was pregnant with Su Mingzun's devil child.

"Maybe you two should keep it low-key for a bit," Lian suggested to Wenyu, nervously.

Wenyu looked at her, incredulous. "And give power to these weird rumors? No way! They're just jealous." She and Su Mingzun began acting in more and more ridiculous ways, sometimes giving each other loud kisses in the middle of class. Lian began to feel far away from her best friend. To Wenyu, Lian felt, she was just one of the envious spectators.

Wenyu and Su Mingzun diversified their antics. Soon it wasn't enough to cause a disturbance with their clothes; they also began pulling petty pranks around the school. Stupid things. They spelled out DOWN WITH THE AUTHORITARIAN SCHOOL GOVERNMENT on the chalkboard with holographic stickers. One of their main targets was their stuffy, buttoned-up literature teacher, Teacher Liao, who had the pinched lips of a much older woman and who was rumored to have been engaged once before her fiancé ran off with her cousin. Her abandonment had translated into bitterness and hostility; she was known to be the harshest teacher in school, specifically when it came to boys. Su Mingzun would flirt with her, complimenting her dull sweaters and her loafers. He and Wenyu snuck into the principal's office one morning and proposed to Teacher Liao over the airwaves. They wrote her love letters from made-up secret admirers and begged her for her hand in marriage. They were suspended once, then twice. Lian might have been inspired by their rebellion, but there was no cohesion to their antics, no higher purpose despite their vague anti-authoritarian bent. It was all just pretty annoying, two people absolutely convinced of their love's singularity and hell-bent on convincing everyone around them of it too.

But it appeared that love, like youth, could not last forever. The summer before their senior year was stressful; everyone was contemplating their future, and Wenyu and Su Mingzun were headed to different places. Su Mingzun, despite his antics, would test into a good university. He hadn't been expelled for the sole reason that he was quite the brilliant student, his exam scores near perfect and his essays controversial but incisive. But Wenyu had always tested in the lower 30th percentile of their class. There was only the slimmest of possibilities they'd end up going to the same school. Wenyu began telling Lian that she and Su Mingzun planned to run away together—to a tiny apartment in Japan, or a plot of land in Sichuan—and Lian saw her friend warping the childhood dreams they had shared into something more desperate. Lian tried to call her back from that brink. She pleaded with her to focus on her exam prep; Japan and Sichuan could wait.

One day in the early winter of their senior year, Wenyu showed up to school wearing a short, tight black dress. Everyone stared; her bare legs were an extra affront in the chilly December wind. Some whispered that she looked like a Korean pop star. Some said she resembled Audrey Hepburn. Ma Zhongshun hollered at Wenyu: "Oh, miss, can you get me a tall glass of beer?" She shoved him playfully. "Shhhh. Get your own beer." Su Mingzun sat in the corner of the room, glowering.

Later, Lian saw the two of them on the field, arguing.

"He asked you to get him a beer! Like you're some cocktail waitress!" Su Mingzun was shouting.

"So what, maybe I want to look like a cocktail waitress! Maybe cocktail waitresses are pretty!"

"Cocktail waitresses are penniless whores! And Ma Zhong-shun is a bastard and a stupid jock and a pimp!"

"Oh please, you'd love to be Ma Zhongshun! You'd love to be a pimp! Maybe I'll date him instead!"

"He's just gonna get you in bed, then forget your name!"

"Fuck you, Su Mingzun! I'll get in bed with whoever I want to get with! Maybe I'll get in bed with every single person at this stupid school!"

She stripped off her pearls and threw them with full force at Su Mingzun's head. The beads hit him limply then flopped to the ground, but the look he fixed on her was so full of anger, Lian felt frightened just watching from across the field. Then he stalked off.

It was, by many accounts, a typical argument between the two of them. Screaming one moment, sure to be wrapped in each other's arms the next. Their fights were as passionate as their sloppy kisses, the storm cloud of anger they'd leave hanging over the classroom as turgid a tension as when they were happy. But the week after, Wenyu appeared on Lian's doorstep to deliver the news that she was leaving for San Jose. She and Su Mingzun had broken up, and she was leaving. She said this with as much dispassion as she said the rest of it—her father's friend, the extra room, the suspensions. Lian wanted to scream, I told you so. I told you you shouldn't tie yourself to someone like him. Look at you now, fleeing across the Pacific. You don't even want to go to America! You just want to go because—because—and Lian had to bite down on her words, push them back into her heart.

It was mine first, she wanted to say. You're just mad at your boyfriend. You're gonna steal my dream just to stick it to this guy?

LIAN LAY ON her bed, thinking about all of this. She could not hear the night over the hum of the air-conditioning. She thought of Wenyu's wide, silly grin and wondered if Su Mingzun was who she'd remembered him as—if that long-ago memory had ignited something dormant inside her. In a way, her class-mates were all the same. Despite years apart, and continents, Ge Zunhuai still approached every decision with the same rigid neuroticism he always had, Liu Bin did the opposite, Zhu Zixi still shouted with the tenor of a man at a bar fight, and Su Mingzun still walked with the swagger of someone convinced he's discovered the secret of life and is living among fools. He had not become someone; he was always still becoming someone, and that perhaps was what made him exciting. Maybe this was the one thing missing from Wenyu's perfect life. A man with his limitless potential still barreling toward something in the distance. No matter that he never got there. As long as his feet never landed on the ground.

As for herself, Lian thought about the way Su Mingzun had so casually called her Guan Yu, slotting her back in as Wenyu's sidekick, and her skin burned. How could she be her sidekick when the two of them had not seen each other in a decade? When she had forged her own path completely independently, when she could barely feel a trace of herself on the new Wenyu? Whatever marks they'd made on each other years ago had long faded.

Her phone pulsed again. She tried to resist looking at it; it was two AM, time to sleep, no logic in responding this late. But she couldn't help herself.

"I hope to live a life without regret. Do you have any regret?"

She rested her phone on her chest, staring up at the ceiling. Did she have any regret? She stared for what felt like hours before she slipped, abruptly, deeply, into sleep. The last image that came to her was a rabbit with its throat cut, blood spurting out in a fount.

3

On Saturdays, Lian and Zhetai played badminton in the morning. They woke up at nine AM, got to the gym by nine thirty, and played against each other for an hour before coming home to a lunch her mother had left for them.

There was something incredibly meditative about swinging the birdie with someone whose habits you knew well. Zhetai was better than Lian, a fact that was as simple and pure as a pearl. He approached badminton with the same methodical precision as his work and had over time developed near-perfect form, his serves and forehands and backhands completed at the optimal angles. Today, Lian watched him stretch, sitting on the bench, his left leg out. He wore a cobalt blue sweat-wicking shirt, basketball shorts, and high white socks. He never let his hair grow out past his ears and it was currently short and tidy, just long enough to part but not long enough to get in his face. He did a few practice swings, smashing the racquet down in swift, dynamic swoops, the side of his shirt lifting to reveal part of his torso. Lian wondered for a moment if all a woman ever wanted was to see her man excel at a sport.

"Lian? Come on," Zhetai beckoned, as he set off toward the farthest court from the gymnasium door. She rose slowly, feeling like her feet were as heavy as lead.

The image of Wenyu and Su Mingzun in the alleyway thumped in her head. She wondered if she should tell Zhetai, wondered what he would say. Well, he'd be scandalized. He'd tell her not to see Wenyu again. Zhetai was a moral absolutist, prone to looking at the world in categories of good and evil. Wenyu would surely fall into the evil category, home to temptresses, floozies, adulterers.

He got into position on the north side of the court—his preferred position, he always played there—and Lian joined, tapping her racquet on the ground. Their relationship fell along simple rules within the confines of the badminton court—he served, she hit it back, he hit it back, she missed, he scored, he told her, Don't worry, you'll get it next time, and then the cycle repeated. Each time, in his calm "don't worry," she felt held by him, reassured, comfortable in the position of student, with no choices to make but how to hit whatever birdie came her way. Each round felt like they were making something together.

Once, years ago, they'd managed to achieve a 287-hit rally, a feat that attracted a small crowd. Amid the cheers, Lian saw a girl tugging on her boyfriend's arm, seemingly pouting, Wow, when will we be like them? Her foot stomping, a tiny envious tantrum. Lian knew that the point was not to keep the birdie afloat—the point was to win—but she felt like this was the winning, the persistent and unlikely continuing. She and Zhetai gave each other coy, jubilant glances as they rallied the birdie back and forth. This was a year into their relationship, that warm, fragile time that teeters between temporary and forever, and by then Lian was familiar with the contours of Zhetai's body, with the way his left shoulder cramped more easily than his right, with the smirk that would play at the corner of his mouth when he was about to attempt a particularly sly serve. That day, it felt like all her knowledge of Zhetai—and his of her—was put to the test. They were teammates, partners, two bodies in a dance that would break if any part of them went out of sync. She relied on his arm;

he relied on her leg. This mutual reliance, this mutual trust: it was never so seamless as during a game of badminton. This was the moment she thought, I love you.

When she finally missed the birdie—he'd flicked it a bit too far to the left, and she dove, but her racquet fell just short—she felt like something had broken in her heart, and suddenly, Zhetai was just Zhetai again.

Today, they started slow, Zhetai lobbing a lazy birdie in a high arc over the net. Lian hit it back in similarly lackadaisical fashion.

She watched as Zhetai steadied his body, placing his right foot in front of his left, turning the racquet face toward her, and hovering the birdie right above it. He typically started in this way, with a low backhand serve. He hit it and the birdie shot toward her. She moved to the left and managed to flick it back over the net. In this fashion, they volleyed the birdie back and forth.

She peered at him, his brow stitched in that portrait of concentration she knew so well. He seemed to have no memory of the previous night at all, had not mentioned anything about the party that morning or on the ride over to the gym. He was focused purely on his current task, the forward-churning train of his mind already on to the next stop.

"Did you have a fun time yesterday?" she asked now.

"What?" Zhetai breathed, hitting the birdie back. "Yeah, it was cool."

"What'd you think of my friend?"

"Oh," Zhetai said, his lips pouting in that way lips pout when something is just okay. "She was nice."

Nice? Out of all the adjectives, this was not one Lian had been expecting. Friendly, maybe. Loud, perhaps. Exciting. Annoying. She waited for him to elaborate, but his eyes were fixed on the birdie falling toward him in a high arc. It shouldn't have surprised her; Zhetai was never one to spend time confabbing about things they'd experienced together; movies and birthdays alike slid out of his mind as soon as the credits rolled or the candles went out. Still, it shocked her a little that he had no more to say about Wenyu, who, in a previous life, would have been the first to hear about Zhetai, the first to dole out her assessment, the first to hold her, tissues at the ready, if something went awry. She supposed she was being harsh. To Zhetai, Wenyu was just any other friend she'd lost touch with. As if he'd read her mind, he added: "She has a lot of friends."

Lian thought about this. There were indeed many people at the party last night. It was impressive, that all of them had flocked to the bar for Wenyu. Lian wondered how many people she'd have at her own engagement party and knew that it'd be paltry compared to the previous night's numbers. No matter the reason their classmates had come to the party—whether for old times' sake or merely out of curiosity over what Wenyu had become—they had still come. Curiosity, although a cold emotion, was still closer to affection than to apathy. When it was Lian's time, Cao Jingqing would certainly not come into Beijing for the event; she might not even invite Liu Bin. This didn't sadden her necessarily; she did not covet friendships that were no longer. People drifted faster when they moved on to new stages of life but stayed in the same place. At every moment, there were choices made, and as the years flowed on, they'd chosen to not attend each other's New Year's parties, or not to invite each other out on trips to Heilongjiang or Hainan, little choices that did not seem so consequential at the time but that after years accumulated into distance.

"Yeah, it was nice to see everyone," Lian said, her thoughts boiling down to one simple fact that was, in its way, true. It had been nice to see everyone. "Her fiancé was quite . . . aggressive," she said next, unsure if that was the best word choice for Thomas's roiling, hot-blooded enthusiasm, but hoping it would prompt some sort of ire in Zhetai nevertheless.

"Americans are just like that," he said, shrugging. "He was shorter than I'd expected. I thought Americans were all as huge as basketball players."

The observation was accurate, if bland. "I just never thought she'd end up with a guy like that," Lian said. "I mean, he's so . . . sanitized. Like a politician."

"You expect her to be with some sort of animal?" He smashed the birdie down toward the right, his hand closing in a celebratory fist before Lian even had the chance to miss it.

She snatched the birdie off the ground, more irritated by his question than by the shot. Her head hurt. She couldn't concentrate on the game before her. "No . . ." Lian said, hovering the birdie above her racquet. She thought of Wenyu and Su Mingzun fighting on the exercise field. "There's just something so shiny about him. He's like a big rubber squeeze toy. I don't know, I don't trust him."

"You don't like anyone's husband," Zhetai said next, lobbing the birdie back over.

Was this true? She supposed he was right. Bo had never worked a day in his life and acted like it; Yang Qinru's husband was spineless. Cao Jingqing's husband—she'd met him once years ago, before they were married—was like an overgrown boy. "Well, maybe my friends should pick better husbands."

"You're being too critical," he stated, like it was objective fact. But Lian thought of what she'd seen outside the bar the previous night, and fiery indignation rose inside her. She was right to question. Wenyu's relationship was not what it seemed.

She purposefully missed the next shot. "I'm tired," she said, and the game was over.

AFTER THE GYM, they toured another condo, this one a larger space in an older building in Haidian. The condo sported more dated furnishings, but it compensated with a sprawling living room and a roomy kitchen. With some work, it would be just as luxurious as the condo at Chaoyang One, and could be a long-term place for them; there was room not only for a baby, but for a child to grow up in. Even two. The realtor emphasized this repeatedly: "You'll never have to move again." Lian could tell that Zhetai liked this certainty, his head bobbing in agreement, his arms crossed and chin furrowed the way they were when he was taking something very seriously.

On the ride home, Lian thought about what the realtor had said. "You'll never have to move again." She pulled up Wenyu's Instagram. Wenyu had posted photos from the previous night; in the first one, Thomas was holding her from behind and leaning down to plant a kiss on her cheek, mimicking the pose in their portrait. "*seeing double <3*" said the caption. Lian scrolled and saw that Wenyu had written more: "*Thank you to everyone who came out to our engagement party! It was the happiest day of my life getting to celebrate with everyone I love—cannot wait for the wedding!*" She swiped through the carousel and saw photos of Zhu Zixi, Yang Qinru, Liu Bin. Her own self stared back in the third photo. She looked happy, genuinely happy, one hand cradling a champagne glass, the other resting on Wenyu's shoulder. Su Mingzun was nowhere to be found.

She kept scrolling through Wenyu's Instagram, ogling the copious evidence of Wenyu's joy: In the following photo she and Thomas rode Mobikes, her sundress rippling off the back of the seat, Adidas tucked into the pedal straps. In a photo from Thursday, she wiped a fluff of beige cake on Thomas's nose. On each was a caption that was both sweet and generic: "*cake's 100 times sweeter with you,*" "*couples who work out together stay together.*"

She seemed so light and unencumbered, her eyes so free from bags and her skin so radiant, her words so full of bliss and expectation, that Lian wondered if she had misinterpreted what she'd seen in the alley, if indeed it had been just two friends catching up, smoking a cigarette after a long and exhausting day.

Her finger hovered above the heart button on the photo of her and Wenyu at the party. She tapped it.

"So?" Zhetai asked, and Lian was pulled back to the world of her reality. The taxi had arrived outside Lian's building. "What do you think? I think it makes sense to invest long-term. Moving is so expensive."

"But . . . how do we know what we'll want in five, ten years? What if we don't like Haidian?"

"You've grown up in Haidian your whole life. What's there not to like?"

"What if we want to try somewhere else one day? Like Chaoyang. Or Fengtai. Or . . . or . . . Shanghai! Or California!"

Zhetai looked at her for a beat, then laughed. "Okay, you know what, I get it. You just want to do what your friends are doing. But you have to think about what's good for you."

Lian didn't respond. She stared down at her phone, at Wenyu's smiling face.

"Maybe you're right," she finally said, then marched through the doors of her building.

AT HOME AFTER LUNCH, Zhetai settled into the couch and put on an episode of "*The Walking Dead*." Lian went into her bedroom and sat down at her desk. She had a lesson. She opened Skype. There was a green circle next to his name. He was online. Had he been waiting for her? She hadn't responded to his question about regret. It was exactly noon. Lian clicked the call button and watched the bubbles ripple. She saw her face reflected in her computer screen and quickly ran her fingers through her hair, smoothing her bangs so they lay flat against her forehead.

"*Hi!*"

It was always jarring for a moment, to speak in English with him. She had to recalibrate her brain, remind herself that this was immersion. They never spoke in Chinese, so it shouldn't have still felt alien, but she always felt a small jolt of confusion when he appeared on screen and the jovial English greeting burst forth from his mouth.

"*Hey, Freddy,*" she said, a name he'd chosen for himself, a kitschy shorthand for the director he so loved. Meanwhile, she called herself *Lily*. She'd picked a new English name for work—*Luna* felt too childish, a name for a witch in a magical place that didn't exist. By the time she remembered that *Lily* was also a name from Harry Potter, it was too late. Freddy was in front of a white wall again, the shiny corner of a film poster visible just behind him to his left. He sat in a gaming chair with a high back and wore a plain black T-shirt, his typical uniform. He always spoke to her through a headset. Today, she felt a little shy looking at his face. He kept his hair tied back, fastened with an elastic so that it formed a little tail at his neck. It was straight and very black, which made his skin seem paler. He wore wire-frame glasses that were a bit too large for his face. When he was passionate, a deep line split his forehead down the middle, jiggling the glasses on his nose. He could not be described as handsome, but there was something about the upward tick of his mouth that made her want to listen to him.

"*So much occurred since we spoke last time,*" he said, the eagerness palpable in his voice. He spoke with jaunty confidence. His grammar was not always perfect and his word choice too formal at times, but he soldiered through, often asking for corrections. He was not embarrassed to get things wrong, a trait that was rare in men. "*I got into a fight with my neighbor.*"

"*What was the fight about?*"

"*I was watching 'The Dark Knight' and she knocked very loudly on my door and told me I was being too loud. I told her that I hear her yell in her apartment all of the time. She got angrier when I said that.*"

"*Why does she yell?*"

"*She has a kid who is very annoying.*"

"*So she <u>has</u> to yell.*"

"*She said that too. She said, 'I need to yell. You do not need to watch your movie so loud.' And I said, 'You do not need to yell. You should give your kid some candy.' She was very angry after I said that.*"

Lian laughed. Freddy had a very funny way of dealing with things. "*She might come back to bother you.*"

"*That is a problem for tomorrow Freddy,*" he said, grinning. She liked that term, "*tomorrow Freddy.*" Two nouns joined together to form an evocative phrase. "*Also, I watched 'The Breakfast Club' this morning. I don't know if I liked this one. Maybe I did not understand it. It was a bit boring to me. Just American teenagers with boring problems.*"

Lian laughed. She thought "*The Breakfast Club*" was a charming film, but she agreed, compared to "*Charade,*" or "*Double Indemnity,*" or any of the noirs they'd found common ground on, it paled in terms of action and drama. She listened as he continued, discussing other movies from the 1980s that he'd found himself dabbling in that month. She loved to listen to him talk. He was someone who pulsed with his own energy, unlike Zhetai, who needed Lian to input energy in order to react.

"*Just because a movie doesn't have three murders doesn't make it boring,*" she said. "*I think 'The Breakfast Club' is an engaging movie about growing up. It's sweet.*"

"*Sweet?*"

"*Yes, like nice. Like wholesome.*"

"*I know what it means. I just don't think sweet movies are my favorite.*"

Freddy had started lessons at GTE six months ago. Lian's boss had asked if she'd like to take him on; Freddy's father was a friend of the CEO and they wanted to make sure his son was taken care of. Freddy had just graduated from Beijing Film Academy and, like Lian, was an old Hollywood enthusiast. He wanted to talk about movies. "*No one else cares as much as I do about film,*" he had said in one of his first messages to Lian. Over video, he was similarly haughty in a way Lian found she liked.

Their conversations were charged, sometimes combative—they disagreed vehemently over Kubrick—and Lian always found herself surprised when the hour was up. Their sessions were only once a week, but in between he would often text Lian, always in English, about their favorite movies, sending her long paragraphs dissecting a Hitchcock film or identifying motifs in Tony Curtis's oeuvre over time. His dream was to attend NYU and make sprawling films about politics and society. He reminded Lian of herself those years ago, her dreams sharp and pointed in one direction.

He loved writing epic war sagas, romances, thrilling tales where good was good and evil was evil. They weren't moralistic, no, he would clarify; instead he viewed his stories with a mixture of admiration and irony, understanding the inherent campiness of "true good." He had a recurring hero, Commander China—modeled after, what else, Marvel's Captain America—who represented the homegrown morals and values of his country, wore a red suit emblazoned with yellow stars, and spent his movies saving damsels in distress. His commitment to saving the citizens of his country was so staunch that he often forgot about all personal ties and commitments. This would come to bite him in the fifth movie, according to Freddy.

He'd been open and forward about his plans the moment he met her. "*I want to improve my English so I can go to America and become a famous film director*," he wrote in his second message. *Famous* was the word he used, which she felt was amusing. Fame was such a bald, ugly desire, but the way he admitted it so swiftly made her like him. Perhaps he was simply misusing it and intended instead to say *illustrious* or *successful* or even *renowned*, but these were words he hadn't learned yet.

As she got to know him, she began to feel that he'd very much intended to say *famous* that first day. He was a boy of many contradictions, someone who seemed to always stay in his room but was obsessed with the concept of perception and what others thought of him. He raged against the lemminglike behavior of the people around him, yet he craved their validation. It was maybe this very lust for approval that kept him shut up in his room. She thought that he must think, If no one sees me, no one can hate me. He talked constantly of the scripts he was writing, but every time she asked to see one, he demurred. He was a butterfly in a chrysalis, fermenting his talents and visions until one day, in New York City, they would erupt into greatness.

His ultimate dream was to direct a Marvel movie and put Captain America in direct conflict with Commander China. This was the direction the world was going anyway, he said.

"*That's a pretty bleak view,*" she said. *Bleak*, meaning *negative*. Meaning *dark*, she explained. "*You would consider America and China enemies?*"

"*Maybe not yet,*" he said. "*They're former . . . friends. Former allies? This is probably the closest to enemies you can be.*"

Now he was asking her if she'd seen the new Yao Chen movie. She had. She and Zhetai had gone to Joy City earlier that very week. The movie was melodramatic—a young mother searches for her kidnapped daughter—but she didn't feel like it had much to say besides, Isn't it terrible when your daughter is kidnapped?

"*Yeah,*" she said. "*It was okay.*"

"*Yes, exactly! I was hoping for more from her. I feel that she is not challenging herself anymore.*"

Lian shrugged. She didn't expect a lot from big-budget films; they usually promised a pleasurable one-hundred-minute experience and not much more. "*I don't think it's her fault. People just want to watch things that make them feel good.*"

"*People are so simple,*" he exhaled now, his face dropping in a way that made it seem like she'd just told him his grandma had died. "*When did life become all about feeling good?*"

The image of Wenyu and Su Mingzun in the alley sprang into her head. She felt a rouge creeping into her cheeks, and she willed herself to calm down; there was no reason she should be thinking of the two of them; there was no equivalency here. She had never mentioned Zhetai in front of Freddy, but she never talked much about her own life, so she told herself that this wasn't a purposeful omission. She simply never had the opportunity to bring him up. There was something blissful and disarming about the way she and Freddy had gotten to know each other, in a total vacuum; basic facts were unimportant here. The only thing that mattered was whether you thought "*Rear Window*" was a masterpiece, whether you thought the purpose of life was maximizing joy or minimizing pain. Freddy did sometimes ask her personal questions, but she'd give brief answers. All she'd revealed in six months was that she, too, grew up and lived in Beijing. About him, she knew that he grew up in Dongdan; his mother was originally from Shanghai, but his father was a native Beijinger. Knowing nearly nothing, she could imagine that they might have walked the same streets, frequented the same malls, watched the same movies in the same movie theaters. She pictured him on the other side of the wall from her, in the very building where she'd grown up; perhaps one day she'd emerge from her front door and run right into him.

Today, however, she found herself testing the waters. "*Where did you see it?*" she asked, a more probing question than usual. She felt reckless; she wanted to stoke the flame of her curiosity. This, after all, is what Wenyu would do, cross that line of propriety, boldly extract what she wanted without worrying whether the replier might be offended. She wondered if he had also gone to Joy City and stopped by the Gong Cha afterward for tea. She wondered who he'd gone with, if it had been with a girlfriend, or a group of friends, or alone. She wondered if he, like Zhetai, sat with his back rail-straight, his hand settled comfortably on the thigh of a girl next to him. He didn't seem like the type of boy to rest his hand on a girl's thigh. He seemed too frenetic, the type to swing his arms up and down at the screen, lamenting a character's bad choices, demanding his money back.

"*At Raffles,*" he said. "*I usually go there.*"

Raffles. The mall on the other side of the 2 line loop. Suddenly, the fantasy she'd constructed in her mind shifted, though not terribly so. He was not on the other side of the wall. Raffles was not the mall closest to Lian, so she did not go there often, but it was not some far-flung, sterile shopping campus in the nether regions of the Sixth Ring. He still lived within the familiar confines of Lian's world. In fact, Lian had gone to Raffles a month ago, when Yang Qinru had wanted to try out a new pancake place. She found herself feeling happy about this.

"*Oh, nice,*" she said. "*They have those great seats.*"

"*Do you go there a lot?*" he said.

"*No,*" she said. "*I live on the other side of the city.*" Now she had shared something from her life. "*Near Baiduizi,*" she continued. "*But I used to go to Raffles a lot.*" She found herself wanting to say more. "*In high school. I'd go there with my best friend sometimes. We stole pens from the stationery store on the first floor.*" Indeed, when Wenyu had gotten bored of the stores near home, she and Lian had traipsed onto new terrain, played with different fires.

"*Wow, a rebel, Lily!*" Freddy grinned.

"*She was the brave one,*" she said. "*My friend. I just followed. She never cared what happened to her. But I cared about everything.*"

She was surprised at herself, surprised that she was sharing anything, and surprised at the way she was describing Wenyu. He nodded. She was scared that she'd shared too much.

But he didn't seem perturbed. "*Did you grow up in Baiduizi?*" he asked.

"*I did,*" she said. "*I've always lived in the same place.*" She felt struck by this statement, as if it were a confession of some sort. It was not so crazy—plenty of people had never moved—but then she thought about Wenyu, about Su Mingzun, about Zhu Zixi— all of them had left Beijing at some point: for college, for work, for love. But she'd never had to do any of this. Never gotten to. Never had to or gotten to, two ways of looking at the same situation.

Freddy, meanwhile, looked surprised. "Really?" he said, slipping suddenly into Chinese. His Beijing accent was thick; his voice was much lower in Chinese. She didn't often hear his real voice, and she relished it every time; it felt like she was hearing the real Freddy in these moments. But he caught himself. "*Not even for school?*"

"*No,*" she said.

"*I always thought you lived in America for a while.*"

"*I didn't,*" she said. "*I just love English. I don't think you need to go somewhere to be good at something—*"

"*I agree,*" he said. "*I'm just surprised, because you're so good at English. You didn't want to?*"

She thought about those long evenings spent at her desk poring over her textbooks, dreaming of a future somewhere in the West, where she'd drive an American car down a wide highway, play tennis, sink her teeth into an ear of corn as big as an American football.

Her phone pinged. Lian looked over and realized they were more than ten minutes past time.

"*I'm sorry, Freddy,*" she said. "*I have to go now.*"

"*Okay!*" he said, in that loud, deliberate way he always did when time was up. He was never the one to end the conversation—and why would he; she was doing him a favor—and Lian swore there was something close to disappointment in his voice every time she had to go, his energy overcompensating for his wish that the conversation wouldn't end. Perhaps she was imagining things.

"*See you next week,*" she said. He raised his hand to wave goodbye. Then she shut her laptop screen. She could hear the sounds of "*The Walking Dead*" echoing from the next room, some half-alive being taking its next victim with a gargle and a screech. She stared at the wall of her bedroom, pausing. A Pompompurin sticker stared back at her. Wenyu had stuck that there so many years ago, and try as she might, she'd never been able to pick it off.

She looked at the notification on her phone. It was Wenyu. "Xidan, Monday? My fans want '*Chinese content.*'"

Those two simple lines surprised Lian threefold: First, because Wenyu actually wanted to hang out. Second, the text was so casual, Lian wondered briefly if they'd already discussed this, somehow agreed amid the haze of whiskey to put their distance behind them and resume their friendship as if nothing had happened. And third, something warm and joyful welled up inside her, and this was perhaps the most surprising, realizing that after twelve years Wenyu could still have the same effect on her.

She wondered how she should respond. "We can't keep the Americans waiting!!" she might have responded, years ago.

Or possibly, "Just upload a rerun of '*Dating with the Parents.*' That's all the *Chinese content* they need!"

"I have work until seven," she finally typed, an hour later. "But after, sure."

WENYU WANTED TO MEET at their "old breakfast spot in Xidan."

"KFC?" Lian typed back.

"Jianbing House!" Wenyu responded.

Of course. KFC was a favorite, but Jianbing House was where they'd most often begun their weekend adventures, fueling up with crispy scallion crepes before hitting the shops. But Jianbing House, along with an innumerable host of other shops, had been bulldozed years ago, making way for the Galeries Lafayette. Lian was sure Wenyu had been to Galeries Lafayette, but perhaps Wenyu had not realized it'd taken the place of their old favorite. Lian didn't know how to say this to Wenyu, so she found herself approaching Xidan, emerging at the north exit, walking toward Galeries Lafayette, wondering if Wenyu was already there, and disappointed.

As she walked, she passed throngs of girls with dyed hair, couples in matching sweatshirts, shiny plastic bags of shoes and dresses. She thought of the way she and Wenyu would come to this square every weekend, haggling with vendors in the gargantuan shopping complex, grabbing egg tarts and bubble tea at the KFC, and ultimately ending up either at the KTV or in the movie theater. It was here that Wenyu had ratcheted up the stakes of their shoplifting, sneaking clothing and jewelry into their backpacks; here where Lian had grown afraid and stopped. Western brands beamed their gluttonous advertisements across the plaza, infusing in them a frenzy for more, for a life outside all of this. This was something that had not changed. The stores were flashier now, but Xidan had always been Xidan.

When she reached Galeries Lafayette, groups of girls were milling about, talking into their phones and waiting for DiDis. She observed one pair, a girl who was tall and boyish, another who was short and a little softer around the hips. The shorter girl tapped on her phone while the taller one carried both of their drinks, frothy pastel things bobbing with tapioca. The taller one leaned her head down to rest on the shorter girl's head, so that she looked like a bendy straw. The shorter girl stood on her tiptoes, relieving the arch of the taller girl's back, and for a blistering moment Lian thought she might cry.

And then suddenly, out of the crowd, Wenyu appeared, her hand arriving first in a wave.

"Hi! Sorry I'm late!"

Lian shrugged. She hadn't noticed. Wenyu was always late; the apologizing was what was new.

Wenyu had transformed again from Lian's last memory of her in the dark bar. Her face was paler, eyeliner spiking small wings off the corners of her eyes, her lips tinted with a subtle cerise rouge. Gone were the fake eyelashes and the bronzer and the thickly glossed lips. She looked like the teenage makeup influencers on Douyin, like a Chinese model refracted through a blemish-clearing app. She had also let her hair air-dry without much product, it appeared, so that it hung wild and bush-like behind her back in a manner that was finally familiar to Lian.

She remembered what Zhu Zixi had said about Wenyu at the engagement party, the disparaging comments about her eyelashes.

Wenyu was disappointed about Jianbing House. "What happened?" she said, staring up at the mall. A pink Zara sweater in the first-floor storefront winked a French word at them: *amour*.

"They, ah, got replaced," Lian said. Years ago, she thought. But she didn't say that.

"That's okay," Wenyu said, tilting her head to the sky, pondering their next move. "Oooh! Lian! I'm so stupid, we gotta do karaoke! Harmony is right there!"

There was something frantic about Wenyu. Lian couldn't tell if it was from the heat, or from any discomfort she might feel, hanging out with Lian one-on-one again. Or if it was because of a secret. Or perhaps Lian was seeing things, and the heat was getting to her too.

Although it was strange to be singing in the middle of the day, Harmony KTV was indeed nearby. They'd gone there after the last day of finals every semester since seventh grade, where, liberated from the scourge of exams and their teachers' hot breaths on their necks, they'd belt out Zhou Jielun and Fahrenheit until their throats were sore. But Lian hadn't been karaokeing in years. Perhaps it was because too many new things had popped up— fusion restaurants, clubs, sound baths. Perhaps it was because karaoke was the terrain of bleeding pubescent hearts, and there was not so much for her to sing about anymore.

"Wow—I haven't KTV'ed in so long," Lian said.

Wenyu clapped her palms together. "Yay!" She beamed and pulled out her phone. "I'm just gonna take some quick video, it's super chill!" Switching on her camera, she observed her face in the screen for a moment, baring her teeth ever so briefly. Checking for spinach. Lian suddenly wanted to give her a hug, envelop her like the tall girl with her short friend. But then Wenyu smiled, and whatever Lian had witnessed had passed, and she was reaching her phone out with one hand and waving with the other. "*Hi, V-fam!*"

Peering at the blinking red light of the recording symbol, Lian realized Wenyu was not the only person on camera, and she quickly looked down at her outfit. She'd worn simple white slacks today, sandals, and a baby tee with a teddy bear logo. Not an ugly outfit, but nothing spectacular. She was momentarily angry that Wenyu had not given her warning, though, of course, she had. That was the entire purpose of this hangout today, she reminded herself, to give Wenyu her "*Chinese content.*" She found herself fussing with her bangs.

"*This is my best friend in Beijing, Lian! Ye Lian!*" Wenyu said, her voice ringing. For an instant, she dragged out the syllables in Lian's name, like Thomas had. Very nearly *Leanne*. But then she corrected herself, the name coming down in a spirited command.

"*Hey guys!*" Lian waved, confident she'd squashed her tones into a perfectly flattened English.

"*We're here at Xidan shopping center, where Lian and I would spend so many weekends just messing around and watching movies, right, Lian?*"

"*Yeah!*" Lian felt her voice rising to meet the tenor of Wenyu's, though she found it exhausting, the forced cheer.

"*Oh my god, remember when we watched 'Seven Swords'?*"

Lian blushed. They'd watched "Seven Swords" in a three-movie marathon after "*March of the Penguins*" and "*Harry Potter and the Goblet of Fire,*" beginning with the birth of a fuzzy hatchling and ending in a graphic, toe-curling sex scene that made Lian and Wenyu giggle the entire way home, giddy with accomplishment that they'd sneaked into such an adult film. "*That was so . . . gross!*" Lian said now, making a face into the camera. *Gross*. Americans loved using this word.

"*Oh my god, yes, so gross,*" Wenyu agreed, and hearing her word on Wenyu's lips Lian suddenly caught herself—why was she putting on a show for Wenyu's American audience in this way? Who cared what kinds of words they loved? She turned away then, pretending to be enraptured by a loose thread in her shirt.

"*Oh, shit—*" Wenyu clicked off her camera and pressed at the hem of her blouse. "*This thing keeps popping up.*" She turned the camera back on. "*And isn't this the cutest top? The peach color is perfect for summer!*" Lian was confused at this tangent. Wenyu put her phone down. "Sorry, this is a sponsored video, so I have to mention the top." She wrinkled her nose. "I hate this color on me."

Suddenly, two girls approached. "Hi," the one with glasses spoke. "Are you . . . Vivian? From *Viv Like Vivian*?"

Wenyu seemed shocked; she tugged at her ponytail in a gesture, Lian thought, of self-consciousness. "Ah, yeah!" she said.

"We're big fans! I'm going to California for school next year, and all I want is to be just like you!" The bespectacled girl giggled.

"I've been trying your açai bowl diet," the other one chimed in.

"Oh, that's so nice," Wenyu said.

"Can we get a picture?"

Lian held the phone and snapped a photo for the three of them, Wenyu's arms around the two girls.

"Does that happen a lot?" Lian asked when the girls were out of earshot.

"Not here . . ." Wenyu said. "That was the first time."

She seemed rattled for a moment, then pulled her phone back out and resumed filming. They walked across the length of the mall, past the UNIQLO, past the H&M, past the Taiwanese boba shop, past the open green space featuring blow-up panda dolls, until they reached the back plaza, a dingy neon sign blinking the words HARMONY KTV. It was one of the only establishments they'd known from high school left in the plaza. What used to be a skewers restaurant was now a Haidilao hot pot. A video stand was now a KFC Express. A day care had turned into a cram center, which cut quite the profile alongside the KTV. Buttoned-up high school students filed in; KTV hostesses in bandage dresses filed out. Lian had only a vague memory of these hostesses from high school: sweet women who gave them plates of sliced fruit and exhausted smiles.

Wenyu flipped the camera so her fans could see the KTV. "*Wow, can you believe this was* THE *place in high school?*" she cooed. "*It looks just like I remembered!*"

That couldn't be possible. Even to Lian, who'd still come here as a college student, Harmony felt different. The entire space was more decrepit, the neon sign duller, and the shiny black lobby floors greasier. A glass tray of mints, which had once so delighted Lian and Wenyu, looked dusty.

The only things that didn't feel older were the girls. Lian made eye contact with the receptionist, whose apricot cheeks bounced in greeting. She couldn't have been more than twenty. "Welcome, ladies!" she cooed. Lian stifled a laugh. Once upon a time she and Wenyu were the children coming to this KTV; now she and Wenyu were the glamorous older ladies. "How will we be paying tonight, ladies?" the girl asked. Lian reached for her phone; Wenyu no longer lived in Beijing, she was a guest, and it was natural for Lian to pay.

But Wenyu beat her to the register, scanning her phone before Lian had a chance to unlock her screen.

"No, really, let me, Lian," Wenyu said, in a tone that irritated Lian, as if it were the most natural thing in the world for Wenyu to be paying.

"How could I? You're the guest!" Lian protested. Wenyu merely waved her off with a flutter of her nails.

The girl led the two of them to a private room. Built-in leather couches gleamed blue-green under the lights of the television. "Two bottles of soju please," Lian said. "Lemon and . . ." she looked at Wenyu, who broke into a grin. "Mango," they said at the same time.

"*Lian used to hate mango,*" Wenyu explained to her audience. "*I broke her will in the end.*"

As Wenyu continued with her recollections, Lian sat back. They were ignoring several things: their broken promises, the time and space that had accumulated between them, whatever it was that Lian had seen in the alley that night. She thought of Wenyu with Su Mingzun, and as the minutes ticked by, her suspicions grew like a balloon between them. She couldn't quite pinpoint what it was about the interaction, but she knew in the pit of her stomach it was not something innocent. The way he had rested his hand on her bag, the way they'd bowed their heads together, the tip of her cigarette lighting his; there was something so intimate about it; her body, ablaze, had reacted in the way it always had the times she'd stumbled in on the two of them sharing some private moment not meant for her.

If indeed something had happened, once Wenyu would have shrieked this in Lian's face, running up to her on the exercise field and stage-whispering it at a decibel loud enough for the whole class to hear. And so every moment that passed without a confession made Lian feel further from Wenyu. As Wenyu chattered on about soju flavors, she also began to doubt her own eyes, to wonder if maybe she was seeing what she wanted to see, some evidence of Wenyu's discontent that she'd fabricated entirely.

"So what'll it be, Lianlian!" Wenyu said, still filming. *"Let's see what song she picks!"* she said into her phone.

Lian grabbed the songbook and flipped through, but she knew what song she wanted to start with. She punched in the numbers, and a look of recognition melted across Wenyu's face. Wenyu turned to her, slapping her arm playfully. "Of COURSE!"

The tinny sounds of the erhu trickled through the speakers, and they let the song roll over them for a moment. "East Wind Breaks." This was their favorite song to sing together. A ballad, one of Zhou Jielun's most romantic songs. When Lian had gotten her first ever MP3 player in high school, this was the song that had come preloaded. "East Wind Breaks" was about the sadness of leaving and the passage of youth, Zhou Jielun reminiscing on his schoolyard love. Every time one of them had a crush, they would come to the KTV and sing this song. Wenyu would always become a more romantic, more serious version of herself when she was in the KTV; she'd commit fully to whatever the mood of the song required. Lian, meanwhile, had always seen the KTV as an opportunity for bravado, belting songs out clownishly until Wenyu would crack and they'd dissolve into giggles.

Now, Lian picked up the microphone, her heart pounding. Wenyu put down her phone, to Lian's surprise. Lian lifted the microphone to her lips and falteringly sang the first line, Zhou Jielun standing by his door, lamenting the time he's let slip by. She looked at Wenyu, who looked back.

And then Wenyu began, holding the microphone very close to her lips and slurring her words. Her voice was deep and rich and full of feeling. Then she stood, her voice crescendoing as she hit the chorus. She infused the refrain with even more passion than Zhou Jielun's original, crying out for the lover who had long ago left—and for time, the biggest leaver of all.

Lian volleyed the chorus back, more energetically now, smiling as she also stood, her voice rising to a clamor. She couldn't help it. "East Wind Breaks" couldn't be sung quietly wedged into a seat. The two of them traded off verses in a fervent dialogue about love and youth and the futility of attempting to make either last forever. Lian found herself erupting into a scream, becoming, finally again, the teenager full of bravado she'd met here in those dingy days, the loud and shameless person she could become only in the KTV, only alongside Wenyu.

And then it was over. They sat down shyly, curling back into their positions. But the song had loosened something between them.

"It's funny, isn't it," Lian said. "We loved singing this song. But we didn't know anything about leaving. Or heartbreak. Or time."

"Maybe we still don't," Wenyu said. She poured Lian another glass of soju and held out hers for a clink. "Lian, I'm so happy you came to the party," Wenyu said. "I was afraid . . . I don't know. I wasn't sure if you'd want to see me."

Lian's face reddened. Were her judgments and desires so transparent? She suddenly felt ashamed for having laughed at Wenyu behind her back. And she felt guilty, thinking about their fallow text chat. Distance takes two, but, if she was honest, it was she who'd first grown distant. Wenyu had gone off and made a name for herself, and Lian didn't want to be just one of the many scrabbling after her glorious coattails. Over the years, she'd considered reaching out. But she didn't know what to say: Tell me about your perfect life. What's going on in mine? Oh, more of the same. Classes. Living at home. Talking to the same sorts of boys. Making the same kinds of friends. She had nothing to report. She could not let the floodgates down, because then she might never emerge again, lost in the coursing river of Wenyu's infinite energy. And Wenyu didn't reach out, either, not in any real way. Lian held on to this over the years, used it as justification for allowing the space between them to freeze over.

"Of course I'd want to see you," Lian finally said, softening.

Wenyu smiled. In the dark, Wenyu looked just like she had remembered, her hair mussed from exertion, a faintly severe emotion in her eyes. Wenyu held her gaze, then turned back to the songbook.

"What is it like?" Lian asked next. She wasn't sure where her question was leading her. There were so many things she wanted to ask. Living the American dream. Becoming a YouTube star. Leaving her. "Being famous." She thought of Freddy, his unabashed proclamation.

Wenyu laughed. "I'm hardly famous."

"You had fans approach you just a few minutes ago."

"It's the same as being not famous," she said, shrugging. "I saw Jason Statham at an airport once and he smiled at me?"

"He was probably too shy to come over and meet his idol."

"Ha! You're so funny, Lian."

"Seriously, though. That was kinda cool, earlier."

"Yeah. That doesn't happen a ton. It's always really nice." Wenyu smiled, but it was stiff.

"Yeah?"

"It's a lot of pressure," she said. "Being this, like, model of 'making it' in America. People message me all the time with every kind of question you could possibly imagine. They ask me about visas. They ask me about birth control. One girl once asked me if American guys preferred to do it in the butt."

"Oh my god!"

She laughed. "And not even for the reason you think—she was like, because there's no abortion there. And then I had to explain that there is abortion, sort of, depending on where you live . . . it was a whole thing." Lian saw her get lost in the memory for a moment, both a stitch in her brow and a smile growing deeper by the second, her laughter ramping. "It's so crazy!"

Lian joined in. "You're like the modern-day reverse Marco Polo. Guide to the magical world of the West."

"I'm too stupid to be Marco Polo! I don't have the answers. I just kind of wing it. They ask me about how to be happy, how to fall in love. Half of their questions are about how I landed a millionaire American fiancé."

"I'm not surprised." Lian laughed. "How is it, anyway?" Her voice grew quiet. "I never thought you'd marry an American." How could I have, she added in her mind.

Wenyu turned her head and looked at her now, so whip-quick Lian wondered if she'd offended her. She stared at Lian, then said, "I know, right? Americans smell really bad."

Lian grinned. "Even with their deodorant?"

Wenyu giggled, then her face grew somber. "It's weird. Sometimes I wake up and see him next to me and still think, who is this man?"

Lian was at turns surprised and comforted; it would indeed feel weird to have someone so different, so not-you, lying so close. Like if a character from *"Friends"* walked off the screen and into your bed.

"It makes every day interesting," Wenyu said next. "I feel like after five years, I've only scratched the surface of who he is. But . . ." and here she sat back, "sometimes it's nice to be around people who I get. You know? That's why I'm back. I wanted to be around the people I know best."

Lian smiled. "So fame . . . good or bad?"

Wenyu looked at the ceiling. "Seven-point-five out of ten. Mostly good."

Lian's phone flashed with a notification.

"I decided to watch all of Yao Chen's movies this week. You were right. Yao Chen is an awesome actor."

Lian grinned, before looking back up and making eye contact with Wenyu, who was holding the other microphone out to Lian. She noticed Lian's phone. "Ooh, what's up?" Wenyu asked, but Lian clicked off her screen.

She considered for one wild beat telling Wenyu about Freddy. But what was there to tell? It was a non-story, a non-thing, and it would be embarrassing to spin it into such. "Nothing," she said. "Just something Zhetai sent me."

"Awwwww, Lian," Wenyu said. "I'm happy for you. He seems so sweet!"

Wenyu grinned at Lian, and a strange feeling overtook her. As kids, Wenyu often understood and articulated what Lian felt even before she herself could. But now, as Wenyu spoke what should have been the truth, Lian felt something slide away, the tectonic plates of her heart shifting out of place.

"Are you guys gonna . . ." Wenyu gestured at her ring, her eyebrows waggling.

"I guess . . ." Lian said, blushing. "At some point."

"What's your favorite thing about Zhetai?" Wenyu asked, grinning.

Lian pondered this, wanting to come up with a good answer. He was handsome and intelligent. He was caring and well-mannered. But these were all clinical words you'd find on a dating profile. "He's never made me cry," Lian finally said, with pride. It was true, and rare, she knew. It was undeniably the mark of a good man.

But there was something faltering on Wenyu's face, and she realized then how sad it was, what she had just said.

"That's a keeper," Wenyu said, kindly.

Lian's face burned. "How was it, seeing everyone?" she asked next, changing the subject.

"It was fun," Wenyu said. She paused. "You know, I'm surprised some of them even came. Zhu Zixi especially. I always thought she hated me."

"Well, now that you're a big deal, of course she likes you." The statement was so reflexive, Lian realized immediately that it might have been very rude. "She was always a starfucker."

Wenyu laughed. "It's true . . ." She sat and contemplated the songbook in front of her. "'A big deal' . . ."

"Su Mingzun seemed the same," Lian said next, trying to keep her voice level. Her gaze was trained on Wenyu's face, wondering if she'd catch something in her eyes.

"Ha," Wenyu laughed. She was still tabbing through the book, but had fallen silent. Then she turned her body ever so slightly and put her hand on Lian's arm the same way she had in the bar. Her hand rested there, her thumb pressing into Lian's bicep, Lian's arm an anchor as it had always been. "Lianlian," she said. "I kissed him."

"What?"

So Lian hadn't been seeing things. In the background, their next song had begun without them: "New Home," the title-credit song of their favorite drama, "Romantic Princess."

"I know, I know! Don't judge me!" Wenyu threw herself against the sofa, burying her face in a pillow. Then she sat up, her hair the wild nest that had always been her signature. "He just . . . looked so good . . . it's stupid, I know."

"What . . . happened?"

"Well, I heard that whole rant of his. God, he's so fucking weird, isn't he. Anyway, Thomas and his friends from Stanford, they left the party early, and I guess I was kinda pissed, so I went outside and I just ran into Mingzun, who's standing there smoking a cigarette. So we start talking, and then Mingzun said we should take a walk around Houhai. I felt bad leaving everyone behind, but he was just like, 'Who cares about those people?' Which maybe might've seemed rude, but I just suddenly felt, well, so relieved. So I followed him."

Wenyu shrugged here. "And we caught up. I told him about San Jose, and moving to Santa Cruz, and then San Francisco. I realized I'd done so many things in those years apart from him. Then I . . . well, then I asked him if he was married. He shook his head, and then told me that he'd kind of just hopped from girlfriend to girlfriend the last few years. There was this woman in Wuhan he met right after he dropped out, an older woman who was going through a divorce. Scandalous, I know. He loved her a lot, but it didn't work out."

She told him about the people she'd dated since him: a charming but philandering ABC she'd dated for several months her freshman year before finding him in bed with another girl; a fellow exchange student from Shanghai whom she'd cried over for months when he went back to China after graduation. Lian was surprised to hear about these people, sketched in such brief but passionate strokes. Each one felt cinematic, worthy of poetry. She wondered what poetry she could write about her and Zhetai's relationship.

"We'd walked around all of Houhai by the time he finished," Wenyu said. "Lian, but then he fixed me with this really intense stare, and went, 'But Wenyu, I've never loved anyone like I loved you.'"

Lian felt her body flush.

"I was so shaken, Lian! I didn't know what to say. I mean—I—felt the same, in a way. I love Thomas, and I loved Yuede and I even loved Eric, but . . . there's nothing quite like the first one."

The image of Ma Zhongshun's hand, doling out his pencil, flashed through Lian's brain. His carefree nod. "I don't need it, take it."

"So then I kissed him. I don't know. It just felt right. I feel like, in life, there are some moments you have to put some punctuation on, you know? A period, an exclamation mark. This was an exclamation mark, for sure." And then a blush flowered over Wenyu's cheeks.

Lian paused. "What are you . . . what are you going to do? Are you going to tell Thomas?"

Wenyu began shaking her head violently. "It doesn't matter, he doesn't need to know, it was stupid. Stupid. I feel like I just had to do it once, you know. To know."

"And? What do you know?"

Wenyu's face crumpled now. Lian could see a million futures pass across it. Wenyu sat up. "It doesn't mean I don't love Thomas. I do love Thomas, that's why I'm so confused. Lian, this is why I had to see you today. Tell me what to do. You're the only one I can talk to."

Lian didn't know how to respond. Her heart pounded; she felt acutely that this conversation was pivotal, that, for some reason, whatever she said here had the potential to change the course of many things. There was something poisonous twisting inside her, glee at the confirmation that the glossy life Wenyu had shown the world these last few years was not so pristine. It was nice when people confirmed who they were. People always came back to their worst vices, and Lian felt a heavy and complicated satisfaction, having been right about Luo Wenyu.

"I . . . don't know," she said. "Are you happy with Thomas?"

"I am. I really am. It's always so funny to find how many

people in life you can be happy with. All the people I loved since I left I never expected to love—it happened on accident. They were sort of all . . . products of experimentation—like, here I was, trying on a different skin, and fuck it, why not go for this dude who I would never have gone for back at home, but I was in California, I was living my new life, so why not! And so I made leaps of faith, all the time. And the thing is—I found myself falling, all the time. I loved a lot. And Thomas was the most different of them all. I mean, you've seen him, I would've made fun of someone like him in high school! But then I found myself falling for him too. It was kind of magical, realizing all the people in life I could love. But Mingzun . . . seeing him again, it's different. I never had to make a leap of faith with him. I was already there."

Bathed in the blue glow of the television screen, Wenyu looked young and angel-like, something extraworldly and vulnerable. The Vivian of *Viv Like Vivian*, of the engagement party, of even one hour earlier, was gone.

"I guess I just feel like, with Thomas . . . there's something that will always separate us. That sounds dramatic. What I mean is, have you ever told someone wo ai ni in a different language? Thomas . . . I tell him *I love you*. Three completely different sounds. I can't tell him wo ai ni, because it doesn't mean as much to him. But what I really want to say is, wo ai ni, wo ai ni. Su Mingzun is the only person I've ever said wo ai ni to."

There were tears in her eyes, and she threw herself back on the couch. "You must think I'm a terrible person!" Wenyu clutched a pillow to her chest, her eyes lifting shyly up to Lian's.

Lian breathed. "I get it," she said, though she was not quite sure what she got. She'd never said wo ai ni in a different language. She'd only ever said wo ai ni to one person. That was one thing she and Wenyu had in common, she supposed, and there was something else they had in common, too, a truth that thrashed about like an eyelash you couldn't see, but that could drive you to the point of tears. This truth, it had something to do with restlessness. "I don't think you're a terrible person."

"Yeah? Really?" Wenyu's voice was so eager, her eyes glimmering. Lian was shocked to see how relieved she seemed. "You know, I never thought I'd get married this way. I mean, you know. With all this." She gestured around her head, at the invisible cloud of fanfare and money. "I guess I thought I'd marry Su Mingzun, but if I didn't marry him, I wouldn't marry anyone. But then . . . I don't know, one thing leads to another. And suddenly you've taken so many steps and changed in all these tiny ways and you look in the mirror and you don't recognize yourself anymore. I'm scared, Lianlian. Being back here, it's like I'm seeing myself, myself-myself, myself at seventeen, again. And I like her. And that girl's not supposed to be getting married, getting married to an American? Living in a fancy house? That girl's not supposed to be blonde!" She grabbed a piece of her hair and stared at it, as if seeing it for the first time. "It's crazy! Don't you ever wonder what life would've been? If you'd done a few things differently?"

Lian stared back at her, and then, bluffly, blissfully, they both began laughing. Another kind of glee arrived, more forceful than the first; suddenly, they were seventeen again, and she was transported back to that exercise field and Wenyu was whispering into her ear, and life had not yet gotten between them. Life had not yet happened at all; life could still be anything. They were still best friends with the world before them, keepers of each other's worst and truest secrets. It was a role Lian knew as well as her own reflection.

She thought about a day the three of them had spent together, the autumn before Wenyu left. One weekend early in their senior year, when the heat still hung wet over the city, Lian and Wenyu and Su Mingzun had gone to the pool, that muggy, dirty place where children peed in the water and elderly women swam breaststroke slowly down the lanes. They arrived late in the day and spent the rest of the afternoon sloshing around in the deep end.

There were not many people at the pool that day, a few older women and a young boy—maybe ten, eleven years old—who was swimming militant laps in the first lane, while his mother looked on, alternatively leaning back in her pool chair and instructing him to do a new stroke every few minutes. An hour before the pool was due to close, Teacher Liao arrived, wearing a bright purple swimsuit with a Gucci logo and goggles, her hair tucked into a swim cap. Lian barely recognized her at first, except that Teacher Liao had such a distinct gait: always walking with her arms swinging as if she were in a great hurry to be places.

"Looks like someone's trying to be Michael Phelps," Wenyu laughed. She swung her arms above her, falling into the water with a great crash. Su Mingzun snickered and dove after her, grabbing at her ankles.

Then they heard the screeching. Wenyu and Su Mingzun emerged, swiveling their heads over to the other side of the pool, where the young boy was pulling himself out. The woman stood over him, screaming. "You call that a good time? I could swim that fast and I'm an old woman. And now you're gonna quit?" The boy stood there, dripping, his shoulders slumped low, giving the appearance of a melting wax candle. He didn't argue or shout or throw a fit; he just took it.

"I can't believe I ever had such a good-for-nothing son!" she concluded, and stomped toward the exit. The boy followed, still wordless.

"What a draaaaama queen," Wenyu said, flinging her eyebrows up. "That poor kid. He seemed pretty fast to me."

Then her eyes lighted on the woman's flip-flops, which she'd left by her pool chair. They were platform flip-flops, bubblegum pink, with a Louis Vuitton charm fastened at the apex of the straps.

In one deft motion, Wenyu had slipped out of the pool, grabbed the sandals, and hid them underneath her towel. "Probably fake, but they're cute."

The woman came back a few minutes later. When she saw her sandals were gone from underneath her chair, she began scurrying around in a frenzy, peeking under every chair, stopping short of turning over every bag. "Oh my god," she kept saying. "My Lou-ees!"

"Have you seen a pair of pink sandals?" she demanded of their trio. Wenyu shook her head, dropping underwater, the cool portrait of a teenager who couldn't be bothered to speak to an adult. Su Mingzun kicked a flurry of water after her, similarly nonchalant. Only Lian made eye contact with the woman, for a beat too long, and her heart began pounding.

"I . . ." she said, realizing that now she'd been staring too long not to say anything. "I think . . ."

The woman was leaning back now, crossing her arms.

"I think someone took them to the lost and found," Lian said. Then she, too, dropped below the water.

Wenyu grabbed her hand underneath the water and they floated there for a second, their legs frog-like and pushing outward so that they descended deeper and deeper, Wenyu's hair forming a long, rippling train. Wenyu smiled and a large bubble cracked forth from her mouth, sending the two upward in rocketing laughter. When they broke the surface of the water, they were still laughing.

Later, in the locker room, middle-aged women stripped naked and put on baggy, faded pink and blue underwear. Lian covered herself with her towel, quickly shimmying out of her swimsuit and into her clothes. Wenyu peered over at the locker next to theirs.

"Oh my god, it's Teacher Liao's clothes," she said, pointing at the distinctive white stripe of the sweatsuit that teachers sometimes wore.

There wasn't a lock on the door. Wenyu opened it and grabbed the sweatsuit, then looked through her clothes. A pair of underwear was folded neatly inside the pocket of her jacket. Wenyu fished it out, tittering.

"Floral? Isn't she a little old for that?" Wenyu wrinkled her nose. Other items in the locker included a pair of running shoes, pants, a fresh T-shirt, a water bottle, and a frilly bra. Wenyu put the bra on and batted her eyelashes at Lian. "Teacher Kong, you look so handsome today," she drawled, running her hand up and down her bare body.

"Ew," Lian said, swatting Wenyu with a towel. Her heart pounded. Teacher Liao could return at any moment. "Take that off."

"Ugh, boring," Wenyu said, letting the bra slip off her arms. She threw it back into the locker. "Comrade Ye, always the good citizen."

Lian finished changing, wordlessly. She wondered if Wenyu was mad at her, if she felt Lian was being a stick in the mud as usual. Wenyu put on her bra and underwear and a bright green tennis dress, then pulled her wet hair into a ponytail and slung her backpack over her shoulder. "Let's get tea. I'm so thirsty."

When they stepped outside into the sticky June heat, Su Mingzun was already sitting on the curb waiting for them. Wenyu trudged up to him, and he wrapped her in a hug. Louis Vuitton charms glittered on her feet—she was wearing the sandals.

Lian followed, her heart pounding. "Wenyu," she said, holding out her bag. "Here."

Inside were Teacher Liao's bra, T-shirt, jacket, underwear, and pants. Wenyu's eyes widened and she grabbed Su Mingzun. "Lianlian! What!"

"I thought we could put her shit in the tree," Lian heard herself saying. "As a sort of fuck-you." She was stunned by the words emerging from her mouth.

"Lianlian!" Wenyu nodded her head vigorously. "WOW! Didn't think you had it in you!"

Su Mingzun grinned and ran under the tree. He gestured at Wenyu to follow and stand on top of his shoulders. Wenyu balanced precariously and hooked the bra onto a branch, slinging the jacket on another. Then she fished inside the jacket pocket, emerging with Teacher Liao's underwear. She pitched it onto the highest branch she could reach. The flowery lingerie flapped in the wind.

Wenyu giggled and hopped off Su Mingzun's back. "Okay, go hide! Before she comes out!"

They ducked behind the KFC. About fifteen minutes later, Teacher Liao emerged.

She was in her swimsuit, her hair wet and hanging in a blunt ponytail down her back. She had tied a towel around her waist and carried her water bottle in one hand, her sandals in the other. If she was troubled by this, she didn't show it. Wenyu and Su Mingzun burst into laughter.

Teacher Liao took a few steps out of the gym and Lian could see her eyes locking on the underwear hanging in the tree. It looked like a ratty dishrag that someone had meant to throw away.

But Teacher Liao only looked for a moment, then continued onward, walking east toward what Lian presumed was home. She left the underwear hanging in the tree.

That night, Wenyu treated Lian to milk tea, getting her extra boba and lychee jelly. Her heart pounded—despite everything, that felt good. It felt good to be the one under the spotlight for once, to be not only an accessory to Wenyu's exploits but the target of her admiration. "How did you do it? I didn't even notice you take it," Wenyu gushed.

"I just grabbed it when you went to the bathroom." Lian shrugged.

"I underestimated you, Lianlian," Wenyu said. "Good comrade's got some tricks up her sleeve too."

The three of them laughed together until late that night. It felt wonderful, euphoric, to be seen as fun, adventurous, exciting: all the things Wenyu wanted her to be, all the things Wenyu had found in Su Mingzun. It was exhilarating to be part of a conspiracy. To be part of something.

WENYU STARED AT her now, her eyes expectant. Her question hung in the air. "Don't you ever wonder what life would've been?" Lian understood the weight of what Wenyu had just confessed. She could crush Wenyu's perfect existence under her thumb; she could dissolve Wenyu's American mirage in an instant. She relished the responsibility of this role; she realized now how rootless she'd felt without Wenyu leaning on her, depending on Lian to keep her grounded. It was Lian who Wenyu wanted to tell her secrets to; Lian who knew who Wenyu really was. She was more than just Wenyu's sidekick, the Guan Yu to her Liu Bei; in fact, they were two indivisible sides of the same person. Wenyu's sun could not exist without something to shine on.

Lian thought about the messages blinking on her phone, the budding seeds of something. They were not the same, no. Freddy's flirtations were paltry compared to the affair that Wenyu had already embarked on. But they spoke to something brewing inside of Lian, a rupture in the blissful snow globe of a life she'd constructed over the last decade. And Lian felt herself wanting, as always, to level the scales, to contribute something to the conspiracy.

"Of course," Lian said. "I think about that all the time." She could feel the floodgates opening. "Actually, I have something to tell you too."

Wenyu broke into a wide grin. This was the expression she'd worn that day underwater; when she'd told Lian about her first kiss with Su Mingzun; when the two of them had sprinted home from the Chaoshifa, pockets heavy with chocolate bars, screaming all the way. A look that said, we're in this together. Lian's two glees collided, vindication and affection converging into a single truth: After twelve years, Lian and Wenyu were back in the same boat, coursing down the same bewildering river. Wenyu grabbed her hands, leaning in. "Tell me all about it."

4

freddy had once stolen his father's credit card and run away from home.

He was thirteen, and he had purchased a flight to Taiwan and made it all the way onto the plane before the flight attendants started asking him where his parents were. He'd said he was meeting them in Taiwan, and that he'd been visiting his uncle, and the thin-lipped flight attendant had warily allowed him to stay on board, but she kept one eye on him throughout the flight. He'd ordered seven cups of instant ramen, and the flight attendant had grown increasingly impatient with every shaky hot-water-laden trip down the aisle.

In Taipei, he checked into a hotel and then hit the streets, drinking and eating everything in his way. He'd made it to the fifth bar by the time his father caught up to him.

Lian told Wenyu this breathlessly, a few hours after her and Freddy's weekly call. They were sitting on a bench in Xidan Square, nibbling pieces of fried potato off flimsy skewers that threatened to snap with every tug of their teeth. He had told Lian he'd seen "*Moonrise Kingdom*" and said that he was just like the little orphan boy who steals into the forest. He'd recounted the story of his Taiwan jaunt with equal measures of bashfulness and pride, and Lian had asked him why he did it.

"*Sometimes, I just get so boring,*" he'd said.

"*Bored*," she'd corrected him.

"Man, I get that," Wenyu said, punctuating her agreement with a loud crunch. "I like him."

Over the last three weeks, Lian and Wenyu had slipped into an intoxicating pattern. Their separate dalliances had continued, and each time either of them met up with their paramours, they'd dial the other afterward, and the two of them would convene at Mingzhu Market and gossip over potato crisps and milk tea. They went cycling at Space Cycle, movie-hopped at Joy City. They spared each other none of the details—steamy on Wenyu's end, mostly banal on Lian's.

The second time Wenyu and Su Mingzun met up, they went to a poetry slam in the basement of an office building, then got drunk on mai tais at a new bar in the hutongs. He fingered her in an alleyway behind the bar, coconut sweetness still on his breath.

The third time they met, the rain ruined their plans. He'd wanted to take her hiking for persimmons, but when they arrived in the mountains, hail was coming down in sheets. They spent the morning in her car instead, fucking in the back seat. By then, she was no longer pretending this would be a onetime thing.

Their fourth date, they began talking about the dreams they'd once had with each other. Remember how we wanted to run away from this city together to the hard-to-pronounce cities and villages in our textbooks? To Reykjavik and Palermo and Oaxaca. Remember our Japan and Sichuan plans? They'd live in thatched-roof huts or beachside hotels. Back then, they were kids; they were broke. Now there was a different kind of barrier. Which was less surmountable?

Lian was not surprised at the swiftness with which they'd fallen back into each other. That was how Wenyu and Su Mingzun had started originally: all at once.

Lian, on the other hand, would recount in meticulous detail her lessons with Freddy, inflating moments that she felt were evidence of flirtation. She learned that he had a soy allergy, that he had ranked nationally in table tennis as a child, and that his mother was doting almost to a fault. She kept these facts like souvenirs on a shelf in her mind, taking them out and looking at them every so often, wondering what kind of person these things made him. Every step of the way, Wenyu listened intently, offering advice and personal experience and sometimes just a wide, wide smile that showed Lian she was right to be excited. She wanted badly to know him, but something remained blocking the path between them. Wenyu swiftly attributed this block to Lian's inability to be vulnerable.

"You gotta tell him something real," Wenyu said. "That's how secrets work. It's quid pro quo."

June felt strangely out of time; they were simultaneously twenty-nine and seventeen again, meeting to gossip and shop and guzzle boba and parting at the end of the day to silently join the men they'd chosen to spend their nights with. Wenyu was totally and utterly unashamed, both in her rapture over Su Mingzun and in her affection toward Lian. "Thank you for being here for me," she cooed over text. "I've missed you." She uploaded vlogs from their hangouts, titled each time: "KTV with my best friend," "the best milk tea with my best friend!," "pretending to work out with my best friend." In these videos, Lian watched them walking with their arms linked, laughing as they raced each other on bikes, taking sips of each other's drinks. She played the videos on repeat, rewatching to catch the little details: the piece of fluff on her shirt that Wenyu picked off; Wenyu screaming as, bicycling, she nearly tipped onto Lian; Lian's own snorts as she choked on tapioca. In the KTV video, she sounded hoarse, off-key (on a return to Harmony, Wenyu had recorded her rendition of the S.H.E. Britney Spears cover "Don't Say Sorry," which she'd really thought she'd nailed), but she wasn't paying attention to the way she sounded; Wenyu's cheers sent pinpricks of joy into her heart. The moments she'd remembered best from each of these hangouts were also what Wenyu had chosen to present to her viewers; they were the moments that Wenyu, too, cherished.

And the comments flooded in, girls in the corners of places like Virginia and Louisiana and Sweden and Morocco scrabbling violently for their friendship. *I'm so jealous of Lian!!!! You two are soooooo cute!!!! I would kill for a best friend like that!!!!* they'd say. With each new comment, Lian felt a searing smugness.

The days blurred together, a happy haze. She and Wenyu found themselves in a sort of honeymoon, linked by their shared secrets. Their friendship as it existed in those few weeks was actually the more blissful version of what things had once been. Once upon a time, Su Mingzun's presence in Wenyu's life meant a removal of her from Lian's. It meant competition, and afternoons previously spent roaming convenience stores with Wenyu were spent alone at her desk while Wenyu ran off with Su Mingzun. Now, funnily enough, the very thing that had torn Lian and Wenyu apart as kids was the thing that brought them back together. For that, Lian found herself grateful for Su Mingzun.

When Lian first confessed her curiosity about Freddy, Wenyu was surprised. Despite her own affair, Wenyu was shocked that Lian's relationship was not as watertight as she'd apparently conveyed. She had the same questions for Lian as Lian had for her, and they ultimately coalesced into one single interrogation: "Have you ever thought about leaving Zhetai?"

In her eight years with Zhetai, Lian had never actually pictured what it'd be like to break up; it was a life she could not even begin to imagine. Who would she watch "*Shameless*" with? Who would she trade Christmas presents with? Who would she stand next to in photographs? It felt silly to think that someone else might take on that role. But the pit in her stomach yawned at her constantly, asking what else life could be; in this way, she was always thinking about leaving Zhetai. "I don't know," she said. "I don't know what it's like to leave."

Leaving was a much harder question than pursuing, and so they did not focus on the leaving. After that first conversation, Lian and Wenyu didn't speak of Zhetai and Thomas in such tones again; their partners instead slotted perfectly into a different box, to be brought up purely during discussions of logistics ("Thomas's aunt keeps saying she wants to visit Beijing while we're here," or "Zhetai and I already watched 'Monkey King 3'; should we check out 'Monster Hunt 2'?").

She still saw Zhetai on the weekends in their customary rhythm, Saturday at hers and Sunday at his, with a dinner somewhere during the week. She had to reschedule a couple of their dinners when Wenyu came calling last-minute, but Zhetai didn't seem to notice or care; each time, she told him she was being held late at work. She didn't know why she felt the need to lie; he would have understood if she said she was seeing Wenyu, but she liked it, the lying. It heightened the already furtive feeling of her and Wenyu's meetings. He never questioned when she said she had work, and he only once brought it up, during a badminton game.

"You've been busy," he commented, whipping the birdie over the side of the net. It was a Saturday at the end of June.

"Yeah," she shrugged.

"Make sure you're sleeping," he said. He only ever had two antidotes—water and sleep. She gave a noncommittal grunt of agreement.

After their game, Zhetai stretched his calves. Lian checked her phone and saw Freddy had sent her a video mash-up of Christopher Nolan's greatest hits. She looked over at Zhetai, then put the phone down. Freddy could wait. She stood and copied Zhetai, reaching toward her toes. She was a naturally inflexible person; despite years of regular exercise, she'd never been able to touch her toes. Zhetai, meanwhile, had always been able to reach the ground easily. He stood straight now and lightly put his hand on her back, so that her fingertips brushed the tops of her feet.

"Try inhaling deeply, then letting the air go. Then let the weight of your arms pull you down," he instructed. She liked him best like this: guiding her. She felt his hand on her back, natural and warm. "Don't push it too much, though," he said, then released his hand. Her back was cool where he'd left it.

She straightened.

"That was good," he said.

"It felt good," she said.

Later that day, during their lesson, Freddy and Lian discussed whether Leonardo DiCaprio was a good actor.

She said no; he said yes—there was no one on earth who could watch "*Titanic*" without crying.

"*Is that all that makes a good actor?*" she asked. "*The ability to make someone cry?*"

"*Yes,*" he responded. "*That is very hard. When you cry for someone, you feel their heart. And isn't that what cinema is about?*"

But she hadn't cried at "*Titanic.*" The story was too unreal, too impossible. She could not imagine feeling that way about someone she'd only just met.

She nodded. "*You are totally right.*"

He told her that he'd picked up work writing copy for yogurt ads.

"*It's a lot of* AHHHHs *and* MMMMMMs," he said, shrugging. "*Who knew yogurt could be so* . . . I don't know how to say it in English, sexual?"

She laughed and could feel herself blush just a bit. "It kind of makes perfect sense," she said. The next day, an ad for sippable yogurt popped up on her Douyin. She screenshotted it. She debated whether to send it to him in English, but decided to risk it, sending it off in Chinese. "This didn't make me cry at all! Is this the death of cinema?" Like they were friends.

"My competitors know nothing of cinema," he responded, also in Chinese. "When you see one of my ads, you will definitely sob!"

By the first weekend of July, Lian found herself asking if he'd like to increase sessions to two times a week, since the TOEFL was coming up. They would be like cram sessions.

"*I was going to ask the same thing*," Freddy said.

"He loves you," Wenyu told her, giggling, as the two of them sat in a darkened theater, watching "*Mission: Impossible*" for the third time.

"You're so bad," Lian said, slapping her on the arm.

Lian and Freddy added Tuesdays to their schedule. The following Tuesday evening, Lian opened her Skype to find Freddy's chair empty.

"Hello?"

"Yeah, Mom, okay, yeah, can we talk later? Yeah," she heard off-screen, and then he was dropping into his chair, raking his hands through his hair. "Hi," he said. "Sorry about that." Then, "*Sorry*," he continued, in English.

"*Everything okay?*"

"*Yes*," he said.

There was a silence; she let it hang there, knowing there was more he wanted to say, but not sure if she was the one he wanted to tell it to.

"*Moms*," she said, just one word, no qualification, but she hoped it sounded something like understanding.

"*She, um. She does not want me to go. To New York.*"

"*It's very far.*"

"*She doesn't even like it when I go to Tianjin with friends*," he said. He leaned back in his chair and put his hands over his face. Then he exploded in Chinese. "It's one train! God!"

He was so much more emphatic than Zhetai; his emotions burbled just under a layer of skin so thin she felt she could slice it open with a fingernail. She wanted to reach out, still his face with her palm, feel the heat there.

"*She'll have to let go one day*," Lian said, and then felt silly. What did she know about letting go and being let go of? The way her mother treated her was not so different than when Lian was a child.

"Sometimes I wonder if I'm running away to America because of my mom," he said. *"She loves me so much. Too much. Maybe that's rude to say. Who doesn't want their mom to love them?"*

"Love is a lot of pressure," Lian found herself saying, though she wasn't sure how much she believed it. She had never minded pressure; what she feared was disappointment. It felt easy to say these things in English. Just like when she'd toss around phrases at work. It didn't mean anything to say *Love is a lot of pressure* in English. It didn't mean anything to say *I'm running away to America because of my mom.* It didn't mean anything to say, *Can we spend more time together,* or *I wonder what you are like in real life,* or something like *I like you.*

"It's probably why I've never made a relationship work," he said now.

"You don't like the pressure," she said.

"I'm used to being on my own," he said.

"Me too," she said, and felt the hinges of her heart swinging open. She thought about Wenyu's words: quid pro quo. Did it count if the secret was a lie? But as she spoke the words, she felt the truth in them too. Despite the people that had surrounded her these last few years—Zhetai, her family, Zhu Zixi, et al—she always felt, in essence, alone. At least for the previous decade.

"Is it still loneliness if everyone feels it?" he said now.

"I think it is still loneliness," she said. *"That's what's sad. So much loneliness in the world, and we can't help each other."*

Su Mingzun told her he'd been engaged briefly, Wenyu said one night as they walked underneath the billboards at Joy City. "When he was twenty-three," she said. "The divorced woman. They really tried, but in the end he was too young for her."

Su Mingzun really was a romantic. "What would have happened had they gotten married?" Lian wondered aloud.

"I guess, none of this," Wenyu said, gesturing at herself. "Or maybe she'd be on her second divorce by now."

Lian laughed. "I'm glad he spared her. What a good guy."

Wenyu laughed. "The rumors were fake, by the way. He didn't have a mental breakdown."

"I figured. They . . . always liked making shit up about him."

"He was just tired of the track he was on," she said. "Didn't like making code all day. Dropped out."

"I don't blame him. But a year to go? Feels like a pity."

"A year can feel like eternity when you've already decided it's a waste of time."

This was true, perhaps. "Does he ever regret it?"

"I'm sure he does. But he seems to be happy, when we talk about it. He actually likes sales. He likes talking to people."

Lian admired this about Su Mingzun, the way he didn't care what others thought about him. If she'd had to take a job that anyone with a high school diploma could've been hired for, she'd have kept it a secret forever. But Su Mingzun was never ashamed.

"Do you think it's . . . some kind of pathology, why we can't let go of each other?" Wenyu asked.

"You and Su Mingzun?"

Wenyu looked at Lian. "Yeah." She took a contemplative slurp of her boba. "Like, are we soulmates, or can we just not let go of the past?"

"I think you'd find it easy to let go if there wasn't something left to hold on to."

Wenyu contemplated this. They walked together on the square, Wenyu moving in a zigzag. "To ward off demons," she'd always say. "Demons can only travel in a straight line."

"Lian," Wenyu said next. "Why do you and Freddy video chat?"

Lian shrugged. "We've always just video chatted."

"But you live twenty minutes apart. Why don't you meet up with him?" Wenyu gave her a mischievous look.

The thought made Lian break into a sweat. "I . . ." She hadn't allowed herself to think about that possibility. Sure, her coworkers sometimes had in-person sessions with their students, but those were held at their offices and clearly delineated at the beginning of every contract; to add in-person sessions midway would be irregular. She wondered about his life, yes, and wondered what it would be like to run into him, but she had never thought to ask to meet up. It made it feel too real, possibly. What she didn't want to admit was, if it became real, then she'd have to contend with the actual challenges of making it real. On a screen, he could be anyone; she could convince herself he liked her. But face-to-face, she wouldn't be so sure. She couldn't be like Wenyu with her careless seduction; she would surely ruin it. "It'd be kind of inconvenient. . . ." She began spinning excuses about how she didn't have time for a commute.

"Aren't you curious what he's like in person?"

"I am," she said. "But it's exciting in its own way, just to . . . just to know this part of him." There was so much about a person that could disappoint you in real life. It was best to keep this a fantasy, one pocket of her mind that would always be wonderful.

"But what if he's better in person? What if it's amazing? Don't you want to take a chance on that?"

"But what if he isn't?" Lian asked. And they played out the philosophical argument, the poles at which they'd always stood: Lian making the contingency plan for inevitable disappointment; Wenyu waving her hopeful flag, asking, perpetually, what if. What if what if what if it's better than anything your mind could ever imagine.

THE SECOND WEEKEND of July, Lian went to brunch with Wenyu, Zhu Zixi, and Yang Qinru. She hadn't seen the other two women in weeks, not since Wenyu had come back into her life.

They convened at a "new American" restaurant in Tuanjiehu, which boasted the perfect poached egg and "wasabi toast," though whatever that was, it didn't sound very "new American." First rule to a girls' day was no boyfriends or husbands or fiancés. Second rule was the divulging of secrets over eight or more collective mimosas. As they sat down at a square table in an outdoor courtyard, lush calatheas tickling their backs, Lian eyed Wenyu and wondered what secrets would spill over the course of the afternoon.

Zhu Zixi chattered on about her belated honeymoon. Apparently she'd missed the memo; Cabo was passé now. Small plates of salmon lox arrived, arranged in spirals atop translucent slices of green toast. Wenyu took out her phone and snapped a photo of her meal, angling the mimosa just so to add a pop of orange to the tableau.

"Is this going to make it onto your channel, Luo Wenyu?" Zhu Zixi teased. Lian suspected a part of Zhu Zixi really did want to appear as a guest star, the better to advertise her new app, or just to glean a little bit of Wenyu's good juju. "Get my good side."

"Oh, I can't afford you, Zhu Zixi," Wenyu volleyed, giving Zhu Zixi a little wink. Nevertheless, she held up her camera. "Say hi, everyone!"

"How's your number one fan?" Zhu Zixi asked.

Wenyu laughed, rolling her eyes. "He sent me a bike yesterday." Wenyu had a new superfan, who had sent her numerous unwieldy gifts: Keroppi plushies, boxes of white chocolates, and now, inexplicably, a bicycle. "Let's ride through the Forbidden City like you do on your channel," read an affixed note. "I mean, it's nice," she said, with a wave of her hand. "But what am I gonna do with a bike?"

"You should be careful," Lian said. "Aren't you scared that one of these guys is gonna . . . I don't know, do something?"

Wenyu gave a little wave. "This happens all the time. But I guess that's one more reason why I'm excited to move into the new place."

"Ooh, yes! How's the new house going? We're thinking of buying in the suburbs too. I'm tired of all this . . . city around me. Need some greenery," Zhu Zixi said, taking out a cigarette and dangling it between two sturdy fingers. She'd picked up smoking at UCSD and now chain-smoked at every outing, though Lian couldn't tell if it was from addiction or commitment to an aesthetic.

"It's going pretty quickly, actually. I can't wait for you guys to see it! Housewarming August 11! Mark your calendars," Wenyu continued. "I'm shooting a big video that day. So look hot! I have a bunch of sponsors I have to mention in a casual, cool way." She giggled. "Thomas wants it to be a classic pool party."

Wenyu had not mentioned Thomas to Lian in several weeks, and Lian was almost shocked to hear his name. He'd had to fly back to SF at the end of June, to deal with some investors who were getting cold feet. She thought of what Wenyu had called to tell her about just that morning. Wenyu and Su Mingzun had gotten a hotel room the previous night, a honeymoon suite. Wenyu had paid in cash. Su Mingzun had brought her a garish bouquet of plastic flowers; real flowers were tacky, he said; plastic lasted forever. He was constantly poking fun at these romantic rites, making a mockery of gifts and gestures, and Wenyu loved it, the sly winking and nodding, but Lian knew that underneath it all, what she loved the most about it was the fact he'd still had to go out and buy the flowers. Plastic flowers, as it turned out, were harder to find than real ones. They'd ordered room service—bottles of champagne and soft-scrambled eggs and Canadian bacon and quiche Lorraine—and made unapologetic love until the sun was creeping up. She'd tiptoed back into her parents' home at seven AM and joined them for breakfast, the only thing amiss her voracious appetite—two large bowls of rice porridge she slurped down, thirsty from the previous evening's events.

She wondered what Zhu Zixi would say about all this. Last year, Bo had cheated on her with a hostess he'd met at a bar. Lian remembered her recounting the event not with any heartbreak or even anger, but instead, a sort of annoyance. "Love is mathematics. Unfortunately, the scale tipped in another woman's favor. What I have to do now is tip it back," she'd said, grumbling. "I had just started cutting my gym days down from six to five. Now I guess it's back to six." She'd been so logical about it. Lian thought about this now and felt a leaden sadness wash over her.

"Oooh! Haven't gone swimming in years!" Yang Qinru said, clasping her hands in front of her face.

"This is what's gonna get me through the next month," Zhu Zixi said. "My mother-in-law has been staying with us and it's killing me."

This was what people talked about at their age. Vacation homes. Housewarmings. Pesky, permed mothers-in-law sensually gripping their sons' necks. Zhu Zixi's mother-in-law was a weak-voiced woman who couldn't steam an egg without having to sit down for a stretch of time, so she did not so much yell and scream at Zhu Zixi as regard her with a wan disappointment, a sad little smile on her face as a carousel of better women swished across her mind's eye. Of course, none of these women actually existed; no woman was good enough for a mother's son.

"She pretended to faint when we went out to Mutianyu last weekend," Zhu Zixi said now, shrugging and plopping a slick scrap of burrata into her mouth. "Bo was so concerned, he put her on his back and everything. Broke a sweat, poor boy. He hasn't exerted himself like that since our wedding night."

Yang Qinru giggled lushly. She was always so charmed by Zhu Zixi's provocative statements. "What about you, Luo Wenyu?" Zhu Zixi asked next. All eyes turned to Wenyu. She, after all, was the only one with a Western mother-in-law-to-be. Did the first Mrs. Straeffer-Kenney expect Wenyu to steam fish and iron chemises and wipe the asses of her parents, if they were still alive, which Yang Qinru had said she'd done in the last three months of her grandpa-in-law's life?

"She's one of those . . . *friend moms,*" Wenyu said, using a phrase Lian had never heard before. "She's really chill, or at least, she wants you to think she's chill. But somehow she's always coming up to San Francisco anyway and asking me when Thomas and I are going to have kids. They're so close, they'll just hop on a plane sometimes and be there in an hour."

"Huh," Zhu Zixi said. "I would die of happiness if my in-laws lived far enough away to have to take a plane."

Wenyu shrugged. "Yeah, it's not too bad," she said, and Lian could see her deflate a bit.

"Luo Wenyu," Zhu Zixi said. She clucked her tongue as she downed the rest of her mimosa. "You really did it right. American parents will let you walk all over them. Then hand you an inheritance bigger than the GDP of Taiwan. I should've stayed and netted a cute white boy like you!"

For Wenyu's sake, Lian was happy Mrs. Straeffer-Kenney was a "*friend mom.*" Wenyu had never been the sort of girl to conform to wifely standards; she couldn't steam an egg for her life, and she'd certainly bleed out her vocal cords feuding with a Chinese mother over her husband's affection. In this way, America had been exactly the right choice for Wenyu.

When it was Lian's turn to bemoan her role as a future wife, Lian found herself straining too. But it wasn't because Zhetai's mother was a "*friend mom,*" but because, in fact, she found dealing with her quite easy. She was demanding, yes, but Lian was very good at—and even enjoyed—meeting her demands. The young girl with the stiff collar was never so alive as she was in Zhetai's mother's home.

"Her birthday is tomorrow," Lian found herself offering. "She loves making a huge deal out of it."

"Jesus," Zhu Zixi said, taking a long drag of her cigarette. "Hey, but you threw that big party last year for her sixtieth. You went all out."

Wenyu was regarding her with a look of surprise. Ye Lian, party planner extraordinaire? Lian didn't like crowds, and Wenyu had always been the one with the big ideas. Evidently, Wenyu was not the only one who had changed.

"Yeah," Lian said, sighing. She'd have to pull out similar stops this time, though this year Zhetai's mother had requested she arrange an intimate affair at home, "just" forty of her closest colleagues and family. "Thank god she wants something 'low-key' this year."

"That sounds so fun, Lianlian," Wenyu said.

"You should come," Lian said, surprised that the invite had so easily tumbled forth.

A ping.

"*NYU isn't responding to my emails. I'm worried . . .*"

"Who's Freddy?" Zhu Zixi asked, leaning over.

"Ah. No one. Just a student," she said, a bit too quickly. She caught Wenyu's gaze out of the corner of her eye, and something hot rustled through her.

Dessert arrived. Tiramisu in a slivered rectangle, strawberry-glazed shortbread with pistachio flakes, chocolate cake. Wenyu's phone rang. She picked it up.

"*Thomas? Yeah, we're finishing now! Wanna come up? They'd love to see you. Okay, yeah. Yeah. Great. Love you. No, stop! Love you, okay. See you soon.*" The frenetic word salad of love. She put down the phone. "He just got back from San Francisco this morning."

"Wow," Zhu Zixi said. "I don't remember the last time Bo picked me up from anything."

"That's what happens when you have a driver!" Wenyu laughed.

"Sometimes Wei will come with our driver to get me," Yang Qinru smiled, and they all rolled their eyes in faux mockery. Yang Qinru was so innocent. She didn't understand when she was bragging, and they couldn't fault her for it.

Thomas bounded up the steps to the restaurant just then, the flaps of his button-down shirt billowing in the breeze. Wenyu stood and held out her arms, and they embraced, Thomas tucking an audible kiss into her cheek. *"Hey honey!"* she cooed. Lian found her palms sweating—this was the first time she'd seen Thomas since her and Wenyu's conspiracy had begun.

"Hey girls!" he waved. A waiter brought over a chair and he collapsed into it. *"How's girls' day?"*

"It's great," Zhu Zixi said. *"We needed a testosterone break."*

"How was San Francisco?" Lian asked.

He waved his hands in front of his face. *"A fucking drag. Flaky tech guys are the worst. But it's all good, I put out the fire."*

Wenyu grinned and squeezed his leg. *"You want some dessert?"* she asked, gesturing at her plate.

He put a forkful of tiramisu into his mouth. *"That's really fucking good,"* he said. With Americans, everything was always *fucking good, fucking amazing, fucking brilliant.* Lian thought the tiramisu was just fine. But Wenyu smiled at him. *"Great choice, babe,"* he said, and gave her another peck on the cheek.

Lian examined Thomas. His button-down hung curtain-like over a gray T-shirt with a LinkedIn logo. He squinted with the eyes of a man who had gotten LASIK. Occasionally his fingers flew to his face to lift phantom glasses. He was a sincere man, a man without a shred of irony, and something needled at her heart as she saw the way he looked at Wenyu, and the way Wenyu looked back, dabbing stray crumbs from his mouth with her finger. For a moment the hotel and the quiche Lorraine and the plastic flowers were gone. This was love, and yet something else was, too.

"So, girls, what was Vivian like in high school?" Thomas asked.

Zhu Zixi laughed. *"Oh my god, she was a total freak."* She and Yang Qinru giggled.

"She was the class rebel," Yang Qinru added.

"A rebel, really!" Thomas said, shocked, his mouth dropping open. He looked at Wenyu. *"You never told me this!"*

Wenyu laughed. "*I mean, it was just kid stuff. I didn't like following the rules.*"

"*She got suspended a few times,*" Zhu Zixi said.

"*She was always showing up in these short skirts,*" Yang Qinru said. She shrugged. "*I thought they were cute.*"

By her recollection, Lian remembered Yang Qinru calling Wenyu a "wannabe Diao Chan, but sluttier" behind her back.

"*Whoa-oh,*" Thomas said, nudging Wenyu. "*Don't tell my mom.*"

Wenyu blushed. "*It was a phase,*" she said.

"*Oh my god, look at this photo,*" Zhu Zixi said now, handing Thomas her phone. It was a photo of their second year class on the last day of school. Their teachers had allowed them to wear whatever they wanted. Lian had agonized over this decision before choosing a pair of jeans with tennis shoes and a varsity-style shirt with the words COOL GIRL PARIS on it; she'd thought the bold-face capital letters telegraphed style and defiance, but she cringed now. Of course, this was the day Wenyu and Su Mingzun arrived wearing their uniforms. "*This was probably . . . senior year?*"

"*Second year,*" Lian piped in. "*Because Wenyu left senior year.*"

"There's Su Mingzun," Yang Qinru pointed, giggling. "King and Queen Troublemakers."

"*What did she say?*" Thomas said, leaning in.

"*Just this guy in our class,*" Lian said, grabbing the phone. She could feel Wenyu's eyes on her. "Wow, Zhu Zixi, you wore a suit to this?"

Zhu Zixi slapped her on the arm. "Shut up, what's the phrase, you gotta dress for the job you want, not the job you have!"

Yang Qinru gasped. "Wenyu, wasn't this the day you punched Liu Bin in the face?"

"Oh my god, yes, it was right after we took the photo!" Zhu Zixi was practically doubled over with laughter.

Lian remembered this—it was funny, a triumphant moment.

"He said something like, 'Where's your stripper dress, Luo Wenyu?'" Yang Qinru tittered, doing an uncanny impression of Liu Bin. "Because it was the one day you showed up in your uniform."

"That was fucking funny," Zhu Zixi cackled. She looked at Thomas. "*Wenyu punched a guy in our class because he called her a stripper.*"

"*Vivian!*" Thomas said, scandalized. "*I can't imagine this.*"

"*It wasn't a real punch,*" Wenyu said. "*I just kinda tapped his face.*"

"*He was bleeding!*" Zhu Zixi added, nearly in tears.

Wenyu shrugged. "*Liu Bin's always been a drama queen.*"

"*You're . . . so sweet usually,*" Thomas said. "*I'm shocked.*"

Wenyu smiled, her lips pulled into an expression even Lian couldn't read. Then she handed Thomas her phone and changed the subject. "*Can you get a video of us?*"

He got up, the matter shelved. He dusted his hands on his jeans and held the phone horizontally.

"Okay, everyone, just eat and then look over at the camera and wave!" Wenyu instructed.

"*I'm recording!*"

Lian watched Wenyu cut herself a corner of cake and fork it into her mouth. "*Oh my god, this is so fucking good,*" Wenyu said. Lian copied Wenyu's movements, faking orgasmic delight at the bite of generic chocolate cake she, too, forked into her mouth. Wenyu pointed at the camera and arranged her face into a dazzling smile. "*We're at brunch! Look at these adorable drinks! Ooh, Thomas, get a photo now?*"

The four of them turned toward the camera, Yang Qinru's shoulders arching regally out of an off-the-shoulder top, Zhu Zixi sitting pin-straight in a black high-neck blouse. Lian had dressed up today, in a strappy violet tank top. This was a portrait of aspirational friendship, adult women who could trade meaningful conversation and look stylish doing it. She wondered what the comments would say about today's brunch. Lian leaned in close to Wenyu.

"*Say 'girls' day'!*" Wenyu cheered.

"*Girls' day!*" came the chorus.

AFTER THE FIVE of them said their goodbyes in front of the restaurant, Lian texted Freddy back. They had their lesson in an hour.

"*What happened with NYU?*"

"*I sent them that email a few days ago. I was offering to send my script. Maybe they are mad.*"

She paused. "*I'm almost home,*" she texted. "*Call you soon.*"

"Maybe I was too aggressive," he said immediately when he appeared on the video chat.

He was speaking in Chinese. She wasn't sure whether to respond in kind. Then he seemed to catch himself.

"Oh, sorry," he said, switching to English. "*Maybe I was too forward.*"

"*They're probably super busy right now,*" she said. Lian had read over his emails; he seemed polite, eager, but not overly so. "*Don't worry. Focus on your application.*"

He shrugged. "*I plan to submit the screenplay about Commander China in Paris. It's an allegory for World War II.*"

"*That sounds funny,*" she said, though she wasn't sure if he intended it to be funny. "*Will you let me read it?*"

He pursed his lips. She was always asking to read his work, and he was always declining in hurried tones, *No, it's not ready, one day when it's ready, you'll see it on the screen.* He suddenly switched again to Chinese. "I can't let you read it."

This time, she allowed herself to relax. She opened her mouth and spoke in Chinese to him for the first time. She knew that her voice in Chinese was more boyish, her consonants less accentuated, harsher. "You know, for someone who loves to judge things, you sure seem to be scared of being judged."

"Whoa, *Lily*," he said. "Your voice is different. I guess this is the first time I've heard you speak Chinese."

"Sorry," she said. "Bad teacher move."

"You have a nice voice," he said. "Not that . . . not that it wasn't nice in English."

"Thanks," she said, hoping her whole face wasn't red. She chewed one side of her lip. Zhetai always told her to stop when she did this, but Freddy didn't know her habits well enough to say anything.

"Anyway, that's exactly why! I know how much of an asshole people can be! They can say nice things to your face, but the truth could kill you. I would know—I'm one of them!"

"I think it'll be good practice. See if you can take what you dish out."

He laughed, then sat back heavily in his seat. He looked up. "What if you hate it and you're embarrassed and you won't want to teach me anymore?"

Lian laughed. "If teachers quit their students every time they did something embarrassing, no one would ever learn anything." If they were speaking in English, perhaps she would have said, *I could never be embarrassed by you.*

He fell quiet for a beat. "Is it stupid, what I'm doing?" he asked. "I've heard the odds of becoming a working director are lower than getting into the NBA. It's stupid, right? To bet on odds like that?"

She paused. "I . . . I think when you're young, you should only bet on impossible odds."

"Is that what you did?" he said. "Bet on impossible odds?"

"Not really," she said now, breathing out. She didn't want to speak about her failure. She thought of their conversation several weeks ago, how surprised he'd been when she told him she'd never studied in America. "I tried," she said. "But I didn't want it enough."

"Hmm," he said. "What do you mean?"

"I had always wanted to study in America, like you," she said. "And everyone thought I was gonna go. I could read Harry Potter in the original English by the time I was ten. I watched so many movies . . . I was just . . . obsessed. But then—" and here she stopped. Then what happened? She thought about the facts. Wenyu moved to California. Lian was rejected by every school. It was too pathetic a story.

"I had gotten accepted," she said, testing the lie on her lips. "Berkeley."

She could see his eyebrows move up, his eyes fly open with surprise.

"But then I pulled this prank," she said, her breath growing faster. "My best friend and I, the one I told you about, we were at the pool." What happened at the pool with Teacher Liao spilled from her mouth, the various details sending tiny needles pricking into her heart. The underwear flapping in the tree. Teacher Liao's head, smooth and wet, her hair pressed flat against her skull in a ponytail. Her straight back as she walked on. Wenyu's sparkling laugh. "Well, the next week, our teacher disappeared. And then the principal came in and told me I was expelled. And Berkeley rescinded my offer." She stated all this flatly, in a rush, worried that if she paused she'd never be able to finish the lie.

"That's crazy," Freddy said, after she was done. "*Lily*, you really are a rebel!"

"It was stupid of me," she said.

"But kinda badass."

"Thanks," she said.

"You never wanted to try again? Going to America."

"I visited once," she said. "The summer after I graduated college. I went to New York City."

"Wait, really? You've never mentioned this."

She hadn't, on purpose. She didn't like to think of that trip. "It was just a vacation." She shrugged. "It was exciting. It was massive. I don't think I've ever been somewhere as crazy as New York. They don't have as many people as here, that's for sure, but there's always something happening. A car honking, a person yelling, thirty different neon lights blinking." Indeed, it had been a disorienting trip. She'd gone with Zhetai, in one of those early-relationship tests of compatibility, bankrolled by Zhetai's mother in her own litmus test–slash–first-anniversary gift. They'd eaten cheesecake at Junior's, watched the Statue of Liberty from a ferry, ridden rollercoasters at Coney Island. She and Zhetai were compatible travelers, she the one with the ideas and he the perfect logistical executor, the king of Dazhong Dianping (they had to get used to a different app in America, the confusingly named "*Yelp*"). But being a tourist always felt a little embarrassing, the whole song and dance of flying over to a country in a plane and riding around in a large red tour bus, the tour guides with their uniforms and the travel magazines with their lists of must-sees, the way tourists always tried to speak in the language of the natives. That was the silliest part. "*Nee HOW nee HOW!*" sweaty Caucasians would say as she passed by them in Wangfujing, their faces open but taunting, demanding her validation. She wanted to avoid becoming this trope at all costs, and refused to linger at any destination, limiting the amount of photos they took and rejecting with breakneck speed anyone who attempted to sell them souvenirs. She wanted so badly to come off as a local, and when, thanks to an insider recommendation from Zhu Zixi, they found themselves at a dessert bar in the East Village jam-packed with trendy Asian American couples who looked just like Lian and Zhetai, Lian smirked, feeling like they had pulled off some sort of charade.

There had been another reason for this trip. A small part of her wanted to go to America to see if something would spark in her, if she'd be newly motivated to apply to grad school. But the trip was harried, brief. Despite her efforts, they only really had time for the highlights, and seeing her dream in such broad, clichéd strokes depressed her, magnifying the feeling she had in the pit of her stomach that she would never truly know America; it would never be hers. While Lian sat on a double-decker bus, Wenyu posted about moving from Santa Cruz to San Francisco, about her new relationship with Thomas. No matter how well Lian got to know America, Wenyu would always be several years ahead of her. Lian was merely one of millions—billions—who had walked America's fluorescent-soaked streets. She came back to Beijing and never spoke of going to America again.

She didn't want to say all of this to Freddy, though. These parts of herself were too ugly; her insecurity and her jealousy could be poisonous for someone who still had so many dreams. Peering at him on the screen, his back straight as he leaned in to listen to her, Lian wanted to preserve that feeling for him forever. The feeling that life could be anything.

"It was beautiful," she said. "You'll love it. I think for me, at that point I'd already set my life into motion. Like a windup toy. I had a job offer. I didn't think it made sense for me to go to America anymore." She didn't mention Zhetai.

He nodded, his eyes narrowing a bit as he stared at her. Then he started laughing. "*Lily*," he said. "You talk like you're forty years old. You're a nineties baby like me!"

And then she was laughing too. "I guess I do," she said. "Thirty feels like forty, in a way," she said. "You'll understand when you're older."

"Thanks, Mom," he said, laughing, then seemed to catch himself. He stopped laughing. "I won't. I'm not a windup toy. I'm gonna change directions whenever I want."

"I think you will," she said. "Just remember to invite me to your premiere."

"Oh, don't worry. When I make it big, I'll say it was all because of my tutor, who believed in me when I was just a nobody."

She laughed again, then grew quiet for a moment. "My job does have a New York office, actually."

"See! Oh my god, that would be awesome!" There was true joy in his eyes. "Hey, if I get into NYU, promise me you'll think about going to New York."

Lian smiled. An image of the two of them in New York City flashed through her mind. It was exciting. "Fine. Deal."

Freddy exhaled. "Okay," he said. "Actually, I think I'm ready to show you something."

He sent over his application essay to NYU. They wanted five hundred words on a formative experience that shaped you as an artist. Freddy's essay was about a stray cat he'd discovered when he was a young boy. The cat had stumbled into the courtyard of his family's walk-up, and Freddy quickly came to delight in feeding it. His father did not like the cat. He thought the cat was vermin, and that feeding it was girlish, and he would stomp his feet loudly whenever the cat came along. Freddy looked up to his father, who worked very hard and had always impressed upon Freddy that it was important to be steadfast about his dreams. Nevertheless, Freddy would sneak away to slip the cat tiny bits of rice, pork skins, and bits of breaded fish. One day, Freddy came home after school and nearly stepped on what seemed to be a fallen piece of newsprint. When he looked more closely, however, he realized that the newsprint had brown fur, and there were streaks of blood matting the fur into a flat sheet. He vomited into the bushes, bile mixing with his tears.

His father found him crying, then said a dog must have done it. "It's as flat as a sheet of paper," he'd said. "How horrible."

Freddy ended the essay like this: "*Heroes in real life are complicated. So I wanted to create my own heroes, on the screen.*"

There was a chill in Lian's spine when she finished reading. The Freddy on the page was so soft, feeding the cat always straight from his palm. The essay was imperfect—there were numerous grammatical mistakes, and the sentences were elementary—but any embarrassment at his technique was swiftly extinguished by the aching in her heart. The fact that he had chosen this anecdote, out of all the anecdotes of his life, to illustrate who he was today left a profound and deeply sad mark on her. It made her feel that maybe love was easy, that all it took to love someone was knowing your heart could break for them.

"It's really profound," she said, looking up.

"Yeah? You think?"

"It's sad."

He seemed anxious. "Was it too sad? I can make it happier."

"No . . . it's. Honest. Which is important."

"Okay," he said.

"I'm sorry," she said.

"Why?"

"That this happened."

He paused. "It was so long ago."

Something occurred to her, and the question left her mouth before she realized she didn't want to know the answer. "What happened? After your dad found you in Taipei?"

Freddy's eyes pinched together just slightly. "He was angry. Yelled a lot." He shrugged. "I was the same height as him by then. Couldn't do much but yell."

Her lip was trembling, and she didn't know how to respond. But Freddy merely broke into a grin. "Oh! By the way, there's this convention tomorrow night. The sci-fi convention. I can't wait. They have these props from the original 'Star Wars' on display at the National Convention Center. Maybe I will get some inspiration from C-3PO."

"That's amazing!" she said.

"Have you ever been to one of these? Conventions?"

"No," she said.

"You might like it."

"I'm sure I would," she said.

"Maybe you should come."

She was startled by the suggestion. "I can't," she said. "I have a birthday."

"You're missing out."

She checked the time. "I have to go," she said. "Fill me in on it later."

"See ya," he said. "I'll send you photos."

She hung up, then realized they'd barely spoken English during their entire lesson.

SHE FOUND HERSELF at the Dia Market an hour later. Since the beginning of their relationship, Lian would steam Zhetai's mother an elaborate spread of pastries for her birthday, spending hours making them from scratch.

It all started because at the beginning of their relationship, Zhetai had once joked that his mother was a tough customer. And so three months into dating, when his mother's birthday rolled around, Lian showed up at his parents' home with a plate of red bean paste husband-and-wife cakes. Her first go had been abysmal, the cakes all different sizes and lumpy so that, stacked on top of each other, they resembled a melting molehill, but Zhetai's mother's face had nonetheless lit up like a full moon. It became a tradition and a source of comfort; it was therapeutic, steaming and boiling and rolling and filling the dough that began tough and always yielded to her hand. Now, her cakes were nearly professional in quality.

She stood in the dried-foods aisle of the Dia and picked out mung beans, which she would soak and boil and smash into a glistening olive-gold paste.

A ping.

"Our conversation inspired me. I'm watching 'A Beijing Native in New York.' Should I get Jiang Wen's haircut?"

He sent a photo of Jiang Wen circa 1993, his hair in a rocker shag over his eyes. Lian laughed, then caught herself, looking at the rows of mung beans in front of her. What was she doing?

She still needed rice flour, powdered sugar, honey. Red beans, taro root, yams. She walked down the aisles, reading each label meticulously. She lost herself in an examination of purple versus white yams. Her hand hovered above a sachet of black sesame. She contemplated slipping it into her purse. The zipper was open; how easy it would be to drop it into the open maw and walk right out the door.

She looked over at the registers. The woman at the checkout was a young girl with sparse bangs and a stout face. Lian wondered now how old the cashier had been the day she'd met Wenyu, and realized with a start that maybe she was only as old as this girl in front of her. In her memory the cashier was old, impossibly old, but what did impossibly old mean to a child? And if the cashier was indeed a young girl, perhaps she hadn't cared very much at all that day, and perhaps she would have had no power to penalize Wenyu, and all of Lian's terror and adrenaline had been exaggerated, a sliver of peril she'd deliberately magnified into something bigger to justify her complicity.

Moments later she approached the checkout and smiled at the cashier. The girl did not return her smile; she scanned the items across as if not seeing Lian at all. When Lian emerged into the stark morning light, she looked down into her bag at the sachet of sesame. It was too late to turn around, apologize, and say she'd forgotten to pay. She turned on her heel and walked toward home, something light jangling in her chest.

ZHETAI'S PARENTS LIVED in an impressive condominium in a slightly nicer complex than her own. Zhetai's father had made his career in natural gas and had worked at China Petroleum and Chemical for years. But the real money came from his mother, who was a lieutenant-ranked official in the Party. Lian's own parents' careers were successful, yes, but his parents' were just a smidge more. And that was what was called a perfect match.

Lian arrived early to the birthday, holding her tower of pastries aloft. When she walked in, Zhetai's mother was at the stove, sniffing some concoction, and his father was pouring a glass of liquor.

"Ba. Ma," she said, the words, after all these years, still cottony in her mouth. "Happy birthday." Zhetai's mother turned around and, seeing Lian, flung her hands to her face, eyes already teary.

"Such a good child," Zhetai's mother exclaimed, squeezing Lian's arm. She surveyed the dessert spread that Lian held before her, eyes glittering, before swatting herself across the nose. "I can't be too greedy," she said, nevertheless popping a rice cake into her mouth. "Mmmmm." She chewed on the filling. "You get better every year!"

Lian smiled and retrieved an apron. Wordlessly, she got to work tending the pot, as Zhetai's mother took off her own apron and rushed to her bedroom to finish getting ready. The action was automatic; years ago Zhetai's mother had stopped asking her to help in the kitchen, because, anticipating the question, Lian had begun doing this handoff silently.

Shortly after, guests began arriving. Lian pulled double duty then, tending to the stove and turning around to smile and wave, wiping her hands on her apron to take the bags and jackets of a fleet of mid-level Party members, family members, and neighbors. She was both the consummate guest and the gracious host. Each of these guests would nod appraisingly and make knowing eye contact with Zhetai's mother—you've got a good one here—and the usual pride would flicker inside Lian.

She turned the heat down to a low simmer and placed the lid of the Dutch oven back on the fish. She'd let this cook down for half an hour and return. She found herself looking around the kitchen for any other signs of disorder, feeling, as she'd begun to in recent years, that this home was her home and so she wouldn't allow a stray napkin or figurine placed at an odd angle to embarrass her. She placed a lemon back in the glass bowl on the kitchen counter and wiped away a few drops of soy sauce. From the living room came a scatter of laughter. Evidently the party had already broken into the baijiu. Lian washed and cut six persimmons into wedges, arranging them as petals around a bowl of sunflower seeds. She carried the plate out to the living room, and Zhetai's mother grabbed her hand and gave it a squeeze. Everyone seated oohed and aahed at Lian's arrangement and gave her that approving look again. Lian poured herself a glass of wine and joined Zhetai by the window, which had a splendid view of the Lama Temple. His hand landed on the small of her back, and for a moment Lian felt peaceful. A waning afternoon glow splashed its sensual colors over the far wall, and Lian listened as Zhetai's mother's colleagues regaled them with tales of her goodwill. Zhetai's uncle complained drunkenly about his spoiled son who had big ambitions and no work ethic. "If only he could be more like Little Lian over here," he said, nodding at Lian admiringly.

Lian peered at the clock and saw the fish was just about done. She moved to the kitchen and turned off the stove. She set a spread of dishes on the counter: spaghettied bean curd, red-braised pork, pig's ear, chili oil chicken, fried leeks, and the glistening sea bream bubbling on a bed of onion. The guests took turns filling their plates.

Then, at eight, there was a ring. Lian went to the door and was shocked to see Wenyu standing before her with a bashful smile. Behind Wenyu stood Su Mingzun. He'd swapped out his baggy clothes for clean-cut khakis and a gray button-down and had brushed his hair back so that it lay flat against his head.

"Wenyu! Hi! You . . . you came!"

"Lianlian!" Wenyu threw her arms around her, then gestured apologetically at Su Mingzun. "I thought it would be weird to bring Thomas," she said. "You know, he wouldn't understand anyone. . . ."

"*Hello*, Comrade Ye." Su Mingzun waved rakishly.

Zhetai appeared behind Lian. "Welcome," he said, ever the polite guy. "And who is this?"

Su Mingzun swung out his hand, locking Zhetai into a body slam. "Su Mingzun. Nice to meet you, man, I went to high school with Ye Lian."

Recognition registered in Zhetai's eyes, and Lian began to sweat. But Zhetai would never make a scene. "Welcome," Zhetai said, stiffly, taking Wenyu's jacket.

Wenyu handed Lian a glossy pink box. "Macarons," Wenyu said. "Hope she likes French desserts?"

Lian took the box to the kitchen counter, where she placed it next to the dessert platter. The box, edged in gold leaf and tied with velvet ribbon, cut an impressive profile beside Lian's home-made plate of pastries. Suddenly, she felt that she should have chilled her dough longer; the crumb could have been flakier; the husband-and-wife cakes were a bit flat.

Zhetai's mother hurried over from the living room, unfazed by the strangers now standing in her foyer. "And who are these nice young people!"

"Ma, this is my friend from high school, Luo Wenyu," Lian said. "And this is my other classmate, Su Mingzun—"

"My boyfriend," Wenyu said suddenly, taking Su Mingzun's hand. The two of them looked at each other with barely contained laughter. Lian tried to make eye contact with Wenyu. What was going on? Zhetai's eyes narrowed.

"How nice! What a handsome man! Come in, come in!" Zhetai's mother, oblivious to the charade before her, led them back to the living room.

Wenyu and Su Mingzun perched on a chaise close to the balcony. Zhetai's uncle continued to hold court, his face two shades redder as he rambled about a new development that had popped up in front of his bedroom window. Lian watched Wenyu appraise the scene. Zhetai's family had an impressive living room with a large balcony, an open kitchen with a direct view of the television, and stunning hardwood floors upon which his mother had draped a 10,000 RMB rug. She saw Su

Mingzun fidgeting with the edge of a Swarovski crystal vase that sat atop the credenza, and she resisted the urge to scoot over and admonish him like Teacher Liao in composition class.

"Lian ah, how about your friends?" Zhetai's mother gestured at Wenyu and Su Mingzun. She turned toward them. "How did you two meet?"

There was a steely pause in the air. Then Wenyu, in her classic bombastic fashion, pulled her lips into a smile and cocked her head at Su Mingzun.

"Well, we're high school sweethearts."

"Wenyu went abroad for university," Su Mingzun said. "And I went to Wuhan." He let his hand rest lightly on her knee.

"We kept in touch the entire time," Wenyu said. "Writing letters. Very traditional."

"She came home for the holidays, and I visited her," he said.

"Wow," Zhetai's mother said. "Very rare to see couples from high school last these days. How precious."

"I moved back a few months ago," Wenyu said. "To . . . work for a . . . consulting company. And we reunited."

"We're going to get married next year," Su Mingzun said next, and even Wenyu looked startled. He took her hand, running his thumb along the ridges of her large diamond. "We have a house in Shunyi. It has a pool."

Lian's spine shivered a little at this, at the casual way in which Su Mingzun had cannibalized the facts of Wenyu and Thomas's life. But Wenyu didn't seem shocked in a bad way; instead, her eyelids fell in a sort of soupy rapture as she watched him talk about the house, the pool, the ring, as if it were all his doing.

"That's so beautiful," Zhetai's mother said, her hands flying to her heart. "Two high school sweethearts, who have stood the tests of time and distance!" Her friends nodded and gazed fondly at Wenyu and Su Mingzun. Lian couldn't see Zhetai's face, but she felt his hand on her shoulder, tense and hard. "What a nice girl," Zhetai's mother continued. "Why have you never come to one of my birthdays before? I've met many of Lian's other friends."

A sad look flitted faintly over Wenyu's face. "I was always out of town," Wenyu said, finally, another half-truth among all the half-truths. "I'm so glad I get to meet you now though." She looked up at Zhetai. "Zhetai is a wonderful man. I'm thrilled for the two of them." She beamed at Lian, and then at Zhetai, and this time Lian twisted her head back to steal a look at his expression. He returned a pained smile, his lips pulled into a straight line.

Zhetai's mother proclaimed it was time to open presents. Lian excused herself to the kitchen to get the tea and desserts ready.

Wenyu followed. Lian couldn't help herself. "What was that back there?" Lian whispered, nodding toward Su Mingzun, who had now migrated to the balcony and was peering over the ledge. He'd rolled up the sleeves of his shirt and undone a button at the top.

"Don't be mad, Lianlian," Wenyu said. "It's just for fun." She opened the fridge, lazily peering inside. Lian felt a bit nervous; Zhetai's mother was particular about her kitchen. She busied herself with the tea. She carefully balanced on a stool and retrieved Zhetai's mother's prized teapot from the top shelf of the cupboard. Next came the two dozen celadon cups, their mouths no larger than a thumb's length across. The cups, as Zhetai's mother often reminded her, had been a gift from the Beijing municipal secretary general, each cup forged of jade mined from caves deep in Xinjiang.

The party chattered on in the next room. Wenyu traced her finger along the lip of a cup. Lian watched her finger. Wenyu continued. "I just . . . I wanted to see what it would feel like to . . . you know, be a normal girl again." She shrugged. "I just wanted to . . . not have to act for once. Not have to explain anything to anyone. I'm sorry, Lian, was that awkward?"

Lian paused. The thing was, she hadn't felt awkward. Zhetai's mother didn't know Wenyu, knew nothing of her real engagement. To her, Wenyu was just like so many of Lian's other friends, a nice Beijing girl with a nice Beijing boyfriend. Lian allowed herself to settle into the normalcy of the moment. She and her best friend at her future mother-in-law's home. And that was what it felt like: normal.

"Aren't you scared Thomas is going to find out?" she decided to say, spooning loose leaf wulong into the teapot.

Wenyu's hand went still. She didn't speak for several seconds, and Lian thought she hadn't heard her.

"Aren't you scared . . ." Lian began repeating.

"Lian, something happened."

Lian looked up from the wulong.

"I got something yesterday. A photo. Of me and Mingzun." Her face was unreadable. There was irreverence, but also something heavier. "It's a shot of us at Club Paradise last weekend. On the dance floor. I think it's the guy who's been sending me gifts. It's the same handwriting." She paused. "He wrote this note . . . uh . . . all it says is, 'I thought I knew you well. Please give me an explanation.' And then he left the same email he always does. No name." Her face was grave for a long moment. And then she laughed. "Isn't that funny?"

Lian was suddenly aware of the voices in the next room, the cold of the teacups in her hands. She didn't think it was funny at all. "Wenyu . . . what? This is blackmail."

Wenyu waved her hand. "Technically, he's not asking me for anything. So is it?"

"He's stalking you. And . . . basically threatening to tell people your secret."

Wenyu waggled her eyebrows at Lian. "I didn't think I was famous enough. To be blackmailed."

Despite herself, Lian laughed. "Please."

Wenyu's laugh was growing. "Mom, I've made it! Are you proud of me now?"

Lian watched her best friend. Thoughts raced through her mind. What did he actually want? "Please give me an explanation"? They were the words of a jilted lover, devastated and entitled; she could picture the man with betrayal lashed across his face, seeing his perfect woman tarnished. But he wasn't her lover. He didn't know her at all. She finally spoke, rapping her knuckles on the counter. "I think you should get ahead of it."

"What?"

"I think you should tell Thomas."

All the color seemed to drain from Wenyu's face. She tried to laugh it off. "Lian! Be serious!"

"I am serious. Isn't this—isn't this what all of this is for, anyway? Isn't that what you want? To be with Su Mingzun?"

Wenyu was quiet. She had been avoiding reality, but Lian knew that this was what she'd wanted to hear. Wenyu needed someone to push her toward a decision, and Lian would be that someone. "Tell . . . Thomas." She repeated the words slowly, digesting them. Her voice grew thick with conviction. "Tell Thomas."

Su Mingzun appeared at the door then, smelling of cigarette smoke.

"Nice party, Comrade Ye."

"Nice khakis," Lian retorted. "What white-collar worker did you have to rob for them?" She surprised herself, the way she was so quickly able to shift into this other, snarky mode.

"Ha-ha. You got funnier. I got them from your nubby boyfriend, of course," he said, winking and nodding in Zhetai's direction. Lian's face burned, peering at Zhetai standing with his back perfectly straight, a triangle of his shirt tucked accidentally into his waistband.

"Be nice, Zun," Wenyu said, hitting his chest lightly with the back of her hand.

Su Mingzun tousled Wenyu's hair. "Did you just hit me in front of company? What'll the parents say?"

Wenyu swatted at his hand, wrinkling her nose. She pushed Su Mingzun to the side. "Stop. Lianlian and I are trying to have an adult conversation." Their dynamic was as Lian had remembered: intense and combative, almost like a male friendship in its playful aggression. It was different from the dynamic that Wenyu shared with Thomas—Su Mingzun did not call Wenyu "babe," did not keep a domineering hand on her waist—but all the same it felt naked, and Lian looked away, her face flushed. A thought flashed through her: Wenyu's stalker must have felt like she did now.

She concentrated on the task at hand. The tea was almost done brewing. Su Mingzun shrugged and loped over to Zhetai. She saw Su Mingzun sit on the couch beside Zhetai's mother. She was holding up a sun-yellow silk scarf. Su Mingzun helped her tie it around her neck. He appeared to be complimenting the scarf; even from the kitchen, Lian could see the woman's face light up like a peach. How powerful was the gaze of a twenty-something.

"He's such a flirt," Wenyu said, smirking as she gazed at Su Mingzun.

"It feels like we're back in high school," Lian said. "You two."

"Yeah," Wenyu said, sighing happily. Her brow furrowed. Then: "I'll tell Thomas."

Lian's heart pounded. "Okay," she said. She poured the tea until each cup was filled nearly to the brim, leaving two millimeters of space to avoid spillage. She placed the twenty-four cups on a long, wooden serving board.

"Can I help, Lian?" Wenyu asked. Lian shook her head, hoping she looked like a gracious host, the kind who would never let her guests lift a finger. In reality, she was afraid that Wenyu would break the cups.

Wenyu stood there in the kitchen, her hands by her sides, and looked quite helpless. There was nothing for her to do. Lian set the tray on the coffee table and hurried back as a chorus of thanks followed her.

Next were the pastries, her pièce de résistance. She'd arranged them in the shape of the number 61. She stuck candles into the top of the 6 and the 1, and carried the platter to the living room, twin flames dancing. Zhetai's mother cooed happily as all her guests began singing "Happy Birthday." Zhetai massaged his mother's shoulders as he sang.

Everyone cheered. "Make a wish, Ma!" Zhetai nudged his mother.

She pinched Zhetai's arm. "I know exactly what I'm going to wish for," she said. Zhetai's mother swiveled her gaze to light on Lian, a twinkle in her eye. Then the woman blew out the candles.

The pastries were a hit. Zhetai's mother ate pastry after pastry, coating her fingers in sticky white powder and licking her lips for every last crumb of mung bean. "You've really outdone yourself, Daughter!" she grinned, giggling. Her friends nodded, enthusiastically reaching for seconds. Soon the 61 had become scattered dots. Lian beamed.

She noticed that Wenyu and Su Mingzun had been quiet during all this, sitting back on the chaise nursing their cups of tea but not partaking in the dessert grab. Then Wenyu walked to the kitchen and returned with her box of macarons.

"Ayi," she said sweetly, leaning down and placing the box in front of Zhetai's mother. "I brought you some macarons. I don't know if they are to your taste, but they're quite beloved in France."

Zhetai's mother beamed. "Zhetai, even Lian's friends are so mature!" Lian found her chest seizing up slightly: it was just like Wenyu, to never let her have the spotlight. Of course her pastries couldn't compete with the professionals' from whatever high-end French bakery Wenyu had no doubt dropped a tiny fortune at.

Zhetai's mother popped a magenta macaron into her mouth. Raspberry, Lian predicted.

"That's my favorite flavor," Wenyu said, smiling.

But a sour look crossed Zhetai's mother's face. "It's . . . quite tart," she said, swallowing and giving Wenyu a meek smile. She took a large sip of tea, draining her cup.

Wenyu's face remained level. She returned to the chaise, and Lian couldn't help but feel pride flower inside her. Zhetai's mother set the box of macarons down on the table and reached for another husband-and-wife cake. The box sat untouched for the next few minutes, until Su Mingzun reached over and plucked a pink one for himself. Eventually, Wenyu made her way to Lian's platter and cut herself a piece of rice cake. Lian watched as Wenyu worked her mouth around the soft dough, then tasted the first morsel of mung bean filling. Her eyes dropped open just slightly, her mouth slowed. Momentarily there was something like defeat painted there, before she looked up and grinned, giving Lian a thumbs-up.

Zhetai sat down on the couch beside Lian. He kneaded one corner of his shirt with his left hand, a telltale sign that he was annoyed. Lian ignored it. Wenyu pulled out her phone. She held it up and said, "Lian, Zhetai, look at me!"

Lian smiled. She was now used to this. But Zhetai seemed bewildered. He dropped his shirt and posed, his hands rigid by his side. "It's a video," Lian said.

"I'm here at Lianlian's future mother-in-law's birthday," Wenyu said, cooing into the phone. Su Mingzun sat next to her, hidden from the camera's lens. "This is Lianlian's adorable boyfriend, Zhetai! Say hi, Zhetai!"

Zhetai gave a small wave. Lian looked at him and grabbed his hand, wondering if on screen they would look like people in love, or if they'd just look like two people sitting next to each other on a couch. He gave her a curious look that Lian hoped translated to a kind of quirky reverence.

Then Wenyu switched off the camera and stood up. "Lianlian, we should probably be going," she said. "Ayi," she said next, in a bright and full voice, turning to Zhetai's mother. "Thank you for having us in your home. It's so wonderful to get to know Zhetai better, and to see that Lian is such an integral part of your family. Happy birthday!" Again, Wenyu sounded stilted and overly polite.

"Thank you, what a sweet girl," Zhetai's mother said. "Take care of her," she said, giving Su Mingzun a coquettish wave.

Lian walked Wenyu to the door. Su Mingzun carried her purse and helped her into her jacket. The action felt so reflexive; in high school, he'd always carried Wenyu's things for her, wrapping her in her tracksuit jacket from behind as Lian trailed them.

"Nice party, Comrade Ye." Su Mingzun winked at her. Lian couldn't tell if he was being facetious. "See ya at my mansion."

Wenyu shoved him. "He's talking about the housewarming. He's coming over afterward. You should sleep over too. Anyway, we're going to Paradise now," Wenyu said, leaning in conspiratorially. "Come join when you're done."

She was surprised that after what they'd discussed, Wenyu would dare go back to Paradise. She tried to catch Wenyu's eye. Something had been set into motion that evening. When was she going to tell Thomas?

As if she'd heard her silent inquiry, Wenyu turned back and showed Lian her palm, a quick flash of celadon, and grinned. A jade teacup.

It was a promise. Excitement bloomed inside Lian, but the feeling was quickly eclipsed by a more present and powerful bolt of worry. She felt protective of that tiny cup. The set was now incomplete. She had an urge to reach out, snatch it from Wenyu's hand, but her friend was looking at her with such glee that she could only return the grin.

THE PARTY REACHED its long arm into the night, and by the time the last guest had stumbled his way out the door and into the elevator, Lian was sleepy. Zhetai carried plates to the sink as Lian stood there, up to her elbows in yellow Latex, scrubbing each dish and pan and teacup. Zhetai's mother twirled about her living room, drunk on happiness and baijiu. There were so many dishes. The hot water and soap mixed with the soy sauce and crusted chili sent up a sour smell that made Lian's eyes water. She peered at the clock. It was ten PM now. She couldn't help but wonder if Wenyu and Su Mingzun were at Paradise, and found herself doing the mental calculus for how long it would take to get there.

Shoulder-deep in the steam rising from the sink, Lian felt herself longing for the open air.

Zhetai wiped down the coffee table. This was their habit, cleaning together the detritus of his mother's parties. In these moments, she always felt a little smug. Yang Qinru's birdlike husband had never lifted a finger in his life. Bo with his sweaty head and thick neck would be sitting on the couch drinking his tenth beer. But her boyfriend always knew to help. He took on the task of cleaning like he did his research: meticulously and almost piously, wiping the table down in neat, deliberate strokes. It soothed Lian to watch him do this; it was like one of those ASMR videos where someone shampoos a dirty carpet. His mother had flopped down on the couch and was watching him too.

"Thank you, dear son," she said. "My darling son."

Zhetai didn't respond, just continued his task as if it were his God-sent mission. Other men hammed it up, said things like, "Anything for you, Ma." His silence implied that her thanks were unnecessary. But of course, this <u>was</u> the real reason Zhetai helped. It was the story of men everywhere. Men loved to be complimented. Golden sons loved to revel in their light.

Zhetai returned from the living room with two glasses and placed them on the counter. His mother rose languidly and went to the bedroom, calling out a muffled good night. The kitchen was quiet now, as Lian reduced the spigot to a light stream and washed the remaining cups. Zhetai leaned against the counter, his face bathed in the cold light of his phone.

"You should have told me you invited your friends," he finally said.

Lian's hand faltered a bit on the rim of a cup. "Wenyu?"

"Yeah, and that guy from the engagement party, Su whatever. What's up with that guy?"

"He's just a classmate."

"She called him her boyfriend? What about her American fiancé?" Zhetai's voice was rising, confusion lacing his words with panic.

"That was weird, I know," Lian said, furrowing her brow. "I think they were just having fun."

"At Mom's birthday? That guy had so many stories. He kept talking about trips they'd gone on in San Francisco, how he'd proposed in a helicopter . . ."

Hearing Su Mingzun's fabrications back, they seemed even stranger. "Yeah, I don't know." She shrugged. "He was always like that in high school. Just making shit up. It's harmless." She felt something thrumming inside her.

"I don't understand why you want to hang out with people like that."

"Like what?"

"People who aren't . . . serious."

"What does that mean? How do you know she's not serious?"

"Come on, Lian," he said, cocking his head and drawing his mouth into a line. "She runs a YouTube channel."

"You don't know anything about her."

"Do you? I've never heard you talk about her. How much can she mean to you if you only just now remembered she existed?" He was clutching one corner of his shirt again, funneling all his anger into his fist.

"I don't have to tell you everything about my life."

"Please, Lian, don't act like this. You're defending someone you don't even know. She turned Mom's birthday into a joke and you're not mad?"

"That's not what happened. You're making this into a way bigger deal than it needs to be. Your mom had a great time!" Her voice was rising, and she was afraid Zhetai's parents would hear them. She turned back to the last glass in the sink and scrubbed it viciously. She was angry at Zhetai's myopia, bitter that despite everything she'd done right today, she now had to apologize for the one thing that she hadn't thought to be on tenterhooks about. And she was, though she didn't want to admit it right in that moment, embarrassed, too, at the way she'd so easily given in to Wenyu's charade, allowed her to enact her little fantasy on the stage of her life. Zhetai was, in a way, right. Why was she defending Wenyu so vehemently?

"Our mom," he finally said.

"What?"

"You said, 'your mom.' She's your mom too. Well, she will be," he said.

"Okay, fine," Lian said. Her mom too. Suddenly the sprawling apartment seemed too small. One day she and Zhetai would live in a place like this, and they would have kids whose girlfriends would come over and make pastries for her on her sixty-first birthday, and it suddenly felt hellish. How could you look forward to a future that was already your reality!

"It's not that big of a deal," Zhetai said next, slowly this time, in that flat, unemotional tone he used when he was trying to de-escalate a situation, but that only enraged Lian further. "I just wish you'd told me ahead of time," he said.

She turned off the spigot and pulled the gloves off her hands. Wenyu's macaron box sat on the counter, largely untouched. She pushed it a few centimeters to the right, desperately trying to find something else to do to fill the silence. Zhetai waited there, anticipating. He needed her to agree with him, to confirm his being, to validate him as a good boyfriend, a good son, a good man. And he was a good man.

"Okay," she said, finally. She wasn't sure quite what she was agreeing to.

He smiled and put his hand on her back, giving it a rub in a wide circle.

She stepped away from him, then moved to the kitchen table and grabbed her bag.

"What are you doing?" he said.

"I'm going home," she said. "Have to wake up early tomorrow." She mustered a smile as she stood there, her bag hanging limply. "When did you realize . . . that this was what life was gonna be? That I was what your life was gonna be?"

He looked at her sharply. "What do you mean?"

"One day we didn't know each other, and then we did, and now we're looking at condos together."

"Yes . . ."

"I just think in life we never really feel like we're making big decisions until later, when we look back, and we realize, oh, that was the decision that changed everything. Do you feel like you chose me?"

"Of course I did. I mean, I walked right up to you."

"That's the thing," she said, her voice sad. "<u>You</u> walked up to <u>me</u>."

Zhetai's brow furrowed. They stood there, staring at each other. He was close enough to touch, but she did not touch him.

"Do you still want to get married?" he finally asked.

She nearly laughed at this. She didn't remember him ever proposing. Instead of responding, she found herself asking, "Why do you love me?"

He pursed his lips. "That's a silly question. Of course I love you."

"I'm not asking <u>if</u> you love me; I'm asking <u>why</u>."

He dried his hands on the dish towel. "I love taking care of you."

She looked at him. She didn't respond. And then, surprising her, he continued. "I love cleaning together. Playing badminton together. My mom loves you." This was as effusive as Zhetai ever got, and she was surprised at this burst of emotion. He was trying, and that was the most anyone could ever hope for from another person, and she felt sad, sad, sad, knowing it was not what she wanted to hear.

She smiled now. "That's nice," she said. "I like that too."

She turned to go.

"Lian—" he began. His question still hung in the air. But she didn't stop; she let the door swing shut behind her.

THE TRAIN ON Saturday evening always carried curious customers. She slid onto a bench and watched the car fill with young girls in neon-colored dresses on their way to the club, men in loosened ties smelling of sweat. An old woman sat across from her carrying a bag of rolls from the French bakery. One of the young girls made eye contact, smiled briefly before turning away. Perhaps she, too, would find herself at Paradise tonight.

She ignored Zhetai's texts, the question marks coming in. A notification pinged on her phone. Wenyu had uploaded her videos on Instagram. Lian tapped through the story, the events of Wenyu's day forming frenetic blips: at the climbing gym, walking through Raffles Mall, buying macarons. Su Mingzun was of course out of frame, but Lian caught glimpses of him: the edge of his shirt, his shoe walking away, even his distant figure, climbing ahead of Wenyu at the gym. These moments felt like little Easter eggs for her, secrets only Lian could unfold. And then Wenyu was arriving at Zhetai's complex. Shots of her macaron box, a pan of the counter of food, Lian's pastries. Su Mingzun lingered in the background of one of these wide shots, part of the larger tableau of people who had gathered for Zhetai's mother's birthday. And then came the ten-second clip of Lian and Zhetai, her nervous smile, the alarmed look on his face.

"*They're so cute!*" she could hear Wenyu saying in the background, a giggle in her voice. It was a sweet statement, and yet it felt diminutive. For the first time since she'd started peering at the mirror of their friendship in Wenyu's videos, she realized she didn't want to be reflected back. The things Wenyu felt were safe—the mall, the party, she and Zhetai—belonged on the screen, but Su Mingzun—her real love, the one she told stories about for an audience of one—remained off camera. Wenyu's real life was not what she showed on screen, but what she hid.

Lian looked at her hands: pink and dry despite the fact that she'd been wearing gloves. She wondered if this would be the rest of her life: dinners, apologies, pastries wrapped in plastic to bring to people you pretended were your parents.

She thought about the way she and Zhetai had met. She and a friend had gone to a screening of a Zhang Yimou movie and bumped into a classmate, who was there with his roommate, Yan Zhetai. She had seen him around campus before but had never spoken to him. They found themselves sitting next to each other in the theater, Zhetai looking straight ahead, his hands folded in his lap, Lian leaning over to her friend and whispering about how hot Tony Leung looked. Zhetai didn't tell her to shut up, which Lian appreciated. After the film, they'd all gone to dinner together, and Lian had found Zhetai to be calm and easygoing, the kind of guy who people like to have in a group because he will affirm and not raise too many objections. She noticed him looking at her, which made a small happiness rise inside her, because her friend was louder and more exciting than she was—yes, she continued having a penchant for loud and charming friends—and yet it was her he was looking at. She ran into him a few days later in the North cafeteria, and they discovered they both had classes in the adjoining building beforehand. They began meeting for lunch every Tuesday, and eventually, over a plate of lamb stir-fry one winter day, he asked her if she would like to be his girlfriend. She thought, Why not? She was twenty-one and had never had a boyfriend, and it was time. So she said yes, and not much really changed except now he held her hand as they walked and they gave each other kisses goodbye and one day, eight months in, they slept together, and after that they would sleep together every week or so when Zhetai could sneak into the girls' dormitory, and it was the most rebellious she had felt since Wenyu.

Later, she discovered two things: one, that they'd both attended that New Year's dinner as babies, and two, that the night they'd met, Zhetai had recently come off a breakup, and his roommate had actually known Lian was attending the Zhang Yimou screening that evening and had told him there was a girl he wanted to introduce him to. Fact number one made her feel that Zhetai was her destiny; fact number two made her feel pursued, like their falling in love was not just a convenient union of two people, but intentional.

For a long while, these two things were enough to sustain her.

She thought about the boy she'd spent one spring and summer obsessed with at university, the moody one in her sophomore-year English class who was the only one better than she was, who'd correct her with a sneer when she said, "*Whom did you deliver this to?*" "*Who do you love?*" "It's '*To whom did you deliver this?*'" he'd say. "It's '*Whom do you love?*'"

You, she'd say stupidly to herself, peering at him from over a plastic plate of eggs in the campus canteen.

She thought about a boy she'd seen on a bus four years ago, who'd held the door open for her as she made a jog for it. He'd splayed his hands out, stepped down into a puddle, nearly fallen in. A boy who was willing to drop into a puddle for a woman he didn't know.

She thought about Ma Zhongshun with his pencil, his easy laugh he'd dole out that she convinced herself was for her alone, even as he laughed with so many other girls.

She thought about her student from two years ago, the kind one with the big eyes who played the guitar and wanted to write songs in English. His songs made her cringe, but he sent her a box of peaches for her birthday, and she thought she might have loved him too.

She thought about all the almosts or not-at-alls of her life, and she nearly cried out. What would it be like to get something you'd actually yearned for? Every single thing she'd ever gotten in this life had come to her without a struggle. With Zhetai it was too easy. Too easy. Everything in her life was too easy. Like rain falling into a pond. She was too scared to really reach for anything, so she settled for what she received.

As always, Wenyu could see a part of her that Lian could not, and it was exactly this third eye that telescoped into Lian, poking her in places that hurt. Maybe it wouldn't be the worst thing if Lian were to pull at the threads of her life. Lian thought of their endeavors at the grocery store, about the first time she'd bucked up and tried stealing something herself. A pink eraser in the shape of a dog. She'd paused in the stationery section, her hand reaching for a stapler with the jaws of a crocodile. But she'd worn a jacket with shallow pockets that day and decided, at the last second, to grab the little pink eraser instead. When she walked out, the cashier didn't even lift her head from her phone. Wenyu cheered for her, but what Lian remembered most was thinking, *That was so easy—why didn't I take the crocodile stapler?*

Lian got off the train early, making her way up the steps and emerging onto an imposing square.

Advent.

Possibility.

Change.

She could hear the music softly blaring, front doors swung wide open to invite in the swarms of cinephiles. She was at the National Convention Center.

5

The convention hall was loud, packed, scores of young men dashing by dressed in their sci-fi regalia. A man painted entirely in gold barreled past; another wearing long robes with pointed elf ears nearly tripped into her. The hall was massive. Neon arrows pointed in multiple directions so that it was impossible to understand where to start. A massive "*Captain Marvel*" poster soared alongside a poster for "*The Wandering Earth*," Brie Larson staring down the red-suited astronauts of China's latest multibillion-dollar sci-fi endeavor. She'd seen both movies; both were bad. But Freddy had admired the scope of "*The Wandering Earth*"—it was always admirable, he said, when a director really tried to do something big. Skinny boys wearing lanyards stood at the entrances to various VR experiences. Despite the crowds, she could tell the event was coming to an end. Vendors were already packing up their tables; half the fluorescents on the left side of the convention hall were off. Her heart caught in her throat—what if he had already left? It was stupid to come here.

She purchased a ticket. "We're closing in an hour, miss," the girl at the desk mumbled, but she waved Lian through. Lian approached one of the VR booths and hurried inside, suddenly paranoid that she would run into Freddy.

It was a zombie-fighting game. A bored teenager handed her a device that looked like a produce scanner, then a headset.

Suddenly she was surrounded by red; she was standing on a rock in the middle of a sea of volcanic lava. Her scanner was now a machine gun, reaching long in front of her. In the distance, she could see figures approaching, hunched things with hollow faces. She was shocked by the eerie realness of the world around her; she tried looking down, but her skirt and shirt had been replaced with silvery armor.

She heard a voice beside her. "Watch out!" She turned to see a man dressed in the same suit as she was, crouching down and firing his gun. And then there was a deafening rumble to her right; she turned back and the zombie was on top of her. She panicked and clicked the buttons of her scanner indiscriminately, launching fiery bullets into the air. One of them made contact and the zombie exploded.

She looked at the man next to her. She swore he smiled at her. Was it Freddy? She huddled nearer to him and they stood back-to-back, facing down the approaching zombies. She was wowed by the details, the realism. She could practically smell the breath of the staggering monsters. But she felt comforted, standing next to this mystery man.

"I'll take this side," she said.

"Sounds good," he replied. Then they faced off, lobbing bullets and watching the zombies dissolve, their deaths punctuated by screams that sounded on the precipice of death and life, some tortured mix of wail and mechanical lurch. She could see why Freddy was so excited to come to the convention. Science fiction was realer than ever.

It took three minutes to defeat all the zombies, and then the VR world powered down with an anticlimactic stutter. She was back in the dark tent. She looked to her side and her face fell. It was just the teenager who'd given her the scanner. He shrugged.

"No one else was in line," he said.

She felt a scorching rod of disappointment. She was so silly. What she was doing was as stupid as a VR game, as unreal as a squad of zombies invading over a volcanic lake. Freddy had probably already left, and she'd paid 400 kuai to play a game with a teenager. She nodded stiffly and walked out through the tent door, the vinyl flapping against her face adding insult to injury.

And then she saw him. He was standing by an artist's table, hunched over, examining a poster. She recognized him first from the small ponytail trickling down his neck, then from the large glasses reflecting holographic light onto the vinyl backdrop behind the artist. He looked slighter than he did on video chat, shorter. His skin was pockmarked, acne scars littered across his jawline. He must have been using a filter on their chats, she realized. He held his body with a slight bent, his shoulders curled inward and his arms by his side, the posture of a teenager. He wore black pants of a thick, cargo-like material, with sandals. It jarred her to see him in the flesh, something living and real. She realized that she had thought him beautiful, on video, because now that he was standing in front of her, he appeared less so. She felt herself sweating.

Lian watched him speak to the artist at the table, a man in his fifties wearing a beret. She could hear his voice travel over the crowd, low and energetic; this was clearly one of his idols, and he'd no doubt been waiting in line for a long time to speak to him. She couldn't quite make out what he was saying, but she watched him gesture, his hands flailing in that same way they'd flail when they spoke on video, when he talked about a new plot point for Commander China, or a movie he particularly hated or loved. The man looked back at him with paternal appreciation—of course Freddy was not the first person to convey such passion for his work that day. Freddy soldiered on with ardor. This was what she'd always admired about him; he was so firmly convinced in the uniqueness of his own feelings. She watched as he asked the artist for a photo. The man gave a quick nod and Freddy went around the table and leaned toward him, lifting his hand in a thumbs-up, a giant smile on his face. It was the gesture of a small boy, and Lian felt that she should perhaps look away; she was witnessing something private and vulnerable and certainly not for her. She forced herself to examine a pamphlet for a filmmaking course on the table beside her, entertaining the eager glances of a young recruiter who offered her a sticker with a grinning purple dog carrying a camera. She was so engrossed in this faux interest that she didn't notice the person come up behind her.

"*Lily?*" came the familiar voice.

She turned around, and Freddy was there. He must have seen her in nearly the same moment that he had said her name, because he behaved as if it were she who had caught him off guard; he nearly dropped his stack of posters. "Oh shit—" His knees buckled as his palms clapped shut on the shifting pile of glossy squares. One lone pamphlet floated to the ground next to Lian's feet, and she picked it up.

"*Freddy!*" she said, and she couldn't help it; she broke into a huge smile.

"You came," he said. "Isn't it great?"

She pulled at her jacket, hoping it wasn't immensely obvious that she had just arrived, had paid for a 400 RMB ticket just to get the chance to cross paths with him. "Yeah, it's awesome. How long have you been here?"

"Oh, all day. Got to talk to so many directors. Guo Fan was here, did you see him?"

"That's amazing! No I, uh, I just got here—my plans ended early."

"Did you come with anyone?"

"Ah—" and she contemplated lying, spinning some group of friends out of nowhere to tell him, I just happened to be here, tons of people told me about this event, you were one of many, in fact, I forgot you'd even told me about it. Make the feelings small; make them disappear.

But instead, she said, "I didn't." She paused. "You made it sound so cool. *So I had to come.*" Just short of, I came here for you.

She followed Freddy to a dozen more booths, watching him speak to his idols, occasionally taking a photo for him. As the night went on, she relaxed, taking his phone to diligently record his meetings, making sure to catch his smile at the right moment. They spoke in Chinese, though occasionally he'd use a phrase she'd taught him. "*Seize the day!*" he declared, lifting his stack of signed posters. Then, when the poor girl at the front had hollered hoarsely into her microphone for the last time—"The convention is now closed! Please make your way to the exit!"—they walked outside, balancing their bundles of paraphernalia.

And then they walked back and forth in front of the convention doors, Freddy talking about how he'd made an ass of himself to a French director that he'd mistaken for someone else.

He asked about the birthday; she was vague. Neither of them mentioned the fact that this was the first time they'd seen each other in real life.

The experience of walking beside Freddy was strange. Lian had never so felt the presence of her own body, of herself as a breathing, fleshy thing. She tended to walk with her arms crossed and her gait wide, something Zhetai had commented on the first month they met. They'd walk to the dining hall from the library, and he said he felt like she was running away from him but pretending like she wasn't. Freddy didn't have any of Zhetai's good posture; he bounded forward neck first—like Wenyu, in a way, except on the body of a man it looked childish. She wondered if he thought she was pretty.

They traversed the lobby area in front of the convention center doors for a long time, both of them submerged in that liminal space after an event when it's clear neither party wants the night to end but no one knows how to prolong it intentionally. It reminded Lian of the way she'd linger in front of Wenyu's apartment building after they'd seen a movie or gone to the KTV, laughing about the evening's events, kicking up dust next to the bike rack outside the building and occasionally eliciting the passive-aggressive slam of a neighbor's window above. They'd take turns shushing each other, until eventually Lian said she had to run along home. She treasured those times, when it was clear both girls wanted to squeeze as much as possible out of the moment.

"Do you want to get a drink?" she finally asked, her mouth dry.

"I, uh, I actually don't drink," Freddy said.

"Oh!" Lian was surprised. She didn't often meet a boy, especially someone right out of college, who didn't drink. But then she realized it must be an excuse. "Ah, yeah, okay." She turned to go, her face hot. Perhaps this would be the end of whatever fantasy she'd spun. It was a stupid feeling; after all, hadn't she felt a bit of disappointment, seeing him in real life? She felt that a disappointment that followed another disappointment should neutralize it, but instead the feeling compounded, washing over her in a funereal wave. Who was she to believe that she could have the same sort of scandalous affair as Wenyu?

"But maybe we could eat," he said next, something nervous thrumming on his lips. "Did you eat yet?"

Her stomach was still bloated from the fish and meat of the day. "No," she said, grinning. "I'm starving."

They walked through the park. The National Convention Center was one of twelve structures that still remained after having initially been built for the 2008 Olympics, and she was struck, as they walked, by how barren the landscape was; flags on light poles flapped dementedly in the breeze, advertising events that had long passed. She remembered the fervor of that time, the summer of 2008. Wenyu had gone; Lian had gotten into Beijing Normal. She had experienced rejection and disappointment but was now to start anew. She felt like she was rebirthing, just like the city, the whole country around her—entering a new era. The sleepy northern expanse of the city quickly transformed into a gleaming Olympic Green. Restaurants and stores advertised swanky celebrity partnerships. The people who'd sit outside the malls in Xidan jangling their cans of change disappeared overnight, and Lian had felt a surge of hope. The Olympics will eradicate poverty, she'd thought; it will usher in a new China.

Only later did she realize where those people had gone, driven out to holding centers in the outer rings before being sent back to their home provinces. The absence that had once suggested salvation now hung ghostly over the squares. Many of the businesses that had flourished that summer had shuttered their doors. And today she and Zhetai played badminton in the cavernous organ of the former Olympic badminton stadium, its showers leaky and walls grungy from lack of polish, the structure straining desperately to justify its existence. Disappointment, it turned out, was an unavoidable consequence of hope.

"Do you remember?" she said to Freddy. "The Olympics."

"Yeah," he said. "It was the best summer of my life."

"Me too," she said. "My mom got into so many fights trying to get us tickets."

He laughed. "I was at the starting line right behind Liu Xiang. I was cheering like crazy when he did that first run. But then when he had to forfeit, I ran out of the Bird's Nest and just booked it all the way home. Missed the rest of the event. I cried for days."

"You were what, ten years old?"

"Twelve, actually," he said, nudging her. "A baby. But I'd cry now too."

She laughed. "I also cried."

He looked at her and smiled. "You were watching?"

"I was <u>there</u>. I was in the tenth row." She remembered sitting breathless in the stands as China's first track-and-field gold medalist—and the world's fastest hurdler—had walked away from the race that should have gotten him his second Olympic gold. A sob had cracked her mouth open in an ugly wail.

"Huh. That's so crazy we were both there." He was silent for a second, and Lian felt the fact settle over them. "You know what that's called?" He said what she was already thinking. "Yuan fen." Destiny.

She breathed, her heart clattering in her chest. She looked away, afraid that she'd see some sort of mockery or indifference in Freddy's eyes. But when she turned back, his gaze was serious.

"You don't believe in yuan fen, do you?" she said.

"What's there to believe in? It's not something you believe. It's something that happens."

She smiled. "Yeah."

"It's crazy enough to meet someone once in a lifetime," he said. "But twice?"

"Nearly impossible," she said, willing herself to hold his gaze. She could feel something rosy unfurling across her cheeks. "Why did you want to take classes from me?" she found herself asking. "You could've chosen any number of native English speakers." It was a silly question. She knew he'd say something like his father had connections with the company; it was the natural choice.

A strange smile tickled the edges of Freddy's mouth. "I didn't think about it at first," he said. "I just liked that you liked movies. After our first lesson, my mom said I should probably switch to someone else at the company who was a native speaker. But I liked talking to you."

Something warm flowered inside her. "Thanks," she said, then added, "I'm glad."

They kept walking.

"So why're you a teetotaler?" she asked next.

He looked bashful. "I made some mistakes a few years ago. Just don't wanna do that again."

With this admission, Lian thought of his father, and wondered, for the first time, if that sort of anger was passed on. She wondered about where violence came from, if it was something you were born with or something that you developed. She thought about Wenyu and Su Mingzun fighting on the field, how when they fought it was an alchemy that could torch everything around them. Freddy must have seen the thought cross her face, because he then hurriedly explained, "It wasn't for anything like that, I swear! I got drunk and tried to enter this guy's apartment, I guess I thought it was mine, and the police came and . . . it was more embarrassing than anything, really. Apparently I opened the front door and sat down on the guy's couch and turned on the TV. The guy found me just sitting there, watching some rerun of 'Huan Le Song.'"

She exhaled a deep breath. "Even when you're blacked out you're watching something, huh!"

He laughed. "I guess so. I don't remember any of it. By the time I came to I was already waking up in the police station. It smelled like piss. And so now I can't think of alcohol without thinking it's gonna taste like piss."

They exited the square outside the convention center and came across a food stand, smoke coming off the grill in sputtering plumes. A man with a cap and blue arm coverings bunched around his elbows roasted pink sausages that bent upward like flapping fish. Wordlessly, Freddy reached his phone over and paid for their food. Lian stole a glance at him, but he didn't even smile, the action was so natural. He held out a paper sleeve of sausages for her before biting into his own, yelping at the heat.

"Fuck!" He nearly spit it out. Lian laughed, and he laughed, his mouth open, trying to blow cool air onto the steaming meat.

"I once burned myself so badly eating a sesame ball my parents had to take me to the hospital," Lian said. "The nurses just laughed at me and said all I could do was suck on some ice."

They ate perched on a ledge outside the gate and discussed all the things that lovers do, life and the past and the movies they had seen and would see. It was exhilarating to feel the question mark between her and another person, and she stared at that question mark, hard, wondering if they had the ingredients for love. He was not as handsome as Ma Zhongshun, not as eloquent as her college crush—he perhaps did not know as many facts as Zhetai, and was not as tall—but if she didn't look too closely, he really could be someone she fell in love with. He was a person who thought about the world, and that was so rare. She watched herself and Freddy leaning on the ledge by the gate and wondered if Wenyu would be impressed by what she had done tonight. As they ate the last bites of their sausages, Lian checked her watch. It was one AM; Wenyu might still be at Paradise.

"A couple friends are at Club Paradise," she said, looking over at him. "Do you want to come with me?"

She couldn't wait to fill Wenyu in on her night. She thought about what she'd tell her. She'd say that Freddy had been adorable at the convention, she'd say that he was kind. She'd tell her the drinking story—she'd be sure to find that hilarious—and she'd tell her that he had paid for their food. She'd tell her that Freddy had said he wasn't much of a partier, but that he was curious what it'd be like to go to the club with her. She'd tell her that she and Freddy had walked together to the subway station, their arms lightly brushing. She'd tell her that when the train arrived, Freddy reached out his arm, inviting her to go ahead of him, and he followed her, and she blushed, knowing that anyone that saw the two of them would think they were dating. She'd tell her that she liked that. And of course she'd tell her about the yuan fen. The yuan fen, she'd tell her most of all.

PART TWO

I

June

The Shunyi Konggang subdistrict supervisor's hair was combed over the shiny pan of his head like latticing on a fly swatter. His neck was as thick as a garbage can, and his fingers fumbled with the edge of a package of Dongbei red dates, which Chen had brought because he knew they were the subdistrict supervisor's favorite. He was a greasy, pontificating man, currently in the middle of telling a story about how he'd slept with three women in one night while he was an army recruit, his yellow kernel teeth glinting every time a laugh escaped from his churlish orifice.

Chen was here to request permission to dig a pool. It was silly bureaucracy, but these types of constructions, private pools and the like, required the extra step. Chen wore a clean, nice suit from the department store, but one that was not so nice that the subdistrict supervisor would think he was attempting to upstage him. He'd left the tie off, in hopes that a more casual demeanor would make for looser generosities.

That morning he'd arrived at the office, a humble three-story building a kilometer away from his worksite, at 10:25, out of breath.

The secretary at the front desk had immediately stood up when he pushed open the front door. She was a stocky woman with a large head and a yellow sweater that was just a shade too bright for the tan-colored walls around her. He remembered a taller, more austere woman in her place the last time he'd come to the subdistrict supervisor for a favor.

"How can I help you?" she said, in a rich, swingy voice. She also sounded different from the previous secretary, who if he could recall was a Beijing native. The new secretary's voice was somehow crisper, vaguely accented. It was familiar, though Chen could not place it. And her breath smelled like mint. He looked down and saw a stack of spearmint Wrigley's on her desk.

"Hello," Chen said, clearing his throat. "I'm looking for Subdistrict Supervisor Ding. I have an appointment with him at ten thirty."

"Of course," she said, hurrying to pull up his calendar. "Mister . . . Song Chen?"

"Yes."

"Would you like some tea?"

"Our meeting is in five minutes, I don't think that's necessary."

"The subdistrict supervisor is caught up in a call. Do you like wulong?"

Apparently, he shouldn't have rushed. He sat down to wait on the lush leather couch, one of two that sat on opposite sides of an imperial, dark wood coffee table. The secretary hurried over with a porcelain cup of wulong tea. He took it from her, giving a cursory smile.

A dozen packages of lemon cookies sat fanned out on a saucer in the middle of the coffee table. Chen grabbed a pack and tore it open, anticipating the citrusy taste.

Finally, twenty minutes after twelve, Subdistrict Supervisor Ding emerged from his office. "Guilin, dear," he called out. "For my evening at the opera with District Leader Qiu tonight, should I wear the green or the blue tie?"

Chen rolled his eyes. He knew Ding was saying this within earshot to make him understand that he was having dinner with a very prominent political figure. As if the expensive leather couches were not enough to get his point across.

"Green," she said, decisively. "It's a friendlier color. You want to make District Leader Qiu feel at ease, correct?"

"You're always right," he beamed, then looped the green tie around his neck. He then called out to Chen, as if just noticing him, "Old Chen! Please come in!"

Chen stood up, brushing a stray crumb of cookie from his lap. The secretary made a little motion with her hand, directing him toward Ding's office. Inside, Ding had decorated his office to look like a British royal's: a heavy wood executive desk, plush seating, floor-to-ceiling velvet drapes.

So here they were. Chen handed the subdistrict supervisor the bottle of whiskey and bag of dates he'd brought. "Just a little something from me," he said. "My wife took a trip to Heilongjiang last month and brought these back."

The subdistrict supervisor beamed. "Very kind of you, Old Chen! Thank you!" He put the whiskey on a side table, nestled next to various other gifts and wrapped packages, but set to work tearing open the bag of dates. "So, what is your inquiry today?"

Chen took a deep breath. "As you know, I am building a new home in your district for some American clients," he began. "Thomas Straeffer-Kenney and Vivian Luo. They're a couple, very successful, very wealthy."

"Yes, yes," Ding said, and Chen wasn't sure if this was to speed him along or to affirm that yes, he'd already approved the project, and what was this additional conversation about?

"Yes," Chen parroted. "We've almost completed construction on the project," he continued, "but there is one final thing the client would love to have. You see, my client, like I said, is from California, and he grew up swimming. The couple would like to have that option at their home in Beijing. He wants something that reminds him of home. Hence this pool, which I would love your permission to dig in the courtyard. It would take up about fifty square meters of space behind the house. My clients would of course be willing to pay whatever is necessary."

The pool had been a last-minute request, some unfastened homesickness on the part of the groom run ashore. They had come to view the property in its near finished form the previous week, and the groom had shyly but aggressively asked if Chen could add this final piece. He'd slung his arm around Chen's shoulder and acted like it was a favor he was doing him—"*I had a thought. What if there was a pool here? Wouldn't that be just perfect?*" Chen's mouth had dropped slightly open—he'd already laid the turf; the backyard was nearly finished—and the American had launched into a speech about how he had been an Olympic hopeful as a teenager. Every morning from the age of six, he'd woken at five AM to swim laps at the local pool. He was the fastest swimmer on every team through middle school and high school. But a knee injury (ironically enough, while playing soccer on land during a break from the swim season) caused him to leave the pool, giving up his Olympic dreams in the process. These days, however, he still loved to swim laps on the weekends.

Chen had listened as the American finished his tale, his eyes nearly glistening as he murmured about some roseate teenage swim competition. "*Of course,*" Chen had replied, using that affirming American phrase, two syllables, one thin, one thick, a full meal of a word (and in fact, *course* was, in some contexts, a meal). "*It sounds perfect.*"

"*Yay!*" His wife-to-be had clapped her hands together rapid-fire, in small patters, her face alight like a child blowing out candles on a cake. "*Babe, I told you!*" She was not an American per se; she was actually from Beijing and had moved to San Francisco as a teenager. She did not look or act like the Chinese girls he saw around him; her spaghetti strap dress revealed tanned shoulders, and her hands danced animatedly about her face when she laughed. He wondered about this woman's story, whether it was anything like his and Fan's. He and Fan had met in America, just like these two lovebirds; the two of them had also once been twenty-somethings with dreams. But he decided swiftly that her story could not be more dissimilar. In his day, it was rare to make it to America; you had to be the cream of the crop, the best in your class. Now, anyone could go to America; the children of his wealthy peers—and there were so many of them—could do anything on Daddy's dollar.

In the office, Ding listened to Chen's speech, his lips pursed. He leaned back in his chair, his green tie slung over his shoulder. When Chen finished, he slowly sat up. "Song Chen," he began. "I appreciate your efforts and understand your coming here today. However, I'm afraid I cannot approve your request. You are aware such constructions are against code?"

Chen feigned ignorance. He knew they were outlawed, but the law meant nothing if he could get the subdistrict supervisor's signature. "I'm aware that residents cannot build any structures beyond their allotted square footage, but this pool would be fully encompassed internally—"

Ding held up a hand. "I have never approved such a request for anyone in the district. It sets a dangerous precedent. Suddenly, everyone will want their own pool. And what's next, their own rock climbing walls? Their own helicopter landing pads? Do you see how this could be problematic for me? Especially as they are American!"

Chen bit his lip, wondering how to navigate this precarious impasse.

"I would never want to do anything against code . . . but considering our long partnership, would you make an exception this one time?"

"Times are changing," Ding said. "The pool makes the property too conspicuous. Opens it to too many questions." His eyes narrowed. "We wouldn't want that, would we?"

Chen gritted his teeth. This bastard was not going to budge. He didn't buy that Ding was worried about attracting attention—the property would attract attention pool or not. Sure, the political landscape was changing, but it had been changing for years and they'd continued their relationship without a hitch. Had he brought the wrong liquor? No, the subdistrict supervisor had downed an entire bottle of Japanese whiskey at their last dinner two summers ago. There was no reason other than that Ding wanted to fuck with him. Maybe his wife wasn't putting out at home and he wanted to feel like a big man. Chen stood up from his chair. "Thank you for your time," he said, hoping his tone conveyed his disappointment. Then he plastered a smile on his face. "I should be going. How's your wife?"

"Eh," Ding said, clucking his tongue and shaking his head. "She's got a bad cough these days. Loud around the house."

"We all get little ailments as we age," Chen said. "Nothing to worry too much about, I hope?"

"Of course not."

"And your son?"

"Doing God knows what in Hong Kong! He's sold four companies already, can't seem to stay still. He turns thirty next month. Time is like an arrow! And you?"

"My son is getting married," he said. He contemplated appealing to Ding's pathos; he did not want to lower himself to begging, but he was desperate. "It would mean a lot if this deal could go through. His in-laws are demanding I buy him a condo, you see."

Subdistrict Supervisor Ding looked at him with an older-brotherly sympathy. "The landscape is brutal right now, indeed."

Was this a glimmer of hope? "You understand."

"Of course," Ding said, rising and flipping his tie back down so that it hung, like a diseased tongue, over the mound of his waist. "But it's good to teach your kids they can't always get what they want."

CHEN EMERGED ONTO the street, ignoring the secretary's goodbyes. Ding's rejection was irritating. The Americans would surely be disappointed; he didn't know what would happen to his payment if he were to go back and tell them he wasn't able to build their coveted pool. They'd paid him in increments, but he was still waiting on the largest chunk at completion. That last payment would determine whether he could purchase for his son his dream home, a condo in the Xiangheyuan subdivision.

It was true, his son was indeed getting married. He turned that fact around in his mind: his baby son, still a child to him, had found a woman he wanted to spend his life with. It was earlier than Chen had expected, but who was he to stand in the way of love? But marriage demanded more than that one emotion; it demanded money, security. It demanded a home, and that was a tall order. Chen racked his brain for how to get Subdistrict Supervisor Ding to change his mind. He'd suffered plenty of setbacks before. But this one felt uniquely sharp, the jagged teeth of the subdistrict supervisor's grimace-smile sawing on the edges of his son's happiness.

He shoved his hands inside his pockets and approached a sidewalk stall for a Coke. Despite the sun's glare, he felt much calmer outside. He purchased his drink, then surveyed the offerings behind the counter. Bottles of neon-colored liquid blinked back at him, boxes of cigarettes, stacks of gum in shades of green and red.

He sat down on a bench next to the stall and stared at the suburban sprawl around him. It was lonely out here past the Fifth Ring, nothing like the honking, towering city he'd left a mere three hours ago. A single bus stop punctuated the landscape, a giant blue-and-white toothpaste advertisement beneath its awning raising the essential question: Who was here to see it? In the distance was the entrance to one complex, a low, beige concrete wall surrounding it, and still farther was the Americans' house. The suburbs were a new phenomenon in Beijing, mere saplings when he had first returned twenty-seven years ago. They were different from the American suburbs he was used to in Illinois, and so different from the urban crush he'd grown up in. Here in these suburbs, developers—Chen included—were building a new sort of China.

Subdistrict Supervisor Ding wanted to power play with him, and he had no time for such games. Chen walked to his car, a 2014 Mazda that in the waning afternoon glow looked quite dirty. He would take it to a car wash on his way home. He dreaded the long slog of traffic that awaited him.

THE SMELL OF spiced carp hit him in the nose when he finally pushed through the front door.

"Can you grab me some ginger!" came his wife's voice from the kitchen. Commanding and clear.

He walked over, squeezing himself through the small doorway off the main hallway, and saw her at the stove with her hands in the air, pepper flakes rolling down her wrists in oily rivulets. Baby hairs stuck out from her forehead energetically so that they took on the appearance of a referee waving numbers on a field. He wanted to high-five her baby hairs. She pointed her chin toward the fridge and he complied, opening it and scrounging around until his hand landed on the gnarled root. He set it on the cutting board.

"Can you cut it, actually—" she said, her back already turned to him as she tended to a fish on the stove. She moved with the clipped efficiency of someone for whom food had always been about survival and not enjoyment. Her dishes were not made with a "mother's love," as the phrase went, but with competence. She'd grown up helping her own mother scale and fillet and smoke fish that her father caught off the shores of their village home, and she approached cooking without any preciousness or passion.

He contemplated reporting his setback but knew his wife would have no sympathy. When Yihong had first told them he was planning to propose, Chen had initiated the conversation about condos with confidence. It had been the first time in years that he'd seen his wife look impressed. But now this was slipping from his grasp. At best she'd shrug it off, say he'd find the money a different way; at worst she'd list all the things he should have done, each supposedly helpful offering a paper cut on his throat. It was the curse of being attracted to smart women. "Putting last touches on the house," he said, carefully balancing the ginger-root on the board, slicing down with the paring knife.

"Oh? Oh, right. That's great," she said, her voice firm on the "great" but not enthusiastic; it seemed to be taking a bit of an effort for her to exude excitement. He thought of the way the American's wife had clapped her hands together. Pitter-patter. When was the last time his wife had been so happy for him? She tossed the ginger into the pan to a sharp sizzle.

"They're gonna send the money over soon," he continued. "Old Zhou should be pretty happy when he hears the update tonight."

"He will be," Fan said, nodding. Then she went still, her right hand on the pan's handle, her left suddenly stationary at the spatula. "I'm going to Illinois," she said next.

He wasn't sure he'd heard correctly. "What?"

Fan was not one to suggest, only proffer. He knew as soon as the words left her mouth that it was not up for discussion; in fact, she had probably already purchased her tickets. His suspicion was quickly confirmed when she barreled on, saying, "I'm leaving tomorrow." Her hands started moving again; she turned the fish with a deft flip and swiveled to grab a handful of green onion. "A Fang, Keqin, you know, the girls, they want to have a reunion."

"But—I'm about to put down the payment for Yihong—"

"I know, I know, but we've been planning this for years, and we finally found a few weeks that work for all of us. I know you have it handled anyway," she added.

"Well . . . shouldn't I be there?" He had not returned to that country since he'd left, nor had he maintained contact with many of their friends, but the lack of an invitation still stung. Even if it had been softened by the suggestion that this was a reunion of girls.

"You wouldn't have fun," Fan said. "You hate it there."

He could not say anything in the face of such certainty. "You really could have told me earlier," he said.

Her back was still turned. "You would have just told me not to go."

Again, his argument was extinguished. He abruptly exited the kitchen and stood in the living room.

There was something else he wished to ask. He knew there was another reason she wanted to return to that country, but he could not choke out the words—he did not want to breathe life into that which had tortured him those many years ago. If he did not speak it, perhaps it was not true. If it was, her simple admission of her plans would have been a slap in the face; he wanted to believe she would not do that to him.

And so he said no more. He busied himself wiping down the table, vacuuming the living room, straightening the cushions. He gulped down half a glass of baijiu, readying himself for the evening's intolerable events. Their place was not particularly lavish—most of his friends lived in larger, more modern condominiums, with better views and better light—but it had felt like a palace when he and Fan and Yihong had first moved in twenty-four years prior. The walls were the palest of sky blues, a color Fan had picked out. The balcony was massive compared to what you could get elsewhere, and Chen stepped out there now, tidying up some fallen debris. The city was never quiet out there on the balcony. Car honks melted into a steady stream, punctuated by sirens and the occasional screech of a pissed-off taxi driver. The balcony had been Fan's favorite part of the apartment, and she spent long afternoons on it these days, tending to her plants. Sometimes he'd find her just sitting there on a bamboo mat with her face arched toward the sun.

"Chen," came Fan's voice. "The door." The words between them now were not words of conversation, but directives, instructions, the logistics of a life. Perhaps he was being dramatic. No romance emerged unscathed from marriage's quotidian demands.

His future daughter-in-law, Rufeng, and her family had arrived, bursting forth five minutes earlier than the agreed-upon time, Rufeng's mother a blotch of fuchsia pink and Rufeng's father swimming in a suit with exposed white threading, as if he were an American cowboy. The parents had driven two hours here to celebrate their daughter's birthday. They tottered under the weight of the gifts they'd lugged with them from the backwoods of Hebei. Yihong and Rufeng followed behind, laughing loudly at a joke Chen would never know the beginning to. People were always arriving and laughing at jokes they never bothered to explain.

Rufeng was a too-loud country girl studying to be a doctor. She wore her hair in perpetual pigtails, and when she met Chen, she'd insisted on calling him "Big Uncle" at a decibel he felt was appropriate only for deaf grandfathers. Her name meant "as a phoenix," a kitschy moniker that advertised too baldly her parents' lofty dreams for their country daughter. But Yihong was simply an entry-level programmer at a tech company with a degree from a second-tier school under his belt. He was not destined for greatness, and Chen worried that the ambitious girl's desires would one day grow too big for his son to handle.

Fan, of course, felt the opposite. It was this contrarian tendency that Chen had once found charming beyond belief. "Women should be surprising," she said, when Yihong had first introduced them to Rufeng. This made sense, as Fan herself had once been the surprising woman, the unabashed girl from a village in Shandong with an impossible dream. But Chen had learned that surprising women had the tendency to do just that, surprise you in ways that splintered you, and he was not sure that that was what he wanted for their son.

Thanks to the baijiu, Chen was inebriated enough to extend his arms in a gesture of welcome to the Zhous. "Sit down, sit down!" he bellowed, ushering them into the dining room. Chen dreaded conversing with these country people; he knew the dinner would be rife with discussions about salaries and housing prices and other numbers they could only begin to grasp in their heads and would never see on their bank ledgers. He wasn't being prejudiced—the Zhous had been the ones to flatten Yihong's proposal into numbers.

"Old Chen, how're things going for you?" Old Zhou poured himself a generous glass from Chen's bottle.

"Oh, good, good," Chen said. The man was asking how Chen's cash hunt was going. "Just wrapping up my latest build."

"Yes?" the man leaned toward Chen, the sleeve of his shirt almost dipping into a plate of vinegared cucumber.

He told the man about the Americans. Rufeng's father's eyes lit up. A line of drool crept down his chin. "So great to hear, Old Chen," he said. Out of the corner of his eye, Chen could see Rufeng chewing rhythmically, not catching on to the coded exchange. Fan, meanwhile, was hunched over, her bowl palmed in her left hand, chopsticks needling in rapid rotations.

"My dad has the coolest clients," Yihong said, puffing his chest. "He once designed Beibei Lisa's house."

It was Beibei Lisa's lawyer's house, but the in-laws didn't need to know that. Rufeng's mother slapped a hand on her mouth. He was surprised the woman hadn't choked to death on a green bean yet with the emotions she was exuding. "I LOVE Beibei Lisa! What was she like? Was she so beautiful in person?"

The only thing the lawyer had said about Beibei Lisa was that she had a lot of faux-snakeskin bags. She was an environmentalist and didn't believe in killing animals for clothing, so she sought out the world's most intricately made dupes. "Only the rich can afford to wear fakes," the lawyer had grumbled. "I'd be laughed out of my office if I showed up with a fake leather bag!"

"Yes," Chen said. "She was a very elegant woman. Even more beautiful than in her movies!"

The woman grabbed a large piece of fatty pork with her chopsticks and plopped it down in Chen's bowl. "Eat up, Old Chen," she said, grinning.

"Ba, tell them about that time you met Bill Clinton!"

"Oh, they don't want to hear about that," Chen said, falsely modest.

Rufeng's mother was shaking. "Why, of COURSE we do! Clinton is so handsome."

Bill Clinton had held a rally in Chicago in 1992, back when he was a young presidential hopeful, but Chen had not met him per se. He and Fan and a few of their friends had driven up to the city, and the future president of the United States had waved in Chen's direction as he arrived on stage.

"He was very kind," he said now, grinning. "He had a firm, presidential handshake. When he shook my hand, that's how I knew he'd be president."

Rufeng's parents howled with glee. "You predicted it, Old Chen!" Yihong banged his glass on the table and Rufeng clapped her hands.

Fan entertained all this with a placid expression. She had long finished her bowl and was now at work wiping her side of the table with her napkin. He wondered if she would bring up her trip. "Okay, settle down," she finally said, laying her hand on Chen's arm. "Who wants tea?"

HOURS LATER, the in-laws left in a flurry. All the gifts had been given, compliments exchanged. Rufeng's parents had brought Chen a towering bottle of brown liquor that Rufeng's father insisted was forty-year aged brandy from France, but Chen was sure was the fermented piss of Fujianese rice farmers. For Fan they had brought a hulking white purse with a gaudy bejeweled rabbit splayed across its surface. Fan had accepted it with enthusiasm, posing with it in the mirror and saying it perfectly matched the dress she had just purchased at Ralph Lauren.

Now the bag sat discarded on the floor.

"Looks like a bag for a child," Chen said, carrying a dish to the sink.

"It was a nice gesture," Fan said, scrubbing.

"I wish they wouldn't bring up the house all the time," he said. "Of course we'll make sure Yihong and Rufeng have a nice place to live. That's to be expected! Who do they take us to be?"

"They want to feel secure, Chen," Fan said, placing a plate on the counter. "It's the most natural desire in the world."

He pretended not to hear, stretching out on the couch. Under the cold blue light of his smartphone, Chen scrolled through images of the American couple. Thomas Straeffer-Kenney and Vivian Luo. An American-Chinese pairing that was becoming commonplace. On their wedding website, Vivian and Thomas stood in a field of flowers, Thomas's arms wrapped around her waist, his eyes lowered and his lips catching her cheek mid-kiss. Between the two of them, they had enough money to retire three times over.

"They're an attractive couple," Chen said. "Almost as good-looking as we were."

He might have said the last part in his head, as Fan did not respond. She simply washed and washed the dishes, the whirl of the water running down the drain the soundtrack of their marriage.

Eventually, she stripped off her gloves. "I have to finish packing," she said. "Good night." She left Chen lying on the couch.

THE NEXT DAY, he drove Fan to the airport. His wife sat with her back straight and tense, her hand resting on the handle of the door as if she were prepared, at any moment, to make a quick escape. The sky was in that blue-yellow hour right before nightfall, the sun sputtering its last desperate breaths as they made their way across the Fifth Ring.

He turned on the radio, tuned to his favorite comedy channel. "Roasts" had taken over the nation, wherein comedians would ridicule other comedians about their accents, weight, and wives. Today, there was a female comedian, what sounded like a young girl with a thick Dongbei accent, talking about her parents setting her up with neighborhood bachelors. "You," she said, and he imagined her gesturing at some other comedian in the room. "How about you marry me? All my mother wants for me is a guy with two legs and two arms, and that seems to be about as much as you can offer anyway." Claps and laughter. Roasting others by roasting oneself. Sublime. Chen let out a snicker. He turned to Fan to see if she similarly found it droll, but she had not seemed to hear the joke; her face was a still mask, her eyes fixed on a point in the distance.

When they had first arrived at Beijing Capital International Airport together those many years ago, returning from Illinois, life was very different. There were not so many cars on the street. There were no radio roasts. There were just him and her, their polos stuck to their skin in the heat, bewildered but excited for a new life. The flight over had been bumpy. Fan had clutched the side of the airplane with every bout of turbulence, but she never made a sound. She'd devoured the airplane food, savoring each bite of the salty pan-fried noodles and green bean salad, which was not so much green as gray. Chen was hungry too and while he thought no one was looking began licking the remaining soy sauce off the plastic box. Fan reached over and tore open the plastic bag containing a single bread roll, broke it in half, and wiped the soy sauce clean for him, handing him a chunk of bread dipped in sauce. It was delicious.

When they landed, Fan brushed her teeth in the airport bathroom and combed her hair into a ponytail and even applied a faint coat of lipstick, as if she were greeting a long-lost lover. Chen, too, wet his fingers and ran them through his hair, so that his thick mane stayed put and orderly. As they walked through the airport's automatic doors, Chen took Fan's hand and squeezed it, before rushing to the curb and sticking his other hand out.

"Taxi!" He waved down a glossy green taxi, whose cost per kilometer had jumped a full two RMB since he left. He turned to Fan and said, "My wife, today we live like kings. Today is the beginning of our new life."

She laughed and he would, so long as he lived, never forget that laugh. It was a laugh so full of trust. They slid into the cab; the seats were upholstered in smooth leather. The air-conditioning was cool on their skin. The taxi driver asked if they had gone on vacation.

"Yes," Chen said. "A long vacation."

They'd been so full of hope. And now? Now there was just life.

He pulled up to International Departures and Fan paused, her earlier eager stance softening into hesitation. She peered out the window, as if unsure that this was her exact destination.

"We're here," he said.

She sat still. "I think we should tell him," she said next.

"Well, of course. He's going to ask where you are."

"No, I mean . . ." She lifted her eyes to him, and there was something akin to sadness there.

"Now isn't the right time," he said, looking back out through the windshield. He watched a man in a yellow vest arrange cones in a neat line, the cones getting smaller and smaller as the man walked away, orange triangles repeating ad infinitum, and he envied him, this man who knew that relief existed at the end of that line.

It had been on a completely unremarkable day that every-thing ended. They had been driving somewhere, and, bizarrely, Chen remembered he had been eating a sleeve of Oreos. Fan had been looking at her phone, and then she had turned to Chen and said, "Let's split." He had thought, for one moment, that she was talking about the Oreos. Fen le ba. Three of the simplest characters in the Chinese language. "Let's separate it." "Let's divide it." And the most laughable interpretation of them all: "Let's share it." But she was not touching the Oreo package and had fixed on him a look that he had only seen a few times in his life: when they'd fought about sending Yihong abroad, when her father had died, and when that other thing, that first betrayal, had occurred.

He had agreed, but on one condition: that they keep it secret from Yihong until after his wedding. He didn't want to rock the boat, give the country people one more bargaining chip. So for the past few months, he and Fan had lived this lie, going to bed each night side by side, an immeasurable distance growing ever wider between their prone figures. Secretly, he had hoped that she'd forget about it; he had hoped that if he could deliver his son a home fit for a king, she'd look upon him again with that old admiration, and the suggestion of separation would become nothing but a blip in the story of their marriage.

Now, he looked at his wife's face. There was no mistaking why she'd wish to break the levee of this news at this particular moment, as they lingered in front of the international terminal. He set his jaw, tightly, and the reason for her trip roared to the front of his mind, undeniable now. The words came out, pristine: "Is this about Qiong?"

Her eyes narrowed and her mouth crinkled upward. He thought that she might yell. But the apparent anger dissipated as quickly as it had come; her lips folded inward, her expression now more solemn than indignant. "See you soon," she said, flipping the door open and grabbing her suitcase from the trunk with the clipped efficiency she'd deployed on everything in this life. And then she was gone.

2

Chen had met Fan in Illinois, on their first day of school. He was about to begin a PhD program in mathematics, while she was about to begin hers in economics. He arrived in Illinois thrilled and eager to prove something; he'd heard of older graduates who'd struck it rich and purchased mansions for themselves or brought their millions back to China to make their own businesses, and he planned to do the same. He made quick friends with his roommates, Meng Haian, a hulking math student who stood 185 centimeters tall, and Jia Yinhao, a neurotic man from Shanghai who seemed to be forever polishing his glasses. The three of them had little in common, Jia Yinhao a child of the Shanghai ex-intellectual elite whose particularity would have ordinarily put Chen off, and Meng Haian the oldest son of eight from a village in the country's northmost tip where no one had ever heard of Illinois. But the nature of being international students in America lent itself to solidarity. They had no choice but to band together, and so they did.

On the first day of school, Meng Haian told him that a few of the Chinese students were meeting at the Black Violet in town. Chen was already the talk of his cohort: that day, he'd been the only person in class able to solve a particularly difficult section of the infamous Feit-Thompson proof. His Chinese compatriots whooped when he pushed through the doors of the bar. Life in America was looking good.

There was a fair-sized group of Chinese students across the disciplines, about twenty in total, but among all the pretty girls cheering for him with their glasses raised, one girl caught his eye.

She stood in a corner, looking tiny behind a monstrous glass of water. The other girls in the bar were very modern, wearing sharp-looking button-downs and white crew socks under square-heeled, leather Oxfords. But she was wearing brown loafers as big as grape boxes, clearly not her size, and her hair was in two braids, like the virginal country girls he'd seen in soap dramas. He felt a pang of pity: the poor girl—perhaps she needed some encouragement or a friend to guide the way.

Minutes later, after the first round of toasts, she surprised him. She marched right up to Chen and stuck out her hand.

"Congratulations on being the new star," she said, in a voice that was almost angry in its admiration. He was struck by her confidence, especially considering her shabby outfit and country-girl hairstyle. Her face was sun-dappled, brownish in patches that soaked in more light and golden all over. Not starkly pale like the other girls'. He took her hand and shook it. It was rough, which he'd later learn was from years in the field, helping her mother plant squash, and on her father's fishing boat, her hands dipping into the cool morning waters of Qingdao Bay, gripping rope, hauling flounder.

She told him her name was Fan.

"'Fan' for prosperous?" Chen asked.

"'Fan' for ordinary," she said, matter-of-factly. "Two strokes and a dot." She didn't seem at all embarrassed in saying that.

Most of the other Chinese students in their cohort were from cities, like Chen, while Fan was from a seaside village, where she was used to skinning fish, not drinking imported beers. She had never been on an airplane before flying to Illinois and had marveled at the way the giant machinery had taken off from the ground. She'd stood in the aisle, jumping up and down to see if she'd feel a pressure change, until finally a flight attendant had told her sternly to take her seat.

She dreamed of being a world-class economist. She'd been obsessed with numbers and systems ever since her village had gone through three consecutive seasons of fish scarcity after a typhoon hit the coast of Qingdao. She was a young girl. Her family had to stretch their meager catch by drying their shrimp and black scraper to sell as flavoring at the market. They survived; other families did not. She and everyone in the village came from a long line of fishers—but she witnessed firsthand the way nature could devastate, and she resolved from an early age not to rely on it for survival. Instead she would rely on herself, and leave her village and the sea behind. Fan was an only child, and she had been expected to stay home and take care of her aging parents. But she fought them stubbornly, insisting that she would move to the United States, become wealthy, and buy them a large house on a large plot of land where fruits and vegetables would grow all year round. Her father would never have to haul fish in the mornings again; her mother's hands would never again have to bleed from skinning them.

"You must have had high marks," Chen said, aware that getting to America from a countryside village was no easy feat.

"Yes," she said. "The best my village had ever seen."

She asked if he wanted to take a walk outside. They stole away to the library, Fan walking slowly through the stacks with an almost devout air, grazing the edges of the dusty books with the tips of her fingers and peering shyly at the chalk scribblings on the blackboards.

"Do you know how many books there are in this library?" she asked him. A smattering of students sat dozing off behind piles of textbooks.

"Legend says it's thirty thousand," he said, conspiratorially. "Or even," he paused, looking from side to side, "forty."

She rolled her eyes. "I'm serious!"

He shrugged. "I don't know. It's funny that you ask things like that."

"I like to grasp the things I see," she said. "I think about things in numbers. I'm an economist. I see a whole room of books in front of me, and it's very impressive, and it takes my breath away, but I can't fully understand it until I get a number. When I went to Huangshan when I was a child, I needed to know how tall the highest peak was, and I needed to know how old the stone steps were that ringed the cliffs. When I discovered there were 60,000 steps built over 1,500 years ago, I started crying—because I was only ten years old, and those ten years felt so important, and 150 times that seemed an impossible amount."

"I understand," he said. "And as a mathematician I suppose I should probably think similarly. But numbers have always seemed very cold to me. I prefer to look at something and accept it for the masterpiece it really is. Do you look at a painting by Qi Baishi and ask him how many brushstrokes it took him to complete it? Do you listen to a concerto by Mozart and ask how many notes are in the piece? I don't. I don't need them to translate their art into something that I can understand in my own language."

She looked at him, a big smile on her face. "An Einstein and a poet, I see," she teased, nudging him playfully. "The most venerable Li Bai."

America in those first few months was a land full of promise. Their contingent of Chinese classmates formed a strong battalion, protecting each other from any alienation they may have felt had they arrived in this country alone. They ignored the gawking gazes of their American classmates and laughed freely on the quad, sharing stories of tyrannical high school teachers, fierce undergraduate rivalries, and crushes they'd kissed or fondled. This was the late eighties; Reagan had granted amnesty to millions of their fellow immigrants, and despite the turbulence of the decade, this felt like a shimmering beacon, a wink and a nod to potential future magnanimousness. They snickered at the bumbling American students with their loping gaits and their swollen cheeks and chins that could only come from a lifetime of Velveeta and football-induced blunt force head trauma. Chen, Meng Haian, and Jia Yinhao lived with one other person, a Japanese kid named Yuki, who never spoke to them and whom Chen would always see alone at the library, and each time he saw him, he would feel twinges of sympathy and pray he'd never end up like that.

The members of Chen's cohort, Chinese and American alike, looked to him for the right answers. And the answers came easily; compared to his cutthroat Chinese education, grad school was a breeze. Half the classes in his first semester were ones he'd already taken as an undergrad; he barely paid attention and got perfect marks.

Fan, too, excelled. And she continued to be bold with him; any time she'd see Chen on campus, she'd march right up to him and ask if he was going to the library, if she could come study with him. Other girls were shy around him, but she never seemed to doubt herself.

Chen felt confident that she liked him, but he also found himself nervous around her, unsure of how to turn their friendship into something more.

As he should have predicted, she solved this predicament for him. One evening, on one of their winding walks home, she turned to him and said, "I like you. What are we going to do about that?"

He gave her a grin and asked, "Why do you like me?"

She looked at him, unsmiling, her brow knitted in intense concentration. She didn't seem perturbed by the question; she only seemed to want to give him the most honest answer. "Because you're the best of all of them," she said, a statement that was perhaps both unromantic in its almost mathematical quality and also the greatest thing anyone had ever said to him, would ever say to him in all his life.

To put it simply: she was always looking for someone to chase. For a while, that was Chen.

Midway through the spring of their second year, Fan invited Chen to come watch her teach. As she stood on the podium at the front of the lecture hall, she looked tiny, just as she had that first day in the Black Violet, her sweater more fit for a child than a university lecturer. She began speaking in her usual confident way, but there was something nervous in her voice; Chen blushed and worried that his presence was making her self-conscious. He tried to give her a reassuring look, but she met his gaze only briefly before her eyes darted back to the center of the room. Behind her and to the side, a man with gelled hair and a pocket square leaned against the blackboard, his arms crossed, nodding paternally, pressing his lips together in assent every time Fan made a particularly impassioned proclamation. Chen disliked him immediately.

After class, Chen bounded down the steps to the podium, trying to catch her gaze again as she collected her papers. But she seemed to be lost in her own mind, her brow stitched, a few words burbling silently on her lips. The man with the pocket square walked up beside her and laid his hand on her shoulder; she turned with a start, and a large smile broke across her face. "*Great work,*" he said, in English, and Chen saw her whole body relax. So it was seeking this man's approval that had made her nervous.

Chen came to a slow stroll as he approached the podium. Fan saw him and gave him a small wave. "Chen, this is my econometrics professor, *Robert* Qiong. Shanxi's most valuable expatriate."

"She exaggerates," the man said, sticking out his hand. Chen smiled stiffly and shook it.

"And *Robert*, this is my friend Chen," Fan said next, pausing ever so slightly on the word "friend." By that point they were more than friends but hadn't told anyone, so the pause made him blush and burst with pride. "He's in applied mathematics. The star of his class."

The man smiled that paternal smile again. "*Good for you,*" he said, using that condescending English phrase, and Chen wanted to sneer. The man looked no older than thirty-five; who was he to be passing judgment—bad or good—on anyone else? "I've heard of you," he continued. "Surprised we've never crossed paths."

"Well, I'm not a star lecturer like Fan," Chen responded, smiling at her. Humility was always a good look. Fan's eyes never left Qiong's face.

Robert Qiong nodded, his lips pressing together in what felt like a practiced gesture of assent. "I've seen very few talents like Fan's." And the answer she sought was reflected in her eyes.

ROBERT QIONG WAS young and brilliant, indeed only ten years older but already a tenure-track professor with a wife, and a daughter on the way. He had come from a village in Shanxi "*with nothing but holes in my pockets,*" he'd always say, in the most consonant-filled English you'd ever heard, the s's coming off in hisses to make no mistake about his words. He'd curated the appearance of an English dandy, his posture rail straight, his hair coiffed and gelled, that preposterous silk handkerchief always sticking out of his breast pocket. Chen thought it was buffoonery, but the women in their group thought differently. Across the table from Chen at the library, Fan gushed about him, calling him *Rah-ber-tuh*, dragging the furry letters of that ill-selected name out into three endless syllables. Shanxi bordered Shandong, so she referred to him, sickeningly, as her "lao xiang." Qingdao is five hundred miles from the Shanxi border! Chen wanted to snap. How in the world are you hometowners?

Still, Chen and Fan grew closer and closer, spending long afternoons walking through the tree-lined subdivisions that bordered campus, admiring the Georgian and Craftsman homes and spinning stories about the people who lived inside. Fan liked to imagine torrid romances and intrigue, while Chen preferred to believe that anyone who could make a life inside houses like these knew only peace and a level joy. But he loved the way she saw the world in all its vivid possibilities. The streets were named for the states of America, and as they walked down Oregon, Ohio, Nevada, California, it felt as if they were making plans for places they'd one day go. They imagined what it would be like to move into one of these houses themselves. Would they build a deck? Would they dig a pool? Would they fight? Chen believed their lively debates would always remain lively. "I'm not scared," Fan would say. "Of fighting with you. I know I'll always win."

In the summer of 1989, tanks rolled through Tiananmen Square. Chen, Fan, and their classmates marched in solidarity protests; they condemned the actions of their country. Fan was livid. Chen felt, chillingly, that a door had closed. Their homeland now seemed heartless—dangerous, even; perhaps America was the only road forward. In their mutual disillusionment, Chen and Fan sought refuge in each other, their American imaginings becoming less and less the stuff of fantasy.

But Robert Qiong hung like an apparition over their romance. Fan began working on a paper of Qiong's her third year, and they continued to work together through the remainder of her PhD. On her walks with Chen, she'd sometimes bring them by Qiong's house, a four-bedroom colonial just three blocks from campus, and rhapsodize about how the city of Urbana had designated it a historic landmark, how Qiong had bested every other buyer with an offer the previous owner couldn't refuse, and how much she wished to live somewhere like it one day. To Chen, the house seemed nice enough but nothing spectacular.

Chen and Fan married shortly after graduation, and Chen moved into the apartment Fan received as a research fellow. They were happy, for a time. But life in America did not continue on in the Elysian way it had begun. The job market proved more viperous than the comfortable academic life Chen had known. At first he tackled the job search with heady optimism. He visited hospitals, banks, mergers and acquisitions firms, labs, X-ray clinics. He could program or compute growth statistics or crunch numbers as an accountant. His peers were being hired left and right; Chinese overseas students were reputed to be highly reliable and efficient. But Chen could not find work.

He didn't tell Fan. The doors kept slamming. Three months in, he told her he'd found a position, and he began leaving the house each morning in his suit to sit in the park, circling jobs in newspapers. He didn't want her to worry, to look at him with pity in her eyes. It was temporary, he told himself. His star would rise again.

Slowly, distance began to settle its tumid body between them, as Fan spent more and more nights on campus, working with Qiong. Eventually, Chen began working late at night as well, but the mutual absence felt all the more searing when he'd stumble home, exhausted, only to find their bed still empty.

So when he finally discovered their affair, he should not have been surprised. Fan's carelessness was almost comical. A lush summer evening. The letter found in the dresser—a dresser they shared. How gauche. His wife was competent at so many things but perhaps not at an affair. He confronted her, tears springing from his eyes for the first time since his childhood. She burst into tears, too, apologizing over and over, the word "sorry" becoming nothingness in her mouth. She cursed herself, said it was over, she had ended it. Bad, bad, bad, she had repeated. I am a bad woman. He did not need to say it for her.

He forgave her, because of course he did. Most husbands would have turned their wives out, thrown them onto the street, called them whores, but he was a magnanimous man. He and Fan's marriage was not meager like most other marriages; it could withstand betrayal. He believed her when she said she no longer loved Robert Qiong.

When his old friend Tao called him with a real estate opportunity, it felt like the universe was giving them a chance to rebuild their family. It was 1994. China had changed, Tao assured him.

It was more than safe; it was thriving. Fan, with her tail between her legs, agreed to return with Chen to Beijing. She left shortly before the conclusion of her research with Qiong. At the time, it felt—for both of them—like the necessary sacrifice they had to make for an even greater opportunity—and for the survival of their family. And it was. Two months after they landed in Beijing, Fan discovered she was pregnant. They took it as a sign. They were meant to come home. Their dear son grew up a Chinese boy. Fan loved Beijing in those first years. She looked at the city with the wide-eyed wonder of a country girl, fascinated by the forever-flashing neon lights and the swarms of bikers thicker than traffic, the way the Forbidden City sat nestled against impressive modern skyscrapers. She found work in the accounting department at the Foreign Language School, where she worked hard at her job and liked her coworkers, who asked her copious questions about America and who made her feel like royalty. Later, she went to work for an American consulting company, where she quickly climbed the ranks and eventually made enough money to purchase a condo for her parents in the outskirts of Qingdao.

And Chen—Chen was a star returning from America. His friends who had stayed in Beijing had done decently for themselves, building their own businesses or nabbing executive roles at large companies, and all of them owned condominiums in the city center, but he was the one they admired. He was the one with the smart wife, the healthy son, the stories about that rumored land, America. His business with Tao took off at a steady clip. The two of them first made their mark in Fengtai, then Daxing, expanding out past the Fourth, then Fifth Rings as Beijing swelled. They began by purchasing older apartment buildings and refurbishing them, then eventually started buying land and building from the ground up. Chen no longer thought of mathematics or academics, happily distracted by his growing bank account. By 1996, he had saved enough to purchase the three-bedroom condominium they lived in now. At the time, it was a much-talked-about purchase; it was a new condo in the swanky Huayuan Road subdivision in Chaoyang, with views of both the Forbidden City and the skyscrapers in the commercial district. The day they moved in, Fan danced around the living room like a little girl, grabbing Yihong's hands and twirling him in a circle. She was happy, and Chen was happy.

What had happened between her and Qiong never happened again with anyone else, and Chen wouldn't expect it to, after her plaintive cries that gray evening. They had gone to America, weathered the storm, then rebuilt their life twofold back in China. It was a life that was more than enough.

Still, their marriage had crumbled. When had they stopped arguing playfully? When had she begun feeling exasperated with him more than inspired by him? Their love had always been combative, expressive, nothing like the cold, well-mannered unions their friends lugged to dinner parties and children's birthdays. But ever since they had moved to Huayuan Road, their marriage had become a frog slowly boiling in a pot—without their noticing, without any real explanation, it was dead. "I know I'll always win," she'd said as a young woman. But it didn't feel like either of them had won.

And now—now he felt that old ghost again, come back to haunt him. She was going back to Robert. Don't go, he'd wanted to say, Don't leave, but he knew that his wife was not one to respond to imperatives.

Chen contemplated all of this as he drove back south on the Fifth Ring highway, turning the clipped facts of their history over and over in his head, returning to every critical juncture and wondering if there was anything he could have done to prevent what followed. Each time he came up empty; he'd done the best he could, and still his wife was now on a plane back to that place. Back to that man. For the first time in many years—and it had taken him decades to rub this image from his mind—he imagined their bodies entwined, Robert Qiong forceful atop his wife's lithe and limber form. He remembered the way Qiong had placed his hand on her shoulder that first day in the lecture hall, how casually he'd made Fan's body his dominion—it had taken Chen months to even touch her arm to get her attention, much less reassure her, soothe her. If Qiong touched her like that in front of forty of her students, how did he touch her when they were alone? Chen thought of this now, and he felt nauseated. And he had simply let her go, let her get on the plane that would take her back to Qiong. The two of them, now free to roam the campus without Chen's envious gaze on their backs, their hands brushing softly as they eyed each other surreptitiously—perhaps Fan would want to duck under the shade of a large willow tree and embrace him, but he'd say, No, not here, I can't be seen, later—and the later would infuse the rest of the afternoon with an irresistible charge—and Chen thought now of the man's wife: Had she suspected too? The man's children—did they know what kind of man their father was? He had never met these people, but in this moment his heart panged for them, the ones left behind.

IT WAS JUST BEFORE FOUR AM when Chen finally arrived home, reeking of liquor. He'd joined Tao and a couple of friends at the Prime Hotel, where they'd drunk themselves into a liquid stupor. Tao had a new mistress, who sat on his lap all night and trailed lip gloss across his neck. Chen knew that Fan had never liked Tao; he certainly was a typical businessman, cycling through girlfriends nearly as fast as he cycled through real estate deals. But Chen liked being around Tao. Tao made him feel like a good man. He walked into his bedroom and slept.

When he woke, sunlight was streaming through the curtains, and he wondered if he had truly been asleep at all. He peered at the clock: it was one PM. Fan would have landed by now. He checked her WeChat, and indeed, she had posted a photo from O'Hare International in Chicago, the same airport they'd flown from on the way home to Beijing so many years ago. The rainbow walkway, its neon lights sending greens and pinks down in streams, looked just as eccentric and out of place as it had back then. "July 1. I am delighted to see that some things do not change. These lights perplex me as they once did. Perhaps I still have the same propensity for wonder." She often posted in this way on WeChat, a platform that she treated with the vulnerability and piety of a diary.

Chen opened his bedroom door and looked out at his empty apartment. Yihong wasn't home. He thought of the way he'd found his wife the previous morning, standing on their balcony as usual, sweeping the debris from her hyacinth plants; the winds had been strong the evening before. He'd watched her for a moment, her hair tied back in the same style she'd worn for decades, her shoulder blades showing underneath a thin T-shirt, her movements rapid and clipped, and he thought she was a perfect machine, a word that popped glaringly into his head; she had always been the kind of woman who carried out her every mission, fifty kilograms of determination. But what he noticed most that morning was the way she stopped, abruptly, and peered out at the city before them, as if the towering building ahead of them with its cascading black vertical buttresses—like all the other buildings in their complex, like their own—was something newfangled to her.

A bowl of porridge had been sitting on the table; hers was already scraped clean, washed, and drying on the rack. He sat down to eat. Fan emerged from the balcony.

"It might be cold," she'd said, matter-of-factly. A phrase undergirded with care, but her voice never betrayed any of that feeling.

He sat down at the kitchen table now and opened his laptop. He typed Robert Qiong's name into the search bar and inhaled before pressing enter. The same angular face filled his screen, his hair still black as pitch, the eyes only slightly downturned. He was too handsome to be an academic, Chen thought. He wouldn't trust a teacher like this. He scrolled through the search results: amid the various scholarly articles he'd published, there was his daughter's 2016 wedding announcement in the *Champaign Dispatch*; there was a photo of him alongside a group of high school students at an event hosted by a nonprofit he'd founded for underserved communities. In 2017, the university had given him a lifetime achievement award. There he was in cascading velvet robes, shaking the Dean's hand, smiling that cheeky smile he'd adopted in Illinois. Chen shut his laptop with a slam.

A ping. Fan had posted another photo, of a woman whom Chen at first did not recognize, before he blinked and realized that it was A Fang, their classmate, once a round-faced girl who cried easily and wore her hair permanently tied with a bow in some shade of pink. Now, her face had grown thin; she was wearing a black sleeveless turtleneck and her demeanor had matured in a way so drastic that she looked a decade older than Fan—but perhaps it was simply the contrast between the girl he'd remembered and the woman who appeared before him. "Wonderful to see old friends again. A Fang was the beautiful one in our cohort, further confirmation that some things never change." He nearly guffawed. Fan was usually so blunt, so painfully honest, but she chose the most ludicrous moments to be saccharine; in no world was this woman the beauty of any group of people anymore.

To him she sent a few words: "Landed in Chicago. At A Fang's house now."

He hunted for signs that she was to reunite with Robert Qiong—in her words, in the photos. A Fang, he knew, had done well for herself after school. She'd landed a competitive engineering position at a local company and married a Taiwanese man she met there. Last he heard they had moved to a large five-bedroom house close to the airport, and from the looks of Fan's photos, they lived there still. The ceilings seemed higher than he could fathom, and he caught the jaundiced glimmer of a chandelier in the corner. This was a house large enough for secrets, large enough to hide a tryst. Chen shook his head. He was being silly; a man like Robert Qiong would not conduct his affairs in someone else's home.

He checked his watch. Later, he had dinner plans at his parents' place, with Yihong and Rufeng. They did this several times a month. The last thing he wished to do was field questions about Fan's absence while his country would-be daughter-in-law chirped—for the second evening that weekend, no less—about her impending engagement to his son. His parents loved her, of course. They loved all the wives in the family.

CHEN'S PARENTS' HOME in West City was a relic of 1960s socialist housing redistribution, three rooms and an entryway, one of eleven units on the seventh floor of their ten-floor building. He and Fan had stayed with his parents for two years when they first moved home in 1994. Now, every time he visited, he couldn't help but think of those first few years, the scrappy years that were so full of promise. They were his second chance—their second chance—at a happy life.

He arrived after Yihong and Rufeng, and by the time he departed the elevators, he could already hear the two of them chattering away, Rufeng's twangy voice bouncing off the hallway walls. Westernization was in that laugh they brought. Since when did Chinese girls laugh at such a decibel? Chen trudged into the apartment, announcing his arrival with a knock on the already open door. His son greeted him with a joyous "Hey, Ba!" and Rufeng followed suit, the word "ba" tumbling from her mouth in a half-joking, half-sincere nod at what was to come. Yihong loved when she did this, tickling her in the ribs every time.

"Chen ah," his mother said, poking her head into the living room from the kitchen. "Where's Fan?"

Chen couldn't conjure an excuse quickly enough. "She's on a trip," he said, hoping his mother would leave it at that, but of course the woman's eyes narrowed, her intuition perennially alert to any signs of marital discord.

"Where to?"

"Just Illinois. With some friends."

"Illinois!" His mother gasped. "Not that terrible place."

"It's just a vacation, Ma. Nothing to get too worried about."

"She's always on vacation these days, isn't she," his mother said, her voice as brittle as chicken bones. Her gaze bore into him. Chen was all too familiar with this look. Indignation welled up in him. She assumed he had done something to upset Fan; why else did wives go away abruptly? But this was a rift that his actions could not quite explain.

His father, already seated at the small, round dinner table, said nothing. He was bent over a teacup, his spine like a watermelon rind, his fingers slender and puckered. Those same hands had once easily wielded a broom, but now they were only strong enough to lift teacups. He watched as his father stood to pour his grandson and Rufeng cups of clear-green Longjing, wiping the porcelain lip with a napkin where he spilled. Age was the most effective tenderizer, wasn't it? The angriest of parents could be the gentlest of grandparents. Chen looked at his son with quiet fury.

The apartment had barely changed in fifty years. The landscape outside had shifted dramatically, skyscrapers penetrating the once-open sky outside his parents' bedroom window, the subdivision around the building ebbing and changing twofold, fourfold. What had once been a stretch of parkway was now another complex, swathes of orange and green flagging the arrival of a new era in the sky. The courtyard in front of the building where he once played with his friends remained, but it had grown prettier since, with new swing sets and seesaws and a cobbled pathway. What used to be a shoe mender on the left side of the courtyard was now a cell phone repair shop.

But the apartment itself was exactly the same. His parents still ate their dinners in the small corridor leading to the kitchen.

There were floor-to-ceiling shelves crammed against the western wall, where his mother stored notebooks and old trinkets and plastic bags stuffed full of dusty sweaters. The railings and doors in the apartment were painted a seafoam green. The paint was fainter now than it'd been when he and Fan lived here, certainly fainter than it'd been in his youth, but the green never failed to make him feel like a child.

He walked into the second bedroom. His parents used it as a storage room now, and the wardrobes and desks shoved into every corner made it feel smaller. Here was where Chen had built his business, where his family had crowded together in a space even smaller than their Urbana studio, but where, finally, Chen had felt hope again.

When they'd first returned, his mother had transformed the room into a marital home, a gold-and-red bedspread stitched with the words "luck and happiness" reflecting the meager light from a small side window. Yihong had slept in a crib on the other side of the room, a mere two meters away, and it was a godsend that he was an easy baby, never prone to crying or waking at odd hours of the night. Fan became the daughter his parents never had. They loved the way she massaged their feet in the evenings, the perfect bowls of rice porridge she'd make, and how she was blunt and straightforward with Chen, snapping a towel at him when he sat down on the couch after a meal. His mother had splurged on wedding photos for him and Fan, pushing several hundred-yuan bills into his hands with a tearful smile the week after they returned. They'd gone to a stylish photo salon in the hutongs, where they'd each selected four different outfits, two traditional and two Western. Fan and Chen posed with matching red hanfu: her glancing at him over a fan, her eyelashes dynamic, and him gazing at her over a cup of tea. They posed as students in the ambiguous West, him in a tie and sweater vest and her in a pleated skirt and knee-high socks. The photographer was a bored youngish man who nonetheless seemed to take his job too seriously, repeatedly yelling at Chen, "You are in LOVE, my brother! Look into her eyes!" He would continuously call out to Fan, "Little sister! Control your man!" And they would strain to gaze into each other's eyes, barely containing their laughter in embarrassment. Thinking about it now, he was astonished that they were able to have such jubilant moments even after her betrayal; was this not evidence that their love could endure anything?

Chen's mother hung her favorite photo above Chen and Fan's bed. In it, Fan smiled demurely at the camera, her skin a blinding airbrushed white against the garden landscape background. She wore a cream-colored ball gown, layers of chiffon spilling onto the floor, while Chen stood behind her in a black-and-white tuxedo, holding her shoulders, his hair combed to one side. The words "happy home" embellished the bottom in sparkling neon type.

The portrait hung there still. They had not taken this one with them when they'd moved out two years later, to Huayuan Road. Fan thought she looked too garish, her lips the red of a spring tulip. Chen gazed at the portrait now, his family chattering in the next room, and was floored by how young they had once been. It hung near the window, the afternoon light illuminating the white dust on the surface. Her lips were so red, her pink tongue just slightly visible. It was the prettiest thing he'd ever seen.

He remembered the first time she'd taken him back to Qingdao, a few months after they returned to Beijing. Fan had been quiet on the car ride. He supposed she was perplexed by the situation; she had gone all the way across the world to leave her village, and now her husband was driving her back to the very place she had spent her entire adult life attempting to leave for good. Still, he remembered how when they'd stepped into the kitchen, Fan had immediately gotten to work helping her mother scale the mackerel, peel the shrimp, and clean the pig her father had killed for this occasion, washing it with a tactile deftness Chen had never seen. Fan rarely cooked in America. Her mother had protested, insisting that Fan sit in the kitchen with Chen, but Fan had swatted her off, rolling up her sleeves with an automatic gusto that could only come from a lifetime of habit. She knew the names of every herb they used to season the pork and helped her mother smoke a few kilos to keep for the winter months. Chen had sat on a small pink plastic chair, nursing a cup of warm beer and politely nodding as Fan's father told a long story about the city kids that had come to their village in the seventies and how they had had to share their food with them, even as they did stupid things like get drunk and leave the gates open so that the goats ran free. Once, he had caught two of them having sex in the chicken coop, and he had chased them for a mile with a hammer.

"Stupid city kids, never skinned a chicken in their life! If they knew how annoying it is to pluck every feather off a chicken, they wouldn't have been so careless!" Fan's father had said. He ate salted prunes as he talked, spitting the tiny pits onto a piece of newsprint at his feet.

Fan's mother had then handed Chen a saucer of pears. "But you're different," she said quickly. "You're American-educated."

His own mother emerged now from the kitchen with a tagine of braised chicken, her hands clad in makeshift gloves made out of old socks.

"This is delicious, Grandma!" Yihong gushed. Chen had once been a bit of a flatterer himself, a trait that Yihong had inherited tenfold. Seeing it thrown back at him now was irritating. His mother grabbed Yihong's cheek and squeezed it, spooning more chicken broth into her grandson's bowl. Yihong had always been adored by everyone around him. When he was a baby, people on the street stopped to pet his curly black hair; as a teenager, Yihong never had a shortage of friends and girlfriends. Fan expected greatness out of him, but Chen felt that he saw his son for who he really was, with all his human failings. There was a lightness about his son, a devil-may-care-ness, a willful blindness to the heavy parts of life. He was not a boy who could take on the world, and so Chen would not expect that of him. Chen was not the kind of father who stretched his child to unreasonable limits—there was no shortage of fathers like these; he'd seen it with so many of his friends and their sons, and some had risen to the challenge, while others had rocketed and fizzled—and therefore his son had lived a blissful if predictable life. What Fan didn't understand was that that was the best kind of life.

"Ma said she went to the state fair," Yihong said, slurping up the broth with a wet smack. "They had fried butter on a stick. Sounds disgusting. I wanna taste that." Chen looked to his mother; at least here was evidence that he had not simply fabricated the America trip to explain Fan's absence. But his mother did not return his glance. He opened his phone and checked Fan's WeChat. "July 2. The Illinois State Fair is as ludicrous as ever. People walk around shirtless holding turkey legs the size of my arm! The only difference now is, the butter is five dollars instead of fifty cents."

"You can't even drink milk," Chen reminded him. "I don't think you would like fried butter." But Yihong was already showing his parents photos of the condo Chen planned to buy for him. It was a three-bedroom unit in the upscale Xiangheyuan subdivision in Chaoyang, its crowning feature the endless amenities: indoor pool, fitness center, computer center, even an on-site daycare. Rufeng held on to his arm as she gazed at the photos, adding supplementary comments, her right hand playing with the edge of Yihong's T-shirt. "Here is where you're gonna fatten me up," Yihong laughed, pointing at the quartz-lined kitchen.

"And here is where you'll work off the fat!" she said, pointing at the fitness room, then at the laundry machine. "And do our laundry, of course!"

"Yes, Sergeant!" Yihong saluted her. Everyone laughed. Rufeng's way with words bested even Yihong. That, coupled with her respectable degree and hardscrabble upbringing, made her the clear family favorite.

Chen plunged his chopsticks into the chicken, the meat falling right off the bones into his waiting bowl. Rufeng offered his parents the largest pieces first. Fan had always done this, given his parents the best cuts, and now Rufeng would carry on the practice. He looked at his son, his head bowed over his bowl as he shoveled rice and chicken into his mouth with relish, a strand of hair hanging down boyishly so that it almost touched his bowl, Rufeng teasing him about a piece of sauce that had gotten stuck on the edge of his mouth, and for an instant he saw a portrait of him and Fan at their happiest. It made him sad; it made him feel that joy was so brief. How would Yihong drive Rufeng away one day?

Yihong and Rufeng left after dinner; they had a birthday party to attend. In the silent void they left behind, Chen heard his mother turn off the faucet in the kitchen.

"If you are fighting, she can always come here," she said. "No need to go all the way back to America. After all, this was her home."

Embarrassment flooded Chen. His mother was no fool, it was true, but he felt slapped in the face by her bald observation.

"What do you mean?" Chen said. "She had a trip."

His mother sighed deeply then, a full-bellied sigh that seemed to empty her whole body and release a stream of melancholy. "Chen ah," she said. "Do you remember playing farmer?"

It had been his favorite activity, playing pretend with his friends in the courtyard. They'd crouch in the dirt outside their building and dig small trenches, dropping in imaginary tomato seeds and using large sticks to hoe the ground. Chen would stand at intervals and survey the horizon, before dropping down and declaring, in a grave whisper, "Rain is coming." And then he and his friends would whip the backs of their imaginary oxen, urging them to go faster, faster, the rain is coming!

He steeled himself, knowing his mother was about to launch into one of her lectures.

"One day," his mother said, "you were playing alone. You planted your seeds, then sat on the ground, waiting for rain. But the rain didn't come. I watched you from this window and I wondered when you'd give up. I went outside and told you to come in for dinner, and you said you were waiting for the rain. Even after an hour, you refused to budge. I was so confused. The rain was fake! I even tried to say, 'Look, rain is coming!' But you shook your head and said, 'Not yet.' I wondered if I should force you to come in, or if I should let you stay there, and teach you a lesson about believing in silly things. I decided to let you stay there."

"And then, right as I was walking back up the steps to our building, the sky suddenly opened and rain poured down. Real rain. You jumped up, shrieking. 'The rain is here! The rain is here!' And then you joined me for dinner."

Chen remembered this. It had been a near holy moment, when the sky, which had moments earlier been blue and cloudless, suddenly darkened in a froth of condensation. Those first few droplets of water on his skin had been nothing less than godly; he had felt that with his sheer determination, he had willed the rain to come. After years of pretending, he had made rain.

"I have often thought of this day," his mother said. "And each time, I think, Xiao Chen, you will be okay, because you believe." She paused, setting the clean dishes in a stack on the counter with a clunk. "But then I realized you are believing in fake rain."

Over the years, his mother had grown increasingly opaque, telling tales that were only tenuously related to the issue at hand, and he felt that now, she had truly lost her mind. "I was a child, mother," he said. "Children believe in things that aren't real."

"Exactly," she said. Then she dried her hands on a towel and switched off the light. "Things won't happen just because you will them. Be a better husband, Xiao Chen. Do not simply let things be."

He left his parents' home and walked to the subway, passing the courtyard where he and his friends had planted seeds, the stump where he'd sat waiting for rain. He boarded an eastbound train. He admitted his mother's tale was not completely absurd. He would not let things simply be. Fan had gone to live out some ludicrous fantasy, but Chen would do what he'd done every day of his life: He would fulfill the task before him. His son needed a home, and so he would buy it. Subdistrict Supervisor Ding be damned—he would build the pool and get the money.

CHEN RETURNED to the subdistrict supervisor's office the next morning, this time dressed in a simple white collared shirt and a casual blazer. The same secretary from three days prior looked up at him, her fringe perfectly curled outward so that her hair presented her face to him like a surprise.

"Hi there," he said.

"Hello! Oh, it's you again!" The secretary smiled, then a look of confusion crossed her face. "Do you have—do you have an appointment?"

"I have a bag of wood ears for Subdistrict Supervisor Ding," Chen said, holding out a tote bag. "They're all the way from Mongolia, and have been known to treat colds in less than twenty-four hours. Tell him they're from Song Chen."

"My, that's very nice!" The secretary gasped and took the large bag from Chen. "You came all the way for this?"

"I just want to make sure Subdistrict Supervisor Ding is happy."

She gave him a smile. "All right, Mr. Song. I'll be sure to get it to him."

As he turned to go away, Chen pretended as if he had forgotten something. "I was wondering, as it is almost lunchtime, are there any good places around here to eat? It will take over an hour to get back to the city in traffic, and I'll be starving by then."

The secretary pondered, then took out a notepad and began writing a list of restaurants. "There are some casual eateries, noodles mainly, if you drive down the main road. There's also a cafeteria, which has many options, though it might be a little low-class for a man of your stature. I typically take my meals there."

He looked more closely at the woman and realized she was older than he'd initially thought. She was in her early or midthirties, probably, though her figure was still very good. Her skin gave her away, as years of caking makeup over her face for jobs such as this must have worn away the natural texture. From her neck dangled a gold pendant in the shape of a heart on a thin chain, and her fingernails were fastidiously painted a garish orange-pink: a younger woman's accoutrements.

"The cafeteria would be perfect! I love to have some variety. Also . . ." Chen then reached into his jacket pocket and pulled out a package of gum. "I noticed you like chewing gum. I always carry chewing gum on me, and I can never get through a whole pack fast enough, so I thought maybe you'd like it. I just got a new flavor. Strawberry."

The secretary's face lit up. "Why, that's so generous!"

"I find spearmint to be a little strong," he said, gesturing at her pile of green packages. "So I tend to chew fruit gum. Try it. You might prefer it too."

The secretary took the gum in her hand and nodded, smiling, then hurried to place the package in her drawer. "Thank you very much, sir," she said. Then she added, "I'm actually about to take lunch in a few minutes. I can walk you down there."

"You're so kind," said Chen with a smile.

THE CAFETERIA WAS in the basement of the building. Various vendors offered spicy rice noodles, hot pot, numbing-spice stir-fry, curry rice, barbecue, and vegetable dishes. Chen decided to get a simple spread of cucumber, pork, and mung bean porridge. He wanted to appear modest in front of the subdistrict supervisor's secretary. But the secretary, meanwhile, purchased a bubbling spicy stew, complete with fish ball skewers.

"Could I dine with you?" Chen asked, his voice nonchalant. "I get uncomfortable around strangers." He looked out at the expansive cafeteria. Around them sat various office workers, their ties undone or slung behind their shoulders, ladies with their feet tucked neatly under their seats.

"Of course!" she said. What an accommodating woman. He followed her to a white table with four orange plastic chairs and set his tray down with an assured plunk. The secretary sat down and swept her shoulder-length hair into a ponytail with one deft motion. He could feel his heart beating in his chest. He and Tao flirted with the women who accompanied them on their dinners out, but those were customary, coed relations within a recognizable framework. It had been a long time since he'd attempted to cozy up to a woman who was not in on the game.

"Ooooooh, yum!" she exclaimed. She grinned like a child setting off a firework. Chen was alarmed by this display of emotion. "Fish stew is my favorite," she said, pointing.

Chen grinned. "You must be from Sichuan."

"I have relatives from Sichuan who came to our home for the New Year one year when I was . . ." she thought for a moment, her chin tilting dramatically, her eyes flitting skyward. ". . . Eleven or twelve. Or was it thirteen?"

They paused as she remembered the exact age. "No, it was twelve. It was my last year of primary school. I was still wearing that terrible red-and-orange skirt uniform."

"Twelve," he parroted.

"Yes, twelve. I was twelve and my mother's brother came to visit with his wife and son. My aunt, my uncle's wife, she was a wonderful cook!" Her eyes glowed as she talked. "She cooked us fish with spices she'd brought from Sichuan, and I fell in love. When I was seventeen I traveled to Chengdu to find work and to live with my uncle and my aunt, and they made me real boiled fish stew for the first time. It was so delicious!" She stopped just then. "I'm sorry, I'm ranting about myself! You must want to eat your meal in peace. I will be quiet now." She made a whisper motion with her finger to her lips.

Chen smiled. The woman was chatty, but he found it a pleasant change from the cool quiet that pervaded his home these days. "No, please go on. It's nice to hear. I don't ever get to eat my meals with interesting people. I'm always scarfing my food down and hurrying on to the next meeting. You've blessed me today with your story! It must have been difficult for a young girl to try to find work in Chengdu."

She nodded. "It was. I was only able to stay in Chengdu for about a year before I went back home. After that very hard year I thought perhaps I would stay at home and help my family with the farm and raise my own family. That sort of life seemed to please most people. But I got restless and decided to try again in Guangzhou and then, later, Beijing."

"What a journey! That's very good," he said. "Beijing has many jobs." Although he normally muttered angrily under his breath at the migrant workers who clogged up the subway and who pretended to be amputees and begged on the streets, in this moment he felt a bolt of sympathy. She and he were not so different. They were both young people who had left their homes and gone somewhere completely alien, who had waged war with that beast, the unknown, and lived to tell the tale.

"Thank you," she said. "I began working in a factory that made rubber phone cases. Then I worked in a factory that made phone screens. I guess I was always working around phones. Technology is very exciting to me. Billions of RMB and hours of labor to manufacture something that can replicate the feeling of walking down the street and knocking on your neighbor's door. And yet it still falls short." She sighed. "Anyway, my boss admired my work ethic and promoted me to sell phones in a market in Haidian. That's where I met Subdistrict Supervisor

Ding. I sold him a new phone and gave him a nice discount because I knew he was the subdistrict supervisor in Konggang. I made it my job to know all of the local politicians in case they ever came into the store, and he was so impressed that I knew who he was that he offered me a job!"

"You're very resourceful. No wonder Subdistrict Supervisor Ding admired you!" Chen said. Ding really was a self-obsessed guy. "You must have been a very talented saleswoman." Tao had once told him the trick to winning over a woman's heart was relentless affirmation. Whatever she said, you agreed with. This tactic had never worked on Fan, who hated hollow platitudes, but for the larger population, it really did help grease the wheels.

"I did have a knack for it. Sometimes I miss the bustle of the sales floor. But this job is a much easier life, and I am learning so much more about bookkeeping and how to keep a calendar and other useful skills."

"Those are all very valuable things to know," he said. He noticed he had eaten most of his food during the secretary's story, and he told himself to slow down so as not to offend her. He took a sip of his tea. "So where is your hometown?"

"I'm from Shandong, from a small town called Ligezhuang. It's very beautiful," she said. "But there was nothing for me there."

Of course. She was from Ligezhuang. A town that bordered Fan's. No wonder her voice was so familiar. He was struck, suddenly, by a wave of nostalgia, the kind of feeling he'd have when he met fellow Beijingers in America. Meeting someone from your hometown, a fellow of the same home, out there in the big world. He had found Fan's voice deliriously charming when they'd first met, her tones always sloping upward in a feeling of perpetual interrogation. This secretary's voice had this exact quality.

"You've only just started working with Subdistrict Supervisor Ding, yes?" Chen said. "Last time I came several months ago he had a different secretary."

"Yes, it's been around six months. I only briefly met the previous secretary, she seemed like a nice girl. I heard she was leaving to get married," she said.

He saw her glance at her watch, an Apple Watch. He wondered how she could own something as expensive as that. It was ten minutes to noon. So far they had not discussed anything of value, and he began panicking.

"I've known Subdistrict Supervisor Ding for a long time," he said. "I've worked on buildings all across his district. I spearheaded the building of the Heavenly Earth subdivision five years ago."

"Those are beautiful homes," she said, politely. "Is that what you came to discuss with him the other day?"

"Yes," he said. "I am building a new home at Heavenly Earth, for an American couple. I came to Subdistrict Supervisor Ding for his sign-off on a recreational pool that they want me to add to the construction."

Her eyes widened. "Wow—American clients! You're quite worldly, Song Chen sir."

As expected, she was impressed. "I work with Americans all the time," he said. "Actually," he found himself continuing, "I used to work there."

The secretary gasped, and Chen saw a flicker of excitement ignite in her eyes. "In America?" she said. "Why were you there?"

"I was a graduate student," he said. "In mathematics. I was the best in my class back in Beijing, the best in my class in America too. It was an amazing experience. I went to see the Niagara Falls, the Sears Tower in Chicago, New York City . . . New York City is unlike any other city in the world. It's nearly as crowded as Beijing! They sell food from carts off the street. And I saw a Broadway show! Tom Hanks starred!" Faintly, these memories pulsed in Chen's mind, memories he'd long buried. He couldn't tell which parts were real and which parts he'd fabricated for the secretary's benefit. He hadn't spoken about his time in America to a stranger in many years, but there was something about Fan's departure that loosened the memories inside him. "Eventually, I became interested in architecture, and when Beijing experienced a housing boom in the nineties, I decided it was the perfect time to come home." What a way to describe his return. It was not a lie, but he was struck by the way a truth could be stated just a bit differently and its meaning could change entirely. It seemed to suffice for the secretary.

"Wow! I would love to go to America," she said, wistful. "Beijing is about as far from home as I've ever been. And Beijing is such a hard place to live. I cannot imagine going somewhere like New York City!"

"What you have done is very brave," he said. "Beijing is its own terrible beast. It's hard . . . it is hard to go anywhere unknown."

She nodded, wide-eyed.

"So anyway," he continued. "As you can see, I have always relished a challenge. My client wants a pool, so I will give him a pool. I'm in the business of making dreams come true." Then he allowed his shoulders to fall slightly. "Sadly, Subdistrict Supervisor Ding wouldn't approve it. He said that it wouldn't be fair to the other residents."

"Why, that seems a bit silly, doesn't it?" she said. Then she slapped a hand over her mouth. "I'm sorry. I don't mean to disagree with Subdistrict Supervisor Ding. But I don't see how this has anything to do with fairness."

"He says it would set a bad precedent. Everyone would start demanding a pool."

"Now I'm even more perplexed! Wouldn't it be so nice if every house had its own pool? In fact," she continued, building in passion, "if such a swimming pool existed in this complex, perhaps the other residents would be inspired to swim themselves. And that would contribute to the overall fitness of our country!"

"Exactly!" Chen said, slapping the table. "Ah, it's too bad Subdistrict Supervisor Ding can't look at a situation from all sides like you can. Not to badmouth Subdistrict Supervisor

Ding. Like I said, we go back many years. But it's good that he has smart people around him to steer him in the right direction."

The secretary blushed. "That's too kind," she said. She steeled her gaze at him suddenly and said, "Maybe I could try to talk to him."

"You would do that?" Chen said, his eyebrows flying up. "I don't want to put you in an uncomfortable position."

"It's not a problem. Subdistrict Supervisor Ding always listens to me. We play chess every afternoon and I let him beat me. And he knows it."

"He's lucky to have company like you," Chen said. He wondered if she'd be offended by his word choice, company. He turned his attention to his plate and quickly finished off the last of his cucumbers. The other workers had begun to clear out. Chen wiped his mouth with a napkin and stood up.

"Well, Miss . . ." he said.

"Guilin," she said. "Surname Xie."

"Guilin, like the national park?"

She nodded. "My parents had always wanted to visit. They never got to."

"They have good taste in names," he said. "'The mountains and waters of Guilin are like heaven on earth itself.'" He quoted the popular phrase. "Thank you very much for this delightful lunch."

She rose with her tray of stew. "I had a very nice time myself," she said. "I will try to talk to Subdistrict Supervisor Ding."

"I look forward to hearing back," he said.

They walked over to the bussing area and slid their trays onto a conveyor belt. Guilin took her ponytail down, then retrieved a compact mirror from her purse to examine her fringe, tucking an errant piece behind her ear.

Chen noticed a tiny spot of grease on her sweater. He felt sad seeing that grease spot. He thought she must not have very many sweaters, and it seemed like a nice one. It was pale yellow, so the grease showed very prominently on the right edge near her collarbone.

They walked up the stairs wordlessly. His phone pinged. He glanced at his screen and saw that Fan had posted a new photo. He looked over at the secretary, who was busy tapping away at her own phone. He opened the notification. There Fan was, standing on campus, wearing a flaming scarlet top that hugged her waist tightly and jeans that he felt were a bit low-slung for a woman of her age. The campus was swollen with green, the trees heaving under their leaves. "*Long time no see*," was all she said. In English. He wondered who had taken the photo for her. Was it Qiong? "*Long time no see*"—did this refer to the setting of the photo or the person Fan was looking at? Had she been on her way to see Qiong at his office, and had they run into each other on the path—he could imagine her yelps of happy surprise— and then had he suggested the photo, Let's capture you, you look beautiful, as young as the day you left, here, pose like this, throw your right arm in the air. Or had the meeting been less frantic; perhaps they had made a date and met each other at this spot and he had taken the photo for her in a more measured fashion. He imagined the man behind the camera just beyond capture, his thumb hovering on the shutter button, beaming at his wife in the viewfinder, happy with the results, happy with his results—for she was a product of him; she had always been a product of him.

"All righty," Guilin said, depositing her phone in her pocket as they reached the landing. She turned to Chen and gave him a wave. "It was nice to meet you, Mr. Song." Then she was off to her desk, her larger-than-average head bobbing up and down as she rushed to answer the trilling of a phone.

3

He kept a slim crew for the pool, just a few of the younger guys to dig and operate the crane, and his water and electrical team. The schedule was tight, and he couldn't wait for Ding's approval to come in; he simply had to start and hope that the secretary would work her magic and deliver good news. And so the Monday after his lunch with the secretary, just as the July heat arrived in Beijing with a humid fury, Chen and his crew started digging. It was not his job, but he liked to get dirty sometimes; it made him feel young again, reminded him of his last years in America, and it was different getting dirty because you wanted to as opposed to because someone else had ordered you to.

They dug the pool in two days, and then it was time to lay the steel rebar. He stood at the edge of the pool instructing while three of his nimbler workers laid in the rebar bit by bit until it formed an undulating chessboard across the concave opening. It was equal parts beautiful and grotesque, this distended steel mass; it seemed impossible now that this thing would ever become something still and relaxing. At noon the sun was high and heavy, and Chen collapsed on the patio.

He called Fan. They had not spoken on the phone since she'd departed over a week earlier. It was nearing midnight where she was, and he felt guilty, for a moment, wondering if he would wake her.

He was surprised when she picked up the phone.

"Hi," she said, her voice alert. She had not been sleeping.

"How's the trip?" he asked.

"It's great," she said. "Sorry I haven't sent many updates. It's been crazy. We're in New York right now. We decided to take the week and go on a road trip. Me, A Fang, Keqin, and Nannan."

New York? Nannan? Nannan had been a cold and awkward girl, a classmate that none of them really liked, one whom Fan on multiple occasions had attempted to befriend, only to be met with hostility. Nannan was the kind of lone wolf who didn't believe that camaraderie fostered anything but laziness. Chen was not surprised she had stayed in America, but he was certainly surprised she and Fan were now friends, and on a road trip in New York together. "Nannan?" he said. "I thought you hated her."

"That was so long ago," Fan said, which was not really an explanation. The passage of time did not automatically make terrible people palatable. "She's living in New York now. Her daughter works for Apple."

Was this what made her more easygoing now? Nannan had achieved the success she'd so desired, and now had time for friends? Or was it that Nannan's accomplishments made her more attractive to Fan, so it didn't matter what her personality was like? His wife really could be blinded by the glittery things. "Well, be safe," he said, suddenly wanting to exit the conversation. These days, every conversation with his wife made him feel that everyone in the world knew her better than he did.

"Okay," she said. "Did you finish the house?"

"Still have a few weeks," he said, softening. "They're having a housewarming on August 11."

"Um, yeah, that's nice," she said, though she now sounded distracted, as if her mouth was far away from the receiver. "Is that one empty?" he heard her say, in the distance.

"Are you out right now?"

"Sorry, yes," she said. "We're coming back from dinner."

"Will you be back by then?"

That question seemed to get her attention. "Right, I forgot to tell you. I'm extending my trip."

"What?"

"I felt it was silly to stay for just three weeks."

"Well, will you be back by then?" he repeated. "The 11th."

There was a pause on the other side. "I'll be back by then," she echoed. Then she hung up.

He gritted his teeth. He didn't believe her. His wife had disappeared into a wrinkle in the Western Hemisphere, and he found it hard to believe she would ever return. She was frolicking around the streets of New York City at midnight with a woman she hated, and he was sitting in an open plot somewhere past the Fifth Ring, his fingernails caked with dirt. The gap between them seemed impassable.

He thought again about those first years in Beijing. Fan had admired Chen's ability to do both the common man's work and the elevated man's, admired it the way she admired the city around her. Once, things had genuinely impressed her.

He thought of the day he'd taken Fan to eat roast duck for the first time. He and Fan dressed up for the occasion, though he did not remember what either of them were wearing, only that they had splurged on a taxi because Chen had not wanted their clothes getting dirty on the bus.

At the door, two lines of girls wearing qipao dresses had greeted them in unison, cooing an enthusiastic "Welcome!"

Fan had turned around, embarrassed, and asked, "Are they waiting for someone important?" And he had smiled and said, yes, and that important person has arrived. She had blushed and for this moment, this Beijing was the place he had promised her, the place she had dreamed of. A city where no matter who you were, you would get a welcome fit for an emperor.

But dazzling things always tarnished over time. The half-life of admiration could be startlingly short. As the years passed, Fan's awe for the city faded. She no longer swiveled her head at the bicycle swarms or the neon lights, no longer batted an eye at the women in qipao bowing in restaurants. Beijing became simply a city she was living in, no longer a tourist destination, and with that change came a more discerning eye. She began pointing out that the waitresses' dresses were cheaply made, that the road infrastructure in Beijing was messy, and that it wouldn't be surprising if she ended up in an accident one day trying to avoid those damn cyclists. She kept a box of her old textbooks in the back of their bedroom closet; once he came home to see them splayed open across their bed, and Fan hunched over, tabbing through each with such focus that she didn't notice him standing at the door for a full minute. He had been confused about what had brought on the sudden walk down memory lane, and she'd gotten defensive, setting off on a rant about how mind-numbing her job was and it was no wonder society was reaching its nadir when its elite minds were treated like human calculators, their potential wasted for the purpose of profit. "The problem with this city," she started saying, "is that everyone is a king pretending to be a Communist." She talked more and more about their friends who were thriving in America, keeping meticulous track of every shiny new position Jia Yinhao attained at Google, at Facebook; Meng Haian's award for his work at NASA; how A Fang's daughter had gotten into MIT at age sixteen. In her tone he could hear the implication: And what, Chen, do you have to show for your decision?

The American couple's lawn was piled high with debris, and he was abruptly overwhelmed by the task ahead of him.

His phone rang.

"Mr. Song Chen?" came the voice on the other end. He recognized the secretary's upward lilt.

"Yes?" he said, not wanting to appear too eager.

"I hope this is a convenient time," she said. "I finally got the chance to speak with Subdistrict Supervisor Ding. He's been out of town this week. But then we played our usual game of chess yesterday afternoon and I allowed him to win, as always. Then I started complaining that the weather was getting warm and that I wished to do some more physically challenging activities, like tennis or swimming. I bragged that I was a star athlete in high school, and Subdistrict Supervisor Ding thought that was quite funny. I think the mention of swimming caused him to think of you, because then he grew sheepish and said, well, actually, you had wanted to build a swimming pool for your clients, but he rejected your proposal. I became very piqued at that point, whining in that way that many men enjoy, asking him why he would do such a thing. He then let out a long sigh and said that perhaps he would reconsider!" The secretary recounted all this with the rush and furtiveness of a spy who has successfully completed a mission, and Chen found his heart racing.

"Why—why—that's amazing, Miss Guilin!" Chen exclaimed. "That's so wonderful to hear!"

"I am happy to help," Guilin said. "The one caveat is, he demands an invitation to their housewarming, should they have one. He loves a party."

Chen was elated. "Yes," he said. "I'm sure that can be arranged! Thank you, Miss Guilin!" The words tumbled out of his mouth, rushing faster than he could think. Perhaps what he said next was a product of Fan's distance, some desperate flailing attempt to stick it to her, enact revenge, send out some sort of siren call so that she'd be tempted to return. "There's a new action movie playing at the IMAX theater at Joy City. I would love to take you there as a gesture of my appreciation."

There was a pause on the phone, and Chen worried that he had offended her.

"I love action movies!" she finally said. "That would be delightful, Mister Song."

THE FOLLOWING SUNDAY, Chen found himself inside a women's clothing store in Joy City. A pop song played on the speakers in the mall, some English-language warbling clashing with various computerized noises. All of Beijing was a mall now. You could not walk out on the street and into a noodle shop without having to first ride an escalator into a shopping complex. He wondered when this change had occurred. It had been a long time since he had bought a gift for a woman.

The saleswoman standing near the rack of coats wore a large smile, too large of a smile for her tiny face. She greeted him with a sparkling "Huan ying guang lin!" as he walked through the sliding doors. She was practically a teenager. He asked her where the sweaters were.

"What kind of sweater are you looking for?" The woman smiled, and he could see her assessing him, calculating how much effort she should put into this sale given the spending potential of her customer. That morning Chen had put on an expensive but casual sport coat, as well as a Cartier watch, which had been a gift from a previous client. She spoke enthusiastically. "Pullover? Knit? Cardigan? Cropped?"

He didn't recognize these words. "I want . . . an open sweater. With buttons. A yellow sweater."

"We don't have any yellow sweaters, sir. We do have some heavier sweatshirts with buttons at the front wall, or we also have a new line of jackets here in the middle . . ." She gestured toward a multicolored display helmed by two mannequins with short blonde wigs. "If you're looking for something a little more fashion-forward."

There were so many options, and none fit the bill. Capitalism had truly failed them all, Chen thought. He made toward the display and gave it a perfunctory glance, fingering the edge of a T-shirt before turning around and leaving the store, hoping the saleswoman was not still watching him.

As it turned out, it was difficult to find sweaters for sale in summer. After four or five stores with similar American pop soundtracks blaring and similar fresh-faced young women ready to pounce on his wallet, he found a light-yellow button-down sweater—a "cardigan," according to the saleswoman—that was not quite the same shade but similar enough that he thought, should she look at it under bright light, Guilin might believe it to be so.

He walked over to the giant Chanel poster outside the Starbucks, the sweater wrapped in gauzy gift paper and dangling from his arm in a bag of an embarrassingly thick material. It made the gift seem very lavish, when in fact the cardigan had been rather inexpensive.

He saw Guilin approach minutes later and could tell from far away that she was wearing the same yellow cardigan. He felt sweat in his armpits.

"Hello," he said.

"Nice to see you again, Song Chen sir!"

"Here," he said, thrusting the bag forward.

"For me?"

"It's—well, open it and I will explain."

She took the paper-wrapped bundle out of the bag and opened it. "What—it's a cardigan! A yellow cardigan!" Her expression was of not-hostile confusion. She took it out and compared it to her own. "It looks very similar!"

"I saw that you dirtied your sweater when we had lunch," he explained. "So I bought you a new one."

"Dirty?" she said, her eyes widening, as she scrambled to find the stain on herself.

Chen's body went cold and he was struck by the rudeness of his gift. "I didn't mean to offend!"

Then she laughed. "I'm kidding, Song Chen sir! I am always getting my clothes dirty. This will keep me from embarrassing myself in front of Subdistrict Supervisor Ding." She folded the cardigan back into its heavy bag and nodded. "That's very kind of you."

They watched the new Tom Cruise action movie in a large, empty theater. Guilin stared intently the entire time, yelping blissfully at heroic moments and looking crestfallen during moments of failure. Chen thought the movie was okay. Tom Cruise was fun to watch, but the plots of his movies were always similar: a spy went on a mission, where he seduced attractive women and had rivals who were nearly as manly as he but not quite. Chen was not a very animated movie watcher, and during the most dramatic moments his face remained as still as a rock, even if inside he did feel anxious or sad or happy for the characters.

When the credits rolled, Guilin remained fixed to her seat, her eyes glued on the screen, her two hands gripping the armrests. She stared and stared until the lights in the movie theater came up and a skinny boy in a striped shirt came out to sweep the aisles. She finally stood, bouncing lightly on her feet as she did, and then walked out of the theater. Chen followed.

"That movie wasn't very good," she finally said, as they exited the theater's sliding doors.

Chen was alarmed. "You seemed to enjoy it!"

"I give myself fully to the cinematic experience," she said. "I like to be as engaged as possible, so that I can always be honest about my opinion of a movie. If I am distracted and gazing off in the distance instead of concentrating on a character, maybe I would later think the movie was boring, but that would be a flawed assessment, because what if I could have liked it, if I had only been more engaged? I once watched 'Finding Mr. Right' with my good friend, but my mind was preoccupied that day because I was going through a breakup. At the end of the movie, when my friend asked me what I thought, I didn't even know what to say, because I had barely remembered any of it! That is why I always put myself in the world and let myself feel what the characters are feeling, and try to catch every detail and dialogue and expression on everyone's faces, so that I know, 100 percent, if the movie was good at the end. And because I have done that I can say that I didn't think that movie was very good. I didn't feel enough for Tom Cruise."

Chen thought about her words. "I agree," he said. "The movie was okay. But I always feel this way about these sorts of action movies. They're all fun but not spectacular."

"You've watched a lot of them?" she asked.

"I used to watch a lot of American movies. 'The Terminator.' 'The Graduate.' 'Taxi Driver.' There's an American movie where two men dress up as women. . . . I thought that was very funny!"

"Oh?" she said, turning to him, her eyes alight. "Which one was that?"

"It's an old movie. It stars Marilyn Monroe. The two actors are very good. There's action and suspense. Romance and laughter. One of the men runs off to marry an old playboy! It's all very ridiculous."

She laughed loudly. She had a high-pitched laugh that was somewhere between a scream and a squeal. Chen found it not unpleasant. He asked if she was hungry. There were many restaurants in the mall she could choose from.

She shook her head. They walked in silence for a while, past advertisements for clothing stores—Vero Moda, MINISO, Mango—and he watched Guilin's eyes light up at the spindly women in blazers and leather jackets. At turns she took out her phone and snapped a photo of an outfit. He noticed that her phone, too, was top-of-the-line, the newest Samsung Galaxy. She caught him staring and blushed. "I like to keep an archive of all the things I hope to wear one day."

"You already look nice," he said.

She covered her face with her hands. "You should have seen me a year ago. Or two years ago. I'm always improving, which is the most you can do in this life."

He saw that her phone background was of a young woman. She looked vaguely familiar, like a celebrity, but he couldn't place her.

"Who is that?"

She smiled. "It's my friend."

"Is she from the village?"

"No," Guilin said. "I met her when I came to Beijing."

A thought came to him.

"Actually," he began, "would you like to take a look at the house I'm building?"

She cocked her head at him, and for a moment he felt ashamed; the invitation could be construed as improper. But then her eyebrows flew up and she smiled. "I am quite curious. Wealthy people fascinate me."

Minutes later, they were in his car on their way past the Fifth Ring.

GUILIN THOUGHT the house was the most gorgeous thing she'd ever seen. She used these exact words, "gorgeous" and "ever"—he was starting to realize this woman loved to operate in hyperbole, but in a way that made you actually believe it was something that could change her life. It was charming—he wished Fan would experiment with hyperbole once in a while, embellish her assessments instead of remaining so stubbornly committed to the tepid truth.

Chen thought there were few things in life more delightful than being in this position, showing an excited woman something newfangled. He thought of Fan and the small gasp she'd made, tasting her first bite of roast duck.

They walked into the living room, which spilled magnanimously out into the backyard. Little Bin was crouched down in the would-be pool, hammering tiles into the bottom. "This will be where they entertain guests," Chen explained, spreading his arms in the open space. He gestured at the soaring ceiling. Then he led her into an expansive kitchen. From the ceiling he'd suspended a large sculptural lamp that Vivian had selected, from Japan. "But I suspect this is where they'll spend most of their time."

Guilin ambled through the house with a pious air. She traced her fingertips across the countertops, her touch featherweight, as if she were scared she might break them. Chen watched her from the other side of the counter. She grabbed the handle of the oven, a 70,000 RMB Miele with a touch display and self-cleaning capabilities, and swung it open. She ducked and gripped some invisible object, then launched herself up from her thighs and sang out in a ringing voice, "Thanksgiving dinner is ready!" Chen watched as she set the imaginary pan on the counter. She leaned over and pretended to smell her roast. "It's so good!" She gave Chen a look, and he smirked, bemused. This woman was a strange one. "Hubby, you want a taste?"

His face reddened, but he leaned over, his body stiff, inviting whatever sat on her imaginary spoon into his mouth with a gauche scoop of his lower lip. "It tastes great," he said, discomfort rising in his throat. Then she laughed and waved her hand in front of her face: playtime was over.

"Did you live in a place like this?" she asked. "In America?"

Chen's chest swelled a bit. It was nice that this woman saw him as she saw the owners of this house, as worldly and unthinkably wealthy. But he suddenly felt an unbearable exhaustion, as if the past two decades of carrying around the burden of being impressive were finally caving in on him. In this instant, staring back at her with her open eyes, he wished to be honest.

"No," he finally said. "I always lived in very small apartments." He thought about his and Meng Haian's and Jia Yinhao's dark first-floor apartment; he thought about his and Fan's drab studio, the bird shit–streaked windows.

Guilin seemed surprised. "Really?" she said.

Little Bin poked his head into the kitchen at this moment. "Do you need anything, boss?"

Chen waved him off. "Just walking around, Little Bin. Keep working."

Little Bin slunk off, and Chen swallowed, wondering if Guilin would continue her inquiry. He found himself wanting her to ask more, his past a marble on his tongue that he wished to excise—that perhaps, if burnished by light, would reveal itself to be a jewel.

"You were saying?" she said, her eyes expectant.

"Yes," he said. "It was very hard in America. The last place I lived . . ." He gestured at the sides of the space around them. "No bigger than this kitchen."

She nodded, but instead of dismissing him with a pitying chuckle, her eyes widened. "Wow . . . you are just like one of those entrepreneurs. Like Jack Ma. He came from nothing and built an empire for himself."

Chen was tickled by this comparison. He supposed he and Jack Ma did have this in common; they were two men who'd built a life out of nothingness. He felt grateful to this woman, who did not sneer in the face of his admission. "That's very kind," he began. "Yes, America is not an endless well of opportunity, like they tell us. It wasn't until I came back to Beijing that I finally lived somewhere nice. America—America is hard. They say it's the place where dreams come true, but I find it is actually the opposite." He had not said so much about his time in America to anyone since he'd left. He felt Fan's absence like a phantom; the more time she spent back in that place, the more the power of its memory seemed to grow in Chen.

"Success is most delicious when preceded by struggle," Guilin continued. "I see my life and its struggle as one grand story. There are my humble beginnings in the village. The kids all made fun of me for being stouter; they'd call me 'ox girl,' and I'd hide away in my mother's kitchen, playing a mandolin my grandfather had carved me. Then my turbulent years selling CDs and handbags in Chengdu and Guangzhou, where I learned to run fast from the police when they'd come to take our wares away. Then my move to Beijing, where I bunked with five other girls and biked twenty miles to work each day." It took Chen a moment to realize she was speaking of her current situation in past tense, already turning present pain into lore. "I tell myself that one day, when I write my autobiography, these will be the chapters that everyone adores, the ones that give my readers hope. Because they will see that even I succeeded." She beamed at him, her optimism radiating in infectious waves. They really were so similar; she, too, was fighting against impossible odds.

Guilin's phone rang. She answered, her voice sugary. It was Ding, and a surprising feeling of rancor rose inside Chen. The man could never let Guilin have a moment to herself, could he. She moved away from Chen, toward the front of the house, and he watched her go.

Chen remained in the kitchen, staring at the veiny pattern on the marble countertops. How, he wondered, had everything changed for him in America? English had dealt the first blow. Ultimately, success among their cohort was determined not by their competence in their field, or even their street savvy and general life skills, but by how American they could become. Their island of Chinese students confronted this question disparately. Chen had never paid much attention in English class back home and had passed the TOEFL with average results. It was a subject that he neither excelled at nor particularly struggled with, and so he never gave it much thought. He did his problem sets just fine; his English reading pace was reasonable. When he first met Fan, her English was abysmal. Fan had only a couple of years of village high school English under her belt and had barely passed her TOEFL. Fan told Chen that her first week of class, English sounded like a storm around her. She went home and read her textbook all night, reciting it loudly into the mirror. "CHAPTER FOUR. ENDOGENOUS AND EXOGENOUS INFORMATION STRUCTURES," she shouted, her mouth twisting around the O's and U's and her nostrils flaring. She did this every night. Fan shared a room with a muscly American girl who spent all her time in the living room painting her toenails, and she'd laugh with barely contained vitriol every time Fan shouted in front of the mirror. Fan didn't care. She would practice her English with

Chen, starting conversations in English, asking him, "*How was your day?*" and he would respond, "*Good,*" but after a while, each time, his face would redden and he would switch back over to Chinese, embarrassed by the silly activity. He hated the way he sounded in English, hated knowing the difference between how he should sound and how he actually did. This was the curse of having a brilliant mind but a stupid tongue; he could always tell where things were wrong, but he could not force his tongue to comply. He'd never known himself to be at a loss for words, but in English he became someone quiet, someone withdrawn. He became a different person entirely. And he didn't see the point. His friends were Chinese, and who knew if he'd even stay in this country past graduation? He was young; he still believed he could have every dream.

Fan began insisting that they speak English at dinner with their classmates, even invited a few American classmates to sit with them. Their cohort reacted in various ways, some eager to practice their English, others wary, electing to sit on the fringes and whisper quietly to each other in Chinese, or, eventually, to break off into a separate table. Fan also gave herself an English name, *Fiona*. As with *Robert*, she loved to enunciate each syllable every time she introduced herself—*my name is* FEE-OH-NAH *Jiang*, she would say. Meng Haian—now *Martin*—joined a local rugby league, and he soon became the most Americanized of all, gleaning inside jokes from his teammates and bringing them back home. Jia Yinhao developed a love for American sitcoms, and many nights Chen would come home from the library in the early morning hours to find him on the couch, his eyes glued to the television.

Chen did not hop on the all-American bandwagon. He had no interest in American friends, so he wasn't going to give himself some schmaltzy American name and pretend he didn't hear their barely contained snickers just to join their inane conversations about football, the war, George Bush, football. These were men who thought they held sway over the matters of the world but, in fact, all they really cared about was football. He refused to play this game. He was Song Chen, top of his class, the one who'd be expected to publish his dissertation immediately after graduating. He did not need to be great at anything he wasn't already great at; after all, his intelligence had brought him this far, hadn't it?

And so he watched his peers Americanize around him. Fan and Qiong got closer as she began teaching sections of his class. In front of others, they would speak in English, their repartee jaunty and full of idioms. To Chen, they sounded ridiculous, and each time he heard them he'd will the Americans around them not to listen, not to pick apart their syntactical inaccuracies, their anachronistic references. The astonishing thing was—even at the height of her English competence, Fan's English never sounded remotely close to native. In any language she sounded always like a girl from a village outside Qingdao, her emphases unpredictable, her sentences forever bobbing on the invisible raft of an upward-sliding second tone. But she never cared. She was not afraid to ask questions when she was confused, often raising her hand and saying, *"Can you please repeat that?"* and ignoring the snickers among her classmates. Embarrassment wasn't in Fan's vocabulary. That was the key difference between Fan and Chen.

His refusal to join the bandwagon did not cost him much initially. The first few years in school, Chen was able to coast on his research and class performance. But as his peers started nabbing internships and interviewing for jobs even before graduation, the gaps began to show. He could no longer postpone becoming American when it came to interviewing; interviewing demanded he be American in every way that he could not; it demanded that he speak, which was impossible. The words on his would-be colleagues' lips were the *Chicago Bulls, Michael Jackson, Seinfeld, Operation Desert Storm, Madonna, Roseanne, Mikhail Gorbachev, Queen.* He could respond passably to the important questions—tell me about your research experience, what is your work history—but when asked to elaborate, he could only stutter out a few words sandwiched between long stretches of silence. It was not enough to perform passably; English was wedded to a furious and specific perfection, and anything less than perfection was tantamount to buffoonery. Each interview ended the same way, with the same kind, pitying look, and five words that signaled the final condemnation: "*Thank you for your time.*"

It was becoming amply clear that to thrive in America, he could not simply be stellar in his own language. He indeed had to, despite what he'd told Fan that first week of class, translate himself into something they could understand.

But he couldn't. He could not be like Fan, or Qiong, who seemed to relish the humiliation, calling himself "*that Chinese guy*"—"*You must be pretty surprised your professor's a Chinese guy, huh?*" was how he kicked off every semester, a shtick that tickled the shameful, stuck-up parts of his students' brains. Robert Qiong prostrated himself at the feet of his American peers, sacrificed his own name on the altar of American fraternity, erased himself to become one of them. He would never do that, Chen had vowed early on. The day he'd met that man and those cloying English words had trickled from his mouth—*good for you*—he vowed he'd never dance for Americans like Robert Qiong.

He thought about a dinner party he and Fan had hosted at her apartment their last year of school. Most of his peers had already settled their post-grad plans, some with high-paying jobs in Chicago or even New York City, others, like Fan, continuing at the university in coveted research positions. Chen's research was coming to a close, and he yearned to be in the job force. It was Christmastime, and Fan had invited a few of their close friends from the cohort over for dinner. She had also invited Qiong. Fan had spent a large portion of her stipend that month on a duck, ham, shallots, clumps of fragrant garlic, fingerling potatoes, and a host of spices she and Chen had never smelled, and had spent the entire day in the kitchen, attempting to make a real American holiday spread. Ham was a pinkish and unruly thing neither Fan nor Chen understood how to judge the temperature of, so she baked it for so long it came apart in crumbles.

Qiong arrived dressed, as always, in his crisp white shirt and suit jacket. He handed Fan a bottle of red wine and his coat to hang. Chen grabbed the coat and delighted in the look of alarm that crossed Qiong's face at the proprietary gesture.

"Careful with that," Qiong then said. "It's heavy." He was finally speaking Chinese, much to Chen's relief.

The party sat on folding chairs and on the couch, crowded around a coffee table Fan had salvaged from the sidewalk. Fan's mother had wrapped her dishes in twelve layers of newspaper and forced Fan to bring them with her to America. That night Fan served overcooked ham on her mother's celadon plates. It was a beautiful meal.

Chen watched Fan and Qiong. Fan turned her body toward Qiong like a sunflower arching skyward, and Chen could see a light in her eyes as Qiong pontificated about the petty drama within the department and his daughter's newfound belief that she was a cat. Fan giggled like a schoolgirl. Qiong spoke of his family's recent trip to Aix-en-Provence, a city Chen had never heard of, and Rome, and a smorgasbord of other cities, some of which Chen had only ever seen in movies or in the little Shakespeare he had managed to understand in school, and others not at all. "Dirty city," Qiong said of Rome, with a dismissive wave, as if Fan and Chen had been planning a sparkling pan-European vacation as well. "Skip it."

Later, while Fan was washing the dishes, and Meng Haian and Jia Yinhao had momentarily stepped away for reasons Chen could no longer remember, he found himself alone at the table with Qiong, nursing matching beers. Chen did not like sitting there with the man and was suddenly jealous of women—women who could live their lives in secret, women who no matter what had ten minutes at the end of dinner to run away and wash the dishes in the kitchen.

Chen took a large swig from his beer. Qiong drank his. Chen suddenly felt that they were having a drinking battle. He looked around nervously, was about to rise to go assist Fan when Qiong put his bottle down and asked, "How do you like it here? In America?"

"It's . . . fine," Chen said.

"Takes a while to get used to. It's so different from home," he said.

Chen could only laugh bitterly. Back in China he'd have absolutely nothing in common with a man from Shanxi. But here, their black hair and mother tongue suddenly made them fellows of the same home.

"What do you feel is so different?" Chen decided to ask.

Qiong gave him a long look. "Well, everything. First of all, Americans just have a little more class. They're not spitting on the ground and squatting on the sidewalk. People help each other out. There is a sense of neighborhood, of camaraderie. And most importantly, in America, things are fair. Everyone has the opportunity to succeed, unlike China, where every little thing has to be greased with cash. Things are simply better here."

The others returned. Fan sat on her folding chair beside Chen.

"I don't know if I would say America is better, or even necessarily fair," Chen said, stiffly. "Terrible things happen here too. Just take that man in Iowa, for instance."

Silence settled over the group.

"Oh! That's a fantastic example," Qiong continued, shaking his head. "That kid. He thought he could buck the system, skip ahead. He thought he could do it with a gun. So sad."

The event had rocked the world of Chinese international students. A graduate student at the University of Iowa had weeks earlier killed three professors, one of whom was his academic advisor; an administrator; and a fellow Chinese student, who had recently won a dissertation prize and research position over him. The news had traveled like fire through a prairie, igniting panic, horror, and heartbreak among their classmates. Never had they heard of a student like them, a Chinese student—not to mention someone who had already completed his PhD, with so many prospects at his fingertips—doing something like this.

"And then he took his own life. A bitter ending to a terrible chapter," Qiong said now, setting his bottle on the table. "But there you go. An eye for an eye—life is fair in America."

Anger sprung up inside Chen. What was so fair about any of it? None of it was fair—from the killings to the suicide to the desperation the man must have felt. He remembered the man's face in the papers, round and solid, his eyes peering out from behind thick lenses, a faint mustache tickling his upper lip. What this man had done was evil, that was obvious, but Chen couldn't help feeling he looked familiar; he looked like all of them.

"What, you would have preferred he walk free? Destroy the lives of more people?" Qiong said next, noticing Chen's silence. "He was a disgrace to the Chinese people. We have to tell them—we are not like him."

Chen was incredulous. He looked at the faces of his classmates. But they reflected back only a sober melancholy, their heads lowered, placid murmurs of assent humming on their lips. He turned to Fan. "Violence is never the answer," she said, softly.

Since when had Fan been the type to spout platitudes? "I didn't say that," he said next, shaking. "I am not arguing that what he did was right. But can't you understand even a little bit how someone might be driven to that point? When you are told every day that as long as you work hard, you will succeed—but then you still don't?"

"No," Qiong said. "That, brother, is not fairness—that is entitlement. It is dangerous to think that violence—that <u>murder</u>—is ever appropriate simply because one does not get what one wants! And for something as silly as a research position? It's ludicrous!"

Maybe so, Chen thought. But it was also human. Wasn't that what America was about? Wasn't that what it had taught them? Grab what you deserve. Fight for it. He thought about rage and its potential, how in its purest, most seething form it could result in the worst tragedies, but how without it, life would merely roll over you, flattening you into the most inoffensive version of a person, someone who nodded and smiled at every piece of shit flung your way. Qiong could only sit here and spout his indignation because the Americans had happened to fling him something juicier.

"See, the thing about America is—everyone has the chance at greatness," Qiong continued, with a final satisfied gulp of his beer. "It doesn't mean we will all get it. But we all have the chance. And that's what makes this country fair."

Chen didn't respond; he stood abruptly and walked his empty bottle to the kitchen. There he leaned over, breathing deeply, until he heard Qiong rising, the lapels of his heavy coat snapping against his chest, strident declarations of thanks and promises to get together again trilling forth. By the time he returned to the living room, the rest of the party had departed. Fan scraped the ham into plastic boxes and gave Chen one to bring home. He ate the man's leftovers for days after.

GUILIN RETURNED. "Sorry," she said. "It was Subdistrict Supervisor Ding. He needed some help with his phone. Where were we? Oh! We were discussing my future autobiography." She giggled. "Please continue. I am so interested in your American journey."

Seeing her, Chen ached; he looked at this woman with her shining yellow cardigan, the hairs from her ponytail slightly frizzing, and he wished to tell her everything, to tear out the ugly parts of himself, to show her that she, too, could one day make something of her pieces.

"It's a crueler country than we are made to believe," he said. "America, it forces you to be a certain way. You have to bow at the feet of people who are stupider than you and thank them for allowing you to grovel." He was spitting out his words now. "That is why I returned to Beijing eventually. I would much prefer to give my talents to my home country, rather than give those bastards a bargain."

Guilin listened with her brow furrowed. "That's so surprising," she said, and of course it was. Here was a woman for whom America would always be some fantasy in a television program. It contained for her worlds of potential, and he found himself relishing the opportunity to shape it for her, to be the one to reveal to her its harsh truths. "It's very patriotic of you."

Patriotic. This was a new word to describe his choice to return, and he supposed it was accurate. He had never thought much about China before he left, and it wasn't until he returned that he began to appreciate everything about it he had missed: the familiar faces, the warmth of his neighbors, the technological advancements, the ease with which he could move through the world. The food. Glistening duck's skin. During his seven years in America, his mouth had not watered.

They emerged outside. The open mouth of the pool stared back at them, a yawning concrete morass. He had poured the concrete the previous day so that the steel rebars were swallowed up, the monstrous cresting web now smooth like sand dunes.

The pool was going to be a magnificent thing: twenty-five meters laid with alternating royal blue and turquoise tiles. With nothing covering it, the pool would always reflect the sky.

"What a beautiful view," Guilin said, exhaling. "Better be careful, Chen, this is even nicer than Subdistrict Supervisor Ding's house. When he sees it, he'll be jealous."

So she had been to his home? Chen's brow furrowed; he did not relish the second mention of Ding in the previous few minutes. A possessive feeling washed over him.

"He has a three-story home in the next complex over," she said. "But his furnishings are not nearly as modern." She looked over at Chen, who was standing stiffly by the doorway. "Don't be so nervous, Song Chen sir," she said, as if reading his mind. "I often run errands for his wife. Sometimes I pick up groceries for the family. I am a 'personal assistant' of sorts."

"It seems a little strange that Subdistrict Supervisor Ding would have his office secretary running around delivering food like any Jingdong driver."

Guilin laughed. "I'm at my core a village girl. I'm no better than a Jingdong driver! Plus, Mrs. Ding always feeds me well every time I help her with errands."

He could feel heat in his neck. He wondered what her real relationship was with Ding. These local politicians were each more perverted than the last, and Chen expected Ding to have no shortage of mistresses.

"Tell me about the owners," Guilin said. "They must be very glamorous."

Chen chuckled. "They're a pretty typical American couple. The husband is in tech. Made a lot of money very young. The wife grew up in Beijing, but went to California for school. She runs a YouTube channel, you know, that video website they watch over there."

"I've heard of it," she said. "Are they good people?"

He was a bit perplexed by this question; he'd never thought, really, to consider the goodness of those who gave him his livelihood.

He paused. "They seem like it," he said. "The wife is very warm."

They walked back inside. Guilin ascended the staircase, running her hand along the banister. "Are you married, Song Chen sir?" She asked it not with the hopeful timidity of a girl in wish of a certain answer, but with a neutral curiosity, as if she were asking for the weather—if it were sunny, she'd wear a short-sleeve shirt; if it were raining, she'd bring an umbrella.

He was shocked by her straightforwardness. Marriage. He thought of Fan's vivacious WeChat posts; the smiles she reserved only for other friends, other men; the frigid space between their bodies as they lay next to each other in the same bed.

"I'm getting a divorce," he finally said as they reached the landing. It was the first time he'd uttered those words. Guilin turned toward him with bemusement.

"I'm divorced as well," she said next.

His face must have betrayed his shock. She giggled. "Is that surprising to you, Song Chen sir? Yes, I was married. But only for an instant. It was over ten years ago, when I was twenty-two, when I returned home from Guangzhou. I did it to make my parents happy. I threw a big party out in the village. But it was mostly for show. I liked him well enough, but I grew bored of him. He was a boy I had known in high school, but we weren't even friends. I left him in the village and came to Beijing. I never saw him again. The first holiday I returned home, I heard that he had gone to Shenzhen."

She spoke the story plainly, like a funny fable that had happened to someone else. But Chen had felt heavy since Fan had left, depressed, the core of his life irrevocably shifted. It chilled him, this woman's nonchalance.

"It was the best thing I ever did, though," Guilin was saying. "I needed to be free to become my true self. Beijing feels like a place where I can do anything as long as I try hard enough. I can always make more money by working more hours, by being more cheerful, by perfecting my accent, by acquiring more skills! At home, there was a low ceiling for what I could accomplish. No matter how hard I worked, I would only ever be just a village woman, someone's wife knitting sweaters for their children."

She stopped speaking, and Chen realized that he had not made a sound for several minutes.

"I'm sorry, Song Chen sir," Guilin said now. "Look at me, going on about the past."

Her eyes were fixed on Little Bin, who had resumed hammering tiles. "I wonder what he thinks of us," she murmured.

"Us . . . ?"

"Do you think he thinks I'm your mistress?"

He was shocked by the suggestion. He had been mildly concerned that Little Bin would be curious about things that didn't concern him, but now that Guilin had put that thought into words, he suddenly felt Little Bin's eyes on him, piercing into his forehead. "I don't think—"

"I wouldn't mind that, you know," she said, moving closer and looking up at him, shyly. Another shock to his system. None of the women he'd been tempted with in the past had been as forward as Xie Guilin. Suddenly, Guilin seemed younger, supple and lusty.

She put her hands on his arm just then and lifted her face to his. Her lips brushed against his; her breath smelled like chocolate. Chen was shocked; his arms stayed frozen by his sides. Her round mouth opened and pushed against his; his tongue, instinctually, responded, meeting hers.

Then he stepped back.

"I think I should take you home," he said.

THEY DROVE, Chen's heart thumping in his chest. The day's events had been shocking. He felt dirty and elated, a strange mixture of emotions. Was Guilin one of the girls he saw on his nights out with Tao, girls who came to the city in search of riches and glory, hoping to become high-society girls, but who ended up hanging off the thick necks of men like Tao and his other friends who seemed to have new mistresses every week? Men like Subdistrict Supervisor Ding. Chen had drank with these girls but had never partaken of this brazen flesh grab—he was not that kind of man.

"I hope that was not rude of me," Guilin said, her eyes trained ahead.

He was silent for a moment.

"I admire you a lot, Song Chen sir," she said. "I wish to learn from your example."

Whatever did she mean by that? Chen felt his penis harden; he pictured her mouth again, and he willed himself to stare ahead at the road. He did not like this version of himself, the leering man, like Tao. He would not do to Fan what she had done to him. But the more terrifying thought came creeping up—and what of it? Wasn't she over there, fucking her old paramour? Skipping down memory lane? Hadn't she already done the unforgivable thing years ago—she, of all people, would understand, no?

"What do you wish to achieve in this city?" he asked now. Outside, CITIC Tower came into view, the skyline rising, the first lights already gleaming in the orange-purple evening haze.

She smiled at him. "I want to be able to spend money however I want to. I want to stay in the city and live in a nice apartment of my own. I do not want to live with five other girls in a cramped dorm space. I want to be wealthy enough that I only have to work forty hours a week and can still send money back to my parents. And . . ." she blushed, suddenly. "I want a car. A car represents ultimate freedom."

He stared straight ahead, his teeth clenched. The smooth leather pulsed underneath his fingers, the steering wheel turning the metal beast ever so slightly off the highway and onto a large four-lane road.

He hadn't realized he was routing him and Guilin to his own complex until he saw the spires of his building. He pulled onto a sleepy residential street just outside the subdivision.

"Would you like to try?" he said.

It was her turn to be surprised. "What do you mean?"

"Having ultimate freedom," he said, gesturing at the steering wheel.

"I—I've never driven!" she said, and for the first time, a look of fear crossed her face, hanging like a question mark.

"I'll teach you," he said. "I'm a good teacher." He'd learned how to drive from Meng Haian. The year before graduating, Chen had purchased a 1979 Mustang off an undergraduate for $600; the transmission gave out just ten months in. But that first day, Meng Haian had wedged his six-foot frame into the passenger seat and instructed Chen on how to shift the car into gear, ease his foot onto the gas, turn the wheel slowly without any sudden movements. A month later, Chen was doing ninety on highways, taking Fan to Chicago to eat at better Chinese restaurants. And then he taught her, too, though Fan was an impatient woman and always hit the gas and brakes too hard, jolting the two of them backward and forward like blades of grass in a storm. He'd get nauseated, but still he'd repeat the same instructions: keys, foot on the brake, check your mirrors, gearshift, ease foot off the brake and onto the gas. Eventually, she became a comfortable, confident driver—too confident, probably, and to this day Chen felt the fear of God inside him any time Fan took the wheel.

He gave Guilin the same instructions now, demonstrating slowly. She nodded and watched. Then they switched places. Guilin sat trembling in the driver's seat. She seemed smaller, though she sat with her back perfectly straight, her arms so rigid and bent at such perfect ninety-degree angles that she took on the appearance of an injured patient in a full-body cast.

"The car is an extension of you," he said. "See the gas as your foot, extending out in a kick. But don't kick too hard. You're more powerful than you think."

Chen watched as she tentatively replayed the steps he'd taught her: check the left mirror, right mirror, rearview, push down on the brake, turn the key in the ignition, shift into drive. She placed her hand back on the steering wheel.

"Ease your foot off," Chen said.

She did, and the car slowly began moving.

"Wait—wait—" Guilin slammed her foot on the brake, pitching Chen forward. "I'm so sorry, Song Chen sir!"

"Not to worry," he smiled. The familiar nausea comforted him. "Try again."

Again she lifted her foot off the brake, and the car continued rolling. This time, she let it roll.

"Now ease onto the gas."

She angled her foot to the right and tapped the gas. The car lurched, and Guilin again slammed on the brake. "I'm! I'm so sorry! I'm so bad at this!" She seemed on the verge of tears.

"You're doing wonderfully!" Chen said. "You're moving, aren't you? A few more times like this and you'll get to the end of the street."

And so they did, pitching forward and backward, until Guilin arrived at the stop sign. A look of pride and relief crossed her face as the red octagon greeted them. Chen let out a cheer. "Yes!" Guilin hurriedly threw the car into park and unbuckled her seat belt, nearly flinging herself from the driver's seat.

"See?" he said, getting back into the car. "You made it."

She was trembling, but a look of immense pride shone through on her face. "Thank you," she said. "You're very patient."

Chen nodded. His phone lit up. A WeChat notification. He opened it, hoping he looked casual to Guilin (and why was he suddenly so concerned with what she thought?), and saw that Fan had posted a photo of the towering pine tree near the economics building. The two of them had spent many an afternoon sitting underneath that tree; he'd often waited there for her for hours while she finished work, tightly cradling bowls of wonton soup to keep them warm. But his heart grew cold, looking at the photo now. "July 29. This tree reminds me what it is to endure; humans are so small, but this tree will live on for thousands of years."

Endure. That persistent verb that time had mangled. Endure, his mother had chided him, when she had detected the first signs of frost in his marriage. Endure, his classmates had said, their empty and unyielding mantra. Endure, the word that had sent daggers into his heart that one night.

He put the car into drive and eased back onto the main road. "That's my place," he said, gesturing at the spire. The waning evening sun hit the building at such an angle that it gleamed. It looked new. It looked like the home of a rich man. He watched Guilin's eyebrows arch. "Do you want to come up?"

He drove toward the entrance gate where the young guard was leaning against the wall, the guard who daily bid him hello with a "Welcome home, Song sir." Chen had always been a faithful husband. There may have been other things he had not done right. But he was not like his friends with their multiple mistresses, their don't ask, don't tell policy at home, their clothes permanently infused with several perfumes. He always came home at the end of the night. He was not Tao. And he was not Fan.

He thought of the letter, that carefully ensconced rectangle of paper he'd found in their dresser one evening in 1994.

After graduation, Chen had moved into the studio apartment the university had given Fan for her postdoc. This apartment was the site of his charade, where he'd shave meticulously at the bathroom mirror before leaving to sit in the park, circling jobs in the paper and delivering résumés to no avail. Fan never questioned him; he never saw her much, anyway. Her research was going well, and he was happy for her, genuinely happy. He did not want to disturb her skyrocketing progress with his misfortune. This went on for several months. One day, he decided to try his hand at a few businesses on the western outskirts of Champaign. It began raining, and he took shelter in a Chinese restaurant he'd never seen before. He was all the way across town, an hour's bus ride from their apartment, his résumés stuffed into the mailboxes of every accounting firm and bank in sight. There was a sign in the window: HIRING BUSSERS. He looked shyly at the men who were cleaning the floors, all of them stocky, whip-quick, probably immigrants from countries he'd never visited. He shuddered to think how someone might end up in a job like this.

By this time, Chen had been living a lie for half a year. And then Meng Haian called him and told him Yuki had tried to commit suicide.

He thought about the evenings he'd spent in the living room with Meng and Jia Yinhao, how they'd laughed with each other as Yuki stole away to his room. He had thought the fourth boy standoffish; he'd attempted, the first week they lived together, to speak to him in English, but Yuki had scoffed at his attempts, responding curtly in Japanese. He would never know what Yuki had said, and he never tried again. Yuki would come in late at night to see Chen, Meng Haian, and Jia Yinhao arranged around the living room, laughing at some new house rule Jia Yinhao had set that evening or joshing Meng Haian for falling in love with yet another classmate. Chen thought that laughter in a different language must always sound like exclusion.

Life in America was so tenuous. But Yuki survived. Chen took the busser job. He started working six days a week, from noon until two AM, wiping the detritus of business lunches and birthday parties into large plastic bins. In exchange, he got three dollars an hour plus an occasional tip. Big Luck Diner was on the opposite side of the city, so none of his friends—or Fan—would ever walk in on him. He ate from their all-day buffet for every meal, and every dinner was a handful of cold fried wontons and a greasy plate of chop suey. The Cantonese owners, Frank and Angelica Tse, insisted on blasting oldies over their tinny speakers, and he hated the fat American women with their golf shirts who came in and pointed at the jukebox and said things like, "*The Chinese like the Carpenters too!*" The whole world liked the Carpenters.

Every night, he'd clock out, his clothes stained with soy sauce and orange chicken. He would change into a new shirt and pants and ride the bus home, where he'd often find Fan already asleep. In the morning, he would tell her that the boss was working him late again, and she would nod and go to campus never questioning him.

Frank and Angelica never spoke to him; their Mandarin was not good, so they only gestured at tables or at spills on the floor that needed cleaning. He almost wished they would just shout at him in Cantonese or even English; he wasn't mute, after all, and hated to be seen as such. But he also cherished the silence; he relished not having to speak.

Once he served an older couple—the man and woman looked to be in their early sixties. He handed them their bowls of egg drop soup and plates of shrimp fried rice and the man smiled at him. "*Hey,*" the man said, pointing at him. "*A lotta you go to the university, huh.*"

Chen nodded slowly. He wasn't quite sure what "you" he was referring to.

"*Young man like you, you should join them! Good to get educated when you're young!*" The man took a noisy slurp of egg drop soup. "*Like this fella!*" The man smashed his finger down on his newspaper, landing on a picture of a man with a head of imperious hair and a tailored suit gleaming out at the camera. The headline: "YUKI NAKAMURA RECEIVES JAMES WADDELL ALEXANDER AWARD IN MATHEMATICS."

Chen nodded again, his head down. Even Yuki. "*Yes,*" he said, softly, though the word came out strangled.

On that evening in 1994, Chen returned to an empty home. It was one of those days when the sun seems never to set, its everlasting light making a mockery of Chen's torment. Fan was still at her office. He had an unbearable urge for a cigarette. He knew that Fan allowed herself a single cigarette in emergencies; she kept a pack tucked behind her bras in the dresser drawer. He shuffled around in there now, fingers tracing over sinews of mesh and lace. But there was no pack. Instead, his hand landed on a piece of plastic. He pulled it out. It was a sheet of hotel stationery from a Courtyard Marriott in Orlando, protected pristinely in a plastic sheath. A wall of English words greeted him.

"*Dear Fiona,*" it began. "*It is my third day in Orlando, and the heat is oppressive. The conference is tedious and I wish you were here to distract me. I am staying very close to Disney World, and every night I can see—and hear—the fireworks from my window. Fireworks are magical the first night, but less so the second night. By now I know I've made my affections clear, but I wanted to write it down for you, in ink, to make it a positive truth. I love you, and have always loved you, and wish every day we had met years earlier when we were not two people already tied to separate posts. Last night I dreamed of a little girl. She was different from my daughter; I think she is the daughter we were meant to have. I woke up thinking about this girl. I imagined us taking her here, to Disney World. She would like to be one of these princesses. So all I ask of you is to wait for me:* endure, endure. *Love exists at the end of persistence.*"

Chen's heart fell away piecemeal with every word. Heartbreak, he realized, was not so much a shattering, but a slow, gradual ache that began in your head and spread to your limbs, until every particle of you panged. It was the same as failure; there were no sudden explosions, just a million little deaths, every day. He collapsed against the bed. His mouth felt unbearably dry. The very thing he'd feared had been true after all. His perfect wife. That bastard. He thought about the long nights Fan had been away, the mornings he'd wake and she'd already be gone. He thought about the way she spoke of Robert Qiong, the adoration, the joy. It was too obvious. She'd dangled it right in front of his nose, and yet he'd still convinced himself that she had chosen him. Him. What a joke! Of course she would love that man with his accolades, his confidence, his perfect, varnished life. People who haven't suffered failure are prettier, it's true. They are kinder, easier to be around. They still believe in the goodness of the world. But not Chen. Of course she wanted to be with Qiong. He wanted to rip the letter to shreds, spit on it, piss on it, set fire to it. He wanted to smear those words until they were mere jest, until they had not been written at all. Those stupid English words.

And then he let out a laugh, mirth curdled into a growl. Of course they wrote to each other in English. They thought he wouldn't be able to read it. This is what they thought of him.

HE RAISED HIS ARM at the gate and gave the young guard a wave. The guard saw him and smiled, good evening, Song sir. He could see him pause for one beat, seeing Guilin in the passenger seat.

He had always been faithful. He had been a good husband. He had never hidden anyone from Fan. This was one thing he had done right, and now he wondered why he'd been so careful— if it was all going to end this way, anyway. Chen should have felt more nervous that the guard might gossip, that a neighbor might see him, sitting in this car with an unknown woman, and tell Fan, spread the rumor around so that every person in his complex would point their finger at him and say, liar, cheater, but in this moment he almost wanted Fan to know, to know that yes, he could be just like her.

4

There was a woman lying on her side in his bed, her hips forming one perfect Grecian mound. It was morning. Chen thought, Since when did Fan have curves like this? He reached out, placing his hand on the exquisite hip, and then realized with a start what he had done.

Guilin had been voracious; their sex had been louche and pleasing. She'd fucked him atop the floral comforter on his bed, giggling and preening, gyrating her body in slow and pornographic waves. He wondered where she had learned to do this. Then they'd both come, one after the other in a serendipitous harmony he'd only achieved a few times in his life with Fan. Immediately after his orgasm he craved the aloneness of that morning. But she had laid her face on his chest, her hair tickling his armpit, and fallen quickly asleep, so he had let her lie there, until he, too, slipped into slumber.

He felt sticky now. He wished that she were back in the dorm she shared with five other girls. The justness he'd felt the previous evening had washed away to guilt, and looking at her breathing calmly, he felt that she was actually quite plain, her face agreeable in every way and therefore unspectacular. But he did not want to hurt this woman; it still pleased him to see her so happily dozing. And he felt that he should do right by her, so when she woke he took her to a different, even better mall than the day before, where they ate sea bream at a Shandong restaurant, and then they walked among the luxury shops, and he saw her eyes alight on a rose-colored silk scarf, so he purchased it for her. He did not want her to feel as though he were retroactively buying her company the previous evening, but with each purchase he felt his guilt lightening, each depletion of his bank account rendering his act transactional and meaningless bit by bit.

He drove her home late that afternoon, and she kissed him sweetly on the mouth. "What a wonderful surprise that was," she said, and he gave a quick murmur of assent. "Will you call me?" she asked, and again the strings of his heart were tugged like a kite's; he could not say no; he had always been weak for those who laid their hearts bare in this way.

"Yes," he said, and then his hand brushed against her cheek, a reflexive gesture that he realized too late must have communicated some deeper tenderness, because she stepped back with a start, and then a wide smile erupted on her face. He regretted it immediately.

HE ATTEMPTED NOT to call for several days.

He finished the pool, and as the water filled its rectangle, he thought that life must be like this: a slow trickling that eventually became something that could consume you. The pool was really the perfect addition to the backyard; in fact, it seemed the entire house had been built around this very purpose; he had, perhaps, subconsciously been preparing for its existence. Vivian squealed with delight when she saw the pool. He swore there was something wet in Thomas's eyes. They sent the payment over with fanfare and a bonus, as he'd hoped. A day later, Vivian texted him a link to the official house-tour video on her channel. She polled her viewers on how she should decorate it, whether she should do dark tones, velvet, and gold; or neutral, mid-century, wood. Chen found himself eagerly anticipating the verdict.

He sent in the down payment for Yihong's Xiangheyuan condo, and gleefully announced the news to his son's future in-laws. They telephoned immediately with thanks and congratulations, Old Zhou shouting about why Yihong hadn't proposed yet—they were ready to ship Rufeng off tomorrow! He dreaded what the next thirty, forty years would look like, these buck-toothed hillbillies gnawing away at every penny Chen had left to give.

Guilin continued messaging him, little updates about the subdistrict supervisor, about the girls in her dorm. He responded laughing, lamenting the long hours and Ding's strange diet and the pettiness of the girls who asked her too many questions about the man who had dropped her off the previous week. He had at first attempted not to respond and found himself quite proud, but then she simply continued messaging him, before finally sending him a moving image of a crying kitten, with the caption "the abandoned kitty is crying!"

A few days before Fan's return, Chen found himself eating in a Shanghainese restaurant in Raffles Mall with Guilin. Guilin was wearing the cardigan he'd gifted her and insisted on sitting on the same side of the booth, so that her hand could rest on his thigh and occasionally travel upward, making Chen squirm with delight and guilt.

His phone pinged, and he saw that Fan had posted a photo of a restaurant's storefront. Her caption: "Ate at a 'Mexican-Korean' restaurant last night. 'Fusion' is all the rage in America right now. I had a burrito with kimchi. Delicious!" And then a strange feeling washed over him, seeing a glimpse of the brown-and-white street signs: the store stood on the corner of Stonebridge and Strand. Where Big Luck Diner used to stand. And so Frank and Angelica had closed up shop, huh. He let out a bitter grunt. He felt vindicated. He imagined the way their snubby faces must have crumpled further when they had to shutter their business, and he barely suppressed a cruel bark.

But sadness unfurled inside him, too. The terrain upon which he'd waged his most pitiful battles, it was gone, and with it all evidence of his struggle. He looked up the new restaurant. It was a popular chain. Where had Frank and Angelica gone?

An earthenware bowl of braised pork came, and he suddenly felt a lump in his throat. It was so hard to last in America. He wanted to laugh—never did he think he'd feel sympathy for those two people, the ones who'd been the chief conspirators to the lowest time of his life. Guilin handed him a napkin. She reached her chopsticks eagerly into the steaming bowl, retrieving a large piece for Chen before serving herself. She really was sweetness incarnate. He had not felt such attention in many years.

"Tell me about your wife," Guilin said, as if she could read the thoughts racing through his mind.

His brow furrowed. His wife. The phrase sounded distant, nondescript; "his wife" could be anyone.

"She is a very intelligent woman," he said. "Very competent. A fisherwoman by birth. Rough. With her hands and with her words. Not an easy woman. We were always very competitive with each other in school." He paused. "She is the kind of woman who is never satisfied."

Guilin stared at him. "And what kind of woman does that make me?"

He paused. "You recognize what you have. That makes you not only an intelligent woman, but a happy one."

She giggled. "You do have a sweet mouth, Chen. Is that why your wife fell in love with you?"

"Perhaps," he said. "You know, I don't really remember anymore. She so seldom reminds me."

He thought about the fight they'd had, the last time they'd fought, really fought. Yihong was applying to college. Fan urged him to apply to school abroad. She'd always regaled him with tales of America, painted portraits of towering skyscrapers and ice cream cones nearly as tall. Yihong would grin and clap as they talked about the big burgers you could sink your teeth into as hard as you wanted and not reach the other side. At first Chen had allowed it, chalking it up to nostalgia for youth. But then her nostalgia soured into bitterness. She missed America, and her antidote for that was to send Yihong there for school. Chen pushed back. He'd returned to Beijing to pursue a better future for his family—why would he send his son to the place they had left behind?

The truth was Chen saw too much of himself in his son. Yihong had never experienced ridicule; he would not know how to survive it. He did not have his mother's thick skin. He did not have her ambition, a fact that had become more and more evident as he grew. Chen supposed it was always a tragic moment when a parent realized his child was simply average. Chen forgot exactly when the realization had come: Was it when he'd read "Three Kingdoms" to Yihong when he was ten and Yihong could not even remember who had won the war? Was it when Fan had first asked Yihong what he wanted to be when he grew up and he had shrugged and smiled, content to be nothing even as an eight-year-old, when he could have been anything?

In the end, Yihong sided with his father. Chen's predictions were confirmed. If he could not make it in America, how could Yihong?

Fan was furious. She could see right through him. "Your problem, Chen," she said, "is that you think everyone is the same as you."

The words hit him like an anvil. They had never spoken of his difficult times, and Fan had never implied that she knew. He'd taken out loans from friends, his parents, anything to keep up the fiction that he had an income. He pretended not to hear her; in the morning she pretended she'd never said it. Her words hung in the air like an apparition, like all the other apparitions of their love.

"Well," Guilin said now, wrapping her arms around his. "I am happy right where I am."

ON AUGUST 10, Chen drove to the airport. Fan was coming home. He should have been happy, but he was nervous. He didn't want to feel her steely cold; he didn't want to see his guilt reflected in her eyes. They had been apart for six weeks, but it felt now like a lifetime. He braced himself for impact.

There were no comedy roasts on the radio today. Advertisement after advertisement blared, but he felt comforted by their stultifying similarities. Shampoo, yogurt, mouthwash, iced tea. Gum, watches, skin whiteners, smartphones. These were the objects that made up a life. It all felt so inadequate.

The arrivals terminal was frenzied, taxis jostling each other, vying for customers. He searched for his wife in the crowd, and when he saw her, the old feeling of discovery clanged inside him. She stood with her suitcase beside her, her right hand shielding her eyes, a white T-shirt billowing at her waist and arms, something colorful splattered across the front, her other hand tucked into her backpack strap. Her brow was furrowed, but what struck him was the feeling of impatience that seemed to surround her, a freneticism akin to excitement. The excitement was strange; he realized he'd been expecting her to be on her phone, sitting, or just simply somewhere else in her mind, already back in Illinois, and not at all worried over when Chen would be there to retrieve her.

He pulled up beside her and a look of recognition flooded her eyes. She smiled.

He emerged from the car. She was already waiting at the trunk with her suitcase. "Good flight?" he asked.

"Terrific," she said, and her voice sounded clear and happy. "I slept the whole way. They had a pretty good stir-fried beef, actually." He opened the trunk and she grabbed the handle of her suitcase and hauled it up, swatting his hand away. Fan never let someone else do that which she could do herself. After she'd settled the suitcase and her backpack and slammed the door, she turned to him and shocked him, giving him a quick hug, her arms wrapping around his back and squeezing together before releasing quickly and falling back at her sides.

They got into the car and Fan buckled herself in. "It's good to be home," she said, smiling at him. She was smiling more than he'd seen in months. He returned the smile weakly as they pulled onto the highway.

On the road back, she peered out the window, in much the same way she had when they'd first arrived those years ago. She seemed to see Beijing with new eyes, and Chen found himself grateful that the sun was gleaming, that the trees were lush, that the traffic, despite the crowds at the airport, was smooth. Fan when she was full of wonder was really the most charming woman.

"Is that new?" She pointed at a tall silver structure, a post-modernist apartment building fringing the Fifth Ring.

He paused. "Yes," he lied. The building had been there for years, but he wanted to remain in this moment of rapture.

"How is everyone?" he asked next.

"They're doing great," she said, encompassing all their friends with that one simple pronoun. "I don't know if you saw, we met up with Jia Yinhao in New York! He has a new wife. She's fifteen years younger than him!"

Chen laughed. He had seen. Jia Yinhao was perhaps the most successful of all of them; the fastidiousness of his youth had translated into fierce financial savvy, and a few calculated investments in the early 2000s had earned him an Upper West Side condo and a country home upstate. His private life was perhaps less successful, as he was on his third marriage, but looking at the photo Fan flung in front of him now as they paused at an intersection, Chen felt that his smile was genuine and perhaps there were sadder things in life than failed marriages.

"Meng Haian is doing well," she said, nodding. "He looked fit as ever, much better than he was last we heard." Meng Haian had been diagnosed with an early-stage cancer several years back, but he had fought it with his typical brand of Meng optimism.

Last Chen had heard, he was a top-level manager at NASA, and his twin daughters lived close to home.

"He was there?" Meng Haian lived in Houston; how would she have seen him?

"Yes," she said. "He came up just for a weekend." Her face was turned away, peering again out the window, and he could not tell if she looked guilty.

He was disturbed by this reunion of all his friends. It was one thing for Fan to go cavorting with Nannan, whom he disliked, but another thing for her to see his two roommates, the ones whom he'd spent seven of the most formative years of his life championing and struggling with. They were his friends. What had really occurred in America? He felt seized by frustration; he might never know.

They pulled up to their front gate. The guard was there; he gave Fan a toothy smile and said, his voice perfectly smooth, "Welcome home, Ms. Jiang." Chen had left the previous morning with Guilin, and the guard had given him the same toothy smile, the same gregarious goodbye that betrayed nothing. He really was very good at his job.

At home, Fan wheeled her suitcase into the bedroom and laid it down on the floor, zipping it open to reveal rows of chocolate wrapped in gold foil. She grabbed a stack and held it out to Chen. "I got you your favorite."

He took the Ghirardelli stacks in his hand, the cocoa smell hitting his nose sharply. She began unpacking swiftly, grabbing handfuls of her clothes and opening their drawers to redeposit them, folded, inside. She pulled a black dress from her suitcase, a slip-like thing. "I got this at Bloomingdale's," she said. "What do you think?"

He pictured her in bed with Qiong, the silk pulling, ripping. The image collided with the memory of Guilin the week prior, her cardigan slipping down her shoulder, his own pallid face that he caught in the mirror in a state of embarrassing arousal.

"It's nice," he said.

"I'll wear it to the party tomorrow," she said.

"The party . . ."

"The housewarming. It's tomorrow, right?"

"Yes." He shook his head. "I'm surprised you remember."

"Give me more credit, Chen," she said, then turned back to her suitcase.

"Well, that would be nice," he said.

This was an unexpected gesture; deep down Chen had resigned himself to arriving at Thomas and Vivian's housewarming alone, the bachelor architect there to smile bashfully and shake his head when the gracious homeowners said things like, "This comes from the brilliant visionary mind of Song Chen . . ." and "We'd be on the street without you!" Instead, tomorrow, he would be attending the party with Fan. He would bask in the glow of who he'd once been: the entrepreneur with the beautiful wife on his arm. They would be the well-matched couple.

THE HOUSE WAS even more beautiful than he'd left it. Seemingly overnight, it was entirely furnished. Vivian's fans had answered her poll and chosen the darker, velvet color scheme. Now an elegant custom royal-blue couch sat in the main hall, a wave crashing in a cavern. Dark wood chairs upholstered in mahogany leather with gold adornments sat perched at forty-five degrees, sentries guarding a painting of a vermilion gash running from the bottom left of the canvas to the top right in rapturous delight. In the kitchen hung the gold sculptural light fixture, wings unfurling midway so it was both bird and surf. There were even champagne glasses in their kitchen cabinets. The party seemed to be in full swing, various men in suits and women in slinky dresses milling about. Chen walked with Fan on his arm, and a burst of pride coursed through him. The black dress was sexy, hugging her hips in all the right places.

Just as she had on the drive home from the airport, she had watched the city with acute curiosity on the way over. She'd pointed out the new development that had started construction down the road, remarked at the same bus stop that had blared its toothpaste ad—now an ad for shampoo—and asked the same question Chen had asked weeks earlier—who in these parts do they think they're selling shampoo to? "Everyone drives once you're past the Fifth Ring," she mused.

They drove into the Heavenly Earth subdivision, and Fan studied the scenery. "The Zhang property looks great from here," she said, referring to a project he'd completed the previous year.

She was being kind, and it had been years since she had been kind. He was grateful and yet suspicious; he wondered when the other shoe would drop. He had not asked more questions about her trip; there seemed to be an understanding that she had revealed some information not intended for him, and they would not discuss it further. But gone seemed to be the heaviness of the last few months; she seemed genuinely happy to be sitting in the car with him, on the way to his big event.

They emerged on the driveway. Chen helped her out of the car. She, like Guilin, stopped for a weighty moment and looked up at the building. Chen peered at it through her eyes.

The house was a Modernist masterpiece, Chen felt—and he was not a boastful man by nature, but excellence was excellence. He'd now spent nearly a year toiling on this house. It was a challenge, with its finicky floor-to-ceiling windows; its asymmetrical split-level structure; its mixture of concrete, steel, glass, and wood that made it look extraworldly and yet traditional, the front entrance imperious and topped with generous eaves that gave the appearance, nearly, of a Japanese torii gate. Vivian and Thomas had wanted something different but traditional, something that was impressive but not excessive—a tricky line to walk. They wanted light; they wanted a grand entrance but an intimate living space; they wanted naturalist details but a modern silhouette. They wanted a portion of their roof to be flat, reminiscent of the new Hollywood constructions that dotted

Thomas's native Los Angeles, so that they could stand on top of their masterpiece and watch the stars. They wanted a state-of-the-art security system; Vivian was a public figure, after all, and had many devotees ranging from the benign to the feral. This was the mark of new money; their desires pointed in a million directions, taste plucked from magazines and conversations atop private rooftop clubs and inside the compounds of richer people over the years. It had been difficult, nearly impossible to accommodate their every desire, but as Chen stepped back and surveyed his work, he was pleased, deeply pleased. This was something he had promised and achieved. A kept promise: There was nothing better in life.

Fan nodded, a smile faintly listing on her lips. Then she looped her hand naturally into the crook of his elbow, and when they walked up the steps, he thought they must have looked like any other happy, stylish couple, here to enjoy a night of levity. She looked up again, her neck craning as she gazed at the red inlaid tiles along the house's facade. "This is well-done, Chen," she said, matter-of-factly. There was no hyperbole here. This was the truth, and his pride swelled.

He nodded, not wanting to soak in the moment too long. As swiftly as a compliment came, a critique could also. They walked into the main hall. She admired the painting, trailing her finger along the velvet couch. "It's so . . . defiant," she said of the painting. "Kind of an odd choice for a newlywed living room."

Then Fan saw the pool, and he caught something hard in her eyes. She began walking with a purpose, dragging Chen toward the courtyard. She slowed as she neared the edge. He waited for the criticism to land. From her high perch, she contemplated the pool. Sunlight glinted off the blue Italian tiles. Puffy white clouds sat reflected in the water, cartoonishly round. The surface of the water was so still it looked as if you could walk right across it.

Fan crouched down and dipped her fingers in. The motion sent a roiling ripple across the surface, the clouds warping.

"It's cold," she said, her hand still moving back and forth in the water. She stood back up, wringing her hand dry.

From here, they could see all three wings of the house at once. Vivian and Thomas's guests lounged on poolside chairs, nursing plates of sashimi. Chen noticed Vivian standing by the kitchen counter, holding a champagne glass. She, like the rest of her guests, was dressed lavishly, in a smart jumpsuit cinched with a belt. Flanking her was Thomas, as well as a small squad of women who were all just slightly less elegant than she, but still pretty.

Vivian clinked her champagne flute and the partygoers settled down. "Dearest friends and family, I left you for the United States twelve years ago. When I left, I was scared. I was excited. I was leaving my family, my friends, my city, everything I had ever known. At the time I saw the trip as a vacation. Just a little summer break to America! I would go to Disneyland! I would go to the beach! I thought that I would spend a few years in America getting my education, and then come home to my family." She smiled and looked at Thomas. "But life is full of surprises. I never thought in my whole life that I would meet someone like Thomas. I never thought someone could love me the way that he does: generously, undeniably. He loves me no matter the day or the weather or the mood. We are so different; we come from such different places, but he celebrates this. He has always made me feel so special, like I'm the most valuable woman in the world."

She blushed, then continued.

"And just like that, twelve years have gone by. Thomas and I have known each other for five. We built a beautiful life in San Francisco and now are going to build another life in Beijing. Never in my wildest dreams did I think I would return and get to live somewhere like this. Thomas and I designed our home together, and we are so honored that all of you have chosen to celebrate it with us tonight. Sometimes I don't believe that I am now a grown woman, with a house and a fiancé of my own. I still sometimes think I am a child, and being back here has let me revisit those childlike delights again. Thank you, thank you," she finished. "For welcoming me home. Wo ai ni."

The crowd applauded and Vivian and Thomas clinked champagne glasses. It was a bit strange of her, to end her speech by declaring her love for all of them, but Chen supposed it was an American affectation. He still felt moved. He wondered if Thomas had understood any of the speech and found himself hoping she'd explain it to him later, her loving words.

Vivian turned and made eye contact with Chen. She gave him a smile and a raise of her glass. And then she and Thomas were moving toward him.

"Chen, hi!" Vivian called out. Chen extended a hand. "Is this your wife? You're so beautiful," she said, grabbing Fan's hand with her right hand, clasping it with her left.

Fan nodded. "Hello," she said, giving Vivian a decorous smile. "Congratulations. That was a nice speech."

"Oh, that!" Vivian blushed. "That's sweet of you to say." She looped her arm through Thomas's. "This is my fiancé, Thomas."

Fan merely nodded again and gave him a smile. Chen was surprised she didn't say more, didn't seize the opportunity to practice her English, demonstrate her gregarious American personality. Perhaps it was because she'd just had six weeks of opportunities.

"*We really can't thank you enough, Chen,*" Thomas said. "*It's even better than we expected.*"

"*It's nothing,*" he said, deploying a phrase he'd been taught—that Fan had taught him, in fact. Americans loved this word, *nothing*; diminishing one's efforts to zero was indicative of a confident ego, someone so assured in his masculinity and competence that he could describe his accomplishments as anything, nothing, and these things would remain undeniable. Chen was surprised at the English he'd willingly deployed; in this euphoric moment it felt like he could do or say anything.

"*My buddies are all jealous,*" Thomas said. "*I'll need to intro-duce you later, Chen, they're clobbering for some of that real estate.*"

"*Your wish is my command,*" Chen said now. "*I am thrilled you are happy.*"

Thomas slapped him on the back. "*Look at this guy, incredible English.*" It was interesting, now, to speak English with the Amer-icans. In this context, any amount of English was impressive, a party trick to make the eyes of the American man light up.

"Your husband is very talented," Vivian said, giving Fan a nudge with her elbow.

"He is," Fan said.

"*Your wife's more of the quiet type, huh,*" Thomas said, in a voice that did not intend to hide his assessment. He realized Thomas must think Fan didn't understand him. He tried to catch Fan's expression out of the corner of his eye, but Fan was looking away from them.

He followed her gaze. "OLD CHEN!" came the booming voice before he even saw him. Subdistrict Supervisor Ding was ambling through the glass doors in a suit that was both too big and too small, pinching him in the armpits and yet billowing out at the waist and trousers. Behind him followed Guilin. She wore a purple dress he'd never seen before, as well as the scarf that he had bought for her. She looked nice. His mouth felt dry. But of course—one of the conditions for Ding's approval was an invite to the housewarming. He had completely forgotten. See-ing Guilin in Fan's presence made his head hurt, and he found himself, just slightly, freezing up under his wife's hand.

"Old Chen," Ding repeated as he sauntered up, slapping him on the shoulder. Guilin held a plate piled high with sashimi. She evaded his gaze. "And the missus!" Ding grabbed Fan's hand and kissed it.

Fan complied, giving him a wide smile. Chen knew she hated Ding, but over the years had muscled through many a smarmy interaction with him and many a sweaty game of tennis with his whine-prone wife.

Chen introduced Vivian and Thomas to Ding and Guilin, hoping Fan and Guilin wouldn't have to trade words in the shuffle. Ding shook their hands vigorously, while Vivian beamed a disarming smile. She handed Ding a glass of champagne. "So nice of you to attend our little event with your busy schedule!"

"Of course, of course. Old Chen over here was crying and begging about this project for weeks. I wouldn't miss it."

She reached out to shake Guilin's hand. "And who's this?"

"My dutiful and brilliant secretary," Ding said, putting his hand on the small of Guilin's back.

Guilin nodded to Vivian. "It's so nice to meet you," she said. "Congratulations."

Fan watched the introductions serenely. Neither she nor Guilin moved to introduce herself to the other.

"Little Mao has been asking after you," Ding said to Fan, chortling. "She misses you on the tennis court."

"How is Little Mao?" Fan asked, fixing her gaze on Guilin. Chen knew she was assessing her, trying to gauge her age and what exactly the relationship was between her and the subdistrict supervisor. He swallowed, feeling sweat trickle down his back.

"She's not feeling too well," the subdistrict supervisor said, "so I've brought her replacement!" He roared with laughter. "I kid, I kid." Guilin finally looked in Fan's direction and gave her a tight smile. "Have you met, Chen?" Ding said next. "My secretary?"

Chen bobbed his head up and down, a bit too vigorously perhaps. "Ah, yes, we met, I think, when I came to your office," Chen said. Guilin lifted her head now and finally gave him a small smile.

"I remember," was all she said, tugging at the scarf around her neck. Then, to his horror, she turned to Fan. "Nice to meet you," she said, extending her hand.

Chen flushed scarlet, and he prayed the rest of the party did not see his face. He quickly chugged his champagne. But Ding had already moved on, gesturing toward the pool. "How charming!" he declared, his voice bellowing.

"That's all thanks to Chen!" Vivian squealed. "I knew it was a big ask, but Chen was so accommodating every step of the way. He never said no a single time. No wasn't a part of his vocabulary!" She laughed, and Ding laughed. Fan's face was as still as a lake in winter. Chen let out a weak chuckle.

"Chen," Vivian said, taking his arm. "I have to introduce you to some of my friends. They love the property. Excuse me, Subdistrict Supervisor."

Chen followed Vivian, and, to his delight, Fan followed him. Vivian led them to the gaggle of women he'd seen earlier, and they all gave him generous, practiced smiles.

"Zhuzhu, Lianlian, Qinru, I wanted to introduce you to the architect, Song Chen," Vivian said.

Chen stuck out his hand, shaking each of the women's hands in turn. The shortest one stepped forward, one hand palming a highball of whiskey, the other clutching his arm. "I absolutely must get your information," she said. She pointed at herself again. "Zhu Zixi. Or you can call me *Zinni*." She handed him a heavy name card, ZINNI ZHU embossed across the front in silver. "I'm so tired of the city," she said, wrinkling her nose. "Everyone and their mother want to live in Beijing now. The traffic, the noise . . ." She turned to Fan. "You get it." Fan smiled politely.

"My husband is the perfect person to talk to, in that case," Fan said. "The suburbs are his specialty." When she wanted to be, she really was the perfect wife.

He made the rounds at the party, speaking to a few more of Vivian's friends, then to her parents and a few of her father's associates. Fan accompanied him. At one point, she fed him a piece of raw fish off a toothpick.

After a while, he heard the scattered sound of laughter. Chen looked in the direction of the noise and saw Subdistrict Supervisor Ding standing over the pool in kelly green swim trunks. Guests were staring and snickering, their faces portraits of scandal and delight. Chen looked at Vivian, whose face registered a moment of shock before amusement replaced it.

Chen was in disbelief. Ding was known for his antics, but this was too much even for him. He watched as the subdistrict supervisor made a run, his paunch flapping up and down, and then cannonballed into the pool, splashing water so far onto the deck it nearly sprayed a few guests. He emerged moments later, sputtering. "That's cold!" he screeched, before diving back down and performing a few slow laps. Chen watched the man's turgid body hack its way through the water, then looked over at Thomas, wondering if he'd be angry that this bombastic man was defiling his treasured pool. But Thomas was simply laughing and clapping his hands, gesturing at Ding while talking animatedly with a group of Caucasian friends. Chen could hear them discussing whether to join—"*Host goes first!*" "*That's not a rule!*"—and some other garbled language he couldn't understand, but in the end, none of the men made any move to strip off their jackets and cannonball into the pool as Ding had.

Guilin walked over and stood beside the pool holding a towel, her face vacant. Ding continued doing laps, switching from freestyle to breaststroke, so that he looked like a large frog bobbing up and down. After what felt like hours of this, he finally arrived at the west side of the pool and heaved himself out. Guilin wrapped the towel around his back.

"Now, get diligent with it," he said, and to Chen's horror, Guilin began patting him dry in front of the entire party, traveling across his shoulders and down toward his legs. Much of the party had returned to their conversations, trying to ignore the spectacle, but Chen remained frozen in place. He felt helpless to change Guilin's circumstance, and he thought of all the times he'd watched powerful men make a fool of him.

Fan stood at his elbow, and he felt her chuckle. "One of these days, I hope one of his secretaries just—" and she mimed the action of pushing—off a ledge into a pool, off a roof, into traffic, he wasn't sure.

Then Fan departed for a glass of water. Chen watched her go before turning his attention back to the hulking figure of Subdistrict Supervisor Ding dripping onto a recliner. "Yow!" Ding yelped. "Refreshing!" Guilin had retrieved his clothes. For one horrific moment, Chen thought she'd help him change out of his swim trunks right then and there by the pool, but she was merely gesturing in the direction of the bathroom. He watched as Ding swayed back and forth, leaning into her. "Telling me what to do now, Guilin? I like this." She swatted him, looking around, a flush on her cheeks. Still she did not look in Chen's direction. Chen could not tear his eyes away, though he could feel the muscles in his hands tensing. He willed himself to relax his fingers. He grabbed a nearby glass of champagne and walked slowly toward Guilin.

Ding trundled toward the bathroom, and Guilin was left standing there, wiping her hands on the towel that he'd dropped on the deck.

"Guilin," Chen whispered, walking past and standing so that he was facing away from her. She seemed not to hear him. "Guilin," he repeated. "Can we talk?"

Her voice reached him, faint. "What is there to talk about?"

She was angry, and he could not blame her. "Can you meet me in the study?"

He then walked swiftly away, hoping that she had heard and that she was willing to come. He emerged into the small study off the side of the living room. Inside, the sounds of the party dulled to a muffled din. Chen's breathing was shallow. He felt that everything was simmering to the surface; he needed to get ahead of it, stop it before Fan discovered that anything was amiss.

He waited and waited. But Guilin never came. At last, he emerged from the study. He saw Guilin standing in the hallway, speaking to someone. She didn't see him. Then Subdistrict Supervisor Ding was calling her name, trundling up to her with water still dripping from his hair and his keys dangling. "Guiiiiliiiiin, I need my chauffeur!"

Chen froze. Suddenly, he regretted ever letting her take the wheel of his car. If he'd known she would have to use his lessons in this manner, he would have denounced the practice, denounced freedom. He watched as she nodded wordlessly and took the keys in her hands, then turned and left with the subdistrict supervisor.

Chen found himself moving toward the two of them, wanting to stop this impending mistake. He stumbled out of the alcove and saw Vivian and her friend standing by the staircase. Vivian didn't seem to notice him, but he murmured an excuse about getting lost on the way to the bathroom. He followed Guilin and Ding outside. "Guilin," he said. "Wait."

"Sir," she said, using her most cordial voice. Her formality shocked him. "Can I help you with something?" Subdistrict Supervisor Ding groaned on her arm. He was so drunk, Chen doubted he'd remember even if Guilin grabbed him and kissed him on the mouth right there.

"You're not ready," he said. "We haven't practiced enough."

She heaved Ding's giant carcass into the back seat and opened the driver's door. "I don't know what you're talking about," Guilin said, and the look she gave him now was neither harsh nor angry. It was simply a little bit sad. "I learned from the best."

Then she got into the driver's seat and shut the door.

CHEN TRUDGED BACK INSIDE, his heart heavy. He had not expected to see Guilin today; he had been content for the past and present to stay in their separate compartments, and he now knew he would have to stop his charade. He would have to speak to Guilin, apologize. He had behaved badly, like a child let loose in a candy store, and he had inevitably hurt someone. He should have either ended it right then and there with Guilin, salving his conscience, or he should have grabbed her, embraced her, told her he wanted no future but with her! There was no good fate for those who stood with their feet straddling two boats.

Fan was standing back by the pool when he returned. He trudged up to her, mumbled some half-hearted excuse about how Ding had left, how he'd accompanied him out to be polite.

"You're too nice to that guy," she said, nibbling on a stalk of celery. "You keep entertaining his stupid shenanigans, you'll always be under his thumb. That's why I don't play tennis with that wife of his anymore."

"You're right, you're right," he said. Power was so simple in Fan's mind. You either took it or you didn't. But there were certain structures that could not be disturbed; it was in America that he had first learned this lesson.

Then she took him by the hand, her palm pressing hotly into his, and said, "Let's go home." They walked together off the property as the women in their silks laughed, as the men loosened their ties, as the champagne went flat and the sun set splendidly over his grand creation.

IN THE EVENING, they slept together on the bed they had always known. She turned toward him, her hand resting on the space between their pillows. He stared at her face for a long time, her lips softly burbling. How deeply he had known this face. Guilin slept restfully, like the dead, but Fan always seemed close to waking. He felt that if he leaned forward, her eyes would fly straight open, though over the years this had never happened. But still he stared, unmoving, his hands also tucked between their bodies but not quite resting atop hers. He wanted to bottle this sweetness between them forever; he never wanted this moment to end. He lay there until morning, when he was jolted awake by the bleating of his phone.

It was Tao. "Chen," his friend said, his voice shallow. "Something's happened."

PART THREE

I

The morning of Wenyu's housewarming, the sky was blue like an anime, Alice in Wonderland-blue. The day was cool for August; God seemed always to smile upon Wenyu. Wenyu had not written the stalker an email, and no blasphemous announcement of Wenyu's infidelity had been made. But Lian and Wenyu had made up their minds. They would tell Thomas and Zhetai the truth. Lian and Freddy had begun seeing each other every few days, meeting to watch film after film across the city. She'd let her hand linger on the armrest between them and he'd let his settle in right next to hers, not quite touching it. It was exhilarating. She had smoothed things over with Zhetai for the time being, calling him the day after the birthday party and chalking her outburst up to sleep deprivation. She did not, however, mention what he had said about marriage. He'd taken the excuse in stride, barely glancing upon it, his desire to conciliate and move on both grating at and warming Lian's heart; oh, how good it was, a person who did not dwell, and how much she craved that, the dwelling. The brief time she'd spent with Freddy had cracked her wide open; she had decided she wanted to chase this possibility, and so she was going to tell Zhetai. Su Mingzun and Freddy were going to join them that night after the festivities, and she and Wenyu agreed they'd tell Zhetai and Thomas the next day. Today she and Wenyu would step forward into their new and different lives. She stood in her bedroom, combing nervously through her closet, changing into dress after dress.

"It's just a housewarming," Zhetai called from the living room. "You don't need to take it so seriously."

Her phone pinged. Freddy. "Excited for tonight!" he'd texted. She responded with an emoji of a bear blowing on a party horn.

The house was indeed everything Wenyu had promised. It was majestic, both modern and classical, the sloping roofs of the second and third floors giving the impression of a Hokusai wave. Wenyu's guests were awed. Zhetai nodded approvingly; Zhu Zixi examined every doorknob, faucet, and crown molding with an appraising and lustful eye, exclaiming at each turn about the price of the fixtures, the authenticity of the Georgian wood. Yang Qinru gripped her husband's arm with the histrionic zeal of the envious.

Lian felt the old covetous pangs, but something different was blossoming inside her too. In a way, she felt that this home was her home; whatever dreams and failures inside Wenyu had made this possible, the same resided inside herself.

This time, Lian didn't have to wait for Wenyu to pick her out of a crowd. Soon after she arrived, Wenyu emerged at the top of the steps, still in her robe. "Lian!" she called down. "Can you come up and help me?"

Lian left Zhetai in the living room.

When she arrived on the landing, Thomas was leaving the bedroom, a cloud of pastel and cologne. There was something stiff in his posture. He smiled at Lian. "*Hey, Lianne,*" he said.

"*Wonderful house,*" she said.

"*Thanks,*" he replied, but did not elaborate in his usual way. Instead, he brushed past her, mumbling about how he needed to check on the drinks.

Lian walked into Wenyu's bedroom. She gazed up at the cathedral ceilings.

"I'm in here!"

Lian followed Wenyu's voice to the bathroom, where she was sitting in front of a massive circular mirror, her hair in dramatic rollers.

"This is insane, Yutou."

"I know, right? I can't believe it's actually done."

Lian gestured around the space. "Your bedroom is the size of my family's entire living area."

"Do you think it's so wasteful?" Wenyu asked, doubt in her voice.

"All wealth is wasteful," Lian said. "Enjoy it while you can. Enjoy it before the Red Guard comes."

Wenyu laughed. Lian cocked her head, examining Wenyu. "I just ran into Thomas. He seemed kind of . . . off."

Wenyu exhaled. "I talked to him last night. I told him I've been feeling anxious about the wedding."

Lian felt her heart thumping nervously in her chest. "Really?"

Wenyu turned from the mirror. "Yeah. I told him being back has brought up a lot of feelings for me . . . I said I might need some space."

"Was he okay?"

"He was sad. He definitely didn't see it coming. But he also gets it. I—" and here she faltered. "Believe it or not, this isn't the first time we've talked about something like this."

Lian was indeed surprised. "You never said."

Wenyu seemed like she wanted to elaborate, but she merely waved it off with a flick of her hand. "You know, wedding jitters. He has a number of divorced friends. Anyway. He's going back to California. On Wednesday."

"He was just . . . okay with that?" She was shocked that Thomas hadn't thrown a fit.

"He knows that pushing me isn't going to help."

Wenyu stood now and walked over to her closet. She selected a cerulean-blue jumpsuit. She untied her robe and slipped into the pant legs, silk cascading down to the floor. She fastened a buckle around her waist. Gucci. She sat back down in the bathroom and began taking down her rollers. Lian helped, making sure not to pull at her hair, loosening the curls slowly.

"I'm proud of you," Lian said.

"Thank you, Lian," Wenyu said, pushing the rollers aside on the counter. She exhaled, a surprising shudder releasing from her as she did. Then she turned and grabbed Lian's hands. "I'm so glad I have you. You make me feel brave enough to do anything."

"You're brave all on your own," Lian said. Her eyes felt wet.

"Everything feels less scary when I do it with you, though," Wenyu said. They held each other's hands, and Lian felt that this was all she ever wanted to be, this right here, two best friends on the verge of something. Everything else—Zhetai, Thomas, Freddy, Su Mingzun—felt far away, even inconsequential.

"*Babe!*" came Thomas's voice. He appeared at the doors, a bounce in his step. There was still some trepidation in his face, but he bounded over and wrapped Wenyu in a hug nonetheless. "*The guests are arriving. You gonna give them a show?*"

"*Of course,*" she said, fastening her earrings. She ripped the last two rollers out from her bangs; Lian watched her hair glide softly into place. "*I always do.*"

WENYU LOOKED GORGEOUS giving her speech. Any trace of the nerves she'd had earlier that evening had disappeared. Everyone clapped when she finished, at which point she began an exhaustive round of greetings. Lian stood next to Zhetai, Zhu Zixi, and Yang Qinru and watched Wenyu as she had that first evening at the engagement party. Occasionally Wenyu would catch Lian's gaze and make a face.

She met Wenyu's other friends, the vociferous blondes and the associates of her father's. She met the architect of the house. All the besuited men blended together in her mind. Then she found herself caught in a conversation on the lawn with first the subdistrict supervisor, who she supposed was here because the house was in his jurisdiction, and then his assistant, a tittering woman with an anxious gait. The woman seemed inordinately enthusiastic, meeting Lian, sticking out her hand with a flourish, and giving Lian's a shake that was much too gregarious.

"Your dress is very pretty," the woman said.

"Thank you."

The woman gestured at the rest of their group. "All of you ladies are dressed so beautifully."

Yang Qinru and Zhu Zixi nodded their thanks. The woman craned her neck toward the kitchen, as if looking for something, then asked if Wenyu would be returning soon. Lian attempted to brush her off, to say that Wenyu was busy with other guests. But the woman did not relent.

"How do you know Miss Vivian?" she asked.

"We grew up together," Lian said.

"Ah, yes," the woman said, as if this were a fact she should have remembered but did not. "You grew up in Beijing?"

"Yes," Lian said. She could not tell where the woman was from; she definitely sounded like she was from the provinces, though she had clearly worked hard to disguise this fact. She was wearing a violet Thierry Mugler dress she certainly hadn't purchased herself. Lian said, "And you worked with her on the house?"

"Well, we worked with the builder," the woman said. "And did you also study in California?"

This woman sure knew a lot about Wenyu's history. "I did not," Lian said.

"I love your bracelet," the woman said next. Lian fingered it self-consciously. She and Wenyu had purchased similar bracelets at Joy City a few weeks prior. The woman looked at her with wide, friendly eyes, though she seemed to be looking through her, too, beyond into the kitchen. Then they heard a great splash and saw the subdistrict supervisor in the pool, the water making a halo of his bald spot for a moment before he blasted back up for air. Unperturbed, the woman moved toward the lawn chair, where she retrieved a towel. Thomas and his friends began cheering and joshing each other toward the pool. Lian only scoffed. These local politicians were always pulling antics like this, peacocking in the hopes of garnering a reputation.

She went back in the house to get some more food. The sushi arrangement had gotten a bit messy, and Lian found herself tidying the dishes. She grabbed a paper towel from a roll beneath the sink and began wiping the counter. Then she saw Wenyu descending the staircase. She was about to call out to her when she saw the woman from earlier hurry up, seemingly from out of nowhere.

"Miss Vivian!" the woman called, pronouncing her name like "vei-vei-an."

Wenyu greeted the woman. "Hi! Was it Miss Guilin?"

"Oh, yes! You remember!" The woman's face lit up like a yellow onion. "I wanted to thank you for a most perfect evening."

"Thank you for coming!" Wenyu said. Lian couldn't see Wenyu's expression from her place in the hallway, but her voice was bright. "Did you get a chance to eat anything yet? I have to say, the toro is quite good. I didn't think you could get good toro this far inland."

"Yes, I did, it's very good indeed," the woman said. "It reminds me of my hometown. I'm from Shandong. Grew up fishing."

"That's so admirable!"

"Is there a lot of fishing in California?"

"Oh, um, I'm sure there is!" Wenyu giggled.

"I don't fish anymore, though."

"Of course."

"Your speech was inspiring."

"Thank you."

The woman paused. "Is it wonderful, being home?"

"It is wonderful," Wenyu said. "There's nowhere like home."

"I haven't been home in three years," the woman said.

"But Shandong, that's not so far away! A few hours by train?"

"Yes," the woman said, blushing. "You're right. I should go home more often."

"Don't wait too long," Wenyu said. She turned to look toward the backyard. "Well, I should probably get back to the rest of the party . . ."

"I'm so happy to meet you!" the woman blurted. Her large head was turned skyward toward Wenyu, making Wenyu look taller than she was.

"Ah—yes—happy to meet you too," Wenyu responded, startled. She was, Lian could tell, starting to get impatient. "Now, I just need to get back to—"

"I've been waiting for this moment for so many years," the woman said. She smiled at Wenyu. Then, with a voice like a gift, "I am a big fan of your channel."

"Oh!" Wenyu nodded, then her shoulders relaxed. "That's very kind of you to say."

"You've helped me through so many dark times," the woman continued. "You are everything I wish I could be."

"That's so sweet," Wenyu said. "You can totally do it!"

The woman smiled, hope mingling with terror in her eyes. "Do you really think so?" Her innocence was a bit unsettling; it was an uncanny portrait, watching Wenyu give advice to a woman several years older than her.

"I'm just a regular girl," Wenyu said. "Anyone can do what I do."

"I have been writing a journal," the woman said. "Maybe one day it can be a YouTube channel too."

"Exactly!" Wenyu said. There was a stale pause as the woman stared. "Do you . . . do you want a selfie?" Wenyu offered, seemingly at a loss for anything else to say.

"What a great idea!" The woman scrambled and grabbed her phone. She turned and pressed her face next to Wenyu's, then reached her arm out and held the phone above their faces. "Eggplant!" she crooned. She snapped the photo.

"Thanks for letting me know," Wenyu said. "Thanks for watching my channel!" She turned to go. Lian watched as desperation flocked across the woman's face. She grabbed Wenyu's arm.

"I . . ." and here the woman sounded close to tears. "I was so shocked when I found out. About your secret."

Wenyu's body froze, and so too did Lian's. She looked around her—no one else was inside the house; everyone was still on the pool deck, enjoying the steadily setting sun. Lian still wasn't visible to either Wenyu or the woman, and she stayed frozen, unsure whether to act or let events unfold.

"It's you." Wenyu finally said.

"Yes! Yes, yes, it's me," the woman said, a bright smile painting itself across her face. "You recognize me!"

"What do you want from me?" Wenyu's voice was low now, coursing with adrenaline. "Why did you come here?"

"I just wanted an explanation."

"What?"

"I thought we could share some secrets. Like friends. Oh, how I want to be your friend!"

"Look, if you want money, I can give you money."

The woman slumped her shoulders; a bra strap drooped downward. Then she sighed, tracing her fingers along the edge of the staircase banister. "I really just want to be friends." She adjusted the collar of her dress and pushed her shoulders back. "Let me tell you a little about myself. I came to Beijing nine years ago, looking for opportunity. I was so lonely. I was twenty-five. I had just ended my very short marriage. I lived in a basement with five other girls. But then one day one of my roommates was watching a video on this American website. She was watching and lying there with a huge smile on her face, even though she had just gotten off her shift at the phone case factory, just like me. We would stand for fourteen hours a day, you know. But this video washed all her exhaustion away. I asked her what it was; she said it was a video posted by a Chinese woman living in California. She called herself *Vivian*." The woman paused now. "You!" She giggled. "I grabbed her phone; I wanted some of her happiness. And I saw you for the first time. This was back when you first started your channel. Your hair was less done up, you had less makeup on, and you were just talking about how you'd cook your favorite meals from back home using American ingredients. You spoke in English, but there was something so soothing about the way you spoke it. You reminded me of myself, speaking in broken Mandarin in Beijing. I could tell that you missed home the way that I missed home. I felt that you were speaking to me, that you were my good friend. I had never used this American website before, YouTube, and my roommate told me she paid 80 RMB a month to jump the firewall. That was half a day's pay! But she said it was worth it, because knowledge was priceless. I became a different woman that day. I began paying the 200, began structuring everything in my life around being able to afford it. Your videos became the number one thing I looked forward to. I would rush home to bed after a shift so I could listen to your sweet words and feel like you were saying them for me alone. You were so honest; you confessed when you were feeling stressed or insecure, and I wanted to reach through the screen to give you a big hug. You accompanied me through my hardest moments, from my years at the factory, where my feet would bleed from standing, to, eventually, when I began to work for Subdistrict Supervisor Ding, and I would sometimes have to be very close to him, as a part of my job. You told me to stay strong and I did. I dreamed of having a life like yours, with a beautiful house and beautiful clothes and someone who loved me. And then, imagine my joy when I discovered that one of Subdistrict Supervisor Ding's contacts was building a house for none other than <u>you</u>! I spent hours daydreaming about how I would engineer a meeting. But the man ended up delivering you right to me! It was so easy to secure an invite to this party. I felt euphoric. Finally! I would meet my best friend! Of course, I got a bit impatient. I sent you gifts. I thought you might appreciate a bike—you're always saying how much you hate exercising, and I thought, biking is a very easy way to move your body without knowing it! I personally love to bike, and I thought it would be so wonderful to bike together. But you never answered any of my letters. Imagine my disappointment when after all this time, my best friend wanted nothing to do with me. I was distraught." She looked at Wenyu with those doleful eyes. "It hurt when you ignored my requests to see you. And then one evening, I was on a late-night frolic through the city—you see, sometimes I like to go where I imagine a young woman with money would go, a club or a nice restaurant, and take photos to look at when I am feeling down or stressed at work—and I happened to catch you and that—that man! I . . . I was heartbroken. I was so disappointed in you. How could you sully your perfect life in this manner? So now that we are finally together, I wanted to ask you: Why did you do it?" She looked at Wenyu, her large eyes round and stunned.

"That's enough." In the course of the woman's speech, Lian had made her way through the side hallway. She emerged into the foyer. Wenyu seemed shocked—even more shocked than she'd been when the woman first revealed her identity. "I think you should leave," Lian said, her heart pounding.

"Oh! The best friend!" The woman giggled. "I've seen you too. Always bouncing through Xidan with Vivian, sharing drinks, laughing, just two girls without a care in the world. I watched you two and wanted that so much. Do you know how many people in the world would kill for something like that?"

"Yes," Lian said. "I do."

Wenyu looked at her. She grabbed Lian's hand.

"You're so loyal. Such a good friend," the woman said. "Vivian, don't you feel so loved? We all love you so much!"

"You don't even know her." Lian's voice had gotten higher in pitch.

"Don't I know her! I know that her favorite ice cream flavor is blueberry. I know that she was scared to have a dog at first but now she loves him. I know that she resents her father for abandoning her family, but she resents her mother more for retreating into herself. I know that she has recurring dreams of horses running in a field and that her greatest fear in life is boredom. I know her! I know her just as much as you do!"

"That's not—just because you know things about her doesn't make her your friend. You're not her friend. You're . . . a fan."

The woman laughed, a joyless thing sputtering into a half cry. "'A fan.' So cruel. What a cruel thing to say." The woman walked closer to Lian. "People like you refuse to admit you've ever wanted anything. You'd prefer to walk around acting like life has just fallen into your lap because of your own righteous actions! I am the only person who's honest about wanting things! I want to be your friend, Vivian Luo! And I'm not embarrassed to say it!"

"Of course we want things! We just don't do crazy things to get them!"

"Don't you!" The woman took out something from her purse. It was a photo. Lian grabbed it; at first she thought it was the photo that Wenyu had received. But when she looked closely, she froze. It was a photo of Wenyu, Su Mingzun, Lian, and Freddy at Club Paradise. The woman must have been waiting for them. She sneered. "Don't you?" she repeated.

Lian stared at herself in the picture. Freddy's arm rested on hers; her face was angled slightly toward him, her desire naked for the world to see. She flinched. "Why are you doing this?"

The woman didn't seem to hear Lian anymore. She looked at Wenyu, her eyes pleading. "Miss Vivian . . . am I just a fan?"

Wenyu looked at her, then at Lian. In childhood, Wenyu would never have given a woman like this the time of day; she'd have laughed in her face. But now, doubt marred her features. "You're just a fan," she said, finally. "I'm not your friend."

The woman screwed her face up and put her head in her hands. "This is such a disappointing conversation." She sagged against the staircase. "I never did anything to you. Why are you so cruel?"

The three of them were silent. Wenyu seemed to have curled into herself; Lian had never seen her so powerless. The woman stood there with her head hung so low Lian could see the shiny top of it, hair product firming it into a flawless bowl. She was perfectly still for one terrifying moment.

Finally, the woman lifted her head. When she spoke next her voice was venomous. "You said it yourself. Anyone can do what you do. You're . . . just a nobody, like me. A nobody who got lucky. Who got rich. Who paid to be beautiful." She looked back down at the floor. "I want to be your friend because you've discovered the secret to happiness. And I want some of that for myself." She paused. "But if you can't give me friendship—well, maybe you can give me some of that happiness."

"What do you mean?"

"Wealth, Miss Vivian," she said. "The secret to a happy life."

"So you do want money. Fine. Fine. Take it. Here, I'll write a check—" There was panic in Wenyu's voice.

"Don't do it, Wenyu—" Lian reached for her.

"I don't want a check," the woman said.

"What do you . . ."

She stood back and lifted one finger, then swirled it around above her head. "This."

"What?" A laugh escaped from Wenyu's lips. "You've gotta be kidding me."

"I'm deadly serious, Vivian Luo," the woman said. She reached into her purse and pulled out another photo. It was another photo of the four of them, taken this time at Houhai, Lian and Wenyu leaning over the stone railing while Freddy stood to the side. Su Mingzun had his hand on Wenyu's waist. She'd been following them for weeks. "I have so many of these," she said. "You can still have everything. Your American fiancé. Your Chinese lover. All of your wealth. Or you can have nothing."

"I can't just give you this house." Wenyu's voice was shaking. "This house is my dream. This house . . . we always said we'd live in a house like this one day . . . away from everyone . . ." Lian wasn't sure, in this moment, which "we" she meant.

"Oh, don't be so dramatic," the woman said. "For someone like you, take away one dream, you still have the entire world. Dreams lose meaning when it comes to people like you. You can't even begin to contemplate the meaning of a dream, because it doesn't exist for you. Not anymore. A dream implies something you can never get. And there's nothing in the world you can't get, Miss Vivian."

"That's not true," Wenyu cried. "There's so much I can't have."

"Lies! You have the world and you still want more!" Hysteria straitjacketed the woman's voice. "You have no idea what it's like to have every dream trampled, every day. You have no idea what it's like to truly suffer!"

"Of course I do," Wenyu said. "I may have money now, but I've suffered. I know what it's like for a dream to die."

"Oh, because America was hard? Because it was hard to speak English?" the woman sneered, her voice mocking. "Try being spat on in a language you understand perfectly clearly. It hurts a lot more."

"That's happened to me too."

Wenyu gripped Lian's arm. The woman watched their faces, flitting from Wenyu to Lian.

"She won't do it," Lian said, squeezing Wenyu's hand. "She's a coward. It's all a bluff. What will telling Thomas even do for her?"

For the first time, the woman's face betrayed a hairline fracture of doubt. But she remained staring back at Lian defiantly.

Lian reached over, grabbing the photo from the woman's hands. "She can't prove that this is you. It could be any girl." And indeed, only someone like Lian, who could recognize Wenyu from miles away, who knew that her hairline crossed in a Z shape when she didn't have time to carefully brush it in the morning, who knew that she liked to rest her hand on a surface and tap it when she was nervous, who knew that she got hot easily and so was always wearing a tank top earlier in the season than anyone else, but had been so ridiculed and called a slut for it that she'd started wearing the sheerest of linen shirts as a cover-up—only she would really recognize Wenyu in this photo. She didn't believe that Thomas could beyond the shadow of a doubt say that this was her, and no one else on earth. "So go ahead, do it." Her heart pounded maniacally. She almost wished for the woman to go ahead and say it; wouldn't Wenyu tell him eventually, after he was back in California? "Do it," she said, and found herself hoping.

Lian and Wenyu looked at each other. They knew what they were risking, saying this. They were jumping into the abyss together. Lian thought of Zhetai, probably mumbling politely on the deck at some confounding story of Zhu Zixi's, and felt a pang. "It could be any girl," Wenyu repeated.

"You—" the woman snatched the photo back, her eyes darting between Wenyu and Lian's faces and the image of the club floor. She turned out toward the pool, as if searching for Thomas in the crowd. Lian followed her gaze. He was still standing with his Stanford friends, all of them hulking Americans in pastel-colored shorts and gelled-back crew cuts. Lian imagined this woman rushing up to that group, trying to stammer out the vicious truth, and almost laughed.

It appeared that the woman thought the same thing. Her shoulders slumped again. "I—"

"Guilin! Oh, Guiiiiiiiliiiiiin!" Subdistrict Supervisor Ding was sauntering toward them, holding his swim trunks in his hands so that they dripped water on every surface. A frosty loss carved its way across the woman's face before she swiftly rearranged it into a smile as she turned toward her leering boss.

"There you are," she said. "I was just thanking the hostess for her hospitality."

"My darling Guilin," he said, putting his hands on her shoulders. "Always so polite."

Witnessing this, Lian felt shame for almost having laughed; she nearly wanted to blurt out the truth herself. The woman turned back toward Wenyu. She reached out her hand, and, when Wenyu did not lift her arm, she grabbed Wenyu's hand with both of hers, shaking it energetically.

"It was so nice to meet you," the woman said. Then she grabbed the subdistrict supervisor's swim trunks and ushered him away, looking like lover, worker, and mother all at the same time.

Once they had exited the house, and Lian could hear the subdistrict supervisor's car starting up, Wenyu let out a giant exhale, practically falling to her knees.

"Oh my god," she said.

"Wenyu . . . are you okay?" Lian stooped and covered her with her arms.

"No," she said. "Fuck. Fuck."

"She was fucking crazy," Lian said.

"Yeah," Wenyu said, her voice trailing. "Was she?"

"Who fucking does that?"

"She's right. I don't . . . I don't need this house. I don't need any of this."

"I think you should rest."

Wenyu sat there on her heels, clutching her arms, her head tucked into her lap so that strands of her hair quivered on the tile.

"Let's go," Lian whispered into Wenyu's ear. She could see Thomas and the men by the pool, the group of them throwing their hands up, making circles that could mean anything: reminiscing about a party they'd all gone to, where Thomas had purchased shots for everyone; a deal that had gone through spectacularly, where the investors had been instantly charmed . . . whatever it was, it was a world far from her and Wenyu's concerns in that moment. She saw that the group was getting rowdier, in that end-of-party way that signals a move to a new location. Thomas took another deep pull of his drink and moved from the dusking light into the kitchen. Lian coaxed Wenyu up; she didn't want to have to see her arrange her face into that perfect portrait again, quip in English with Thomas at a moment like this. "Let's go," she repeated, and Wenyu obeyed, standing slowly, her breath steady and shallow.

She turned her friend toward the staircase and the two of them ascended. Wenyu pulled off her heels as she went, and Lian collected them in her hands. "I'm so tired," she said.

"I know," Lian said.

They reached the landing, and Wenyu raked her right hand through her hair. "Thank you Lianlian," she said, taking Lian's arms in her hands. "I'm just gonna lie down for a second."

"Go," Lian said, and stayed where she was. Wenyu walked into the bedroom and shut the door behind her.

"*Hey!*" She heard a voice down below and turned to see Thomas gesturing up at her. "*Where's Vivian?*"

"*She's just resting for a second,*" Lian said, pulling her own mouth into a toothy smile. "*Too much champagne.*" She twirled her head in a mimicry of drunkenness.

"*I get you,*" he said, laughing. "*We're just gonna head into town, all right? Let her know. Boys wanna go to Paradise.*"

"*Sure,*" Lian said. She felt a swell of pride, that she could be the one to wear Wenyu's mask for her now, could bear the burden of the portrait. It hurt her mouth to smile, but the pride was worth it.

WENYU EVENTUALLY CAME DOWNSTAIRS. Lian could tell she'd washed her face, redone her makeup. No one mentioned her absence. Zhetai left shortly after. Lian told him she'd be staying with Wenyu tonight; she would see him later. It was past ten when Zhu Zixi and Bo stumbled out of the house and Wenyu shut the front door behind them with a cheery wave.

And then she and Wenyu were alone. Wenyu immediately stripped her heels back off, so that the hems of her jumpsuit trailed on the ground. For a moment she looked like a child again, wearing her mother's too-large clothes.

"What a day," she said. "I'm gonna get changed."

She seemed rejuvenated from her nap, the events of the previous few hours scrubbed from her mind. Perhaps this was how Wenyu had to operate, a shark constantly moving forward. They set off for the second floor, nearly running up the stairs in their excitement. Now that Thomas and Zhetai had departed, it was time to get ready for Su Mingzun and Freddy. Wenyu unclasped her belt and exhaled. "God, that thing was so heavy." She changed into a blouse and cotton shorts, and Lian did the same.

They cleaned quickly and thoroughly, as if ashamed of the excesses of the party that had just transpired. The champagne glasses went rapidly into the dishwasher, the plates of picked-at sashimi were dumped and taken out to the trash bins.

Freddy showed up first, carrying a bottle of wine. He was wearing a dark gray button-down shirt, and Lian saw immediately that he'd missed the middle button. "Hi," he said, in his straightforward manner, holding out the bottle. "I didn't know what Wenyu liked or what . . ."

"Thanks," Lian said. "Thanks for coming," she added.

"Hey, Freddy!" Wenyu burst forth from the kitchen, wrapping Freddy in a hug. "So nice to see you!"

Lian felt her face grow hot; she'd still never hugged Freddy in this way—emphatically, lushly. He took the hug in stride, though, and replied, "This is a nice house."

"Thanks," Wenyu said, and waved him inside. "What's your drink?" she asked, moving toward the kitchen and placing Freddy's wine on the counter.

"He doesn't drink," Lian reminded her, quickly.

"Right, well, why don't you take Freddy on a tour of the house?" Wenyu said, smiling.

Freddy followed behind Lian as they walked through the kitchen into the living room and then the rec room, then up the staircase, politely craning his neck and pointing out details.

They paused on the landing, looking down at Wenyu in the kitchen, wiping countertops with her typical brand of Wenyu brashness, furiously and broadly, with no attention to detail. "That chandelier is so cool," he said, gesturing at the fixture hanging from the ceiling in the kitchen.

"Check this out," Lian said, pushing through a pair of double-doors. "This room has the best view." She gestured out at the sparkling lights of the city, and only then did she remember that they were in the bedroom.

He continued his polite narration. "Rich people love to have nothing in their bedroom, don't they," he said. "Except a huge bed."

"Minimalism," she said. "The more you have, the fewer things you're allowed to show you have."

She led him to the balcony, which overlooked the pool. "Ta-da," she said, half-facetiously, half-genuinely. It really was a beautiful view.

He stopped and stared down at the pool. An evening chill startled the surface of the water; the slightest ripples billowed outward from one green leaf.

"You think you could jump into the pool from here?" Freddy asked.

"I don't think so . . ." Lian said, her brow furrowing. "It's high."

"You're right," he said. "Those things are usually pretty shallow."

At this moment there was a persistent ringing at the front door. "Hey!" came a bark. "The party's here!"

Lian and Freddy exited the bedroom and made their way back down the stairs. Su Mingzun had arrived. Wenyu practically pounced into his arms, covering his face with kisses. He looked up at Lian and Freddy.

"Hey there, Comrade Ye," he said. "And Student Freddy, where's your backpack?"

"Be nice, Mingzun," Wenyu said.

Freddy ignored him, loping past into the living room. Wenyu mouthed a "sorry" at Lian.

Freddy sat down on Wenyu's velvet couch. Lian took a seat gingerly beside him.

Su Mingzun brought out a bottle of tequila. Wenyu clapped her hands, then saw Freddy's bottle of wine on the counter. "Should we break into this?" Wenyu held it up. Lian immediately felt a bit self-conscious. The wine was superfluous; clearly they would be drinking tequila tonight.

"Maybe later," Lian answered, then turned to Freddy. "Wine makes me so sleepy." He shrugged.

Su Mingzun poured drinks, mixing tequila liberally with dashes of soda. He held one out to each of them.

"He doesn't—" Lian began saying, but Freddy took a glass.

"Maybe just a little bit," he murmured, shrugging.

Su Mingzun collapsed onto the couch. Wenyu draped her arms around Su Mingzun's shoulders and nuzzled her cheek into his. Again Wenyu's love floated off her like steam, its heat lapping at everything around her, and again Lian was the frigid one, sitting alone with her arms folded, at a distance from the one she should be touching. But this was not Zhetai. The context was entirely new, and that made all the difference. She glanced over at Freddy, who gave her a knowing smile, bashful, and she was shot through with a thrill. In that stare he acknowledged a hundred things: I am a man, and you are a woman, and we're sitting here looking at this man and woman in love. I am a man you've invited here. I am a man you've been talking to for months, and, let's be honest, it's not just because you're very invested in teaching me English. It's embarrassing and also exciting to watch these two do their romantic little dance because that's what I want to do to you, but later. Later.

"So how was the party?" Su Mingzun asked, and took a big pull of his tequila. "The real party."

"This is the real party," Wenyu said, knocking his foot with hers.

"What party?" Freddy asked.

"Just a thing she had with her parents," Lian interjected, not wanting Wenyu, or, god forbid, Su Mingzun, to go into a whole explanation. She'd told Freddy she and Wenyu would be busy earlier in the day, but would he like to come see Wenyu's new house? Freddy knew that Wenyu was a YouTuber in America, but she hadn't told him about Thomas or Wenyu's engagement, just as she'd never told him about Zhetai. More omissions did not make a lie, she told herself.

"It was nice," Wenyu said.

"Did the Americans have a good time? Feel right at home in this good ol' American suburb?" Su Mingzun looked around, made an exaggerated shiver with his body. "Makes me feel like I'm on a movie set."

"What are you talking about? This is nothing like a normal American house!" Wenyu said, pouting.

"Okay, okay," he said. "You're right, most people in America live in the ghetto." He paused. Then, softening a little: "You did all this yourself?"

"Yeah," she said, beaming. "Two years of blood, sweat, and *Pinterest*."

"Did the Americans do something stupid? Get naked in the pool?"

"Actually, Subdistrict Supervisor Ding went for a swim."

"Ooooooh," Su Mingzun said, in faux admiration. "How daring."

Wenyu ignored his sarcastic tone; she poured herself more tequila.

"I still don't know how you don't feel gross," he said, stroking her arm. "Cozying up to all these politicians, these brands."

Wenyu shrugged. Lian could see her shoulders stiffen even as she did so. "I know it's not what you would do, but it's a job."

"But it's kind of a bit, too, right? Like you're sticking it to them, in a way?"

"Yeah," Wenyu said, her tone nonchalant. "They don't own me."

"You know what would be so sick? If you posted a whole takedown of all the brands you get money from. You have more money than you can count now, don't you? Why don't you just say, fuck it! You know, pull back the curtain and air every last bit of dirty laundry."

Wenyu chuckled. "That would be fun," she said.

"And that supervisor guy, whatever his name is, I'm sure he's got some sicko skeletons in his closet."

"Yeah," Wenyu said. But her voice was getting quieter.

The tequila was starting to heat up inside Lian. "Why don't you go into politics, Comrade?" She found herself sneering. "You can clean up the whole damn system."

Su Mingzun grinned. "Oh, Comrade Ye, the old change it from the inside out. I'm not naive enough to do that. Cleaning up politics is like trying to mop up an oil spill with a cotton ball. Especially Chinese politics."

"Do you think there's another country where politics are better?"

His smile turned wolfish. "No," he said. "There is no current system of government that works well for all of its citizens. But there are certainly people who thrive in every single country in the world."

"Yes," Lian said. "And your problem is you think you're not one of these people, but you are." She turned to Wenyu. "What do you think, Wenyu?"

They were in a silent tug-of-war for Wenyu's loyalty, as they always were. Wenyu looked shyly up at Su Mingzun. "Lianlian is right, Zun. You're always complaining about rich people, but, I mean . . ."

"What do you mean?"

"It's not like your family is poor."

"How could you say that?" His face wore an expression of genuine hurt.

"I mean, before. I mean before . . . that. When we were kids and stuff. We were all the same. Like, doing okay."

"You've really bought into the grand Communist mythos, haven't you!" Su Mingzun sprang up now, releasing his arm from behind Wenyu. His face was the color of crawfish inside a soup of numbing spice. "The grand 'middle class' created by Mao Zedong, thank you so much. Let's completely forget about all the government officials who hid their riches and passed them down; let's forget about the boom in the nineties when some of our parents got fucking rich and some of them lost their jobs and had to go do <u>hard labor</u> . . ."

"Please! Mingzun! You know it wasn't like that. Your dad got fired because—"

"Don't talk about my dad."

Freddy looked from Su Mingzun to Wenyu. "My dad got his first company taken from him. By his friend. Real '*Social Network*' type of situation."

They blinked at him.

"Like the movie. About Facebook," Lian said. "You know, Mark Zuckerberg fucks over his friend . . ."

"I don't know who that is," Su Mingzun said. "I don't worship Americans."

Lian rolled her eyes. "You don't know who Mark Zuckerberg is?"

Freddy put up his hands in a gesture of surrender. "I'm just into movies. Not necessarily set in America."

This seemed to set Su Mingzun off most of all. "Movies. Oh, you're a <u>movie guy</u>!" The emphasis on the last two words was mocking.

"Yeah, he's going to film school, right, Freddy?" Wenyu chimed in, seemingly desperate to change the subject.

It wasn't helping. Lian watched as Su Mingzun heaved a great sigh and trudged off to the kitchen. "Kid's going to film school and he's trying to relate to the masses." He gulped down a glass of water then trudged outside, sliding the glass door closed behind him with a slam. He stood by the water, just watching it.

"What's his problem?" Lian said.

"He's just stressed," Wenyu said. She turned to Freddy. "I'm sorry."

Freddy shrugged, then fell back against the sofa, clutching his glass in front of him. It was nearly empty.

This pattern was classic. Su Mingzun made a scene; Wenyu made excuses for it. Why did she have to apologize every time he ruined the mood? She almost seemed to take pleasure in it— he's a disaster, but he's my disaster. She became smaller in Su Mingzun's presence, her fire still bright but less so in comparison to his wildly flailing inferno. Lian watched as Wenyu lit a cigarette, her fingers trembling, her eyes darting every so often back toward the pool. She hadn't seen Wenyu smoke since that evening in the alleyway.

"I didn't realize you smoked," she said.

"Just sometimes when I drink," Wenyu replied, waving a plume of smoke away from her face.

Wenyu was always a mystery around men. She was someone Lian could never fully see, like a shard of glass reflecting one million shadows with every tilt. Once Lian had left her textbook in the classroom and run back to retrieve it. She walked in and saw Wenyu and Su Mingzun in the corner, Wenyu's eyes red, Su Mingzun leaning over her with a tenderness she'd never witnessed in any boy. When Wenyu saw Lian, she immediately whirled toward the back of the classroom, hiding her face. Lian slowly backed out of the room with a mumbled, I'll be outside.

In this moment Lian realized there were things about Wenyu only Su Mingzun would ever see—only men would ever see—and she'd be forever locked out, peering at Wenyu through a window. And seeing Wenyu's face obscured by smoke now, Lian was reminded of all the other times in her life when she stumbled in on someone else's private world, and how lonely that felt—so lonely that she'd gone and made her own.

"Tell me more about film school," Wenyu said now, gesturing at Freddy, but her eyes remained trained on the pool.

"Well, some good news," Freddy said, turning to Lian. "I managed to get ahold of a professor. She—she said she read my sample and liked it. I feel like my chances are good!"

"That's awesome!" Lian said.

"I'm jealous," Wenyu said, smiling politely. "I love New York City. I would kill to live next to Washington Square Park!"

"I hope I get to," he said.

"You know what, sorry," Wenyu interrupted, rising and putting her cigarette out. "I'm just gonna check on him . . ."

They watched her go. She walked up to Su Mingzun and wrapped her arm around his waist; he put an arm over her shoulder. They sat down on a recliner, Wenyu coiling into the crook of his armpit.

Shyness settled over Lian and Freddy. She took a heavy gulp of her drink.

"I'm excited for you," she said.

"Thanks, Lily," he said. "I don't wanna get my hopes up, but . . . someone wise once told me I should only bet on impossible odds."

She grinned.

"You've really made me feel like I have something interesting to say."

"I haven't done anything. You already did."

He smiled. "When you come to New York, I'll take you everywhere," he said. "I'll get you a . . . big apple."

She burst into laughter. "Oh, that's what you think the *Big Apple* means? That they have a lot of big apples?"

"Yeah!" he laughed.

She took another large gulp of her drink. She was looking at his lips, wondering what those lips would taste like. His eyelids were dropping just slightly, and he looked back at her. Then she kissed him.

Freddy's eyes did not flutter open in surprise. In fact, he met her mouth with a larger force, pushing his lips into hers, his tongue—soft and wet—grazing the edge of her lower lip. They kissed like this for a long moment, their necks outstretched, hands still in their respective laps, as if their bodies couldn't quite believe what their mouths had just done.

His mouth tasted like meat, the remnants of an earlier meal oily and hot on his breath. A twinge of mint smacked shockingly, briefly, against her tongue.

His hands moved toward her now and her hands moved, too, meeting and interlacing with his. They sat there, holding hands and kissing. It was sweet. Then they disentangled their fingers and moved their hands onto each other's bodies. It was a dance; it was synchronized swimming; she was most surprised at how they both seemed to understand what would happen next.

It was different with Zhetai. The first time they had had sex, they had stripped naked before even touching, and he had looked at her body with the clinical curiosity of a scientist. He had palmed each of her breasts like he was offering fruit to an ancestor. When he kissed her, it felt as if his lips were searching for an answer.

There was no looking here; she let her body lead, possibly for the first time, and it found its destination quickly. His fingers moved to her waist and then up her arms, rubbing them; she put her hands on his chest, feeling his heat through his shirt.

Then she heard Wenyu's voice. It was plaintive, agitated, carrying from outside. "Then do it!" She heard a piercing laugh, the kind tinged with disbelief. A Pavlovian response tugged at her. Wenyu was in trouble.

She felt herself slowing, pulling away. Freddy seemed hurt. Then his face registered detection; he heard the voices too.

"I'm sorry," she said. She peered behind Freddy, at the pool.

"They're probably fine," Freddy said. "I'm sure he's just ranting about something again."

"I'm sorry," she repeated. "I just have to . . ."

She got up. Freddy's lips twisted into a knot; he looked down and finally noticed the undone button. He looked at her shyly, probably thinking she'd been the one to undo it, a misconception that brought her almost to laughter. But she didn't have time to contemplate; she was already walking toward the glass doors.

Su Mingzun's figure loomed over the side of the pool. Wenyu crouched at the edge, her arms wrapped around her knees. Lian slid open the door to a stilted heaviness in the air. The usual shyness crashed over her; perhaps she shouldn't have interrupted.

"Wenyu?" she managed.

"We're fine," Su Mingzun barked, annoyance jittering through his voice.

"Hi Lianlian," Wenyu said. She seemed okay, though the rings around her eyes told Lian she was right; Wenyu had been crying. "We're okay."

"Okay . . . uh . . . I can go back inside . . ."

"No no, come sit," Wenyu said, waving her over.

Lian sat down next to Wenyu on the pool deck, let her feet tickle the edge of the water. Freddy followed, sitting down in a recliner behind them.

"Are you okay?" Lian whispered to Wenyu.

"Yeah," Wenyu said, after a pause that felt too long.

"She won't leave him," Su Mingzun said, his voice like death.

Lian started. She looked at Wenyu, who didn't meet her eyes.

"Zun. I'm not talking about this right now—"

"When will you talk about it, if not right now? There's no more time. You're gonna . . . you're getting married." His voice was solid and low, almost trancelike.

Wenyu stood and crossed to the other side of the pool deck, her hands on her hips. She bent at the waist before crouching down, her hands moving to her mouth to stifle—what?—a scream? A sob?

"Is it because of the money? Is it because I'm not as rich as him?"

"Zun! You should know me better than that. I don't care about that!"

"Really? All you talk about when you talk about America is how you guys bought this house or went on that vacation or how fucking good life is. You love the money! Admit it! You never had any money and that's why you love it! You were just a poor fucking asshole too." His voice crescendoed then retreated; Lian couldn't tell if he was on the precipice of an explosion or a surrender.

"Su Mingzun! Can you just shut up for one second! It's not because of the money. I have my own goddamn money."

"What is he talking about?" Freddy whispered, scooting closer to Lian.

"It's . . . complicated," Lian said. She watched as Su Mingzun moved toward Wenyu, pleading. Lian, too, was surprised and confused. Wasn't this the day that their lives were supposed to change? Wasn't it a happy moment? When had Wenyu had this change of heart? She thought about the stalker, remembered the timidity in Wenyu's voice.

Lian rose. "Su Mingzun, just . . . lay off for a second—"

"Ye Lian," he said, his voice shaking. "Please. Let me talk to Wenyu."

Lian didn't say anything else. She watched him watch Wenyu.

He took a deep breath. "Okay. I'm sorry. It's not because of that. But if it's not . . . what does he have that I don't have? How could he possibly understand you more?"

"Mingzun," Wenyu said, and her voice was a harsh whisper, saliva cutting her off halfway. "You always think you know me best."

"But I do!"

"Su Mingzun—" Lian stepped toward him.

"Ye Lian—I don't need your assessment of the situation for one fucking second, okay?"

"Don't talk to Lianlian like that," Wenyu said, turning to face them.

"You just can't let us fucking live, can you." Su Mingzun advanced on Lian. "Anywhere Wenyu is, you're always fucking <u>there</u>!"

"Hey, man, you don't need to talk to Lily like that—" Freddy stood and pressed his hand to Su Mingzun's chest. He was shorter than Su Mingzun, and Lian felt herself cringe.

"Oh, you're so innocent," Su Mingzun snapped at Freddy. "Look at me, I'm a big hero. I write movies and I'm gonna save this damsel in distress!" Su Mingzun jabbed his finger into Freddy's shoulder.

Freddy slapped Su Mingzun's hand away. "Don't touch me."

"Whoooooooeee, big guy!" Su Mingzun sneered. "Wake up, dude. You're defending someone you don't even know. Let me tell you, man to man, she's just using you too!"

"What? What are you talking about?"

"Don't listen to him—" Lian said, putting her hand on Freddy's arm.

"Stop thinking you're so high and fucking mighty, Ye Lian. If it wasn't for you, Wenyu would've never had to leave."

At this, Lian's blood ran cold. She looked at Wenyu, who had crouched back down, her face hidden from view.

Lian's skin burned. Her throat felt tight. "You're the one who kept getting her suspended, because you can never not be the center of fucking attention!"

"And you really wanted that, too, didn't you? Except you couldn't handle the heat when you got it. And then on top of everything, you abandoned her when she left."

"I didn't abandon her! We both stopped talking!"

"Well, I stuck around."

Wenyu had pulled her knees up to her chest now, and her voice came out muffled. "Zun . . . this doesn't matter . . ."

"What is he saying?" Now Lian was confused, and she looked at Wenyu.

"Yeah, that's right, Comrade Ye. I bet she didn't tell you we kept talking. We never stopped talking. I was talking to her up until the day she got fucking engaged."

Lian's heart stiffened. "Yutou . . . is that . . . true?"

Wenyu kept her back to them, her arms wrapped tightly around herself, her shoulders hunched upward as if she were protecting herself from a deep chill. She was painfully still. When she finally turned around, her face was a sea. "It's true, Lianlian, it's true, I'm sorry, I didn't mean to lie . . ."

"Don't apologize to her! I'm the one you lied to!" Su Mingzun's voice was sharp.

"I didn't lie to you! Everything I ever said to you was the truth!"

"What? That you'd come back here, that we'd be together, that we'd live in this fucking house, that we'd have a million babies and be together forever, forever!" Su Mingzun was sobbing now, too, tears mingling with snot. "Was that true? Was that true!"

His sobs rang out in the open courtyard. Freddy shifted beside her. "What is going on?"

"Shut up! Shut up shut up shut up!" Su Mingzun's face was contorted in the way that woman's had been. Desperate people all looked alike, didn't they? He grabbed Freddy's shoulder. "There is no happiness on the other side of this, my brother! See this bitch?" He jabbed his finger at Lian. "Ask her about her basic little boyfriend of, what, a decade? Then see if you wanna play knight in shining armor."

Freddy looked at Lian, his face a portrait of bewilderment. "What? Who?"

"Don't listen to him," Lian said.

"Come on, Comrade Ye! I thought you were better than this. You're gonna straight up lie now? Come on, go ahead, tell him!"

Freddy's gaze turned hard.

"I . . . Freddy, look, I'm just . . ." She didn't have an explanation. Giving an explanation would necessitate delineating whatever the hell it was the two of them were doing, and she couldn't do that, not here. "I don't know what I'm doing."

"So it's true. You have a boyfriend."

"I do," she said. "But I—I don't know if I—if I want it . . . want him . . . look, I don't know, you're going to New York! I didn't think that this—that any of this—would happen—I—"

"See?" Su Mingzun said. "These girls are just using us because they're having a quarter-life fucking crisis. We're just pawns in their little game. And you fucking bought it—you stupid idiot. You're a little boy coasting on a dream! You don't see the truth right in front of your fucking face. Wake up, little boy! Wake up!" He lurched closer to Freddy, until his breath fogged Freddy's glasses. "Paradise is a myth, and you bought into it. Idiot! Dreams don't come true! You grow up and everything becomes fucking boring and the love of your life marries someone else. Wake up, you stupid. Little. Boy!" He was shaking him now, Freddy taking the jolts like a rag doll.

And then Freddy lunged at Su Mingzun, pushing him into the pool. Freddy dove in after Su Mingzun and grabbed at his neck.

"I'm not. A little. Boy! I'm not a little boy!" Freddy screamed.

Su Mingzun surged upward, trying to break Freddy's grasp, flailing his arms. Freddy's hands locked into a choke hold and held Su Mingzun under the water.

"Stop! Stop!" Wenyu shouted. "Get off him!"

Lian heard her own voice as if from far away; it was a screech: "Freddy! Freddy! What are you doing! Freddy!"

"I know what I'm doing," he shouted. "You're the fucking stupid one!"

"Freddy," Lian pleaded, as Su Mingzun's arms began to slow, as the spray settled, Su Mingzun's shirt parachuting upward in the water. "This isn't you."

Freddy looked up at Lian, and in that moment, he really did look like a little boy.

"Stop," she pleaded, her voice hoarse.

He let go. Su Mingzun surged to the surface, thwacking him in an attempt to retaliate. "What the FUCK was that, man!"

"Stop it!" Wenyu was still screaming. "Get out of the fucking pool!"

Freddy swam to the edge and heaved himself up. It seemed to take quite some effort, his slim arms quaking under the weight of the water on his clothes. She wanted to rush forward and help him, but she was frozen in place. Freddy collapsed onto the deck, then slowly rose, before turning back and reaching out a hand to Su Mingzun.

"Fuck you." Su Mingzun spat. He hoisted himself up, his head hung low, his T-shirt pasted to his chest.

Freddy looked at Lian. She saw fear in his eyes, and she supposed it was a reflection of what he saw in hers. The figures from his essay flashed in her mind, the disemboweled cat, the violent father. He wiped his face with his wet sleeve. His glasses had fallen off in the tussle. Lian wondered—who was this person in front of her?

As if he could hear her question, he turned toward the water. His glasses were on the pool's bottom. He sat down on the edge and slipped in again, gingerly this time, and ducked below the surface for a long beat before he reemerged, glasses in hand. When he lifted himself back onto the deck, he wouldn't look at Lian.

"You know, I've always liked older women," he finally said. "What's the phrase? *Fool me once, shame on you. Fool me twice...*"

They had never spoken of their romances, and it shocked her now to hear this confession.

"Freddy . . ." She wasn't sure what she was trying to save. The beginnings of something? A way out? "I just. I just really wanted to know you!"

"Well, now you know me," he said. "Is this everything you wanted?"

They stared at each other. She held his gaze, unmoving, not wanting to make a decision, her brain assessing all the new information that had presented itself to her in the last five minutes—if only she had more time—

He looked away. Then he nodded almost imperceptibly, a bobble of the body that could have been merely a shiver in the suddenly cold night air.

He went into the house. She watched him retrieve his jacket from the sofa. He looked back at her and gave a little wave. She wanted to run to him, give him a hug. Then he walked through the front door and was gone.

Su Mingzun's voice cut through the quiet. "I need a cigarette. Fucking punk." He rose slowly and stripped off his T-shirt to trudge, chest bare, across the deck toward the house. He grabbed the handle of the sliding glass door.

It was just Wenyu and Lian now, crouched by the side of the pool. They huddled together, looking up at the house. All the lights were on, casting aureate streams onto the pool's surface, now still. It struck Lian, the brevity of rage, the way it ignited and sputtered so rapidly you could almost miss it.

"Wenyu . . ." Lian began. "What changed?"

Wenyu peered up at her, flyaways coming loose from her curls. She looked somehow younger than she had in high school; she looked like that little girl Lian had first encountered in the grocery. Uncertainty lashed her face.

And then there was a sound, like wind traveling rapidly through a tunnel. The smell of smoke hit her nose like a blow.

2

The blast was reasonably small, but, as it turned out, the house was made of paper. The kitchen and guest bedroom went up in seconds; the hundred-thousand-RMB light fixture that had hung so imperiously over the kitchen was attached to mere plaster. It came down swiftly, right on top of Su Mingzun.

She saw the blaze almost immediately after she smelled the smoke. The fire refracted through the glass panes seemed almost to ripple. And then she heard Wenyu screaming. And then she was rising, following Wenyu as she ran toward the door.

Smoke smacked at Lian's eyes.

"Mingzun! Zun!" Wenyu's cries were bloodcurdling. The kitchen and doorway to the first-floor bedroom were ablaze. The light fixture lay on the ground in a pile of debris, and underneath it was Su Mingzun. His hands were curled toward his face; the bulk of the fixture rested on his left shoulder. Lian's breath caught in her throat when she saw red blooming from his forehead.

"Zun! Zun!" Wenyu stumbled toward him. She grabbed the light fixture and hoisted it off, adrenaline rendering her superhuman.

"We have to get out of here," Lian said. The kitchen was on fire. Flames licked their way up the wall next to the fridge and scorched black rings into the ceiling. Lian and Wenyu grabbed Su Mingzun's feet and pulled him toward the glass doors, just as another great crash resounded behind them; the rectangular window above the archway to the bedroom came down in a brilliant shatter. Su Mingzun was heavy. She wondered if with every pull they were cutting him on the glass that had already fallen on the ground. Lian managed to wedge her hands underneath Su Mingzun's armpits and hoist him up while Wenyu grabbed his feet, and together, they lifted him through the doorway, his body sagging in an undignified U so that it scraped the threshold. It was so hot—fire was so hot, she thought dumbly. She stepped back, nearly into the pool itself, before pivoting and collapsing on the lawn. Inside the fire licked its way up.

What the fuck had happened. What the fuck what the fuck. She fumbled for her phone.

"Mingzun, Su Mingzun! Wake the fuck up!" Wenyu was cradling Su Mingzun's head and crying. "Wake up!"

She dialed 120.

"Zun, please, wake up—I'm sorry, it's all my fault—I'll marry you, I promise—I fucking hate you—you stupid fucking idiot—who do you think you are!! Wake the fuck up!!" Wenyu yelled in Su Mingzun's face.

The operator picked up. "Hi—there's been an accident," Lian said into the phone. "An explosion, a man, something fell and hit his head, he's unconscious. Please come. We're at 48 Sutton Place." She surprised herself with her cool efficiency. Everything around her seemed to warp; she was no longer in her own body but staring down at the figure kneeling on the lawn, speaking into the phone, her clothes smoky and stained, the unconscious figure of Su Mingzun next to her, suddenly as vulnerable as a baby.

"It's my fault," Wenyu kept repeating. "I'm sorry. I'm sorry. I'll marry you, yes, I'll marry you. Please wake up. Please just wake up."

But he didn't. His head lay tucked in the crook of her elbow, his face turned toward the sky, utterly peaceful. One of his socks had a hole in it. Lian felt suddenly ashamed, seeing the flesh of his foot peeking out from inside.

"Stupid, stupid, stupid," Wenyu screamed, shaking his body. "Why are you so stupid!"

"Wenyu," Lian said, grabbing her arm, steadying her. "Keep him still."

The paramedics came. Firefighters, police sirens, men with pens and hats asking them questions. The crew managed to put the fire out within half an hour, but the damage was done. Large black stains marred the walls of the kitchen; the floorboards had warped and burned. The second guest bedroom sat right on top of the ground-floor bedroom, and the fire had burned through the ceiling to the second floor. The fallen light fixture left a hole a meter wide.

Lian watched as Su Mingzun's body was lifted onto a stretcher, one side of his baggy pants burned so that shreds dangled off. She had a wild thought that he might like that, might find it high fashion. Wenyu followed him, her hands lingering on the stretcher, tears running down her face, streaming in a current that her dimples could not catch.

Then there were questions. Police with their notebooks and vulturine curiosity. Lian observed Wenyu talking with an officer. She'd collected herself almost instantaneously in a startling quick-change that unsettled Lian. She could hear the officer ask Wenyu if there was anyone else at the house that night.

"No," Wenyu said. "I had a housewarming, but everyone left before ten." She lied so convincingly Lian felt suddenly frightened.

"What was your relationship to the injured?" he asked next.

"A classmate," Wenyu called him.

The police suggested they stay elsewhere that night, then departed, with promises to return the next day for further investigation. Lian and Wenyu were left alone on the front steps, unspeaking. Wenyu had stopped crying. All her tears had left with Su Mingzun. All the feeling that had just coursed through Lian's body, the desire and excitement and anger and fear, had withered into cool embarrassment. What she and Freddy had been doing seemed like childish fumbling now.

Lian put her arms around Wenyu. The smoke lingering in the air made her head pound. Questions raced through her mind. How had the fire begun? Was it an accident? Or had someone done this? Would Su Mingzun be okay? She could barely comprehend all that had happened in the previous hour. How did their lives change so suddenly?

"Wenyu," Lian said, landing back in her body. "What happened?"

Wenyu was silent. What happened? It was a big question. What happened here tonight? What happened the last few days? The last few weeks? Lian supposed she was asking about all of it.

"I hated America," Wenyu finally said, her voice thick. "When I first arrived. I was so lonely. I could barely speak. No one talked to me. My host mom's kids, they were the meanest. They'd ask me the stupidest questions about China, laugh when I couldn't understand the question. I hated those kids. I wasn't surprised. It wasn't anything unique. I knew this would happen and that's why I'd never wanted to do it! I missed home so much. I missed you so much." She paused. "And our texts, they were a life raft. I could still be home, in a way. I could still be with you. But then we graduated, all of you went to such great schools, and meanwhile, I felt completely lost. I was at school, but I couldn't make a single friend, and I didn't know what I wanted to do with my life at all. So when you and I stopped talking . . . I thought, okay. We've moved on."

Lian was incredulous. "I only stopped talking to you because I thought you were too busy with your amazing life."

Wenyu hugged her knees to her chest. "'The other mountain is always taller,' or whatever it is they say."

They laughed. Lian swallowed a lump in her throat before continuing. "I didn't—I didn't mean to stop talking."

Wenyu nodded. "It's funny. It's like Mingzun could feel it. Right around when you and I stopped talking, he emailed me. This was sometime in college. And we started sending emails all the time. He became the life raft. We said we'd be together again one day. And then as the years passed, we'd fall in love with other people, we'd stop talking, but then we'd always find our way back. But when I met Thomas, I didn't stop talking to him. I think, weirdly, it's because Thomas was different. I think I knew it was going to be something that lasted, and that's why I kept talking to Mingzun. Like if I stopped talking to him I knew it would be for good this time. So I didn't. And things got better for me, over the years. And so he wasn't exactly a life raft anymore, but just someone I liked talking to. I liked peeking at my old life through him. And then when Thomas and I got engaged . . . he sent me a long message, pleading with me not to do it . . . so then I stopped responding. I really tried to cut it off." She paused. "But when I landed here I was just filled with this, this need to see him. It didn't feel right to be here without him. And so I invited him to the engagement party. And it was like no time at all had passed. I saw you, and I saw Mingzun, and I thought I could recapture myself. And for a moment I could. And it was amazing."

Wenyu smiled, and tears sprang back up in her eyes.

"It really was so good for a while. I let myself love Mingzun again, without thinking about what was going to happen next." She paused. "I really did think I was going to do it. Choose him." She chuckled. "Su Mingzun hated America, too, as you know. Everything about the West. And we ridiculed it all the time. It was so cathartic. But he also never wanted to hear anything good. He didn't really want to hear about the things I'd discovered or learned; I'd mention somewhere I'd gone in America or someone I'd met and he'd grow quiet and just not respond, or call me brainwashed. So I tried to be who I was when I was seventeen for him. Or who I would have been had I stayed. I tried to live as I thought a Chinese woman in her twenties should. I tried to be like you, Lian."

She looked at Lian now, and snorted. Lian's heartbeat felt electric in her chest; what did Wenyu mean—why would she ever want to do that? "So stupid. I couldn't. I'm not good at it. I'm not good at pretending. And then I realized this is how I felt those first few years in America, when people would meet me with blank stares, when I was forced to do everything possible to hide everything about my past and where I'd been. To make myself exactly what the people in front of me wanted to see. And today, when that woman said all those things . . . I realized that that was all I was anymore. This vessel for other people's expectations. I am everyone's dream woman, and that woman isn't real. So when Mingzun backed me into a corner, I knew I couldn't do it again. I couldn't push yet another part of myself below the earth. It was almost impossible to do it the first time."

She laughed now with her whole chest, a wailing laugh, emptying out a decade of hurt. The guilt inside Lian clamored; it was deafening. She looked at Wenyu, sitting there with her hands wrapped around her shoulders, and wanted Wenyu to hit her. After all, this was her fault.

She thought back to that week after the pool, when Teacher Liao's chair was empty, when a man with dirty fingernails came in to take her place. She thought of Principal Li walking into class the day after and telling them solemnly that Teacher Liao was gone and was not returning. He then described what had occurred at the pool and demanded that those responsible stand up. She thought of the beating in her heart, the way she swore Principal Li could see right into her skull, see the guilt eating at her from the inside. She turned her head slightly to catch Wenyu or Su Mingzun's eyes, but Su Mingzun had his head down in his sweatshirt, as always, and Wenyu was staring at some unspecified point in the distance, seemingly lost in a trance.

What should she do? Should she confess? No, she couldn't confess right then and there; what would her classmates think of her? Maybe the principal would never find out and would just drop the whole thing. But what about Teacher Liao? Lian hoped she was okay. She thought about Teacher Liao cutting through the water in the pool. No, she would go to the principal after class and tell him the truth.

"No one? If no one confesses, I am assigning every single one of you Saturday school every weekend until your Gaokao. And I will have each of you write an apology note to Teacher Liao, and you will write it every day until she returns. I don't care if it takes a year. I don't care if it takes ten years."

"That's not fair!" "I was in Daxing last weekend, it wasn't me!" "I already do Saturday school . . ."

The murmurs hung in the air like rain.

Principal Li looked around at every student in the class, his eyes landing on each person and lingering. When he got to Lian, she squeezed her arms to her body, praying that he couldn't tell she was sweating through her shirt.

"It was me. Obviously." Wenyu stood up, abruptly. "If I'm not afraid to do it, I'm not afraid to say it."

Quiet settled in around them. Lian's heart was racing so fast she thought she'd be sick.

"I was bored, okay? My dad made me swim laps at the pool and I thought it'd be funny. I didn't think it would be such a big deal. I'll write the apologies, whatever."

Principal Li's mouth was a flat line. "Come to my office, now."

Wenyu was expelled, the prank the last straw in a long line of offenses. Teacher Liao never came back to school. There were rumors she'd drowned. Lian pictured Teacher Liao sinking down into dark waters in that very same Gucci swimsuit, and she told herself every day after Wenyu stood up that she would go to

Principal Li and confess. But one day turned into two, which turned into weeks. She listened to her classmates gossip about Wenyu, how she'd really done it this time, how she was an attention seeker, how she wanted to get kicked out because she was so stupid. Lian listened and did not say anything. She was a silver herring, used to traveling in a school, fish bodies forming an iridescent snake traveling upstream to their destination. She would always go where the river took her.

So Lian stayed quiet, just as she always did, and allowed Wenyu to fall on the sword she had pulled in hopes of impressing Wenyu with its gleam. And when the rejections came for Lian, she saw it as a reckoning, due payment for what she had done, and when Luo Wenyu emerged with those millions of dollars and subscribers years later, Lian told herself that in the end, it had all evened out, there was no harm done, there was no harm done.

Karma.

She looked at her friend now and felt that no amount of apology could turn back the clock, could rearrange things so that everyone got the life they'd bargained for. "I'm sorry," she wanted to say. "I'm sorry. I've always been a coward. I'm sorry I didn't stand up for you. I'm sorry I stopped talking to you. Because I was ashamed. I was embarrassed. I was jealous." These were the words she should have said those many years ago—that she should have said now. "You shouldn't have to do that," she finally stammered. "You shouldn't have had to do any of that."

Wenyu looked at Lian, her eyes wet. "Mingzun and I, the last time we fought back then, it was because he wanted to go to Principal Li and tell him it was you. And I wouldn't let him, and he got so angry."

"You should've let him do it."

"You were destined for great things, Lianlian! I would've never let something as stupid as this ruin that. Me . . . well . . . it was no loss for me."

"I lost a lot, losing you."

Wenyu smiled and took her arm, squeezing her bicep. "It's so crazy—that you're jealous. All I've ever wanted was a life like yours. Someone who loves me. Family. People who understand."

"There's not much about my life that's so great."

"There is, Lianlian! There's so much! You don't see it because you've never had to lose it. You know, in America, it's obvious to feel out of place. Everyone around me looks so different; they speak a different language. It's not a surprise to me anymore," Wenyu said. "But here? It hurts more to feel like a foreigner in your hometown. That woman . . . Lian, she was right. Feeling like an outsider in your own language. It hurts the most."

As she spoke, Lian could see something turning inside Wenyu, some invisible hinge clicking into place, so that she no longer knew if Wenyu actually believed what she was saying, or if she was simply telling herself these things so that they became incontrovertible.

They got up from the steps and walked back into the house. The fire was out, the doorway to the first-floor bedroom roped off. Wenyu had explained a decade's worth of things, but there was still the mystery of tonight and what had really happened. They both stared, wondering.

"That light was really fucking expensive," Wenyu finally said. There was nothing to do but laugh.

Wenyu texted Thomas. She grabbed a tissue and dabbed at her eyes. A rose of black blotted the tissue, her mascara bleeding. "Lian . . ." she began. "When Thomas gets back, can you play along with me? I'm going to tell him that Mingzun was just a classmate. Please don't let Thomas know the truth. Can you do that for me?"

Lian swallowed. She felt unbearably sad, and for whom? Su Mingzun? Thomas? Wenyu?

"Of course," she said.

They walked into the living room. Lian picked up the ash-tray, retrieved the cocktail glasses, and washed them in the sink. It seemed farcical. Half the house was a charred ruin and they were worried about cocktail glasses. But together they cleaned, wordlessly undoing the events of the night.

After the living room, Wenyu undid herself. She went into the bathroom, wiped off the rest of her mascara, patted her cheeks dry, swept her ponytail back up so that her baby hairs tucked in neatly.

Lian returned to the pool deck, staring at the empty expanse of the Fifth Ring. It stretched into blackness, dotted fitfully by gold.

Thomas arrived shortly after. Wenyu emerged from the bathroom, her face serene.

"*Thomas!*" she cried when she heard his keys at the door. She flung himself into his arms, and he held her tightly. She let herself cry a little bit, but Lian could tell these tears were different. These were the tears of a frightened woman, not of a woman who had just possibly lost the only man that had ever truly known her.

"*What happened, baby? Oh my god, you're in shock, baby, come here.*" Thomas comforted her, his large hand palming her back tightly and guiding her into the living room. Lian watched him look around incredulously at the damage. She approached the two of them, and he pulled her into a hug. "*Thank god you were here, Lian.*"

"*Of course . . .*" Lian said. "*Girls' night,*" she added, her body stiff, and feared she sounded fake.

He and Wenyu settled in on the couch. "*I'm so sorry that fucker had to ruin things,*" he said, his teeth gritting, anger thickening his voice.

"*It was so scary,*" Wenyu said, sniffling. "*Maybe it was my fault . . . we had seen each other again at the engagement party, and I was so happy to see everyone since I'd been away for so long. He'd always had a crush on me in school, and I was just trying to be nice. Maybe he mistook that for affection, I don't know.*"

"*That doesn't give him any right to follow you to your own home in the middle of the night,*" he said, now nearly tearing up himself.

What had Wenyu told Thomas? Lian's spine was full of ice.

Wenyu wept into Thomas's shoulder as they sat on the couch. *"I guess he tried to set the house on fire. So scary to think what could have happened,"* Wenyu said.

"Thank god you weren't inside," Thomas said.

Lian felt sick. Suddenly she did not recognize the woman who sat in front of her.

"Are you all right, Lian?" Thomas turned to Lian. *"Did he scare you?"*

Lian stared through him, at the exposed brick wall behind his head, at the fifty-thousand-dollar finger painting hanging above the fireplace. She could feel Wenyu's gaze boring into her, begging her for one more lie. And Wenyu knew she would do it; since that day in the grocery store, she'd always known that that was what Lian was: the perfect accomplice.

Lian knew this would be the last time they protected each other. The gauzy world they'd re-created this summer was never meant to last; it was a miracle they'd been able to resurrect it at all. Wenyu had chosen her allegiances, she'd chosen her life; some shift had occurred when they weren't paying attention, and she'd crossed over into a territory she could never come back from. Perhaps this shift had occurred when Wenyu made this single illuminating choice. Right now, in telling Thomas this lie. Or perhaps the shift had occurred earlier, when she'd told Su Mingzun she couldn't marry him. Or earlier still, when she'd discovered her favorite jianbing shop was now a mall. Or even further back, at some moment in Wenyu's American journey, when the scales tilted toward the other side, when arriving in San Francisco suddenly felt like arriving home. Or maybe there wasn't a single moment at all. Maybe it was just the accumulation of days, the result of so many subconscious and oppressive accumulations, the accumulation of uncomfortable encounters and dreams crumpled and reshaped and nights spent missing her life and days spent squashing those feelings to fit the box of her new life that all added up to a wholly changed person. Seeing her now with those same dimples, that same flagrant, careening hair, Lian was shocked at the way a person could seem so familiar, and yet be critically altered within. Wenyu had tried to come back, but she could no longer.

If she had stood up that day in front of Principal Li, would the story of their lives be completely different? Would she have stayed in school, tested into a respectable local university, graduated, met a nice man, and bought a condo within the Fourth Ring? Would she have stayed with Su Mingzun? Would she have had Lian's life? She thought of what Wenyu had said: "I tried to be like you." She hadn't thought that maybe Wenyu felt the same about her. Could Wenyu have had her life? Would she have lived it better? Lian wondered what would have happened had she stood and screamed, "Ma Zhongshun! You are a pig! Yang Qinru! You wish you were one-tenth as pretty as Luo Wenyu! And Su Mingzun! Wenyu is not yours. She is brighter than the sun and she cannot be captured by any of you." She wondered if then Wenyu, even if she had left for America, would have found her way home faster.

But she had not said any of this. And as she sat there now, with the American's eyes trained on her with such severity, she wondered if they would ever arrive in the same place again, or if Lian had cursed them to a forever of passing by each other.

"*He's always been a little intense,*" she said. "*Just so obsessed with Wenyu. But I'm okay. He didn't scare me.*"

"*So resilient,*" Thomas said, squeezing her arm. *Resilient.* This was a word she had heard a few times, usually associated with failure, with rebirths that followed the crushing heartbreaks of life. And so she nodded now, and pursed her lips solemnly, giving the Americans what they wanted to see.

3

The drive to the house was the longest he'd ever experienced. It was a perfect August day; the rains earlier that week had cooled the city down, and Chen felt that the perfect weather was taunting him.

Tao had told him there had been a fire at the house. A man had been critically injured when debris collapsed on him. Most of the kitchen had caught immediately; the authorities were now investigating not only the source of the fire but also why so much of the house had gone up so quickly. Chen's heartbeat became a frantic thud as he listened—after all these years, finally, his choices had come home to roost.

The sea of cars swam around him. He gripped the steering wheel, feeling nauseated by morning light. He should have drunk some water, grabbed a Coke. When he left, Fan had still been sleeping, and he received a text from her now: "everything all right?" He clicked off his screen. Everything would be all right. A fire was not his fault. His breath quickened as the gold letters of the subdivision rose above the horizon, throwing a sharp glare onto his windshield. As he slowed to a stop in front of the house, he saw a police car idling in the driveway.

A few officers stood outside. He introduced himself as the builder of the house and made his way through the front door.

He gasped. The kitchen doorway had completely caved in, and black scorch marks ran up and down the walls. The light fixture that had been dangling from the ceiling had fallen, one corner cleaving the floor. There was a smear of dried blood about a meter from where the fixture had fallen. How had his pristine creation become the site of such tragedy?

"Poor kid," he heard a voice say. An officer walked up behind him, his hat in his hands. "Just snapped, huh?"

The officer handed him a newspaper. "The youth in this country have gone crazy. I blame the internet." Chen read the headline: "LOCAL MAN SETS RMB 15 MILLION HOME OF INTERNET CELEBRITY VIVIAN LUO ABLAZE." There was a blurry black-and-white image of a young man. His eyes were piercing, beady; his hair was buzzed short, giving his face a hardness. He didn't recognize this man—what was he doing in the home of Vivian Luo and Thomas Straeffer-Kenney?

"Who is he?" Chen asked.

The officer shrugged. "Just some fan. You'd think they'd have a security system to keep people like that out."

"There is a security system," Chen said.

"Oh yeah? Let's see." The officer walked over to a man who looked like his superior. "Guy says to check the security tapes."

"Security wasn't on last night," the other man said, shrugging.

This accident was more and more confusing to Chen. "Who was in the house when this happened?"

"Just the lady of the house and her friend," the man replied.

"The fire wasn't an accident?"

"We found gasoline all over the floors and doorway. Looks like foul play. Seems like this guy went crazy and wanted to light her house up. Guess he just got himself." He chuckled. "Good thing the fire guys got here before anyone else was hurt."

"Is the man alive?"

"They're still working on him," the officer said. "He's in the hospital. Coma."

Chen nodded and walked back out. When he emerged into the air, he suddenly felt his lungs expand; he could breathe again.

He opened his car door and looked back at the house. It seemed alien to him, an uncanny valley version of what he'd basked under the light of a mere sixteen hours ago. The large overhanging eaves formed a menacing smile. He sank into his seat, his heart uneasy.

Chen drove back to the city. He thought about what would happen next. The police, if they were competent, would run tests on his materials. They would know immediately what Chen had done. But his materials were meant to survive usual wear and tear; for the average homeowner, they made no difference. He could not have factored in an act of arson. Who would want to do something like this to Vivian and Thomas?

His phone rang.

"Hello, Mister Song Chen," came a voice he didn't recognize.

He introduced himself as a lawyer for the Su family, the parents of the man who was now lying comatose in the hospital. They were filing a lawsuit against him for unsafe building practices to pay for physical and emotional damages.

Chen couldn't believe what he was hearing. How could this possibly be his fault? His mind whipped between sympathy and indignation. "I'm very sorry that this has happened," he said, choosing his words carefully. "But it was not my fault someone started a fire."

"Your construction proved unsafe," the lawyer said. "The police discovered the usage of wood-plastic composite panels, which were banned years ago for their flammable nature. This caused the fire to spread at twice the rate that it otherwise would have, leading to the collapse of the metal structure that critically injured our client. But I'm sure you don't need me to go over the logistics of your profession," the man added, a condescending slick to his voice.

"These safety measures are in the jurisdiction of the subdistrict supervisor," Chen said. "I detailed the specifications of my project in my contract, and he approved it knowing the regulations. I don't believe I can be held fully responsible for this." He convinced himself as he said it; it wasn't his fault.

"I have already called his office," the lawyer continued.

"Okay, good," Chen said. "Then you should know—"

"Subdistrict Supervisor Ding never approved this project," the lawyer replied.

Chen's heart dropped.

"What?"

"I called Subdistrict Supervisor Ding and was told he had never approved the project. You are on record as having met with him about the project, and he is on record rejecting your proposal. I'm sorry to say, our suit stands."

Of course. After their yearslong partnership, of course the man would come back to fuck him in this manner. That's what all these politicians were about, covering their own asses. Nausea surged in him.

"How much are they asking for?"

"Four million RMB."

Chen hung up the phone without responding.

CHEN AND FAN had been living at his parents' home for a year when Chen heard from a real estate connection about the possibility of fudging on certain materials. It was rumored that local officials tended to look the other way for materials that were "nonessential" to the structural integrity of the house—paints, crown moldings, non-load-bearing columns and beams. He and Tao had just secured a new deal that would be costly to build; this discovery would widen their profit margins significantly. And so Chen had approached the subdistrict supervisor at the time (a man named Zhang) and sent the proper bribes; the deal had gone smoothly and the apartment complex had gone up without a hitch. The money he'd saved went toward purchasing their home in Chaoyang, which he was able to afford a mere six months later. Without this discovery, they might have languished in his parents' guest bedroom for several more years. He and Tao continued to make the same deals as they grew their business. Vivian and Thomas's house was no different. The corners they cut were paltry compared to what their competitors did; if Chen had really cared about profit, he would have built on unstable land, would have used noxious dupe materials bought for pennies and shipped from factories in Gansu. He did not. He would never do anything to harm a client. He was just playing the game that everyone played. This is what they all did in the business, and yet—why was he the one who had to pay? Why did the other shoe only drop for him!

Four million renminbi. That was more than the total amount of money he'd received for the entire build. He'd already paid the down payment on the Xiangheyuan condo—this lawsuit would bankrupt him. Chen sat in silence after the phone call, his car idling by the side of another bus stop advertisement. It was madness—he'd done everything he had to. He'd done his job. He had done nothing out of the ordinary. Was he really to blame?

He put the car in drive and headed onto the Fifth Ring highway.

He pulled up outside Guilin's apartment. He had still never been inside, never seen the conditions of her bunk bed, her five roommates, the small window that one could barely fit one's head through to see a view of a drab and crowded parking lot. The memory of their encounter the previous night thudded against his skull. A dozen emotions clashed inside him: the object of his guilt now fractured and redirected, he was unprepared to face her; but in this moment she was his last hope. He called her.

"Guilin," he said, hoping he sounded cheery. "I was just in the neighborhood. Want to go to lunch?"

Ten minutes passed, and she emerged downstairs, wearing the yellow cardigan he had purchased for her from Joy City. She got into Chen's car. She did not look at him; she was still upset, and rightly so. He drove.

They went to Nine Majesty Hotel. He wondered when he would be able to treat her in this way again. A line of hostesses stood at the door, their viridian qipaos emblazoned with rose-pink phoenixes. He demanded the largest private room with the best view.

They sat with a heavy tablecloth cool against their legs. He ordered whole pheasants, eel soup, scallops, stewed fish, jumbo shrimp, jellied wood ear, and pork hock. The platters overwhelmed their table, waitresses arriving in twos and threes, porcelain clinking as they turned the heavy lazy Susan. Guilin gazed upon the dishes, her eyes bewildered. "Chen, slow down, I'm not too hungry today—"

"We can always have leftovers," he murmured, sinking his teeth into a crunchy pheasant head, picking bones from his molars with a greasy pinky. He felt famished.

Having Guilin there beside him, the heavy tablecloth at their ankles, felt comforting to him. She was such a sunny force; he felt he wanted to weep right then and there, and she would hold him, rock him until the tears ran no longer. A slim waitress brought them miniature bowls of Buddha jumps over the wall soup.

"Drink up," Chen said. The soups, chock-full of fish and abalone and tendon, cost over 300 RMB a bowl. Chen spooned some sea cucumber into his mouth, relishing the way it slunk down his throat as if still alive.

Guilin picked up a slice of tendon and nibbled on it. "This is so decadent," she breathed. "My parents never ate anything so decadent in their whole lives."

"This is nothing," he said. "Wait until I take you to eat raw mitten crabs."

"Song Chen sir," she said. "I heard what happened."

A sea cucumber went still in his mouth. He chewed quickly and swallowed. "Yes," he said. "It's unfortunate."

"The man was young, wasn't he?" she said.

He nodded.

"Will you be okay?"

"That's—that's a good question, Guilin," he said, turning to her. "I was actually wondering, if you wouldn't mind—if you could—if you could talk to Subdistrict Supervisor Ding again. You see, I got a phone call this morning, a bit of a disturbing call, the family of the victim, they're filing a lawsuit because, well, it appears as though Subdistrict Supervisor Ding never approved the project at all."

He finished his explanation and stared at her, dry mouthed. She looked back at him, her eyes wide.

He continued, his words tripping over themselves. "I mean, you were there, of course he approved the project. He was a bit stubborn about the pool, sure, but you got that handled too! At any rate, would you please talk to him again?"

"I don't know, Song Chen sir," she finally said, softly.

He slurped his soup. He felt so parched. "Is this because of what happened yesterday? I'm sorry; I wasn't expecting her to be there, I didn't even think she'd come back, to be honest. I really, really wanted to take care of you, Guilin. I still want to. You're such an amazing girl. I want to give you a great life. But I just need this one thing, please." He spoke so passionately he wasn't sure if he was attempting to convince Guilin or convince himself. He thought it would be so easy, if he could settle on her, decide to love her and only her. She would give him joy and uncomplicated love. Maybe the path forward was right in front of him. He grabbed the bottle of wine and filled her glass, pushed it toward her.

But she merely stared at the glass in front of her. "Subdistrict Supervisor Ding is a very shrewd politician," she said. "He does what he has to do. He puts his bets where he knows they'll pay off."

Chen leaned back against his chair and stared at Guilin. "Guilin! Oh, my darling, the man has brainwashed you, please don't listen to a word he says. He approved the project, so now he must stand by it. That's what a decent man does, stands by what he says. I'm a man of my word, I carry out my promises. That's how I've always lived. He should take a page out of my book. Please," he said, taking her hand and placing it on his palm. He was surprised by how small it was, an island in a sea. "We could be together, Guilin. If I can just sort all of this out. I have a beautiful balcony. I'll get you a mandolin, you can practice out there and charm the whole neighborhood. This dinner, see? We will have many more of these. You know, I saw a car the other day that I think you would love . . ." He was babbling now, throwing Hail Marys into the air.

"Song Chen sir," she said now, her voice hard. "You promise people the world. But you can't do it."

"I . . ."

"I've seen scores of men like you. I've had many, many boyfriends. Yes, is that surprising? Most of them were wealthy. They promised houses, cars, jewelry, jobs. When I was younger, I was more trusting. I let them string me along. One was a millionaire who made it big in Shenzhen and who had a wife. One was a perennial bachelor who gave me bags and shoes and nice dresses but who never took me to see his home. As I've gotten older, I've learned to see through it. The money and the nice dinners and the promises. You're all the same. You are all envious, prideful men."

"No, Guilin, you don't understand, I am not like those men. I want to protect you."

"Protect me? You can't protect yourself."

He looked at her, sitting there, and she was suddenly so large and looming. He was hit with a terrible realization.

"You spoke to the lawyer today," he said.

She stared into her bowl of soup. "Yes."

"You told him Subdistrict Supervisor Ding had never approved the project."

"Yes."

There was a heavy silence.

"I too have had to learn where to place my bets," she said. "You might be able to give me a mandolin, a nice time, even a car, but Subdistrict Supervisor Ding has given me a job, has promised me a future. He's a powerful man. He cannot take the fall."

"So that's that," he said, bitterly. "You've chosen the man you want."

"Don't flatter yourself." She looked at him with an intensity he had not seen before. "You were never the one I was looking for in the first place."

He was bewildered. "What do you mean?"

"I overheard your conversation with Ding that first day. I couldn't believe my ears—I have wanted to meet Vivian Luo for as long as I can remember. So when you asked about lunch, I saw my chance."

A poisonous ache filled him.

"Turns out Vivian Luo was just like you. People who spit on nobodies like me. City people who spit on country people. Rich people who spit on poor people. Until we're convenient to you, at least. No matter how I try to level the scale, it will never be even." She seemed close to tears. "The silly thing is . . . I did like you."

He did not say a word. He needled his chopsticks into the white tablecloth. How had he gotten here? Everything he'd done had been for Fan, but somewhere along the way something had become twisted.

She stood up and walked to the window. There was a brilliant view of the entire west side of the city. Her voice softened a little bit as her eyes seemed to land on the glowing lights of Joy City, where they'd had their first date of sorts. "You are a kind, sweet man, Song Chen sir. I really enjoyed every minute with you. I laughed and smiled a lot. But I can't survive off that."

He didn't respond. He merely stared at her figure, so foreign to him now, as it blurred into the background of his hometown.

Then she retrieved something from her bag. The silk scarf he'd bought her. She placed it on the table. One corner of it was charred.

She leaned down and grabbed one more piece of fish maw, grinding it softly between her teeth. She picked up the soup bowl and drank the umami broth down in one gulp. "Thank you for this lunch," she said, and gave him a kiss on the top of his head. And then she was off, swinging the handle of a purse he had never seen before.

HE STARED OUT through the windows of the hotel. Taillights made their way down Chang'An Avenue, inching toward Princess Grave, toward Apple Garden. He realized he'd been gritting his teeth, and he willed himself to relax. He already missed the playful touch of Guilin's hands. He looked at the scarf. There was a faint smell of burning in the air. What did this mean— what did any of this mean? Life had so few answers. Guilin's words echoed in his mind: No matter how I try to level the scale.

He sat and sat and pondered Guilin's words as the seafood around him grew pungent. He put his face in a heavy cloth napkin and cried.

She was right. He had made promises, promises that he could no longer keep. What could he do? How would he give his son a home now? His bank account would be drained by the lawsuit. Chen wondered, bewildered, how anyone on this earth kept their promises. Circumstances changed. The previous week a bus driver in Chongqing had driven a bus full of people clear off a bridge into the Changjiang. Surprises happened all the time. He was sure that bus driver, when he took his oath as a bus driver for the city of Chongqing, had not thought that one day he would drive a bus full of people off a bridge into the longest river in China. Building this house to buy his son a home, that was the first thing in years he'd done that he felt Fan had actually been proud of, and now it was slipping from his grasp. He didn't want to see that old disappointed look on her face, the look that said he'd confirmed her worst suspicions about him. Since Fan had left for America, since they had fought over Yihong's college prospects, and earlier still, since he'd made the choice to bring them back to Beijing, he had been trying to save what was left between them. This house was his last and best attempt. Hope was a brittle thing, and he felt tired thinking about all the times hope had entered his life, only to break again.

He thought about the conversation they had had about a year ago. She had discovered some of the accounting paperwork from the first few homes at Heavenly Earth, had confronted him about the large profit margins the spreadsheets showed. He had pushed off her concerns, telling her he had a deal with the vendors; he could get electrical and water piping for pennies because of his long-standing partnerships. She hadn't bought it and had asked more and more questions until he'd snapped, shouting that she never trusted him—and why? She was the one who couldn't be trusted!

He thought of the way her face had crumpled that evening, how he had cursed himself, because he was no better than she— he, too, was a liar.

He thought of that morning in spring, back when hope was still plenty. The ginkgo trees were a deep green, and all the students lounged about on the quad, sweat wicking off their bodies in lusty tendrils. He walked, sucking in the perfume of the emerging milkweed. The milkweed didn't smell like milk at all, but like jasmine. Those same little white flowers bloomed all over Chen's childhood Beijing, and if he closed his eyes now, he almost felt like he was at the beginning of his life again.

This was before Big Luck Diner, before the months of pretending and applying and doors shutting. Before he discovered

Fan's betrayal. It was the day of his dissertation defense, and none other than Robert Qiong was on the committee. He wasn't looking forward to staring the smug man in the face and presenting his research in English, but he would do it, because it was all that stood between him and his diploma. Finally, he could say he had a degree from an American institution. He'd have his pick of jobs. Every bank in the country would want him, the city government—no, the state—even Washington! He wore the navy suit that Fan had purchased for him at Marshall Field's; she'd bought it with money she'd received when she won a departmental prize earlier that year. That morning, he'd ironed it carefully, steam hissing off it in emphatic spurts.

He would wear the suit again three weeks later. He was planning to propose to Fan on graduation day. He, too, had saved up money, for an engagement band.

On the committee sat his advisor, David Aimes, a graying man who had always been kind if preoccupied, his head on his own research and on birding instead of on his students; Lukas Koenig, another veteran with a specialty in high factorials; and Robert Qiong, who was the youngest of the three. It was a bit of an anomaly that Qiong was on the committee, as he was a professor in the economics department, but unfortunately Chen's research involved econometrics, which was Qiong's specialty. Today Qiong had put an inordinate amount of hair gel into his coif and had chosen an absurd shade of purple for his pocket square. He greeted Chen with a firm handshake and a *"Nice to see you, Chenny,"* a gross Anglicization that he'd taken to calling Chen around the department.

"Morning, Chenny," the other men echoed.

Chen nodded, inhaling deeply. His research focused on set theory and combinatorics; Chen had always loved finding patterns, groupings, categorizations. He was not in love with numbers the way Fan was; he loved mathematics despite the numbers. He loved it because he felt it had much to say about the world, about people and populations, about history, even about literature. He was no good at the rote memorization that social science classes demanded of him, no good at excavating meaning out of poetry and literature, and so he had flocked to math. Combinatorics, particularly, sought out generalizations. But it also sought out specifications. It sought to find general patterns among specific groups, which was, in essence, what Chen believed was the stuff of life. Finding commonalities between disparate factions. His party trick among his cohort had always been to guess the astrological signs of his peers—and he was often correct. It was, for instance, easy to tell when someone had been born in the year of the dragon; dragons were blessed with an unparalleled ambition and charisma. He'd guessed that Fan was a dragon right away.

For his defense today, he had practiced his speech painstakingly, sounding out the vowels the way Fan had always done, stretching his mouth into ridiculous shapes in the mirror and continuing even as red spread across his cheeks. "*Failure to satisfy the axiom of choice is a more common phenomenon than we may think . . .*" he recited, surprised that "*axiom*" was not as difficult to pronounce as he had feared.

Now he recited it all again, more clearly than he ever had. He watched the faces of his professors light up; Lukas even nodded approvingly at some portions. Qiong stared, his body unmoving. His face was entirely unreadable; Chen liked to think that he was furious, indignant that Chen could pull off such a performance. Take that, he thought. You are not the only brilliant man in Fan's life—and certainly not the first.

The questions were harder—Chen could understand David and Lukas, but he had a much more difficult time answering. He fielded questions about Woodin cardinals and the Suslin hypothesis, stammering through without grace. His face flushed. But his professors were encouraging nevertheless. When it came time for Robert Qiong's question, the man looked at him with a cold and curious gaze.

"*Thanks for this presentation,*" he began. "*My question pertains to the Kunen theorem. Can you explain how your research creates exceptions to the rules laid out in the Kunen theorem, whereby strong cardinals exist when there is an elementary embedding, in which M is closer to V?*"

Chen flinched. A stone formed in his mouth, weighing down his tongue. The concepts were crystalline in his brain; this was the entire crux of his research, a simple system through which to understand large cardinals, and in Chinese he could talk circles around the concept. But strong cardinals and embedding were concepts the English words for which fled his mind.

He stammered out a cursory answer, his hands gesturing, hoping the circular motion would make the concept clear. Elementary embedding was a useful tool to demonstrate the existence of strong cardinals, which in turn heavily implied the existence of large cardinals. He grabbed two dry erase markers and held them up to each other, trying to suggest that the existence of the blue dry erase marker implied the existence of the black marker—although they were separate entities, one could reasonably assume the other given the former's existence. The words did not come out this way, but he refused to admit he could not say them.

Luckily, the message was clear.

"*I think we're good here,*" David said after a while. Chen had many a time flown into an emphatic rant about strong cardinals in meetings, so perhaps he didn't need to prove himself again today. "*That's a good example, Chen,*" he added.

"*Very evocative,*" Lukas added, smiling.

"*I'm confident that we can send a pass declaration up to the department,*" David said, already rising from his chair. "*Congratulations, Chen.*"

David and Lukas left the room. Chen let his shoulders fall. His body was tingling. Finally. Finally. He had done it. The product of his five years in America—he had achieved it.

Only Qiong remained in the room.

"Chen brother," Qiong began, as he gathered his jacket. "Can you explain the exceptions to the Kunen theorem again?"

Chen turned around. "I've already explained it."

"I wanted to give you the chance to explain it in Chinese."

"Well," he began, annoyance rising in his throat. "The existence of strong cardinals, which the Kunen theorem can prove with a simple embedding equation, implies the existence of large cardinals. Kunen states that ZFC plus phi can be either consistent or inconsistent depending on assumptions about the large cardinal."

"Right. Right. It's a concept you know well. Just like the rest of your research. I am a bit perturbed, however, that you couldn't explain it to the committee."

"Evidently, my explanation sufficed."

Qiong bowled right through him. "It makes me wonder how you were able to so clearly articulate these topics in your actual dissertation. Large cardinals is a complex subject."

"I've spent many years writing it," he said, and swallowed.

"Of course," Qiong said. "Then why couldn't you explain Kunen's theorem?"

Chen paused, willing himself to steady his voice. "There was some vocabulary I forgot in the moment. My apologies. If your intention is to humiliate me, don't bother."

Qiong exhaled in a long stream. "My intention is never to humiliate, brother. It's to find the truth." He looked at him for a long beat. "Did you have help with your dissertation?"

The stone on Chen's tongue now fell into his heart. He slipped his notes back into his folder, then slotted it neatly into his backpack, moving slowly, his back turned to Qiong. He did not want him to see his face, the truth written there.

"What are you implying?" he asked, his brow furrowed.

"I think I've made myself clear," Qiong continued. "Did someone else write your dissertation?"

"That's a terrible accusation," he said.

"It happens more often than you might think," Qiong said.

"Well, I wrote it myself," Chen said, turning to him now, his face a portrait of steely resolve.

Qiong looked at him. There were creases on the sides of Qiong's eyes, a streak of gray tickling his temples; he wore contact lenses, a frivolous expense that Chen felt was the epitome of this man's folly, hundreds of dollars spent for an aesthetic choice. "What was the beginning of your defense again?"

"What?"

"Can you start the defense again, explain to me your research? In English."

"I'm not entertaining this."

"If you don't, I'll assume I'm correct, and I'll have to report my suspicions to the committee."

"Why would you do that? What good does that do?"

"It's truth, Chen. The truth is always good."

Chen gritted his teeth. "*Large cardinals have often been thought to be the only exception to the axiom of choice. However, in the early twentieth century, Ernst Zermelo and Abraham Fraenkel posited a theory of sets free of paradoxes. Zermelo-Fraenkel set theory, shortened* ZFC, *which includes the axiom of choice, does not allow for the existence of a universal set. A universal set, of course, is a set containing all sets—an impossibly large thing to think about. Imagine all of the tennis balls in the world. Now imagine all of the tennis courts containing all those tennis balls, and parks containing those tennis courts, and neighborhoods containing those parks, and cities containing those neighborhoods. And on and on—*"

"See?" Qiong said, cutting him off. "You've memorized a script."

"It's called being prepared," Chen said.

"It's called reading off a script," Qiong said. "Can you rephrase this in a different way? Explain it to me again?"

"This isn't an English defense," Chen said. "I'm not entertaining this. I have to get to the South Quad now," he said, hitching his bag onto his shoulder and pushing past Qiong. "I don't have to prove anything to you."

"Meng Haian used the same example in his defense earlier this morning," Qiong said now. "*Tennis courts.*"

Chen stopped. Through the window of the classroom he could see a few undergrads, all of them careless blond boys, throwing a football around on the quad. Their lives were so easy. One of the boys fell to the ground, then threw a handful of grass in the air. He was so close to joining these people; what separated them was a matter of meters. He needed only to turn the handle of the door and walk through.

He turned around. "What are you going to do?"

Qiong stood at the front of the room, looking at him. "I don't want you to fail, Chen," Qiong said. "But my hands are tied."

"You can choose not to," Chen said, desperation leaking into his voice. "You can choose not to fail me. We can pretend like this never happened. You don't have to do anything."

"You know I can't do that."

Chen gritted his teeth.

"I'm sorry, brother," Qiong said. "But this isn't just about you." He leaned against the desk and crossed his arms over his chest, heaving a great sigh. "We are at a very important precipice in history, brother. We are supposed to be the role models. We need to prove to them that we can make it in this country the proper way. We don't need shortcuts and special treatment. Only by doing things the right way can we finally prove our place here."

"But what about loyalty?" Chen's heart was racing. His opening was closing; the grand dream he'd constructed, that free life out on the grass, the proposal, the job at a bank in his navy suit, the money sent home to his parents, the phone call from his mother where she'd finally say, Chen ah, you made the right choice . . . all of it was fading into white noise. "What about lao xiang?" He spat the last words out. "You act like that means so much, but it means nothing to you! How will any of us ever win if we're not allowed to even try?"

"Loyalty is important. Of course. It hurts me to do this. I don't relish bringing down a brother."

"I think you love it," Chen said.

"I don't, and you willfully misunderstand me if you think that. Every day, I want for every Chinese man to wake up and make their mark honestly. That's why this is so disappointing to me, Chen."

"Come on," Chen said. "You know I know the material. This is important research. So what if I couldn't write some of it in English!"

"You could have told the department, we could have gotten you help—"

"I don't believe that."

"I cannot allow you to cut corners like this. What would that look like? Everyone would think I was doing it only because you're Chinese. Making exceptions for my own. Even beyond the legal ramifications, I'd be seen as a fraud."

"No one needs to know."

"But I would know. And you would always know. That you got a lucky break, you took a shortcut. I can't allow that."

Tears flooded Chen's eyes; he could not believe that after his five years of struggle, Qiong would be the final immovable roadblock.

"I'm sorry, brother."

He wanted to sock him in the face, wipe that word from his mouth. They weren't hometowners and they certainly weren't brothers. "Fuck you," he said.

"Profanity won't help your case."

"You're so fucking proper," Chen said. "Tell me, how does it taste, the white man's asshole?"

"*Chen brother, I've been nothing but polite to you. Please don't be vulgar with me*," he said, switching again, inexplicably, into English.

The sounds of the man's syllables slipping deftly out of his mouth were nauseating. The way he flattened his words, tried so hard to squash his tones, the way he clearly looked so proud to be able to speak these stupid little English words, all of it sickened Chen.

The next thing he heard was the crack of the man's jaw on his fist.

The thing after that: Fan's gasp as she swung open the doors, carrying a single gold balloon. It said, "CONGRATULATIONS."

HE STOOD UP from the table, the dishes in various stages of whole and consumed, a kaleidoscopic graveyard of seafood slowly sweetening in the air. Thousands of renminbi of barely touched food. Nausea rose in him. Thinking about that time was so stupid. It gave him no catharsis; his years in America were a pointless tale leading nowhere. He had hoped that his grand construction would have been the conclusion that threw the rest of his life into sharp relief, the ah-ha moment that would have made it all worth it. But here he was again, for the nth time, at a dead end.

Yes, he had been driven to do ugly things in America. He'd lied and cheated and put his hands on people. All in the name of—of that dream he'd been sold! America had driven him to desperate places, and his desperation surfaced now. America, China: Living was shit, wherever you were. He would never be a Qiong, would never be a Subdistrict Supervisor Ding. These men were the lucky ones. They all lied and cheated and lived above the law, but Chen was the rotten, stupid one who got caught, every time.

He was suddenly hit with a pang of sadness for the young man lying in the hospital, who may have been an intruder and may have been innocent, and if he had been an intruder Chen would have applauded him, for maybe this man was a cheat and a liar too. This was the only way to live, and a cry choked him as he thought of this man with his wild eyes. Maybe he had wanted nothing more than a different life.

He pushed through the gilded doors of the restaurant's private room.

"Sir, is everything okay?" the slim waitress asked.

"Yes, yes, just need to use the restroom," he said, stumbling down the hall. He would not turn back. At the end of the hallway, he started running through the carpeted corridor, until he burst onto the street.

The afternoon air stung him like a wasp. He remembered the look on Fan's face that spring day, how she had immediately rushed to Qiong's side, how there had been venom, pity in her eyes. And Chen had wondered then if it had all been a mistake for her to trust him, for him to have promised her anything. If he could go back and erase it now, maybe he would have walked away then, tried to live up to someone else's less lofty dreams.

But he had not. He had stood there, his fists clenched, defiant. Qiong did not return the punch; he did not even look angry. Chen wanted the man to fight him; he wanted to feel the sinews of muscle on his face; he wanted to be battered by something he could batter back. He had loved fighting in the courtyard of his childhood home, all his friends piling up on each other and slapping dirt on each other's faces. Fistfighting was a delight; there was nothing simpler on earth than connecting your fist with an enemy who was standing right in front of you.

But Qiong wouldn't fight back; he merely stood and dusted off his coat. He would not even consent to participate in a competition with Chen. Amid Fan's cries, he fixed on Chen a chilling look, and Chen braced himself for the truth to come. He thought about the ring in its velvet box, sitting in his dresser. He thought about the proposal he'd planned, kneeling on the quad in his graduation robes, their tassels intertwining as they kissed. All of it was fading.

"What's going on?" Fan's cries pierced his heart.

"We were arguing about Kunen's theorem," Qiong finally said. "Things got a little heated." He forced a laugh. "We disagree about the evidence on large cardinals." He shrugged, and slapped Chen on the back. "And who said mathematicians aren't passionate?"

Chen was stunned that Qiong didn't tell her the truth. He couldn't muster a word.

Fan's face was a portrait of confusion, a deep stitch in her brow. Chen took the balloon from her, gently. "Thank you, dear," he said. He looked at Qiong as he spoke to her. "It went great. I passed." He managed a smile. "We're just finishing up over here."

"Okay," she said, nodding. "That's . . . that's good. I'll wait outside."

She departed. The silence in the room was heavy.

"Why didn't you . . ." Chen began.

Qiong was already gathering his bags. "I will have the truth," he said, after a pause. "And I will leave you your reputation. That is what I can do for you."

Chen nodded. His temples were tight.

They agreed that he could walk, and it would remain a secret between the two of them. Qiong would wait until after graduation to discover, quietly, some other inadequacy in Chen's dissertation. At first he did not understand this magnanimous gesture. Later he'd tell himself that it was because when Qiong took Fan from Chen, the man wanted to feel he'd battled on an even playing field.

And so part of Chen's dream still came true: the donning of robes, the taking of photos, the kneeling, the proposing, the intertwining tassels. As they kissed in front of their friends, Chen momentarily forgot about his failure. When they moved into that studio together, Chen heaving the mattress into its doorframe, Chen managed to convince himself it would all be okay. He still had a brilliant mathematical mind. He would still find a job. For a moment, a joyful future still seemed possible.

HE BEGAN WALKING along Chang'An Avenue, feeling the cars zoom by. The day, formerly so temperate, now pressed its heat into him. Buses zoomed past him, their passengers rattling. He stripped off his jacket. His knees ached. He caught a glimpse of himself in a passing taxi and he was shocked at how old he looked.

He walked and walked, past Xidan shopping square, past Tiananmen West, past Tiananmen East. Guards stood, their backs straight and their eyes conveying nothing. They formed an olive battalion, protecting one hundred acres of pavement from the people of this city. When Yihong was a child, the people could still come here. Chen would take Fan and Yihong to the square to fly kites. Fan would wind the kite for their son and kneel next to him, helping him anchor the butterfly that soared high above the square. It would sometimes dance so high that for an instant it would disappear, before catching a breeze and nearly bowling little Yihong over. He would cry and then Fan would scoop him up, and she would end up flying the kite for him, delight animating her as she watched the butterfly valiantly attempt an escape. But no kite had flown over Tiananmen in years.

He passed Wangfujing, with its throngs of tourists, its neon lights blinking erratically. This place, too, had been a favorite of Fan and Yihong's when they first landed back in the city, the smell of fried dough irresistible as they passed by on the 1 bus. Over the years, they tired of the crowds and the overpriced street food—scorpions and frog's legs meant to shock foreigners—and Chen stopped taking them to Wangfujing too.

He thought of the call that finally came, over a year after graduation, after his sophomoric hope had fizzled into nothingness, after the rejections and the months spent mopping the floors of Big Luck Diner had flattened his joy into a dull monotony. It came on a blisteringly sunny weekend when he no longer had any expectations.

An old friend from high school, Tao, had rung him on a rare afternoon he had off. Tao had just had a couple of friends strike gold in the real estate industry—money was flowing like Evian water in China, and he wanted to know if Chen would return to Beijing and start a real estate business with him. One of their classmates had started his own agency and two months in was already picking up big accounts for foreign corporations that wanted to develop on Chinese soil.

"Old Lu, the really weaselly one," Tao said, and Chen could picture him sneering on the other end of the line. "If that fucker can get rich, so can we! If I have to see him driving that stupid Lexus around one more time, I better be seeing it sitting in a Bentley!"

He and Tao had always been a madcap if turbulent duo, constantly getting into fisticuffs in high school but sticking up for each other when it counted. His old friend's voice was a beacon in the dark. Another future flashed before his eyes, and Chen could see it all: He and Fan would move into a sprawling penthouse condominium in the city center and eat congee packed with thousand-year egg for breakfast and braised short ribs for dinner, and he and Tao would create an empire, and they would buy a house in the suburbs and a vacation home abroad, and Fan would be the most stylish wife in all of Beijing. Back home, he would find his rightful place again.

"Let's do it," he said to Tao on the spot. But when he set the phone down, he knew it would be impossible to convince Fan. She would never give up her American dream. His fantasy began dissolving before his eyes and he could not bear it; he could not stay there an instant longer.

He knew in that moment that if she insisted on staying, he would leave regardless. He would leave her behind. He would start anew on his own.

And so when he discovered the letter shortly after, it was heartbreak that he felt, but also relief. The double-edged sword of relief, both in that his suspicions had been vindicated, but also that she would have no choice but to leave with him. And she would believe their return was because of her. Their marriage would remain intact; he would not have to suffer the guilt of the runaway husband, the cheater, the fake. Instead, he'd return a martyr, a man who'd made sacrifices, who'd given up his American dream so that his marriage could have a second chance. He would be a hero.

HE WALKED. Beijing in the summer was relentless. Sweat dripped down his face, soaking his collar. Guilin's words pounded in his head; who was this woman? He saw some of himself in her, that desperate flailing heart, and he wanted to cry—for her, for him. He had fallen in love with Fan at the prime of his life, and then had spent the rest of it trying to hold on to the hope that they could make something of this love. Now hope, that brittle thing, was lifting from him. How freeing it felt, to have no more of hope.

He passed Jianguomen. He passed Guomao. He walked until his feet felt like lead, until he'd sweated so much that his throat was parched. When he reached Dawanglu he turned around. He had one more place to go.

4

When he arrived home, the sun was beginning its crawl earthward.

Fan was standing in front of the television. The news played. The intruder's face filled half the screen; Vivian took up the other, her brilliantly white teeth forming a crescent. Fan was wearing the thin T-shirt she always wore to bed, her hair swept up with a clip. The smell of fried eggs and bitter melon filled the room. She had been texting him throughout the day, but he had not responded.

She looked over her shoulder at him. On another day, there might have been anger in her eyes, but instead, she merely asked, "What happened?"

"There was an accident," he said.

"He tried to set their house on fire?"

"Maybe so," he said.

"I heard they went to high school together," she said. She paused. "The people you know always have more of a vendetta against you."

Chen didn't respond. He walked to the kitchen, opened the fridge. He got a beer and popped the cap. He watched his wife watch the screen, her butterfly claw loosening on her head, strands of hair forming a halo, her hands perched on her hips so that her arms formed defiant right angles, her back slightly hunched and her brow furrowed. Fan was a woman consumed by anything she watched; like Guilin, she was a relentless participant. How he would miss this view.

"I made a mistake," he announced. Fan's eyes were still fixed on the screen. He waited.

"Fan," he said, louder. "You were right. I shouldn't have kept doing it. But I just wanted us to have a good life."

She turned around and looked straight at him, a stitch between her eyes. "What do you . . ."

"They say the house went up in minutes," he said, pausing. "I was still using those materials. You were right," he repeated. "I shouldn't have kept doing it."

She was silent. He looked at the photo of the glowering man on the screen.

"They're suing me, the family," he said. "If we still want to get Yihong his place . . . that's everything we have." He crossed his arms, steadying himself. "So—" and then he reached into his jacket pocket and pulled out a sheath of papers. "Here." He slid the papers over to her.

She didn't move. "Chen . . ." she said.

"You should go. I don't want to keep dragging you down with me. I don't blame you for wanting to leave," he stuttered. "I don't blame you for wanting to go back to Illinois. To see Qiong. I'm a failure. I'm a bad man. You should have left me years ago, I—"

"Chen," Fan interrupted, turning now so that she faced the balcony. She walked over to the kitchen table and pulled out a chair. She was still facing away from him, looking out over the balcony, so that she was gazing again at the black buttresses, or perhaps beyond those, at something he couldn't see. Then she turned back and looked at him in a way he had never seen before: there was something heavy, something sorry, something fearful. Something loving. "Robert Qiong is dead," she said.

His breath caught in his throat.

She continued. "I went to America for Robert Qiong's funeral. I'm sorry I didn't tell you, but at the time, I didn't have the words to describe my actions. I was worried that you would think that I still loved him. I mean, I'm stupid—you thought that anyway." She paused. "Chen, I want you to know, I was happy for years. I loved being here with you and Yihong. But Beijing . . . Beijing is a tough city. When we lived with your parents, life was busy. It felt normal for me to take care of your parents, take care of Yihong, go to work. But when we moved in here, life changed. We had achieved everything we'd wanted in many ways, but in other ways, it was nothing like I'd imagined. I had none of the friends I'd had in Illinois. This was your city, and I didn't have much in common with your friends. I'm just a girl from a Shandong village to them, after all. I was lonely. I went to work, I was good at work, and at night I cooked for you, and I called my friends who lived in other cities, other countries. It was a good life. But I couldn't help thinking what would have happened, had we never left Illinois." She looked up at him, and in her face he saw a glimpse of the woman he'd met that first day in the Black Violet: a woman with the world at her feet. "This is normal. I know you've wondered that too."

He nodded. He remained in place, standing by the kitchen counter.

"After we fought about Yihong going abroad, I was so angry. So I emailed Robert. It was petty of me. I think I was looking for an excuse to talk to him." The words landed on him, confirmation of a fear he'd held inside for so long. "I'm sorry. I just wanted to know how he was. I felt that I had reached my life's terminus, I had hit the ceiling of what it was going to be, and I wondered if he had, too, and what that looked like. I wondered what his daughter, his son, looked like. I just sent him a simple email, how are you? And he responded. It wasn't as if we rekindled a romance; he didn't respond like he'd been waiting by the phone for years. He was just happy to hear from me. He said his daughter was in her final year at the University of Chicago. His son was about to start at Boston University. He was very proud."

A daughter. He thought about Qiong, sitting in their living room, talking about his feisty firstborn, who could speak full sentences by the time she was one. She was destined to be a lawyer, an actor, someone whose wit was as fast as her tongue. His son had still been an infant when they'd left; he was just a bit older than Yihong.

"He'd had a few papers published and he was still teaching his same classes. He seemed to have a good life, though in a way he, too, had hit his ceiling. He seemed happy about that, though, and it drove me nearly crazy, the way that he was happy and yet I was not. Why, I asked myself, was I not happy? And I kept returning to that decision that changed my life forever. Would I have felt more fulfilled had I stayed in Illinois, had I followed my economics career, had I become a professor like him? I don't know; I will never know."

She was frantic now; she'd stood and had begun busying herself in the kitchen, grabbing cups off shelves and slamming cabinet doors. She stood over a boiling pot of water, her back hunched.

"We kept in touch over the years, sending updates," she finally continued. Her nail worked its way into a packet of tea. "It was friendship. I rationalized this to myself, and so I never told you. I never told you because it really was nothing. We . . . never talked about what had happened between us." She set a cup down on the counter in front of him. The tea was flaxen, chrysanthemum flowers floating up and down like jellyfish. She sat back down at the dining table.

"And then a year ago he emailed saying that he was sick. Cancer. He didn't seem too sad; he said he'd lived a very good life. His daughter was pregnant. His one wish was to live long enough to meet his granddaughter."

It was a slow-moving cancer deep in his esophagus. He'd had it for years but it had lain dormant until suddenly, the previous winter, it had come to claim him with a fury. He had died back in March, actually. But the family had kept the news private—this was, Chen realized, why he hadn't seen anything about the death when he'd searched Qiong's name online weeks ago—until the memorial in July, for the friends who couldn't make it there right away.

As Chen listened to Fan, triplet emotions buffeted him. First, a thread pinched loose inside; finally he could feel himself breathe. The man who had dogged him his whole life had died. The second emotion came swiftly: shock like a knife. All these years she'd kept him like a secret under her pillow, mere inches from Chen's face. With shaking hands, he took a sip of tea, wincing at the heat.

"I cried for a very long time after I received that email. Robert, he wasn't a young man anymore, but sixty-six is still too young to die. I felt that the world was unfair, and I felt that the questions I had asked myself were so petty and inconsequential in the face of death. He was dying, and I was healthy. Wasn't that proof enough that my decision had been right?

"We emailed often in that final year. The last email he sent me, he told me that he thought I would have been the most brilliant economics mind of my generation, and that one of his life's regrets was loving me—if he had not loved me, perhaps I would have stayed. It was shocking, the fact that he would bring this up, and I didn't know how to respond. So I left it there. I wanted to take time to give him the right response."

She choked up. "He died two weeks later. His wife called me. I am not sure how she got my information, but I suspect she'd gone into his emails. She wasn't angry though. She just seemed tired. I'm sure she had called so many people by the time she got to me. I started planning my trip to Illinois the next day. I told you it was a trip to see friends, and that was true too. I told myself if I was going to go back, I would make a trip of it. I would see everyone I hadn't seen in years. I would really allow myself to envision what kind of life I would have had had I stayed."

He remembered the moment she'd first brought up the divorce. Five months ago. March. Now the third emotion landed, soberly: a ragged sadness at the finality, the unrelenting certainty of death.

Frank and Angelica, moved to some unknown place. Big Luck Diner, gone. Robert Qiong, gone.

"Being back on campus was so strange. It felt exactly the same. The old math building seemed even to have the same ivy trailing up its front. They have some new buildings, a very nice computer science building, yes, but other than that, things were just as we'd left them. Even the students were the same age, which of course they are, but for a second I half expected to see myself with a backpack slung over my shoulder. Anyway. His memorial service was that weekend, held inside the church. There were many, many people. He had a lot of friends. His wife was smaller than I remembered. She didn't cry. His daughter was the one who was crying. He'd been doing better in the month leading up to March. So she was back in San Francisco when it happened. It was so fast. No flights available. And his son was in Boston."

She looked at Chen, searching for understanding. "Neither of them made it back in time."

"America is such a large country," he said. "Too large."

"They played his favorite song at the memorial. 'Every Time You Go Away.' I remembered he used to hum that while writing problem sets on the board. Kind of an odd song to hum, if you think about it." She paused. "I kept thinking, during the memorial service, that he would walk through the doors and up to the front and start lecturing about employment theory. Isn't that silly? And then I saw friends. Many friends. It was so wonderful to see A Fang again. Nannan is quite sweet now, actually. All month long, I compared myself to these friends, measured my life against theirs, compared houses, compared husbands, compared children, compared faces. Everyone asked me how you were."

He was surprised at this, though it must have seemed peculiar that Fan had been at the service without him. No one—to his knowledge—knew what had transpired between her and Qiong, but he was sure many suspected. This was why he'd found it difficult to face the friends with whom he'd once shared every dream, why he'd avoided calling Meng Haian for years, until he'd gotten sick.

"They all praised you. They've always praised you. They always knew you as the doting husband. A Fang said so many times, I wish Old Yuan was like Chen. And I felt proud. I've always felt proud. My husband was the best; I've always known he was the best."

He was shocked to hear this. "I thought A Fang always hated me."

"Are you kidding? She couldn't stop saying all the things Old Yuan was doing wrong. I think she has a little crush on you."

She was being so generous. Why was she being so generous?

"You know . . . Meng got pushed into an early retirement after his sickness. A Fang hasn't worked in fifteen years. Jia Yinhao's first three businesses failed. It seems like only young women want to date him because they don't understand that the money runs out." She laughed, mirthlessly. "Being there, I realized that failure can come for anyone, anywhere. Perhaps I would have been happier had I stayed; perhaps I wouldn't have. All I have is the choice I made. So I thought I'd come back, see if I could have one last good weekend with you, see if I could try just being happy."

He looked at her. She looked back. That damned emotion, hope, swelled back up in him. He wanted to tamp it down, but that's the thing about hope—it grows fast, even when you're smart enough to know you shouldn't let it.

"And then I saw you talking to that woman last night. The secretary."

He froze.

"I saw you talking outside, on the driveway."

"Fan, it's not what you think—"

"I saw you with her and realized: Is it really fidelity that matters so much to you? For years, I felt like such a bad woman. I had hurt the person I loved the most, and yet you had still forgiven me. All you asked of me was to come back home with you. My mother had only ever had one dream for me and that was to find a good husband. And I thought, if nothing else, I had this. But over the years I have realized that even you didn't care anymore about what had happened. You didn't care that I had loved him, only that he was better than you, richer than you, smarter than you. And that same jealousy extended to me. You couldn't stand to see me win. So you clipped my wings, Chen. And I let you."

"Fan, no—" He wanted to shout. He wanted to say that he'd always loved his brilliant wife. He wanted to describe the pride he'd felt, watching her lecture, winning awards and praise. He wanted to say that he was driven crazy by the thought of the two of them, Fan and Qiong, achieving together, grabbing more and more of the dream, and where would that leave him? It would be only natural for Fan to leave him in the end. He thought that if she had been a lesser woman, he might have let Qiong take her. But her kingdom was too big. He couldn't handle losing it.

"Chen, I know your degree was rescinded."

His heart dropped.

"I found out a few months after our wedding. We were talking about work, and it just felt like you never wanted to talk about your job, which was unlike you. You loved bragging about work." She laughed. "And so I asked Robert; I made him tell me. He tried to keep it a secret, he did. And when I discovered the truth, I waited for you to tell me. I waited and waited. For years I waited. And then when I found that paperwork and I asked you—and you denied it—I realized you would never tell me the truth. You would never be honest about failing. Chen, I just wish you could have talked to me!"

He wanted to walk to her and wrap her up in an embrace. He moved toward the table, managed only to place a hand on the back of her chair.

"I was ashamed," he finally said. "I didn't feel good enough for you. You needed a great man, and I just always fell short."

She had tears in her eyes. "Do you know why my mother named me Fan? Everyone in the village thought she'd lost her mind—sure, we were used to calling our kids Little Dog, Little Bastard as nicknames, but as an actual name? 'Ordinary?' They felt like she was playing a joke on them. But my mom said that ordinary was the stuff of life. Most people are ordinary. Ordinary is good. I was angry when she explained this to me; I thought she was trying to limit me, make me a conventional woman, keep me by her side in the village all my life. She never wanted greatness for me, and for years I fought this—I would go to America, be someone great. I'd tell people my name was Ordinary and dare them to confirm; it was obvious to everyone that I was anything but ordinary.

"But now I realize that my mother was right all along. Greatness is elusive; it is not meant to last long; even when you attain it you spend the rest of your life trying to keep it. I chased you because I thought you were extraordinary, then I chased Robert because I thought he was. Greatness always ends, with time, with distance, with death. But ordinary is everlasting. Ordinary is the morning light. Ordinary is a wave to your neighbor. Ordinary is the fact that Robert got to hold his granddaughter two months before he died. Ordinary is our son, our wonderful son. My mother wanted me to be proud of who I was already, someone ordinary. She did not want me to wager the worth of my life on what I could achieve, on who I could become. I was already her beloved daughter, her ordinary daughter. And now I finally understand this."

She looked over to the stack of papers on the counter. "Thank you, for this."

He turned and gazed upon their home, its white crown molding, its brown oak floors, the French doors leading to their bedroom. He thought of their old studio in Illinois and the mattress he'd found lying on the sidewalk outside of a dumpster. It had been gaudy and massive, a hulking body bulging out of a collage of gold and silver thread. He'd dragged it across gravel and concrete for a mile and then up three flights of stairs. As he discovered later, it was a *"California king"* and barely fit in their studio. After what seemed like hours of maneuvering, he managed to squeeze it between the window and the front door. Part of the mattress heaved into the doorframe, necessitating an aggressive slam every time they entered and exited the apartment. But the bed served as a perfect couch and dining room table; by night they made love beneath their polyester quilts, and by day they sat atop the perfectly made bed, the quilt smooth and the pillows fluffed, eating their meals as they watched their neighbors across the way, a young couple just like them, who'd often dance together in their living room as music Chen and Fan could only imagine flowed from their stereo.

He thought of their wedding day, a sweltering day in July, Chen in leather shoes he'd borrowed from Meng Haian, Fan in a pair of beige heels her American roommate had thrown away years ago, shoes she'd fished from the dumpster and kept in a plastic bag in her closet. She wore a white blouse and a white skirt that was a little too big. It was a courthouse ceremony, and when they emerged, it was pouring. They ran across the street to a Subway, where they ordered two footlong sandwiches stuffed with steak and cold bologna and cheddar cheese and lettuce. They hated the taste of cold meat, but they were ravenous and devoured their sandwiches all the way down to the bread nubs. Fan loved mustard—it reminded her of the pickled vegetables she would eat back in Shandong—and emptied two full packets onto her sandwich. That day, he thought their life would always be like this.

"I'm going to move back to my parents'," he finally said.

"What do you mean?"

"It's the perfect solution. I'm going to sell this place. My half—I'm going to use it on the lawsuit and on Yihong's condo."

"Chen . . . it doesn't have to just be you. We can split the cost."

"No," he said. "I can't ask you to sacrifice anything for me again."

She was silent. She sat back down at the table and stared out at the city, now black. He saw a woman leaning over a stove in a starkly lit apartment across the way. She was cooking herself a meal and looked peaceful. He envied that she didn't care who saw her.

"Can't you see, Chen?" Fan said. "We could have had everything, if you would have just leaned on me."

"Let me make this one last mistake," Chen said. "Keep the money. It's just enough to start your life over again."

5

There was less to take than he'd thought. Chen stood in their bedroom. He had known this space so well, and now it was no longer his. He opened the top drawer of their dresser. Here was a program for a musical he and Fan had attended in Chicago. Here was a photo of Yihong grabbing at his mother, his fists chubby, Fan's face a portrait of delight. Here was his notebook of handy English phrases, the pencil marks still pristine, having not seen the sun in nearly thirty years. "*English,*" the inside page read, in Chen's neat handwriting. The date in the corner was December 1990. The second page: "*Loud and confident speak,*" which had been crossed out in red pen and replaced, in Fan's messier handwriting, with, "*Speak loudly and confidently.*"

Here was the photo he'd had a street performer take for him in Times Square. It was off-center and overexposed, but it shocked him to see how happy he was, standing amid the lights and the pale faces and the towering steel bodies. His second Christmas vacation in Illinois, he had taken a twenty-hour bus ride to New York City. He sat awake the entire ride, stuffed between snoring teenage runaways, and had stayed in a hostel for nine dollars a night. He barely slept a wink that weekend, so excited he was to see as much as possible of the city of dreams.

He'd always believed that if he worked hard enough, he could do anything. But he'd worked hard and failed anyway. He'd always thought that winners could only exist where there were losers. Between him and Fan, who was the winner? And who was the loser? Out of all of them, Qiong must be the winner. But as Chen thought of him lying in that hospital bed with his wife weeping over him, all alone, his children on both coasts of that vast country, he wondered if there were any winners at all.

Why was it so hard to leave a mark on that country? Despite every struggle, every victory, every concession you made, in the end America was always unchanged by you, and yet you held the years inside like a cancer, just like a cancer, until it spread over your entire body and in the end took you for its own. America didn't swallow you whole, no—it chipped away at you, tiny nibbles at a time, until you were gone.

When he'd returned home he'd resolved to make a different dream. In this dream he had his wife, and his son, and their life in Beijing. So he'd put his photo from Times Square into his notebook and wrapped the whole thing tightly with twine, and never opened it back up: his old dream, boxed in like a corpse, the light shut out.

He looked at himself in the photo, so young, his smile so stupid and wide. He had nothing in the world, nothing in the world to lose. And he had never been so happy.

HE WALKED THROUGH the morning hordes at Yuan Dynasty Capital City Wall Site Park, wheeling behind him the first of many suitcases. Fall had come suddenly, as it often did. Wind bit at his nose. On the trees in the park hung dozens of white papers, each with a typed-up résumé. "Male, 37 years old, never married. Has car, has house, makes 10,000 a month." "Female, 25 years old, accountant. Beijing hukou. Wanting: a clean, smart man with a master's degree or higher, car, and condo." "Female, 32 years old, divorced once. No kids. Wanting: a man with a kind heart."

He wondered what his matchmaking poster would say. Guilin's would read: "Female, 34 years old, from Ligezhuang.

Secretary to a prominent local politician. Hardworking, funny, pretty. 155 centimeters. Associate degree. No kids. Mandolin player. Wanting: male 30 to 59 years old. Beijing hukou. Has car, has house, makes 10,000 a month or more."

No, more like: "Wanting: a man who can keep his promise."

"Wanting: a car. Absolute freedom."

"Wanting: a home I can call my own."

What would Fan's say?

"Female, 55 years old, from Linjiacun, Shandong. Financial analyst. Smart, beautiful, capable, stubborn. 160 centimeters. American-educated. Postdoctoral fellow in economics at a top-ranked American university. Left for family. Left for love. One son. Many friends. Charming, witty, impatient. Fantastic cook. Loves: seafood, reality television, travel, taking fast walks in the park, playing volleyball. Wanting . . ."

What did Fan want? Fan didn't want anything from anyone when she met him, not anything he could give her, anyway. In 1988, she would have said: "Wanting: a smooth six years of graduate school. Friends to guide me along the way." What did she want now?

He thought of Fan leaning on the balcony with her phone to her ear, laughing, laughing, so far away from him, wearing loose pants and a padded vest and chewing on sunflower seeds, each shell popping between her molars like twigs beneath a truck's tire on an open road. He thought about who she would be at the end of life. Would she be that same village girl, skinning pigs and stir-frying gailan and eggs? A girl who spent her nights measuring the points between stars in the sky, between ants on the ground? Would she be that girl counting books in the library or approaching strangers with all the confidence in the world? Or would she be someone else entirely, someone Chen had never met at all.

SHORTLY THEREAFTER, he stood before the seafoam door of his childhood again.

The peeling green paint, the concrete floors, and the polluted wind that blew north to south left him breathless in a bad way. He stood in the parlor, which was also the kitchen, which was also a dining room. He'd grown up in these twelve square meters. He faced the door to his old bedroom.

He was fifty-seven and back at home. For his return, his parents had pushed the desk to the far-left corner, and the dresser closer to the window. The Luck and Happiness comforter was gone, but the portrait still hung there above the bed, the blank spot still visible on Fan's cheek, where weeks ago he had swiped away dust. The floor was still cracked in the place where he had shattered a vase when he was twelve, and the ceiling was still scratched where his father's broom had scraped it.

Fan had departed for her hometown the previous week. That morning he had folded his shirts and two sport coats and three pairs of pants into a suitcase, along with his divorce papers and the photo of Yihong grabbing Fan's face. At Mudanyuan Station he'd swiped his pass, shuffled into the station with the hundreds of late commuters, then gotten on the 10 to the 1. He'd ridden the line thirteen stations with one transfer, and gotten off at the Military Museum stop, where he'd exited from Door C and emerged to be greeted by the garish yellow sign of the McDonald's that had been new when he had first returned. He and Fan had frequented this McDonald's—it reminded them of America. They'd wait in lines as long as the Changjiang for the familiar taste of hamburgers and fries. So much of Beijing had changed in the three decades since then, but this had stayed the same. Teenage couples still crowded its fluorescent interior and enjoyed the hamburgers with equal fervor. They probably thought their love would last forever too.

Had Guilin loved him? Had Fan loved him? Or were both of them merely trying to survive? Perhaps love was but a frivolous addition to the hefty work of staying alive.

He looked again at the portrait hanging above the bed, at

Fan's smiling airbrushed face, the skin as white as bone. His tuxedo fit perfectly. They had been modern people.

He took a handkerchief and dusted it fully, so that their young faces shone.

That morning on WeChat, Fan had posted a photo of a line of trees outside her mother's apartment in Qingdao, that crescent-shaped city that yawned its giant mouth around a fistful of the Yellow Sea. The leaves were so red they looked almost artificial. "Nothing like autumn in Qingdao. Have not seen this in many years," read the caption. He thought about the eulogy she'd given for her father a few years back. A longtime heart disease had killed him in the middle of the night. Fan's mother was convinced he'd choked. The coroner found a grape seed on his tongue. "Old Jiang," she wailed, "I told you not to eat before bed."

Fan did not cry when her father died. She organized his funeral, tended to his cremation, then went with her mother to spread his ashes at dawn into the Yellow Sea.

"He lived his life on this sea," she said, standing on the gray rocks leading up to the sand. "He was born here, and when his father died, he took over his fishing boat. Each morning he would wake up at four and go out to the water. He'd haul sardinella in the fall and anchovies in the spring, and he was happiest in the winter months, when the salmon would emerge. He never left Shandong all his life. I used to think that was small-minded of him, that his life was small because of it. But as I stand here now," she said, peering off into the distance, at the sun softly cracking through the horizon, "I realize it was boundless."

He hoped that she was home now, that she considered that city by the sea her home. He wondered if she still thought of that street in Urbana, and he wondered what else he could have done to bring them back to that home on Huayuan Road. Fan would say that wondering was exactly the problem.

HE WAS FIFTY-SEVEN. He had left his country and had worked for pennies and had tried his best to pinch and mold himself into the kind of man who could make it in America, make it back home. He had gotten divorced, and his son, engaged. He had glimpsed love, then lost it, then fallen back in love and out again.

He had given up his home so that his son could have a home, and now he was to live again within the crevice of his youth, fitting his body into a childhood story, a bygone era. He was sad, but in this sadness he thought of the sound of his son's voice as he dropped the keys into his hands. "Really, Ba?" It was resonant, apologetic, and full of joy.

His phone buzzed. It was a wedding invitation. In the photo Rufeng and Yihong sat on the floor of the Xiangheyuan place, wearing matching, nice blue clothes and smiling radiantly at the camera.

As he stood in the space, Chen could see the outline of yet another new housing development through the haze of the city smoke. The orange-and-green of the complex across the way had begun to fade. Perhaps life was an everlasting process of leaving one home for another, but he would never fully leave his. It was okay. He took the Times Square photo from his briefcase and placed it on his desk, alongside the photo of Yihong. His son reached his chubby fist upward, toward Fan's face, toward the sky. These were the things he'd lost. These were the things he'd gained.

6

Su Mingzun woke up five months later.

It was a brilliant morning at the end of February when Lian heard the news. That morning, Lian was astounded by the cloudlessness of the sky. Blue engulfed the city.

She opened her WeChat to see a photo of Su Mingzun smiling, along with a link to a blog, where he had begun writing his thoughts after waking up in the hospital. She clicked on it. He wrote:

"On January 12, I woke from a coma. It's the strangest feeling, waking up from a coma. I felt like I was waking up from a very long nap. There was this crazy blinding light and suddenly I could hear all these people around me, shouting. I was so fucking confused. I had no idea where I was or how I'd gotten there. People told me I'd been in an accident. Something hit me. There was a fire. It all sounded like the kind of shit you see in a soap opera. When I woke up my parents were sitting around me. My mom was crying. I started crying. It was insane. Then they told me I had been the lead suspect in an arson case. I couldn't believe it. I thought I'd been at a party. Nothing was adding up. I tried to sit up and I felt like my whole body was made of sand. For weeks, I could barely stand. But I'm getting better. I'm doing physical therapy. I learned more about what happened that evening, and I'm happy that the world understands that I am innocent. My last memory was of falling into a pool; I just remember feeling so wet and heavy. And I remember seeing someone I loved standing above me. That's the last thing I remember."

His blog had already racked up thousands of followers. Su Mingzun had become a bit of a celebrity in the months since he'd been asleep. Investigators had pursued him as the lead suspect in the arson case. Old photos of him were splashed across television screens all over Beijing, where he glowered behind shaggy bangs he'd yet to cut. Swarms of women sent their sympathies, blaming Wenyu for seducing him and leading him on. When the investigation eventually petered out and all charges against him were dropped, his fan base only grew more vociferous, indignant about how their hero had been framed. They began a campaign looking for the real perpetrator, though that search was never fruitful. Lian had her suspicions, but she couldn't be sure.

As his blog grew, Su Mingzun told his story in more and more fantastical tones, spinning thousands of words about how inside his coma he'd dreamed he was a medieval knight galloping through an Irish town during the plague. He was a Qing prince in the waning days of the monarchy, refusing to give his country up to the Japanese. He was a farmer who'd been visited by a rain spirit who told him he'd be blessed with a thousand wives if only he did not drink the water in his well. All his stories had something to do with the deterioration of society, with how lust, greed, and an overabundance of resources and inequality in distribution, combined with authoritarianism and unjust democracy, had perverted the very core of human connection. Sometimes Lian agreed with him; other times his words went completely over her head. He wrote many stories, but he never told the truth about Wenyu.

Lian was sure he'd disappear from his blog the way he'd disappeared so many times over the last decade; he was never one to seek the attention of the faceless masses. But perhaps adoration was a currency no one could resist. Eventually, he turned his posts into a novel.

The novel told the story of a pair of star-crossed lovers separated by the forces of capitalism, geography, and greed. It sold 500,000 copies and made Su Mingzun into the kind of rich man he'd always hated.

He called it "Rabbit Trap."

SHE SAW WENYU one more time before she left Beijing, one unseasonably cold day at the end of summer. It was one of those days where everyone felt, even at their age, that school was about to begin. Wenyu came over to her house for the first time since she'd been back, and they sat on her bed just as they had when they were seventeen, when Wenyu had made her announcement. She asked Lian to forgive her for lying. "What if he dies?" Lian asked. "Won't you feel bad for slandering the dead?"

"It's better than slandering the living, at any rate," she said. "And Mingzun's used to that, anyway."

Lian had so many questions, and in many ways, Wenyu had already answered them. Wenyu had gone off again and made a world without her, and again Lian was left alone to create her own.

Wenyu lay on Lian's bed, picking at the Pompompurin sticker pasted on the wall next to her desk. Crumbs of white sticker paper speckled her floor in a snowfall. Then Wenyu gave her a note, folded into a square.

She waited until Wenyu had left to open it.

It was the first four lines of a poem by Gao Shi, one that she had loved in high school.

Thousand-mile yellow clouds obscure the setting sun,
The north wind blows, trading geese for snow.
Do not worry about strangers on the road ahead,
For who won't know you under the sky?

Gao Shi had written the poem for his friend, Dong Da, when they had parted as young men. Dong Da was worried about the future and whether he would ever again find someone who understood him. And Gao Shi had comforted him, saying, Old friend—you are beloved everywhere. Who won't know you under the sky?

It was a poem they'd learned as children, and it had always been Lian's favorite. She'd written these lines down and tucked them into Wenyu's suitcase the day she left for America. Wenyu had never mentioned it until now.

The next day, Wenyu and Thomas were back in San Francisco. Two months later, Lian watched them get married in a live stream from a beautiful estate north of the city. It was four in the morning, and Lian had crawled awake, pulling up the video on her phone. She crouched next to her bed, using her knees as a phone stand.

Wenyu had chosen a simple silk gown that looked soft and billowed out in the wind. She'd woven flowers into her hair. Lian watched as Wenyu walked slowly up a grassy slope, her feet grazing white rose petals as scores of classmates and friends watched from wooden folding chairs on either side of the aisle. A long veil streamed behind her, and she held peonies in her hands. A romantic folk song played, an American song Lian had never heard. Their attendees were a spread of Americans from all corners of the world. But there was no one from Wenyu's old life in attendance. No one there to gossip about her, to place bets on her happiness and whether she'd gotten here by choice or by mistake.

The whole ceremony was in English. They wrote their own vows, Thomas choking up as he spoke about Wenyu's kindness, love for life, and curiosity for the world. Wenyu, too, got emotional as she spoke about how they'd met, how Thomas had been a life raft during a hard time. *"Life raft"* was the phrase she used, and Lian wondered which of the three of them—Thomas, Su Mingzun, or she—had really kept her afloat, or if they all had, and without one of them, Wenyu would have slipped into a crack in time. Her voice was clear and high and nearly devoid of any trace of her Chinese self. They'd weathered many storms together, she said, and she wanted to hold his hand through rain and shine forever.

Was it Thomas that kept her in America, or was it America that kept her to Thomas? She and Wenyu would never know.

Vivian Straeffer-Kenney was the most beautiful bride. Standing there in her flowers and her silk, she looked right where she should be. Lian knew now that to thrive in America meant to tell a constant lie, tell it until you believed it to be gospel. Wenyu had always been a good liar, but none trumped that of the night at 48 Sutton Place. She'd uploaded a video shortly after returning to California, her face gravely serious, telling her fans that she was safe and that she was home. Lian wondered if she told herself this truth enough that even she believed it. The facts were so adjacent, so almost true; Su Mingzun had been obsessed with her; he had been the one to reappear in her life like a flash, nearly destroying everything. So when a year after Wenyu left, Lian heard of another instance, a man who broke into their San Francisco home, who stole seventy thousand dollars' worth of jewelry and electronics, who left for Wenyu a single chocolate Hershey's Kiss, she questioned the reality of that crime. Perhaps there would always be another adoring woman, another Su Mingzun. Another Lian. All of them, forever searching for an answer inside Wenyu. She posted a video shortly after, saying they were moving to Los Angeles, and Lian wondered if this would always be Wenyu's life, chasing the fragments of herself, trying to piece together someone she still recognized.

LIAN READ Su Mingzun's post all the way through. She peered at the photo of him smiling with something haunted in his eyes. She thought about that last snapshot before he'd blacked out. Someone he loved, standing over him. There would be much debate in the comments about what he meant—many believed this was Wenyu, while others believed he'd been dreaming about someone else. Then she put her phone away. She had a busy day. She strapped her backpack on and walked out her door and onto the elevator, then the street, and down into the subway. She had to stop by the shipping store; she needed boxes. Her body swayed as she gripped the blue plastic handles of the 10 train.

She was going to pack up all her plushies and posters and stickers. Her clothes, her pens, her socks, and her shoes. Her favorite mug, her computer, the blank lined diaries she and Wenyu had stolen together and never used.

She was moving out.

THE CONDOMINIUM her mother had found was spectacular. There was nothing she could pick at. It faced south; it was on the eighteenth floor. On a clear day, it had a view of the Forbidden City. It had brand-new appliances and real hardwood floors. Zhetai fell in love instantly and by the next day was already contemplating what color to transform the kitchen. He wanted a light, summery green.

She said yellow, and so they went with yellow.

After the fire, Zhetai had called her, worry in his voice. She had told him, again and again, "I am okay." Then she did not see him for three full weeks. He tried to call her, and she let the phone ring.

Finally, in September, Lian found herself back at the badminton court.

Zhetai was practicing his smashes by himself, hitting the birdie against the wall with a cold and unshakable focus. He didn't look different at all. She didn't know what she'd expected— for him to be thinner? Paler? To be so racked with worry at her disappearance that he was but a shell of himself? But the thing Zhetai was best at was rolling on; he was always better than her at moving through life. She walked up behind him. She could see a bead of sweat traveling down his left cheek. She could hear the clanging sounds of cymbals reverberating out of his AirPods.

She reached out her racquet and caught the birdie coming their way.

He snapped toward her, his hand flying to his ears. "Lian."

"Hi," she said.

She bounced the birdie on her racquet. "I'm sorry I've been distant."

He grabbed another birdie, hit it against the wall. "You've been more than distant."

"I'm sorry I haven't talked to you," she said. "I should have been honest with you. I needed some space to think about what I really want with my life."

He didn't respond.

"You think I don't think about that, Lian?"

"What?"

"We all think about what we want with our lives. But I chose this a long time ago. And I want to stick with it."

She nodded and continued bouncing the birdie. "Wenyu went home," she said, and then flinched at the easy way in which "home" had slid off her tongue.

He paused. "Probably for the best," he said. Someone else might have said, "I'm sorry," or "I'm glad you two got to see each other again." This is what she had hoped, but of course Zhetai was not someone else.

"Yes," she said.

He smashed the birdie into the wall. Instead of bouncing back, it fell to the ground. He picked it up. "You know what I think? You always think that others have more than you, so you can't possibly fathom having the power to hurt anyone. But you do."

She didn't respond right away. She threw the birdie into the air; she smashed it at the wall, right next to Zhetai's arm. He was right. She had hurt him. And she felt an ache, just a little bite in her heart. Her eyes were wet. *When you cry for someone, you feel their heart.* It was something Freddy had taught her.

"I'm sorry," she said again. He reached out and handed her the birdie. It was light in her palm. He did it in such a way that said, Here you go; do with it what you please. She could walk away if she wanted, drop the birdie, drop the racquet, and never turn back.

"By the way," she said next. "The answer is yes."

His lower lip dropped just slightly. He knew what she was talking about. "Yes?"

"Yeah," she said.

He nodded, then motioned toward the net. "Let's do a round before we go?"

She did not speak to Freddy again. She almost did, many times. She typed up countless messages on her phone, ranging from Hi to Can we talk to What the fuck was that. She pictured herself in New York. How she'd ride the subway with Freddy, how they'd sit in Washington Square Park together. This girl would wear rings and platform shoes. This girl would wear ripped jean shorts and dye her hair with streaks of blonde. She would flirt with her teeth bared and her painted nails flying. This girl would have a different name, one whose syllables dragged on forever. This girl would love Freddy, and she might love many others. She was struck by how wonderful it must feel, sometimes, to have only one option in your life, and not limitless ones. So that you weren't always crushed by the volume of life you could have lived. The girl with the blonde streaks in her hair would have a wonderful life, too, Lian knew. In the end, this was precisely why she could not get on the train of this choice. She would not ride the train, see the views rolling outside its windows, would not ride it wondering if it would take her so far from home she could never come back. Others could do it and return unchanged. But Lian was not like Zhu Zixi, who could recycle countries like boyfriends; not like Freddy, who lived vicariously through the heroes in stories. Actually, she was most like Luo Wenyu, who was not a chameleon, as Lian had always thought. Wenyu was more of a butterfly, who had evolved irrevocably, sloughing off a skin she'd never recover. What would Lian have to lose in exchange for a possibility? Others could change colors as many times as it took to find happiness, but Lian knew that she could not.

THEY WERE MOVING that weekend, Lian with her various boxes—and oh, how many boxes there were; who knew what it took to transplant yourself from one location to another! A small bag for your lotions, yet another bag for your cleansers, and another for your charging cables and toothbrushes and guest toothbrushes and spices and cleaning sprays—and Zhetai with his, the two of them coming together to build a life.

That weekend, she and Zhetai would unlock the door to their new condominium together. They would stand in the glowing hardwood space and stare up at their high ceilings, look out their windows at the city, their city. If they squinted, they could see the Forbidden City to the south, the Bird's Nest to the west. Yonghegong sat closer. On a clear day, they could see the little curlicues of incense floating upward from the temple, hordes of people crowding into its halls and lighting up a ten-kuai wish, wishing for just this: a home in the sky with someone they loved.

They would move in their boxes and mingle their silverware. They'd laugh at the repeat rice cookers and the missing shampoo, both of them thinking the other would have brought some. They'd scrub the tiles and the oven and the toilets (two of them!)

clean, then collapse on the floor on their makeshift couch, three suitcases pulled together and pushed against the wall. They'd accumulate things: pots and pans and a television and a rack for their shoes. They'd be gifted spider plants and ceramic ladle holders and Gudetama night-lights.

They would be married in a small ceremony in a botanical garden, and at the reception, photos from their various birthday parties, vacations, and anniversaries would play across a screen. The photo of the two of them at the New Year's dinner when she was one and he was three would end the slideshow and everyone seated would coo and a few would shed happy tears.

They'd meet their neighbors, other couples, some with babies on the way. The couple in the two-bedroom across the hall would be a man with a big grin and a woman with a big laugh. He would dress in basketball shorts at all times, like Su Mingzun in his prime, and she would wear gaudy sweatshirts with American slogans. They would always wave. Eventually Lian and Zhetai would invite them over for dinner, and they'd learn that the girl was studying to be a doctor, and the boy was an engineer. Sometimes Lian and Zhetai would see their families come to visit, a pair of loud countryside people in fake designer clothing, and other times, a no-nonsense woman carrying a mountain of groceries, and at other times, a man with a slight slouch, each arriving on their own, the woman brusque and full of life, and the man quiet, always quiet, before he entered the door. He looked familiar, but Lian never could place him. But once the door opened his voice would grow loud and boisterous, and Lian would wonder which of these versions of him was real.

They would have a housewarming and attend housewarmings and pregnancy announcements and baby showers. One day Lian would have a child of her own, a little girl with a sharp, inquisitive mind. She would grow up in the second bedroom, which did not have its own balcony but had a corner by the window where she could devour books. They would host dinner parties and spend weekend evenings watching sitcoms and period pieces with beautiful men. They would watch a film that had gotten some media buzz at the Berlin Film Festival by a daring new director named Han Xiaofei, and Lian would be astonished and happy when she looked him up and saw a familiar face staring back. The film was about a superhero who falls in love with a woman he meets on an alien planet and learns later that she is actually from his hometown but has stayed so long on this planet that she can't return to Earth with him. He has to make the choice between staying on this new planet and returning home. She would look up an interview the director did with *"Screen International,"* and hear him describe the journey of his titular character, Commander China:

I've been developing Commander China as a character for my entire adult life. I used to be very obsessed with what made him Chinese specifically. I saw him as the antithesis to the macho, faultless superheroes made by Hollywood. But eventually I became more interested in Commander China as a transient figure. Commander China's central trauma is his rootlessness. He's a character who leaves home at an early age and loses the ability to return. It's something I saw all around me, and it's something that I later experienced myself. This was neither a Chinese nor American condition, but a modern one. I studied film in Beijing, then went to New York for my graduate studies, and then I went to Argentina, and France, and now, Germany. I don't know when I'll stop. I don't miss home, not yet, but if you told me I couldn't go back, I don't know what I'd do. In an era when people are displaced every day by war, poverty, racial and ethnic strife, the concept of a homeland has become just that: conceptual. People are homes; memories are homes; land can sometimes no longer be a home. So Commander China's struggle in this film is essentially between the created homeland and the actual homeland. I don't know what the right choice for him is, myself.

In the end, Commander China would choose to go back. Lian would cry, watching the movie, and Zhetai would put his arm around her, and her daughter would say, "Does Mama want to go to the alien planet?" And she would say no, she wanted to stay right here.

And then she would have another child, another girl, who would look up to her first and copy her in all ways. She would teach her daughters the English words that had kept her company all these years—*jalopy, morose, mimeograph, desiccated. Beatification, gentrification, glorification, transformation.* Her first would tire of these exercises while her younger would wrestle them around in her mouth, spit them out in defiant wails. Her first would be her younger's guiding light, and Lian would hope that the younger could find her own way one day. And she wouldn't have to worry; the younger one would quickly, too quickly perhaps, grow a mind of her own, and she'd run faster and farther than any of them. She'd leave one day, maybe, leave Lian and her father and her sister behind, and Lian would let her go, hopeful for her but worried about everything she would lose in leaving.

Sometimes she'd drive out to the suburbs and see the house. A blue tarp covered half the facade. For a year or so after Wenyu left, she'd sometimes see a light on in what would have been Wenyu's bedroom. She'd wonder if it was that wild woman, if she'd finally gotten what she wanted. And then, after a year, the building was demolished and an apartment complex was built in its place.

She would see Wenyu again one day, on a family trip to California, another decade later. Wenyu would have three kids by then, two boys and a girl, and they would trade sly exhausted smiles, because they would know that yes, between the two of them, it made more sense for Wenyu to have sons but it really made no sense for either of them to have boys. Wenyu would allow her children to run on the cliffs of the Los Angeles coast as she lounged on a pool chair in the sun. She'd cut her thumb making guacamole, and she'd give up halfway and order takeout. The two of them would indeed nurse martini glasses of cold shrimp as they discussed the years that had passed. Wenyu would still be beautiful in the same torrid way, and Thomas would have gray hair by then, and Wenyu would tell him he looked distinguished, and privately she and Lian would laugh at the way Americans grew old so quickly. Lian would peer closely at Wenyu's children, looking for signs of her friend, and see the telltale dimples in her daughter's face, the devil-may-care crinkles at the corners of her older son's eyes, the diamond-shaped indent between her younger son's eyebrows that grew somber when he was distressed. But she would have to look harder than she wanted, as the children were brown-haired and green-eyed, barrel-chested in that way that Thomas was, and when Wenyu introduced her, they called her *Aunt Lianne*, their voices loud and definite, without a trace of song. And Wenyu would attempt to correct them, but the children would loll their heads back and run off to the surf, and Wenyu would trade conspiring looks with her, throw her hands up as if to say, I tried. Lian liked to believe they could only see each other during these delayed, intense intervals, because otherwise their collision would be too much; either of them would stir up too many maybes in the other. Or perhaps it was just the logistics of life that kept them apart.

BUT THAT WOULD come later. Now, Lian stood on the subway, feeling the shake of the machine around her, watching a couple in matching yoga clothes huddled around a pole, a balding man napping into his own shoulder, a teenager on her phone scrutinizing a makeup tutorial, frowning as she pondered how to make her face beautiful, how to be beloved like the woman on the screen. For now Lian would stand, wonderfully alone, barreling into the infinite ahead of the black train tunnel, and the future was currently nothing at all.

A Note on Italics

All languages foreign to my protagonists are denoted in italics in the novel; therefore, any English is in italics (English that is spoken or thought—of course, the novel is written in English). The English-speaking West is the exotic in this novel, so I wanted my usage of italics to reflect that and to poke cheekily at the Western literary practice of italicizing non-English words.

To avoid confusion, I've found other ways of typesetting words and phrases that are conventionally italicized. Emphasized words are underlined. Titles of films, books, magazines, and other works are presented in quotation marks—and italicized, again, only when my characters use the English titles.

Some words I've left in the original (albeit Romanized) Chinese, unitalicized.

References

p. 75: Lian refers to the 2018 film《找到你》(*Lost, Found*).

pp. 147–49: This scene was inspired by the virtual reality game *Zombyte*, created by Hologate, that was once available at Two Bit Circus in Los Angeles.

p. 215: Chen describes the 1959 film *Some Like It Hot*.

p. 350: The lines of poetry here are from Gao Shi's "Farewell to Dong Da," translated from the Chinese by Claire Jia (the poem in the original Chinese appears in *Reading Poetry of Tang Dynasty*, compiled and with commentary and introduction by Yi Zhongtian, Shanghai Literature & Art Publishing House, 2018).

Acknowledgments

When I got all four of my wisdom teeth out in college, I, waking up from my anesthetized stupor, pleaded desperately for my mother to thank the dentist. Apparently, I love thanking, and I hope here to do it well.

I never thought I could write a book. I always thought writing was for other people.

Thank you, therefore, to my agent, Sylvie Carr, for taking a chance on me as a mere twenty-two-year-old and giving me that critical thing: a belief, however delusional, that I could write and be a writer. Without you, my novel would've lain fallow on my old PC forever. Thank you for pushing me to excavate the very best version of it, and for our friendship. Thank you to everyone at Parse agency for your work. Thank you also to Hillary Black, for first reading me and bringing me to Sylvie. Thank you, Mary Pender, for coming on this journey with me.

My novel took ten years to finish. Thank you to my editor, Elizabeth DeMeo, and to Tin House for believing in my book and for making real a decade-long dream. I could not imagine a better home. Elizabeth, working with you is utterly life-giving. You have always seen me and seen my story. Thank you for your incredible eye, for so kindly handling my persistent indecision, and for your infinite thoughtfulness. Thank you to Beth Steidle for the dazzling cover, and everyone at Tin House for your faith and care: Becky Kraemer, Jacqui Reiko Teruya, Nanci McCloskey, Masie Cochran, Isabel Lemus Kristensen, Justine Payton, and Sydnee Ellison. Thank you to Jessica Roeder and Rebecca Munro for your crucial copy edits and proofreading.

Thank you to my teachers and mentors. Amity Gaige, I began my novel in your class at Amherst College; thank you for teaching me how to write, and for encouraging me to dive into Hollywood headfirst. Thank you, Judith Frank, for advising my novel and believing in me. Thank you, Kim Townsend, for the spirited conversations. Thank you, Andrew Poe, for generously reading my entire first draft after meeting me so briefly. Thank you, Shen Tong, for the lessons in Chinese and in life. Thank you, Liz Santiago and my classmates at GrubStreet, for your enthusiastic encouragement. Thank you, Elizabeth Irwin, for your early guidance. Thank you, Kerry Williamson—I struck gold on bosses with you, and I cherish your enduring support and friendship. Thank you, Pavel Machala, for telling me to live dangerously.

Thank you to Belinda Huijuan Tang, Hanna Halperin, Emily Feng, Jade Chang, Cleo Qian, and Alexandra Chang for your incredible praise. Thank you all for your generosity and enthusiasm, and for your fantastic writing.

I would have neither a novel nor dreams nor poetry nor laughter without my friends and family. I am such a happy duck.

Thank you, Lisa Deng, my partner in so many things, my twin (but one twin is six feet and the other is "five-eight") flame. You have seen this novel and me through too many iterations to count. Thank you for your brilliance and your whims; thank you for catching me down every spiral. I am the luckiest to get to write and clown about town with you. May we take so long sending emails it takes us the rest of our lives.

Thank you, Willa Zhang: perfect editor, sublime writer, glorious 哥们儿. The last tier of my Maslow's hierarchy of needs is you taking my hand and saying "I loved it" when you first read my novel. Thank you for constantly saving this book, for forcing me to view mountains, for sweating and stomping through this life with me. In every universe we are scream-laughing somewhere on a couch together at three AM.

Thank you, Marie Lambert, whose writing strikes me and whose friendship sustains me across decades and coasts. Here's to fourteen years of madness together and to a forever more.

Thank you, Jon Shestack and Portia Iversen, my Los Angeles parents. Thank you, Jon, for our wonderful ten PM dinner conversations and impromptu movie nights. Thank you, Portia, for fearlessly running our writing group and for the immaculate prompts. Thank you to our whole group, especially Stephanie Yu, for those early novel thoughts and Los Angeles years, and Zoe Kurland—reading you and being read by you is astounding.

Thank you again, Cleo Qian, for our thoughtful and thought-filled long-distance friendship. Thank you for leading the way as I blindly stumble through what it means to be a writer.

Thank you, Wendy Wei, for our nonlinear conversations, our summers together, and the Flamin' Hot Cheetos. If you're a poser I'm a poser. May we stay thinking chaotically.

Thank you, Joe Abriatis, for your boundless support, for my perfect author photos, and for hand-making the most beautiful embroidered first ever physical copy of *Wanting*. Thank you for your love.

Thank you, Jen Kim. Life is so fun with you. Thank you for giggling and singing with me, for your excitement, and for always being ready to do something unwise together.

Thank you to my friends who have generously read pages or talked me through plot knots and life knots, and to my treasured group chats: Andrew Haworth, Christina Won, Emma Hickman, Emma Weissmann, Ginny Hogan, Jacob Shenker, Jeanette Lim, Jennelle Fong, Jenny Zhou, JinJin Xu, Kimberly Han, Lexi Cary, Lilia Paz, LV Frazier, Nancy Yun Tang, Rachel Nghe, Rekha Mohan, Robin Alexander, Sarah Han, Teddy Dief, Walker King, and many more whose love, support, and humor I am forever grateful for. Thank you also to Saba Karimeddiny and Michelle Ngo for your invaluable mathematics expertise.

Thank you, He Shujing, for your friendship, for my perfect epigraph, and for showing me life in Beijing as a young Chinese woman. I wrote this novel, in a way, to see if I could be that woman—if I could, like Wenyu, embody a life that was not mine, but that I longed for. I couldn't, but because of friends like you, I got close.

Thank you to everyone I interviewed while researching this book. Thank you for helping me to build a community in Beijing, to build a community in you. Thank you to the 2018 expat crew for one of the most wondrous seasons of my life. Thank you to Li Yingcan, my first friend in Beijing; Ruolin Feng; EJ Mitchell; Nikki Huang; Bao Xu; Yu Siqi; Tian Yuanquan; and to many others I will not name here for privacy reasons—I treasure the privilege of your time and vulnerability, and I hold your stories with me dearly.

To my family: I am so lucky; thank you for your stories, your support, your love. Thank you, 舅舅, for taking us to eat the greatest food Beijing has to offer. Thank you, 姑姑, for your wit and for *Friends*. Thank you, 叔叔, for teaching me how to make a perfect scrambled egg. Thank you, 姥姥, 姥爷, 奶奶, and 爷爷, for the afternoons walking laps on the university track memorizing Tang poetry, for the evenings in front of the television drinking 绿豆汤 and watching war dramas. I learned Chinese so I could speak to you. 姥姥—我是最棒的!

Thank you, 妈妈, 爸爸, and Panda, for being the greatest cheerleaders, for loving me, for everything. Thank you, Panda, for the Mansion and the Treehouse, for your aesthetic wisdom, for being the first person I told stories with. Our adventures are everlasting. GMH! Thank you, Baba, for your ceaseless hilarity and encouragement, for beng jia/ka cha/etc., and for showing me that growth is forever. Thank you, Mama, for being my safe haven; for being joy, sunshine, hope, love, and curiosity incarnate—you ask the questions I spend my life seeking answers to. I am always coming home to all of you.

Reader's Guide

1. Watching and observing—especially as means of comparing oneself to others—are big themes in *Wanting*. Who are the characters being watched, and who is doing the watching?

2. What do you think of Wenyu's and Lian's decisions to stay with Thomas and Zhetai at the end of the novel? Would you have chosen differently or done the same?

3. Do you believe Lian and Freddy had a real connection? Was there any point in the book where you felt Lian would choose to pursue Freddy?

4. As the story unfolded, who were you rooting for most?

5. How would you characterize the friendship between Lian and Wenyu? What does it mean, in the context of this novel, to be a good friend?

6. In your opinion, could Chen and Fan's relationship have been salvaged had Chen not pursued a relationship with Guilin?

7. Who is to blame for Chen's failure to make a life in America? Is it a combination of factors?

8. While reading, did you see Robert Qiong as a villain or merely an adversary? How did you see Guilin?

9. How would you describe Wenyu as a person? What about Fan? How do you think each woman's vision of herself would differ from the way she's presented in the novel, from Lian's and Chen's points of view?

10. How do Lian's and Chen's storylines resonate with each other? Is there thematic overlap between the two? And why, in your opinion, is the story told from their perspectives?

11. At the very end of the novel, we see both Lian and Wenyu as mothers. Lian speaks throughout the book about her complicated pleasure at assuming roles that are expected of her (daughter, girlfriend, daughter-in-law). What do you think her feelings are about motherhood? Why do you think Wenyu decided to become a mother? What lessons do you think the two of them will pass on to their children?

JOE ABRIATIS

CLAIRE JIA is a writer from the suburbs of Chicago. Her work has appeared in *The New York Times* Modern Love column, *The Rumpus*, *Reductress*, and more. She writes for television and video games, including the 2024 Peabody Award-winning *We Are OFK*. Her family is from Beijing, and nothing puts her at peace like haggling in a chaotic Beijing marketplace. She lives in Los Angeles with her friends.